Upamanyu Chatterjee is the author of the novels *English, August: An Indian Story* (1988), *The Last Burden* (1993), *The Mammaries of the Welfare State* (2000), which won the Sahitya Akademi Award for writing in English, *Weight Loss* (2006), *Way to Go* (2011), which was shortlisted for the Hindu Best Fiction Award, and *Fairy Tales at Fifty* (2014); the novella *The Revenge of the Non-vegetarian* (2018), which was shortlisted for the Crossword Jury Award; and *The Assassination of Indira Gandhi*, a collection of his stories written between 1985 and 2018.

In 2008, Upamanyu Chatterjee was awarded the Order of Officier des Arts et des Lettres by the French Government for his contribution to literature.

Also by Upamanyu Chatterjee

English, August: An Indian Story
The Last Burden
The Mammaries of the Welfare State
Weight Loss
Way to Go
Fairy Tales at Fifty
The Revenge of the Non-vegetarian
Villainy

The Assassination of Indira Gandhi

Stories, 1985-2018

UPAMANYU CHATTERJEE

SPEAKING TIGER

SPEAKING TIGER BOOKS LLP
125-A, Ground Floor, Shahpur Jat
New Delhi – 110049

First published in India by Speaking Tiger Books in 2019
This paperback edition published in 2022

'Othello Sucks' was first published in the March 2015 issue of *Granta*.

'The Killings in Madna' was first published, in a slightly different version, in the October 1987 issue of *London Magazine*.

'Bombay, 1984' was first published, in a slightly different version, under the title 'Desolation, Lust' in the October 1986 issue of *London Magazine*.

'Three-seven-seven and the Blue Gay Gene', 'Girl' and 'Can't Take This Shit Anymore' were first published in the 11 January 2016, 9 January 2017 and 8 January 2018 issues, respectively, of *Open*.

'Sparrows' was first published in the Summer 2017 issue of *Berlin Quarterly*.

'Robertus Heimric, Welcome Back' was first published on Granta Online on 17 September 2017.

'The Assassination of Indira Gandhi' was first published, in a slightly different version, in the June 1985 issue of *London Magazine*.

ISBN: 978-93-5447-089-9

10 9 8 7 6 5 4 3 2 1

Typeset in Garamond Premier Pro by SÜRYA, New Delhi
Printed at Chaman Enterprises, New Delhi

For Chitra Palekar

Contents

History Lesson

Notes for a skit in ten episodes.

In Episode I, an ambassador of a foreign power decides to call on the Conqueror of the World. So far, so good, this happens all the time in history. The Conqueror has barely heard of the country that the ambassador represents—it is some sort of island far far away—but he is unfailingly courteous even with the inconsequential. There is a lesson to be learnt there in his unceasing mannerliness, for history remembers him less for his caprice and his incompetence than for his graciousness; he is whimsical but courtly, for example, when he watches a thief being trampled to death by the royal elephants, and when he has visitors, his cupidity is always masked by his civility. For insatiably greedy he is for gifts but only the veteran courtiers can tell in advance which caller's offerings will please him; only that visitor will be blessed with the imperial favour.

The calling-on takes four months. It is delayed in part by an antecedent, subsidiary—but almost as important—matter of precedence. The ambassador arrives at Surat by ship in September, is not received by the natives, he feels, in a manner befitting his status—no gun salutes, no pennants, no foot soldiers standing at attention for hours in the coastal sun—is miffed, and bickers for weeks with the governor of the province over who, between them, should, as per protocol, call on whom first and secondly, how dare he, a piffling governor, ask his venal customs officials to ransack the effects of an ambassador and his entourage for dutiable items.

'In my world, my dear sir, a governor always first calls on a visiting ambassador.'

'But this is not your world, silly fellow, this is Surat. And till you call on me, I shall have my customs officials seize your effects.'

'That would not be advisable, my dear sir. I should then have to request my drunken sailors to call on the customs house.'

'Oh. What say you call on me this evening and I return your call tomorrow morning?'

Of course, they are not speaking to each other face to face because officially, one hasn't called on the other yet. Further, it is not to be forgotten, ever, that each speaks in a language that the other does not follow. The ambassador uses English and the governor Persian. In English, therefore, the ambassador whines his outrage to his translator—or his linguist, as they call them. The linguist is European. In his other, bread-and-butter life, he is an agent, a procurer of calico and indigo and clove for his company. He knows English and thirty-seven phrases of Persian. These he has picked up neither at the imperial court nor at any university but during his business interactions in the bazaars, factories and bordellos of Agra, Ahmedabad, Burhanpur, Broach and Surat. He chooses amongst the thirty-seven those that approximate to the ambassador's chagrin at the absence of a sense of protocol in the world's second largest empire; he then trots off in a tonga the ten miles from the diplomat's residence, which is a creaking ship at Suvali harbour, to Surat town to convey, orally, his version, in Persian, of the views of the envoy to the governor's linguist.

That functionary is Indian; he has grown wise in the service of four governors. He speaks Persian, his native Surti Gujarati and fifty-three phrases of Portuguese. He is a little taken aback by the sentiments of the ambassador as couched in the Persian of the agent; they sound rather like a trader in tobacco shrieking at a drunk who seeks some favours for free. The Indian linguist converts the message into a Persian suitable for the governor's ear and conveys it to that organ. The governor takes umbrage and responds in a huff.

On the return journey, the conversation between the two high functionaries takes the same route. The governor's translator transforms the master's expletive-filled abuse into a sonorous Persian dusted with some of the Portuguese that he has picked up in the harbour; the ambassador's linguist follows only every fourth word but gathers its general drift from his interlocutor's expression. It is that play of features that he, ten miles later, renders in English for the envoy's edification.

In this manner, governor and ambassador (or, mindful of alternative orders of precedence, ambassador and governor) exchange four sentences a day; they are moreover not their own. The footwork of their diplomacy—one step forward, two steps back, a side feint, a mini-tackle, an about-turn, a back kick—and the elocution attendant on these moves, forms the subject matter of Episode II.

It could well fill several sheets of someone's memoirs; the ambassador himself, detailing the manoeuvres step by step, devotes over twenty pages to this topic in his journal, and his letters and despatches home. On September 22, for instance, the governor sends a message to the ambassador on his ship, saying: 'Hey, let me know the day when you want to come ashore (and call on me) and I'll send thirty horses and my commanders to escort you. And if I find an empty house in Surat, it's yours.'

'You are too kind. In fact, I do spot some fellows on terra firma. Your reception committee? Ah no, they are customs officials. I am given to understand that they even search each nook and cranny of the clothes that one is wearing. I shall not tire myself of repeating, my dear fellow, that I am an ambassador from a mighty king; I insist on claiming my privilege.'

Back and forth in this manner for a while and then: 'Okay, land your merchandise. We'll *count* the chests but not open them. For now.' And after a bit: 'But we do have to inspect your goods to see what gifts you have for the Conqueror of the World. And the Prince. And me. Whether they are of a certain standard, you follow me?'

Eight full days after arrival, on September 26, the ambassador descends the gangplank of the *Lion* to formally set foot on the land to which he intends to be accredited as envoy. He is accompanied by the captains and merchants of four ships and preceded by a hundred rifles. They form a court of guard in his honour and the ships shoot off their cannon. Trumpets sound and drums roll to impress upon the assembled just what's what. The who's who of the Surat bureaucracy await the ambassador under an open tent, upon good carpets and in grave order. He approaches them slowly and dignifiedly, they do *not* scramble to their feet in awe of the event, he stops. He summons a linguist and sends word that he will not budge an inch until the assembled company stands at attention to receive him; lo and behold, it does. He then, composedly, moves forward to sit, knees cracking, on the carpet in their midst.

Speeches from both sides, perforce long-drawn out, with frequent pauses for the linguists to butt in and declaim whatever they like. 'You are great, we are great, welcome. The Conqueror of the World conveys in turn his best wishes to Your Most Esteemed Majesty.' 'They love and honour each other. Many thanks for the horses into town.' 'It is a privilege to be able to help. And now may we search your persons for anything of value? It is the custom of the country.' 'A poor play upon words, sir, and the occasion ill-chosen.'

In a sulk, the ambassador and his entourage decide to return to their ships. 'Convey to this rabble,' he directs his linguist, 'that I shall complain to the Great Mughal that they are eager to lay their grimy hands on the gifts meant for him.'

On the return journey to the harbour, his retinue is followed by messengers from the governor. They have a proposal for the ambassador. 'Choose five of your aides, any five. Them we will not frisk. The others we will but in such a ceremonial manner that it will appear as though we are embracing them.'

'Sir,' a seasoned merchant cautions the ambassador, 'be forewarned. I experienced their embraces last year at Swally Road. They groped all of us, *very* familiarly, to the bottoms of our pockets, and nearer too, modestly to speak it.'

The ambassador is in two minds. If he returns to the ship, he will never get anywhere. If he turns about and proceeds to Surat, on the other hand, he would at least, at last, be on his way to calling on the emperor.

'You will lay your hands on my remaining men not with intent to search but to embrace them: I accept those conditions.' He pauses for the exhausted linguist to convey whatever he wants to, then turns to his weary compatriots, 'Master Boughton, Master Berkeley and some three others may take horse with me. The rest will follow after our hosts. Gentlemen, onward to Surat!'

In his despatches home, describing the events of the day, the ambassador writes that the cavalcade had moved some distance when it was disturbed by a Master Wallis rushing up to them from the larger group of white men bringing up the rear.

'Sir sir, under pretence of stopping for rest and a drink, the blackguards have taken hold of our horses and begun not to embrace but to search us!'

The ambassador turns and rides back to the rescue. His rage does not cool by the time he reaches the group of dusky beggars. 'What do you intend by treachery so base, you varlets? If any of you dare touch anything or anyone belonging to me, I bid you speak and show yourself.' And he lays his hand on his sword.

Protests from the dusky. 'Don't take it so ill! We hugged them but in friendship! These are Persian embraces! Think of Chinese whispers!'

The ambassador calls for a case of pistols and hangs them by his saddle. '*These* are *my* friends,' he announces, 'in them I place my trust.' He pats them throughout the linguist's haywire rendering of his threats.

A pause in the game while the ambassadorial brain ticks away. To return to the ships would be to display pusillanimity, no, they've burnt those boats. Surat it is to be, Surat in pursuit of advancement and justice! 'We will continue towards the town. Our charming hosts will lead though, and we will follow. Is that understood? Translate please.'

But time now, really, for the ambassador to be given a name and a personality. He, to quote the job profile that the Company has sent to the government, is required to be a man of extraordinary parts; he is to reside at Agra, at the king's court, to prevent any plots that may be wrought by the Jesuit Portuguese to circumvent England's trade. The nobleman finally chosen is of a pregnant understanding, well-spoken, learned, industrious and of a comely personage. He is the grandson of the Lord Mayor of London and has attended Magdalen College, Oxford. That, three hundred years later, would be almost as good as St Stephen's College, Delhi. The year is 1615 anno domini and he is Sir Thomas Roe, England's first ambassador to Hindustan.

And so the adventure continues. An hour along the dusty and rutted track, the envoy's entourage passes the group of Surti bureaucrats slacking off under the trees. 'For repose, refreshment and reflection,' they explain. 'Sir, please grace us by accepting this banana.'

'On your guard, gentlemen. Perhaps they intend to embrace us from behind.'

Onward. The river Tapi is to be crossed before they can enter Surat. The ambassador, Master Boughton and the other four chosen take their places in the boat. The less fortunate are first embraced by the natives. The envoy, like a shepherd, stands guard to oversee proceedings.

During the crossing, the dusky players smilingly change tack. The Honourable Ambassador must first call on the governor before going to his new residence.

'Not really. I am weary and unfit for visitation.'

'But it is the custom, sir.'

'As per *our* custom, I cannot look in on the governor until he has visited me first.'

Back and forth, the ball in play amongst the four—envoy, Surti bureaucrat and the linguists—till they arrive at the ghats of the town. The governor's brother and many attendants wait at the steps to escort the ambassador to the castle. More exchanges, then the governor's brother, who seems a little normal, bids the envoy welcome and says that he should rest that evening because he must be very tired: the morrow would be fitter for ceremony. Thanking him, the diplomat mounts his horse and winds his way through the alleys of the town to the house allotted to him.

He is too exhausted to describe his surroundings or his new residence; besides, he has other things on his mind.

'But where are my necessaries? We had sent them on ahead, hadn't we?'

'Your—our—effects have all been kept at the Alfandica, sir.'

'Speak English, my dear man, to an Englishman.'

'From the Portuguese, sir, which itself is from the Arabic alfandega: custom house, sir.'

September 27, the next morning, the saga continues. The ambassador sends for his stuff to the Alfandica. It is refused him. 'You come here and we'll open the chests in front of your damned eyes.'

He protests. 'I am the greatest, my King is the Greatest, I shall complain to the Great Mughal.'

He is still fuming when he receives a message from the governor. 'Come visit me and all your desires shall be fulfilled.'

'Not possible. I am better than you.'

'Rubbish. Here, *I* am better than you.'

'No, as governor you stand in for the Prince. Whereas as ambassador I represent the King. A king is greater than a prince, so that makes me better than you, you follow? Tell you what, if you drop by first, I shall show you my Commission with the King's seal and everything and *your* emperor's firman on how to receive an ambassador with all due respect. How about that?'

'Grow up, nobleman. Come to my house and I'll come out and receive you in the dewan-e-aam. That is one hell of a concession, I might add.'

'You may add all the hogwash you want, my man. Why don't we accidentally meet in a third, neutral place? At which we will both arrive on horseback, fortuitously, at the same time.'

Thus ends September 27. The governor orders the town to sell to the white trash nothing except food and imprisons those traders who disobey.

Early next morning, the merchants announce that they, having had enough of the ambassador's struggle with the governor for precedence, want to return to their ships. 'Very well,' replies the envoy, 'I shall not give in on a matter of principle; I shall play the great game alone.'

It is not that easy though for the merchants to simply slink away. They have first to fend off some questions from the governor's linguist. 'Your ambassador makes such a fuss of my governor visiting him first. What jewel or diamond will he offer to make it worthwhile?'

'We've already sent you a gift from the ship,' respond the merchants. 'A set of knives it was. Or that box of coarse coral.

A token of course. The quality of presents in future would naturally depend on how our ambassador feels he has been treated.'

Two days pass. The governor's brother looks in on the ambassador. Unhurriedly, haltingly, by means of the linguists, they gossip and bitch about privilege, custom and the Portuguese. Both sides agree that the Jesuits are truly unspeakable. The governor's brother lets drop that it would be most unfortunate if, to land their goods, the English were to bypass Surat in favour of Cambay; the governor of the latter is very chummy with the Jesuits and Surat after all is the port of the prince. This idea takes an age to be conveyed across three feet. Exhausted, the ambassador offers his guests a drink. They decline, pointing out that it is Ramadan, but add that they will come and chew the fat with him daily once the fasting is over.

Things happen on September 30. Overnight, the ambassador sends a piece of advice to his captains: 'The Suratts are worried that we might altogether toss them aside and move up the gulf to Cambay. A good thing, let them stew.' In the morning, he gets the news that the governor would visit him after dinner and thereafter at night, call on the captains in their ships. During the day, the ambassador learns that the governor has sent a gift to Captain Keeling and changed his mind: he will skip the envoy altogether and visit just the ships. After bursting a blood vessel, the diplomat sends a message to the governor: 'To ignore the ambassador for the captain is just too, too insulting. It is *not* going to happen, the captain has been instructed *not* to receive you. Your move, you scroundel.'

In the evening of that very day, the governor, dressed to kill, arrives at the ambassador's doorstep. The envoy receives him, leads him in. The governor slips past his host so as to be the first to arrive at the foot of the stairs. The diplomat, annoyed, shoulders past his guest but is pulled back by one of the governor's servants who hisses that the ambassador cannot precede his master. Wonder of wonders, the governor pushes his servant back and docilely follows the ambassador up the stairs.

Sir Thomas thus comes out on top in this his first lesson in Indo-Persian diplomacy. That first adversary of his, the governor, by name Mahmud Beg, is the erstwhile body-servant of Hindustan's most powerful prince, Khurram. As is well known to all save those completely out of it, a body-servant is a euphemism for you know what. Mahmud Beg in fact massages so well that he has been given a posher name, Zulfiqar Khan, and appointed governor of Surat. Not once in his memoirs, however, does Sir Thomas let slip that he would have made efforts to learn Persian had he been dealing with someone genuinely more aristocratic.

He takes more than a month to leave Surat. To call on the Conqueror of the World, he intends to make his way some four hundred and seventy miles north to Ajmer. Planning and providing for that journey takes its own time; carriages for the accompanying merchants and men are needed, and carts for provisions and the hundreds of gifts both impressive and trifling; rations too, and horses, provender, mounted and armed guards, firearms and ammunition. It is a third of a ship on the move, bearing with it, moreover, a conspicuous amount of wealth in merchandise and luxury goods. The roads are unsafe, deserted save for brigands and bandits.

Trade in such quantities and in all these provisions, in horses and ammunition, and even oil and vinegar and salt, is not possible without the consent and involvement of the man at the top. Sir Thomas *needs* Zulfiqar; they and their linguists begin to pass the time of day together in civil intercourse. Sir Thomas sends word to Zulfie that he would like to call on him but doesn't have horses: could the governor loan him half a score of his?

'They will not fail to attend you,' is the reply. It does not specify when. They arrive four days later, in the evening of October 7 and in number are not commensurate with the status of the ambassador. He grins and bears it. Riding them a week later past the Alfandica, he learns that Zulfiqar is inside, ransacking the coffers of the diplomat, picking for himself whatever he likes and whipping almost to death a servant of the English for protesting. Roe does *not* go in. He sends word that the guards and servants in the pay of the English are to leave Zulfiqar to his rapine and come away, that the rogue is welcome to all of it, that he, Sir Thomas, will never accept the other's leavings, and that he will depart for Ajmer with complaints instead of presents.

The civil intercourse however continues. The governor asks the ambassador to show him the coach and the virginals that are among the principal gifts meant to impress the Conqueror of the World. True to his personality, Sir Thomas refuses. Zulfiqar of course sees them the next day. He is charmed by the musical instrument but scorns the coach. *Little* and *poor* are the words he uses. To decorate the interior of a carriage meant for the emperor, he scoffs, the English buy the cheapest velvet from the Chinese; they need to take lessons in generosity from Portugal.

'And what,' he adds, 'do you plan to gift the Most Honourable Prince Khurram?'

'He isn't *really* the one on my radar, you know,' is more or less Sir Thomas's answer.

And as it were to show that he should be, Prince Khurram sends instructions to Zulfiqar on October 18: *For the exclusive purpose of trade, the English may unload only one ship and stay just for one month at Surat. They cannot however have any residence in town.*

Oh. Time to go.

But if a prince can dictate a diktat, can the monarch be far behind? On October 30 arrives a firman from the emperor. It is a command to all his governors to attend the ambassador with sufficient guard and not to meddle with anything that belongs to him.

At last, after a few more days of struggle with the local satrap for their *own* possessions under seizure in the Alfandica, the entire cavalcade—carriage, carts, horses, coolies and porters—leaves Surat on October 30. The wagons carry all except the merchandise, mainly cloth, a huge amount of it, that Zulfie has found it impossible to part with. But it's not for me, it's for the Prince, he is ready to explain when asked. No one asks.

Episode III will, while providing necessary background information on the central character, cover his journey to Ajmer.

Sir Thomas, for the three years that he spent in India, was paid six hundred pounds per annum. That, four centuries later, amounts to some ninety-six thousand pounds annually. Any employer would naturally want results for that kind of money.

In his meticulously maintained journal, his regular despatches home to the East India Company, his frequent letters to the high and mighty in London and his correspondence with diverse agents and factors at Surat and Ahmedabad, Roe successfully gives the impression that if those expected results are not happening, it is certainly not for want of trying on his part. He is the hero of every paragraph that he writes. He fights with a governor so as not to pay the host country's custom duties, he defends his homeland's honour against those mighty in their ignorance, he writes threatening letters to the Portuguese at Goa asking them to behave or else (he receives no reply). He falls ill with fever and the flux but soldiers on. He ticks off the Company for not giving him more authority over its business and its factors and advises it on where and when to ambush the Jesuits at sea. He maintains his cultural identity at all costs, refusing, for instance, whenever he can, to even attempt to sit on the floor and insisting on a table and chair at all times. He does not hesitate to counsel on matters of state even his own monarch. He is the first crusader for empire. And he does not fail to point out, on every page, how much he is respected by emperor, prince and governor, how he has bowled them over, even though he cannot follow a word of what they say. If it crosses his mind from time to time that one may smile and smile and call an uncomprehending guest a pest and a sonofapig, he, being an intelligent man, is careful to keep that notion out of his journal.

When Prince Khurram speaks, what *do* you hear, Sir Thomas, while you wait, with a diplomat's half-smile on your comely lips, for the linguists to translate? When he or anyone else mentions the emperor's favourite queen, Nur Mahal, by name, you hear Normall. If someone refers to her father, Itimad-ud-Daula, you jot down Etiman Dowlett. Prince Khurram himself is Coronne and his notable grandfather, to you, goes by the incomprehensible name of Ecbarsha. In the three years that you spend in India, you hear Persian, Turkish, Konkani, Marathi, Gujarati, Rajasthani, Marwari, Khari Boli. You find them amusing, you mishear every word that is uttered in your presence in a foreign tongue. In your journal and your despatches, the river Narmada is Darbadath, Chittor Cytor, Mukarrab Khan Mochrebchan and Khan-e-khana Channa Channa. And yet, after your years on the Continent, you are aware, or ought to be, that diplomacy's great games are not won by monolinguals. And you yourself are at home in English, Latin, French; you know some German, a little Spanish, a phrase or two of Portuguese. But on a continent older and larger than Europe, the languages of which you do not care to learn, what games will you win with your ears stoppered and your mouth shut?

To go four hundred and seventy miles north to Ajmer, Sir Thomas and his cavalcade first travel some hundred miles east to Nandurbar. They average fifteen to eighteen miles a day. The envoy looks out of the carriage at the fields of jowar, the barren earth, its inhabitants, cattle, carts, goats, mules, horses and hovels and sees nothing that he can put into his journal. For the past few days, he has been experiencing—been insensible to everything but—the three features of the country that will dominate the accounts of its chroniclers for all time to come. Heat. And dust. And dysentery.

Episode IV of the skit will show two ordinary folk just outside the town of Nandurbar. They stand by the wayside watching the diplomat's unending entourage pass. They are Pandurang, male and Gangabai, female. Their ages are not quite known even to themselves. They are cowherds and folksingers. Carts, wagons, riders on horseback, coolies on foot, moving from right to left, pass them by at snail's pace. An ageing horseman, without stopping, asks them in Marathi for the nearest water source. They together point to the mango trees behind and to the left of them. Three white men, heads lolling, half-comatose in the heat, crawl by in a carriage. All at once—*just imagine!*—Pandurang and Gangabai begin singing in Ahirani, screaming really, at Sir Thomas for not writing about them in his diary.

It is okay, perfectly acceptable; people have been known since the dawn of history to protest against being excluded. In the case of the Nandurbar natives, only their one cow and two bullocks appear to hear them; ears flick and tails swish in response, and some flies, disturbed, rise up only to settle a few seconds later on some calmer expanse of bovine skin. The screaming definitely is not heard by Sir Thomas; he would not have followed a syllable of Ahirani, he jots nothing down. But of course that is history's first lesson; that something has not been recorded certainly does not mean that it did not happen. *Write about us, about us!* chant the cowherd-folksingers,

> *and how we live*
> *Amidst the rhythm of the seasons.*
> *What we eat, how we marry, how few of our children survive childbirth,*
> *What we sow, what we reap, how we die.*

Then the refrain:

> *Oh, okay, perhaps that is not going to interest anybody.*
> *Then of cholera and snakebite and smallpox and the plague, write about that,*
> *How our young leave our villages never to return and how we waste*
> *Away our lifetimes of two decades waiting for rain.*
> *And breaking wind.*
> *And of our wider world in which our dialects*
> *Change every fifty miles and wherein we trudge*
> *Twelve miles a day to our livestock fairs to barter*
> *Our goats and our cowdung and in extremity our daughters.*
> *We are unemployable.*
> *We know nothing.*
> *Despair and fear is what we know best of all,*
> *At the arrival of the zamindar's marauding henchmen, at a life in bondage*
> *To the landlord and the moneylender,*
> *At the spell of the shaman who won't cure your child of the shits*
> *Until you give him your wife.*

Again the refrain: *Too boring. Too true.*

'Here, get them to stop screaming, throw them these coins... That's better. Ask them how much they'll sell that starved cow for. Saheb has the shits bad and wants some beef broth.'

'Not clear. Apparently, it isn't theirs to sell. They seem to sort of follow my Marathi but this dialect of theirs is incomprehensible. I'm a townsman, you get me?'

'You're useless, you get me? What am I to tell Saheb when he asks for his broth? That I didn't have the skill to procure some meat for his table?'

'Cook it up. They are banias, tell him that, who couldn't bear to sell their revered mother. Anything that can move from mouth to mouth will do.'

The message does, sort of. In mime, the Indian cook informs the English cook of the fact of the matter. The English cook mulls it over and apprises Sir Thomas on his surfacing from his stupor. And the diplomat does note, against November 6, in his journal: *'though the Country be plentifull, especially of Cattle, by reason of the Banians that will kill nothing, inhabiting all over, yet by the same reason they would sell us none.'* Short and sweet. And wrong. As always, he's on the ball, Sir Thomas, but off the mark.

It takes forty-four minutes for the diplomatic caravan to disappear forever from the lives of Pandurang and Gangabai. The swishing tails marking time, they chant Sir Thomas onward to his next adventure. Their singing loses gusto only during the moments they take off to chase the occasional coin flung haphazardly in their direction.

Emperors and princes,
What need have we of you? It is you
Who need us, us, our grain, our beasts, our land, our labour, our lives.
Oppression is our recompense,
Starvation, and pillage, and bondage that lasts
Seven generations.

These however are not the thoughts foremost in Sir Thomas's mind when he arrives on November 14 at Burhanpur.

In 1615, Burhanpur, on the banks of the Tapti in central India, was a happening place. It was the headquarters of the Mughal army and of its governance of the Deccan. The commander-in-chief of the armed forces was located there, as was his nominal boss Prince Parvaiz, the Conqueror of the World's second son.

Sir Thomas has been advised to call on both.

That is to say, Kerridge, the Company's man at Ahmedabad, writes to him in October 1615 that he must, for form's sake, even though the prince is a bit of a wimp (*whose Cappacitye beinge weake and he given to womanish pleasures, there is no hope either of honour or Content from him).* But the diplomat, ever wishing to make history believe that he does not act on just *anyone's* bidding—when he does, it is only at the beseeching of the high and mighty, and for the greater glory of empire—records on November 18 in his journal that he goes to call on Parvaiz 'for many considerations, as well to see the fashions of the Court as to content the prince, who desired it, and I was loathe to distaste him.' He feels—but does not add—that frankly, the prince should have called on him first.

Episode V. Sir Thomas likes the setup at the Red Fort at Burhanpur. It's just his thing. A hundred-armed horsemen in rows, gentlemen all, waiting outdoors to salute the prince. Or perhaps the ambassador, who can tell. Inside, a high gallery, canopies, carpets, in great but barbarous state. A slipper-licker type apparatchik approaches the diplomat and asks him to take his hat off and, presumably upon meeting the prince, touch the ground with his head.

The nerve.

An ascent of three steps to where Parvaiz, enthroned, is surrounded by the great men of the town with, Roe notes, their hands before them like slaves. Rich canopies, more carpets. Sir Thomas bows to the prince who returns the courtesy. Like a great stage seems the setting to the envoy—who is after all a good friend of Ben Jonson and an avid theatregoer back home—with the prince sitting in state above the rest like a mock king.

Sir Thomas to his linguist in English: 'Tell the Prince, I, being an Ambassador from the King of England to his father The Conqueror, was passing by and could not but in honour visit him.'

Linguist, in his version of Persian, to the assembled nobles and in particular to Parvaiz's secretary, 'Hail to the Prince who is brighter than a thousand suns. We bring you greetings from the mighty King of Great England.'

Parvaiz to his secretary, 'Who is this man? Ask him why he is wearing so many clothes.'

Secretary to linguist, in Persian that he thinks the latter can follow, 'He is welcome.'

Sir Thomas to his linguist, 'I don't like standing beneath this gaggle of whoresons. Ask the Prince whether I can at least come up and stand beside him. See and be seen, that sort of thing.'

Linguist to secretary, 'The ambassador most kindly wishes to remind the Prince that he is his equal.'

Secretary to linguist without bothering to turn to Parvaiz, 'He must be off his rocker.'

Linguist to Sir Thomas, 'Even if the king of Persia or the great Ottoman were here, it would not be admitted, sir.'

Sir Thomas to linguist, 'I am most aggrieved but keep that to yourself. This wretched prince, for the Ottoman or the Persian, would have jumped down from his high horse and crawled all the way to the gates of the fort to lick his boots. I can't keep standing here like some slave of his. I demand a chair.'

Linguist to secretary, 'My feet are killing me.'

Secretary to linguist, 'No one sits in the Prince's presence unless he wants his head chopped off. Your funny man can go and lean against that pillar there. Or any other pillar. We are not particular.'

Linguist to Sir Thomas, 'We had better keep this short, sir.'

Sir Thomas to linguist, 'My feet are killing me. Yes, on with it. Tell him that we want to open a factory and station an agent here in Burhanpur. If he would kindly issue a firman to that effect, please. And we would need carriages to cart onward to Ajmer the king's presents.'

A version of the gist is conveyed. In response, the secretary to the linguist, icily, 'And are there no gifts for the Prince?'

There are. Sir Thomas ceremonially hands them over one by one. They include two magnifying glasses, a set of sharp knives, a large telescope, a velvet tablecloth folded to hide its most faded square and a case of Spanish red. The sight of the last turns Parvaiz entirely into another personality. He suddenly mumbles something and gets up. Everyone comes alive and begins to bow and scrape. Parvaiz gestures to Sir Thomas as though to say either Come with me or Go away, but swivels and leaves the hall with his entourage before the diplomat can react. An attendant scurries after the prince with the case of wine. The secretary scurries after the attendant. The hall begins to resemble a modern classroom in a government school which the teacher suddenly exits for the toilet. In stately fashion, Sir Thomas climbs the three steps to go and stand by the throne, look around and feel like a monarch of all he surveys. The secretary returns in a bit to tell the linguist: 'The Prince will be occupied for a while with matters of state. You may take your leave now and return some other time to continue your visit.'

On November 19, the ambassador sends the commander-in-chief of the armed forces (the Channa Channa) a small present but does *not* call on him because he expects him, Mirza Abdurrahim—naturally—to visit him first. That does not look like happening. Sir Thomas then twiddles his thumbs for a further five days at Burhanpur for the two items that he has requested for, the firman and the carriages. That long wait takes its toll, depresses him terribly. He feels that he is wasting his time. Then, to top it all, he falls ill once more. The *feevor* it is on this occasion. It knocks Humphrey Boughton out too, Boughton who has been with him all those weeks since Surat. He can't sweat it out or fight it off, poor man, and on November 25, Sir Thomas buries his good companion at Burhanpur. Two days later, it is a chastened, wasted and sombre diplomat who leaves that part of the world (*a country all slavish...here your swine lie better than any man*) on a litter carried by six men.

He *has* been wasting his time, most unfortunate but true, and in more ways than one. He has for instance been calling on the wrong royal son.

The Conqueror has many such. The history books record the names of only five. Half-brothers, all of them. The eldest is Khusrau, born to Shah Begum (nee Man Bai). He is the one who tries a coup against his father in 1605 itself, the year of his accession, botches it and is blinded in punishment—but that is botched too, so he retains some semblance of vision. He remains under house arrest in Agra until he dies in 1622 (poisoned by Khurram, says everybody).

Parvaiz, whose acquaintance has just been made and who was born to Sahibi Jamal Begum of Herat, is the Conqueror's second son. Having failed his father in the military campaigns that he was asked to lead against the Deccani kingdoms, he is now the mock king of Burhanpur, the alcoholic who prefers Sir Thomas's wine to his company. Eleven years later, he dies where he drinks, in Burhanpur itself, of his lifestyle. One fine day in 1626, he becomes delirious, falls on the floor and into coma, comes to, has head wounds that need to be cauterized, sinks again into unconsciousness and finally gives up the struggle to surface for air. Everyone again suspects Khurram.

Khurram, the third, the rising son, conspicuously ambitious

and unscrupulous even by the high benchmark of the Mughal dynasty, has already, as the overlord of Surat, made his presence felt in Sir Thomas's life. It is him whom the diplomat should have been sucking up to from Day One. It would not have been easy; Khurram is contemptuous of Europeans in general and in particular prefers the Portuguese to the English. They give better presents, he explains.

His mother (like Khusrau's, a Hindu) was a Rajput princess by the name of Jagat Gosain; after marriage, she became Taj Bibi Bilqis Makhani. His lineage however does not prevent Khurram from going after pesky Hindu kingdoms like Mewar; his other notable success though is against a convert to Islam, the troublesome Ethiopian Malik Ambar at Ahmednagar. His military exploits impress his father; year after year, his star continues to rise and shine. In 1628, he takes over as emperor and within a month, has some nephews and Shahryar, his younger half-brother and the Conqueror's fifth son, executed.

The fourth son is Jahandar. God knows what happened to him. He didn't even make it to the footnotes of the textbooks.

Three weeks later, Sir Thomas encounters another—one of the emperor's fourteen illegitimate sons, so claims the worthy himself—one fine day outside the township of Chittor.

The diplomat's cavalcade, winding its way north, unmindful of time, covers the seven hundred-plus kilometres from Burhanpur to Ajmer in twenty-six days. *Miles,* Sir Thomas would've said, four hundred and fifty-odd miles, not caring to use kos as a unit of measurement of distance, particularly since its length itself varies from kos to kos, it could be one-and-one-eighth of a mile in one place and two miles in another; an infernal country.

Episode VI takes place outdoors.

Hot as hell the Deccan is during the monsoon, stifling the day. It is only when they near Rajputana that the nights, sensing the desert, become cooler. In the evenings, they pitch their tents in a circle and then light their fires to deter the lions and wolves from ravaging the livestock. Dinner is late, it has to be cooked first. They eat surrounded, always encircled, by native servants, in the day to swat the flies away and at night the mosquitoes. It is Sir Thomas's first sustained encounter with the latter. He is impressed.

End-of-the-day talk, of the climate and their ailments, of home, the Company as paymaster, the latest from Agra, the next ship out. Of the Portuguese and their clout in the court of the Mughal, and how to counter it; and the venality of the Dutch, and the blessings of their base in Masulipatam for the trade with Batavia. Of Surat versus Cambay versus Syndu versus Bengal as the ideal hub from which the English should expand operations. Of the great Mughal and his caprices, Nur Mahal his bewitching queen, even more beguiling because none of them will ever see her in the flesh, and her father and brother, that coterie of three that, aided by Khurram, actually runs the empire.

'Laws they have none written, sir,' sadly announces the factor William Biddulph, helping himself to a generous pinch of snuff from Sir Thomas's pouch, 'it is the king's judgement that is binding on all. He sits and adjudicates with much patience, once a week, both in capital and criminal causes; and sometimes he sees the execution done by his elephants, with too much delight in blood.'

Sir Thomas listens, contributes a phrase here, a chuckle there, and squirrels away material for his journal. He is a well-travelled man—he has been to Guiana and up the Amazon in search of El Dorado, he has visited Trinidad—and even though its variety seems to assault his senses with something new every day, he refuses to be overwhelmed by huge and bewildering India. Every week he has come upon plants foreign to Europe—the coconut palm, the aromatic tulsi, the enormous mango tree, and animals too, domesticated elephants, king cobras, camels as beasts of burden; every week he runs across a different race or religious group. Hindoos and Mahometans and Jews naturally, each group with its own rituals and customs, and Persians, Tartars, Armenians; plus the Europeans of course, the Portuguese and the Dutch, the occasional Genoan, and in the bustling centres of trade, Chinese, Burmese, Malays and Japanese. He might not jot any of it down in his memoirs but he does store it away. All experience is grist for the diplomat. If in the years to come he again has the good fortune to represent, protect and nurture His Majesty's interests in the foreign lands of distant empires, at Isfahan or Constantinople, he should be able to look back with pleasure and profit on his involvement with the great Mughal. He must achieve something here. He must be *seen* to have achieved something here.

'God's bodkin, man! What was that!!'

That is the barking of a dog, the sudden neighing of horses, a shout, a rifle shot, and some frenzied, frightened yelling in a language that Biddulph cannot even pretend to identify. The yelling and the barking continue in pleasant counterpoint for a while; both abruptly end in different kinds of yelps. Conversation stalled, the diplomat and the company's agents, expecting a dramatic entry, look away from the fire towards where the horses have been tethered for the night.

'Angels and ministers of grace defend us!'

The syce and the senior guard have dragged in something half-human, a half-naked, half-mad fakir. His hair and beard are matted, filthy; he wears a tattered rag that barely covers his torso. He is otherwise noticeably naked but that is fine, it is not the Jacobean stage. He stinks. In that day and age, everyone stank. His custodians thrust him forward. Contrary to expectations, he does not resist the push but allows its momentum to carry him onward, past Sir Thomas to within a foot of the fire; there he proceeds to warm himself, to tremble and to reek.

In the succeeding lull, Sir Thomas stares icily at the head guard. Biddulph translates.

'Caught him trying to steal some of their dinner from the dogs, sir,' explains the guard, unfazed by all that iciness, in a near-incomprehensible mix of Marwari and Gujarati. 'Then seeing that he was a eunuch, we remembered that—' indifferently raising his arm here in the direction of John Hall the ambassador's chaplain '—Sahib had so wanted to see one in the flesh. And very much in the flesh he is sir as we all can see.'

In the next succeeding lull, Sir Thomas stares icily at the chaplain. The eunuch is led away to be clothed and fed before being brought back to the fire for the edification of the company.

That does not happen that evening, for the beggar falls asleep while gorging on his meal of the leftovers of leftovers. The next morning, though, Sir Thomas learns by way of his apothecary that their visitor of the night before is the emperor's eldest son. 'He assured the syce last night that he would not forget our kindness when he ascends to the throne of Hindustan.'

'Please convey to him in advance that His Majesty is too munificent. All we ask in return is that he throw the Portuguese and the Dutch out of his domain.'

The beggar, straggling along behind the caravan, continues for a couple of days to edify the company at third hand. He is from Sylhet, he confides to one of the coolies, where it is customary for the people to make eunuchs of some of their sons and give them to the governor in lieu of revenue. It is only natural, it is inevitable, so difficult these days to tell the difference between taxation and emasculation. And if you are attractive to look at as a eunuch, who knows, you could be profitably employed even in the private chambers and retiring rooms of the emperor.

From a myriad such different sources, from roadside beggar

to factor's servant, Sir Thomas hears far too much every day. And almost all of it is in translation. It is necessary to separate the wheat from the chaff for posterity. Not an easy task, for the truth is so inextricably muddled up with fantasy, myth and traveller's tale; but he has to do it, he *will* do it. If *he* cannot, then by Gis and by Saint Charity, who else can?

'The present Mughal and his ancestors have brought all the splendid cities of Hindustan to ruin, have dispeopled them and forbidden their repair! Beyond their own beginnings, these horse breeders from Samarkand would have nothing remembered that was great, as if the Mughal dynasty and the world itself were coeval.' This notion is the beggar's parting food for thought, delivered one morning to the syce before he sidles off to join a gaggle of pilgrims en route to Ujjain. 'It is to be hoped,' had continued the eunuch sage in a shout, 'that these white sharks who have invaded us from across the waters will prove to be kinder to Hindustan than those Central Asian soldiers of fortune in search of a fiefdom. I hope so but I have my doubts. These sea denizens appear to be even greedier than the progeny of Timur the Lame.'

Sir Thomas curls his lip at the allusion to white sharks but likes the analysis of the destructive capacity of the Mughals. He slips it into his journal as part of his entry for December 18.

On December 23, he arrives in Ajmer—alas!—again in a litter on the shoulders of six able-bodied men. It is not the entry that he would have hoped for.

Arise, arise all for Episode VII and behold, at last, the Conqueror of the World!

Before his coronation in 1605, he had been merely Muhammad Sultan Salim. Just another prince sulking after having tried to usurp his father's throne. That is genetic, it runs in the dynasty. Once he became emperor, however, he renamed himself Nur al-Din Muhammad Jahangir Padshah Ghazi and felt much better. Then, from Day One itself, he was torn between governing his empire and writing about governing his empire. Literature, much the softer option, won the day.

The *Tuzuk-i-Jahangiri* is over seven hundred pages long and is written—dictated, more accurately—in Persian. The emperor knows Turkish too and Arabic, Braj Bhasha and the stray phrase of Portuguese, but for these discourses to posterity in the great family tradition, Persian it is to be.

The *Tuzuk* comprises the recollections of a man in love with himself. In it, Jahangir emerges as generous, short-tempered, capricious and a prodigious lover of wine, women, gifts, elephants, lions, horses, European mastiffs and poetry, particularly of those poems the subject matter of which is the emperor himself.

Speaking of the time in 1608, for example, when Khurram's maternal uncle, Raja Suraj Singh, had called on him, Jahangir writes that the Rajput chieftain had been accompanied by an unnamed Hindi poet who had tremblingly placed before the emperor a poem. An offering. A translation (at three removes from the original) follows:

If the Sun had a son, 'twould always be day
And never night,
For at sunset, the son, in his father's way
Would give the light
To the world. For blessing the sire with such an offspring,
God above be praised,
Upon the father's death, no night, no mourning,
For the light the son has raised.

Few Hindi verses of such freshness of purport, writes Jahangir, have ever reached my ear. As a reward for this eulogy, he continues, I gave the poet an elephant.

After he is satisfied with what he has written of the first twelve years of his reign, Jahangir compiles the first volume of his memoirs, has several manuscript copies made and distributes them to the People Who Matter. Khurram is bestowed with the honour of the first copy. Sir Thomas, still floating around India at that time, gets none.

A pity, even though it wouldn't have been of much use. Language problem. He would have opened it at the wrong end, Roe, and begun reading from the last word backwards. And as for the first English version, garbled, inaccurate, full of interpolations and inconsistencies, he'd have to wait a little over two hundred years. *But* if he had had it translated and read out to him, the *Tuzuk* might have helped him to understand a little the world that he was trying to penetrate and dazzle with his sagacity. A thousand things big and small might have become clearer, why, for instance, they all—king, prince, noble—loved so much to receive gifts and why, to take another example, when the capital of his empire is, say, two hundred and thirty miles away at Agra, the monarch may live, for two years or more, in a tent in Ajmer or Mandu or Kabul.

The capital first. Simply put, the Mughal court is wherever the emperor is.

His predecessors, Ecbarsha in particular, have built royal palaces right across the Indo-Gangetic plain—Lahore, Agra, Fatehpur Sikri, Delhi, Mandu—and Jahangir, like his father, rarely stays in one place for more than three years at a go. He needs a change of scene, he needs to escape the weather, or be nearer a military engagement that some incompetent prince has fucked up, he needs to show off the splendours of imperium in every corner of his domain. So like his ancestors, those wanderers from Samarkand, he likes to move.

Since 1613, he has been in Ajmer to oversee the campaign against Rana Amar Singh of Udaipur.

And the tent royal—

But to describe the tent, one would first have to introduce Edward Terry.

Fellow of Corpus Christi, Oxford, chaplain to Sir Thomas since 1616, thereafter rector of the church at Greenford, Middlesex, England and the redoubtable author of yet another memoir, *A Voyage To East India: Wherein Some Things are Taken Notice Of, in our Passage Thither, But Many More In our Abode There, Within that Empire of The Great Mogul,* Edward Terry adores the ambassador and follows him around the million and a half square miles of kingdom, taking notice of and recording whatever the diplomat misses. If Roe covers the incident, Edward provides the backdrop. For a more rounded view, therefore, of the expatriate life in the time of Jahangir, the adventures of Tom and Terry need to be read together.

So there lolls Jahangir in state, either in a fort or in a city of canvas at least five miles long, says Terry. The emperor may be perched high up in a balcony to see and be seen, or be at court in his durbar hall passing judgements that instantly become law, or conferring, discussing matters of state with his ministers and commanders, or watching some miserable creature being flogged or trampled to death, or drinking like a fish and passing out in his harem. Durbar hall, public court, privy chamber, retiring rooms, harem, they can all be made of canvas. The other tents are off-white in colour, the emperor's are in red. The emperor is the centre of the universe, his tents form the heart of the camp and provide it at all times its pivotal point of reference. They are surrounded by those of his nobles in concentrically increasing order of unimportance, all reared up, writes Terry, in such a due and constant order that wherever the camp is pitched, in whichever season and region of the empire, the same arrangement is maintained, the lanes between tents are laid down in the same way, the bazaars, eating houses and places of recreation are in identical places and follow everywhere a matching layout.

For close to three years, one sees Sir Thomas, two or three times a month, make his way through that maze of stone or canvas, that swarm of humanity, horses, camels and carts, to visit the court and call on the emperor. He is not alone, he never is; he has with him faithful Terry, Biddulph or some other factor—several of them—a couple of agents who know their way around, their attendants to do the running about, and always a handful of guards to protect his, the ambassador's, idea of himself.

While the great brain reflects on the great game and how he doesn't seem to be winning it, it is Terry who keeps his eyes and ears wide open and jots down what his readers back home would want to know. So it is from him that we learn, for instance, that Roe and Co, to maintain cultural otherness, wear silk, and retain their mode of dress even in temperatures of forty degrees Celsius plus.

'For my lord Ambassador and his company, we all kept to our English habits, made as light and cool as possibly we could have them. His waiters in red taffeta cloaks, guarded with green taffeta, which they always wore when they went abroad with him, myself in a long black cassock; and the colours and fashion of our garments were so different from theirs, that we needed not, wheresoever we were, to invite spectators to take notice of us.'

And it is Terry once more who completes the picture, time and time again provides the details of what his ambassador's stiff upper lip cannot divulge, on the subject, for example, of the rowdiness of the English themselves when let loose in public.

'When my Lord Ambassador first arrived at Surat,' discloses Terry, 'it so was, that an English cook he carried with him, the very first day of his coming thither, found a way to an Armenian

Christian's house, who sold wine in that place. The cook had his head quickly over-freighted with it, and then staggering homeward, in his way, met the brother of the governor of Surat; the cook made a stand, staying himself up upon his sword and scabbard, and cried out to the governor's brother: *Now thou heathen dog.* He not understanding his foul language, replied civilly in his own: 'What sayest thou?' The cook answered him with his sword and scabbard, with which he struck at him, but was immediately seized on by his followers, and by them disarmed and carried to prison.'

One drunken English cook reeling in the lanes of Surat, waving his sword at a local big dad, spending a night in prison. Hardly material for a diplomat's official journal. Keep it out. A stately ambassador at the Mughal court, concentrating mainly on being stately because he can't follow a word of what is going on around him. Keep that out too. That is, give it a spin.

On a typical visit to the emperor, Roe's problems might begin at the gates of the court itself. It is a truth universally acknowledged that only neanderthals, since time immemorial, in all the civilizations of the world, have been chosen to be palace guards. They know fuckall, they *like* to obstruct, they are suspicious of people who use words of more than one syllable, they are happiest when someone loses his temper.

'Hey you, white trash, where d'you think you're going?'

The linguist of the day, by way of some attendant: 'The great ambassador, His Majesty's envoy, calling on The Conqueror of the World,' et cetera.

Neanderthal stares at the diplomat. Roe though can outstare anybody.

After a bit: 'He can go in but him alone. No one else.'

Protests. 'We shall complain to the great Mughal.'

'And not from here. He can't enter from here. Use the door by the south gate where the horses are being fed.'

Protests. 'But that is used by footmen, nautch girls, syces and elephant-dung removers.'

'What is his business? Explain to this whoreson that as an ambassador, I am fully the equal of any of those syphilitic noblemen who use this entrance. And of course I would need my linguist with me. I mean, am I going in there to play pall-mall?'

First round to the diplomat. Next, in a palace corridor or in a lane between walls of canvas, the linguist to Sir Thomas looking stately and lost: 'This way, sir.' They join a sort of unruly queue of noblemen before a door manned by three other neanderthals in posher uniforms. Each nobleman stops before a guard and exhales forcefully and noisily into his face and then waits while the guard, shutting his eyes to concentrate, wrinkles his nose—or sometimes gags—at the quality of the breath. In a moment, the nobleman is either allowed to pass through the door or pushed gently but firmly to one side.

The linguist to the ambassador: 'An alcohol test, sir. Can't be avoided. You can't go in if you've wine on your breath. Unless you want a whipping in front of the emperor. He'll watch, of course. *He* can drink, naturally, but he alone. Sometimes he allows some of the others to toss off a glass or two in his presence and then forgets that he's given permission. So they get drunk, then they get flogged. It's complicated, this court.'

It's a fucking madhouse, that court.

The ambassador's journal creates the impression that the lure of his personality is such that Sir Thomas is a head-turner wherever he goes, that in the emperor's private audience chamber, for instance, Jahangir never fails to notice him; at his entry, the monarch stops whatever he is doing and, over the heads of the others, beckons the diplomat forward to come over and say hello and chew the fat. In sign language? Or maybe Latin? Whom is Roe kidding?

Jahangir sits enthroned a couple of tiers above the world, smiling and daydreaming while pretending to listen to fourteen people at the same time. Noblemen, grandees, governors, ministers, commanders, all clamour together for fifteen seconds of his attention. Milling about the hall, separated from their superiors by wooden rails and another set of neanderthals, gazing up and about at the lights, the tapestries and canopies, and tripping over the carpets, are secretaries, squires, retainers, attendants, escorts, stewards, servers, bodyguards and servants; the confusion is frightful.

Muttering *Rule Britannia* to himself—a full hundred and twenty-three years before the rallying cry becomes a byword, so prescient is he—Sir Thomas pushes forward. He is thrust back by a silky, pointed, Persian elbow. He shoves again, he begins to jostle and shoulder his way towards his goal. Will he make it this time to the royal ear? Before its possessor suddenly gets up and goes off to get laid? Or watch his elephants dance on some poor sod? *Onward, Christian soldiers.*

Of course, Sir Thomas does make it to the front row on the good days.

'Now what have we here?'

The nobleman nearest to the emperor, to Roe: 'Yes, please?'

Roe's linguist, an Italian on that occasion, by name John Veronese: 'The Honourable Ambassador from His Majesty the glorious King of England.'

Nobleman, bored: 'No presents?'

Linguist: 'A coach all the way from England for your travels, sir, and a rare musical instrument, traditionally played by *young* women, for your listening pleasure.'

Jahangir, perking up: 'An *invisible* coach? I don't see it.'

Linguist, shouting above the surrounding din: 'It is outside, sir. The emperor's mere wish to see it would be our command.'

Jahangir, suddenly lacklustre: 'What I would really like is an English horse.'

Linguist, stumped, to Roe in a loud whisper: 'The beggar wants a *horse.*'

Roe, without losing his stately expression, to the linguist: 'Is he nuts? No horse would survive the storms and the confinement of a sea passage. And by land, depending on the route one takes, the Turks would grab it either at Buda or Aleppo.'

Linguist to nobleman: 'Not possible, sir. Horse die and eaten by Turks.'

Jahangir, just a little impatient in the face of such stupidity: 'Not one but *six.* You put six horses in a ship. One would survive the voyage. Think of the six faces of a die. The beast will arrive here lean and miserable but we'll fatten it nice and slow.'

Roe, feeling that it is essential that he change the subject: 'I will write home to advise my government of Your Majesty's request.'

Jahangir: 'Good, you do that. And what else do you have to say?'

At last. Thought he'd never ask! Roe clears his throat and gets down to it. In a minute, Asaf Khan—Jahangir's brother-in-law and one of the unholy trinity that runs the empire—realizing how long the narration is going to take, pulls John Veronese away so as to break his flow. The linguist falters but momentarily. Roe pulls him right back in place; the translation, sporadically accurate, continues.

So what does Roe want, exactly? What's all the fuss about?

Well, for one, he—they, his lot—want a treaty. A good solid agreement signed by Jahangir on the one hand and—they being of the same level—by Roe on the other. Enough of this firman crap; firmans are short-lived, practically interim, orders, valid only till the next one comes along, hardly worth the paper they are written on. Whereas a treaty, especially of the sort that Roe covets, with clauses that would cover every facet of his nation's greed, and a sonorous preamble that would speak of good and perfect love and peace to endure forever between the two parties, the kind of document that could be waved for decades under the noses of uncooperative and uncomprehending officials to make them toe the line, that was a consummation devoutly to be wished. It would provide the English free access to all Mughal ports, including those of Bengal and Sindh. They, the English, would *not* be frisked when they disembarked, would be allowed to remain ashore without any harassment, to buy and sell goods without restriction and to rent factories and appropriate housing at fair prices. Further, gifts that they bore for the emperor would not be impounded by the customs riff-raff.

In return, they, while ashore, would behave.

In addition, they would do their best to provide rarities for the Mughal and upon payment, supply him with any material for war that they might have, but only for use against an enemy to the common peace.

And those Jesuits. The Portuguese are to be invited to participate in this agreement, but if they do not react within six months, it would be *quite* lawful for the English 'to chastise the stubbornness of an obstinate enemy to peace...in taking any of their ships, boats or goods, without any offence to the said great king of India'.

Of course, Roe and the Italian are not allowed to prattle for too long. Asaf Khan intervenes to say that even if they went on all night, it would still end up in the ambassador having to give them a written draft that they could examine, so would he please?

The emperor, mainly to avoid Sir Thomas, then rises. It isn't however that easy. Roe, loudly and rapidly, to Jahangir, and prodding John Veronese to translate simultaneously: 'Your Majesty! Your Majesty! Yesterday, for the feast of the Navroz, you were magnanimous enough to allow me to stand behind the throne. It was a great privilege and I shall be eternally grateful for your kindness. But unfortunately, Your Majesty, I saw nothing of the splendour of the ceremonies, just the back of the throne I saw. A magnificent sight of course but I was just wondering, next time may I stand *alongside* where you are seated? It would be so wonderful and I would see everyone and everyone would see me!'

Jahangir, after a moment, to Asaf Khan: 'Let him stand wherever he wants. On his head too if it makes him happy.'

Roe attends the Navroz the next day and stands to the right of the throne; to its left are Khurram and Karan, the eldest son of Amar Singh of Udaipur. The ambassador is all cock-a-hoop, naturally and, in his words, observes all evening 'presents, elephants, horses and many whores'.

He takes a full week to draft the treaty; when he is satisfied, he has it translated into Persian by his team of language experts and goes and, with much ceremony, hands it over to the emperor who *instantly* hands it over to Asaf Khan. Good Old Wily glances at it and at once says that it is far too long. Roe gives him a full five days and then asks him if he has had a look. Not yet, is the reply.

Three days later, on April 3, 1616, Asaf Khan says that the demands of the English, as presented in the draft treaty, are unreasonable. He does not however elaborate. He does not want to, he does not need to, *all of it* is unreasonable. Roe concludes that the brother-in-law wants a bribe.

Well, he is *not* going to give it. He will wait a while and then go and whine to the great Mughal. Meanwhile, he will not let the grass grow under his feet, he has other work to do. Take up, for instance, with Khurram the continued depredations of Zulfiqar Khan against the English in Surat. Though the chances of that ending satisfactorily are about as good, says Roe to himself, as of the treaty being signed.

Meanwhile, life of course goes on as usual. And death even more so. On April 23, four thousand two hundred miles away at Stratford in England, a playwright acquaintance of his from his Mermaid Tavern days in the late fifteen-nineties dies of suspected syphilis. Roe doesn't hear of his passing till several months later when the mail comes in with the next ship. He is acutely depressed and remembers with a heavy heart how much he had enjoyed *The Merry Wives of Windsor* and the antics of Bottom in *A Midsummer Night's Dream.* Letters from home always make him feel low, and not because of the news of the deaths alone. They make him feel left out, banished from the meaningful, the real, life, condemned to perish amongst unfeeling, uncomprehending aliens.

The wiliest of whom, on April 29, at the durbar, asks Roe to excuse his sluggishness and not to worry about the draft treaty, that he will get it signed and have it sent, that he takes to heart all matters concerning the ambassador, that he needs no reminding other than his affection for him. Sir Thomas's head swims, and heart sinks, at all that gush.

With reason, because on May 4, Asaf Khan tells him that some of the articles in the draft are obscure but not to worry, he's on the job and he isn't of double heart. 'But you know,'—glancing reproachfully here at the ambassador—'how come you never bring nice stuff for the Emperor, curious toys as do the Portugali?'

'Just say the word, sir! It would help though if we had a list of preferences.'

'Now you're talking! And as for the list, please note the following: One, pictures. Two, basins and ewers in brass. Three, coloured French muffs. Four, cloth embroidered in gold or silver, preferably gold. Five, wall hangings. Six, a good saddle with a nice caparison and to go with them, seven, an English horse... Say, have I ever told you what a magnificent sword you have?' He reaches out and withdraws the blade from Sir Thomas's scabbard. Turning it over in his hand, holding it up against the light, he continues till the ambassador gets the point. 'I *have* to admire the quality of its metal, its grip and the sharpness of its edge. It isn't often that one comes across workmanship of this high order. You know, I've so often wished...'

So Sir Thomas, telling himself that he is not *giving* Asaf Khan a bribe, the other is taking it, gifts him the weapon. 'It is at your service.'

'No no no! To take a sword from so good a friend is in our world deemed unlucky!'

'Your excuse, sir, is not strong enough against the affection with which it is offered.'

'Small persuasions from you will serve! Thank you so much! Thank you! You must come to dinner one evening!'

Sir Thomas waits for the other to name a day. He waits, then he leaves. At home, he receives a return gift, the first from Asaf Khan, of twenty musk melons.

The weeks pass. Roe is, he writes, in every way afflicted—fires, smokes, floods, storms, heat, dust, flies and no temperate or quiet season. And more deaths. His cook and his chaplain John Hall. He writes to Surat for a replacement. This is when they offer him young Edward Terry.

And the treaty. On August 2, Asaf Khan says that it was to have been sealed without delay but it's been mislaid by a negligent servant and so, could he have another copy, please, and also a 'rich' present for Prince Khurram? On August 16, never say die, says Sir Thomas and enquires again. Asaf Khan responds, 'Tonight, I swear by Allah, tonight or latest, tomorrow!' On August 27, the ambassador visits Wily but can't meet him because he is in his harem and 'comes not that day abroad'. Roe asks Jaddow the broker to keep watch and catch him *no matter what the hour*. Jaddow grabs Asaf Khan at night and delivers the familiar ultimatum: *We shall complain to the great Mughal!* The draft is being vetted by Normall, learns the broker, and Asaf shall speak to his sister on Sunday.

On September 1, Sir Thomas is told that nothing can be

done for two days because everyone is busy with the king's birthday. And on September 4, after five months, he gets the draft treaty right back.

Asaf Khan's objections, clause by clause, are indicated in the margin. Why a treaty? A firman from Khurram would do for Surat and in any case, you will never be allowed to trade in Bengal or Sind. And it is way too long, the draft, and the very idea of a treaty itself would offend the Emperor.

And Khurram as well. You think that if and when this accord is signed, you can ignore and bypass the Prince and his government at Surat? Don't you get it, Sir Thomas?

Of course he gets it. He may be an ambassador but he is not a fool. To bypass Khurram and his myrmidons at Surat is precisely what he had in mind. The rest of it he gets too. *The Conqueror of the World doesn't, from up there, sign treaties.* And certainly not with the envoy, practically a trader, of some obscure king of some funny little island four thousand miles away.

Thus from September 1616 on, the ambassador's journal moves away to other topics, to the next chapter of the epic struggle with the governor of Surat to recover for the Company its dues. To talk of the emperor moving his court to Mandu to better oversee operations in the Deccan (this last Sir Thomas doesn't much like; it would be cumbersome and expensive to follow the monarch and yet pointless it would be to remain in an Ajmer from which the emperor has withdrawn; a play without the prince).

And in mid-October, in Episode VIII, to the arrival in Ajmer, from Isfahan, of Muhammad Raza Beg, the ambassador of the Persian emperor.

Roe sends a guy to spy on the event so that he can then compare notes. His sharp eye on the entire visit is that of the wife's on the comportment of the suspected mistress. A reception committee, he writes, with a hundred elephants and musicians awaits Beg outside the town to lead him in. Beg himself has some fifty horses of his own, all decked in cloth of gold, besides forty armed guards and two hundred peons and attendants. Roe with a shudder recalls his own arrival in Ajmer, half-dead on a litter, a good ten months ago and steels himself to record that he had not demanded a reception outside the town on that occasion because of his wretched dysentery.

In the evening at the durbar, to greet the emperor, the Persian ambassador does three taslims and one sijdah, that is, he places the back of his right hand on the ground and then, standing up, its palm on his head, three times, and then the sijdah: he prostrates himself flat on the ground and knocks on it with his head as though, notes Roe later, he would enter in. Jahangir, pleased, gifts Beg a handsome turban, a vest of gold and a girdle. Beg gifts Jahangir twenty-seven Arabian and Persian horses, nine large mules, twenty-one camels laden with grape wine and seven others with velvet, two chests of Persian hangings, forty muskets, five clocks, eight silk carpets, five swords and seven daggers all set with stones, seven Venetian looking glasses and two rubies.

The Conqueror of the World is pleased. When he speaks to the Persian ambassador, writes Roe, Beg dances to the tune thereof. Of course, a common language makes all the difference and his rival, notes Sir Thomas, delivers his own business with so much flattery and obsequiousness that it pleases as much as his gifts, ever calling Jahangir King and Commander of the World, forgetting that his own Master has a share in it.

Sir Thomas, one must not forget, is both Elizabethan and Jacobean; that great stage is in his blood. So when he meets the Persian ambassador a few days later, it is only natural that he finds him to be a juggler, a jester, not a person of any gravity, running up and down, and acting all his words out like a mimic player. Of course, between him and his rival there is a vast, fundamental gulf that in part explains why the empire treats them differently. Unlike Roe, Beg is not a bania, he hasn't come to Ajmer to do trade, to further the interests of the commercial company that is paying his wages; Beg has been sent on proper ambassadorial business. He has orders from the Sophy to give content to the great Mughal, that is, to suck up like crazy and while *pretending* to plead a peace for the kingdoms of the Deccan (the protection of which the Shah Abbas ostensibly takes to heart; in reality, he doesn't give a damn about them, he is far more worried about the aggrandizement of the Mughal empire), while pretending, actually to touch Jahangir for funds for the neverending struggle of the Safavids against the Ottomans.

Mughal, Safavid, Ottoman. So what does Jahangir himself think about that trio? About the fate of more than half the known world in the hands of a triumvirate? Sir Thomas has been wondering about that for a while and he finds out for himself, later in the year, at Mandu.

September 9, Episode IX. Jahangir on his elephant, riding out to the river Darbadath to take the air, passes Sir Thomas's house. The ambassador, as is the custom, rushes out to meet him. It is also customary to gift the monarch something even when he is passing by, perhaps even when he is going to take a shit, who knows with emperors? This one, this darting out with a present, is called mubarak, blessedness. As usual, miserly Thomas has nothing to offer. He cannot go out empty-handed, he cannot not go out, perhaps he has the shits, this is the kind of crisis in which the diplomat finds himself entangled every day. So he picks up a book, his personal copy of the latest edition of Gerardus Mercator's *Maps of the World,* races out, bows and hands it up to the Conqueror.

'I have nothing worthy but to a Great King I offer the world in which he has so great and rich a part.'

Jahangir, hand on his (own) breast: 'Everything that comes from you is welcome. I have some wild fat hogs sent to me from Goa. If your mouth is watering, I shall send you some.'

Roe, bowing: 'Anything from Your Majesty is a feast to me.'

For what the Conqueror of the World thinks of Mercator, it would be more profitable to leaf, not through Roe's journal, but through Edward Terry's Observations.

Terry disapproves of these grand-sounding titles that the Mughals give themselves. The chaplain believes that the Conqueror of the World is not Jahangir but Jesus. He traces the genealogy of the dynasty, almost accurately, for seven generations and notices that the closer he gets to his own time, the more extravagant the epithets become; and the Conqueror of the World just about takes the cake.

So the cake-taker a week later, in Episode X, in his durbar, Mercator in his hands, turning its leaves over, gazing at it from all angles like a dimwit.

Roe to Jahangir, as per Terry: 'The book describes the four parts of the world, and the several countries in them contained.'

The linguist of the day, summing up: 'You are in it, sir.'

Jahangir: 'Show me.'

Panic.

Roe, the linguist and two noblemen glance at one another, shuffle forward, pause. Four pairs of hands hesitantly reach out for the atlas, withdraw. The ambassador suddenly finds himself alone alongside the throne. He clears his throat preparatory to clearing his throat. Jahangir looks up at him and repeats: 'Will you show me, please?'

Roe bends over the page on which the known world has been longitudinally sliced to form two circles which, in the process of being prised apart and flattened out, seem to have run out of space; at the edges of the page, the last third of the two circumferences have been turned inward towards the equator to make the outer ends of the circles resemble (Roe chastises himself for such unworthy thoughts in the presence of royalty) buttocks; he jabs—always a safe thing to do—vaguely at the centre of the page: 'That is Your Majesty's domain, sir.'

Jahangir peers at the map, understands as much of it as the diplomat and in turn points to the same general area on the page: 'And this? Whose is this?'

'That is Persia, Your Majesty, Safavid territory.'

'And that?'

'Ottoman, sir. They regrettably possess a larger part of the globe than Your Majesty.'

'And that?'

'Tartaria, Your Majesty. It borders your domain.'

The Conqueror glances about him, two attendants scurry up, lift Mercator up from his lap and, holding the book open at the same page, at eye level in front of the monarch, stand stiffly before the throne. He wiggles his fingers, the attendant on the left releases a page, it curls forward in slow motion, the attendant on the right grabs it, pulls and secures it to reveal a new world. 'And this?' In this manner, page by page, emperor and ambassador travel the known world together. 'And this?'

'Hapsburg, Your Majesty. The Mediterranean, Your Majesty. The Muscovites, the Ming in China, Your Majesty, Palestina, The Holy Land...Virginia, the Americas, Your Majesty...'

Slowly, page by page, Sir Thomas watches it dawn on the Conqueror that the other maps do not add a whit to his empire. Jahangir appears for the moment downcast. The ambassador hurriedly, to distract him, says: 'Mercator is full of errors, Your Majesty. For example, he shows the Indus emptying itself into the sea at Cambay whereas you and I know that it should be Sind. If you will allow me...'

Politely, civil till the last, the emperor responds, 'Unfortunately, no one here—neither my people nor me—understands the language in which Mercator has prepared his book. Therefore—and further because I would not dream of robbing you of such a jewel—I thank you for allowing me to leaf through it and feel honoured to return your gift to you.'

So they do return presents, the Mughals, especially when the gifts make them feel small; at other times, their own stuff that they have used and are bored with, they give away to some lucky sod; the recipient on these occasions is advised to look grateful. Thus one evening in the November of 1616, Khurram calls for Sir Thomas and then as usual keeps him waiting while he fucks around, first in his harem and then at cards. After an aeon, he comes out with a cloak of gold, his own, that he has worn a couple of times and which he, ceremonially, has placed around the diplomat's shoulders. Sir Thomas remembers to look honoured and makes reverence—he writes—most unwillingly. What he recalls though, in a flash at that moment, is a vision, two decades old, of the Elizabethan stage, of Khurram's *own* forefather, eight generations removed, strutting about on it, and raving and ranting, at the Rose Theatre in London.

...the Scythian Tamburlaine,
Threatening the world with high astounding terms
And scourging kingdoms with his conquering sword.

'This golden cloak that you have given me, Prince,'—that is the thought that the language barrier prevents him from sharing with Khurram '—would have better draped the back of the actor playing Marlowe's creation. I thank you for it, nevertheless; perhaps I can bequeath—better, sell—it to the King's Men for use in another tragedy, yet to be penned, on some other member of your illustrious dynasty.'

The archives are silent on what Roe does with that cloak,

whether after his passing, by some quirk so common in history, it ever reaches, in a mere sixty years, the actor playing Khurram's son and successor in John Dryden's *Aurungzeb.*

Succession—daydreaming of it, making it happen—poisoning the competition, for instance, or trying the usual tricks, insurgency, insurrection, if it doesn't look like working out—takes up a large amount of the waking hours of the typical Mughal prince. Khurram outshines and outstrips his brothers at the game and so eleven months later, after he has been victorious against the Deccan kingdoms, his father receives him at Mandu with the love that is usually reserved only for the very successful.

'After he had paid me his respects,' writes Jahangir, 'I called him in at the window and with the impulse of excessive paternal affection and love, I immediately rose up and took him in my arms. The more he expressed his reverence and respect for me, the more my tenderness increased towards him.' 'Now in consideration of his present service,' the father orders that henceforth, a chair should be placed for the son in the court next to the Emperor's throne. Further, the Conqueror of the World, on that occasion, confers on his son the title of *King* of the World, Shahjahan.

Sir Thomas, meanwhile, continues to roam around the country for another two years and four months before finally leaving India for home on February 17, 1619. Twenty-eight months is a long time. An expensive time too, at six hundred pounds per annum plus allowances. Plus the services of a chaplain, a physician, an apothecary, a secretary, a cook and several attendants. So what's he been up to when he's not been dictating his journal?

For one, following the emperor. From Ajmer to Mandu, that's five months gone. Up mountainside and through forest, searching for camels and for water after watching, for a start, in November 1616, on Jahangir's orders, the camp at Ajmer go up in flames to compel the people to follow their king. In December 1617 then, from Mandu to Ahmedabad, where Sir Thomas suffers and survives the plague. And in September 1618, when Jahangir leaves for Agra, the diplomat parts ways with the emperor; he returns to Surat to wait four months for a ship to take him home.

The last recorded entry in the ambassador's journal dates from January 22, 1618; the rest of it, as so often happens, is lost to history. Succeeding events, though, have been reconstructed, from his letters, from the despatches of other agents and from the records of the Company. Over the centuries, white historians have agreed with the opinion that Sir Thomas had of himself: he really was the cat's whiskers. Sir William Foster, for instance, historiographer, India Office Superintendent and editor of the diplomat's journal, can hardly breathe for awe before the colossus: *Roe was the first of the long line of remarkable Englishmen who by their ability, their force of character, their unselfish adherence to lofty aims, have built up the British dominion in India; and looking down the ranks of his successors, it is not too much to say that few have equalled, none has surpassed him.*

His contemporaries though would have written a different appraisal.

On March 12, 1619, a month after the *Anne,* with Roe on board, has set sail, the factors at Surat—Thomas Kerridge, William Biddulph, Giles James and Thomas Rastell—write to the Company in London, asking it to 'be ascertained of the mean grace his lordship,' that is, Roe, 'stood in with the King and prince that, even after, three years' attendance, could not procure the gift of a house nor ground nor licence to build us a habitation'.

However, the letter goes on to elaborate, housing for the factors is not the only area that Roe's incompetence has touched and tainted. Debts remain outstanding at the court for items picked up by royalty and not paid for and—to touch only upon two instances—the ambassador's draft treaty was danced on several months ago by the royal elephants. All we have to boast of after three years, says the letter, is one firman from the emperor, a second from the prince and a handful thereafter. They are all useless—that you may perceive from the fact that the Company's goods have been rotting, detained, at the Surat custom house for the last six months. So Sir Thomas goes and plays the hero at court and gets a firman issued but the local vermin here get different orders from other sources and are also told which ones to obey.

Before his very eyes, suggest the factors, other Europeans in India have played the great game better but he has not learnt from them how to deal with the locals. 'These are a people that curbed will be brought to any reason and if suffered in their own ways grow insolent and insupportable.' They however dare not try any tricks with the Portuguese who 'encroach as much on them and do not permit any of their ships to sail without a licence'—just imagine, having to pay a foreign power a tax to ply your ships in your *own* waters, how much we can learn from the Jesuits! Even when the vessel is owned by Normall the beloved Queen, it pays its duties at Diu port. Fabulous!

And finally, the factors just don't trust the guy.

A case of doubting Thomas, 'to whom (in the *Anne*) we have delivered a box sealed, mailed and covered, containing the accounts, letters and registers and invoices and sundry other writings, both from this and the Agra factory, directed unto your worships, *which we hope he will safely deliver in the same condition; others of your servants, distrusting that conveyance, have delivered theirs to Captain Shilling, master of the ship.*

That is not the note on which an account of the adventures of so seasoned a diplomat should end; better to add that he arrives in England in September 1619, is met by the Company and his wife (whom his journal, being an official document, has all the while carefully kept under wraps), and towards the end of the month, goes to Hampton Court to call on King James, report on his embassy and hand over Jahangir's presents. These include 'two antelopes, a strange and beautiful kind of red deer, a rich tent, rare carpets, certain umbrellas and such like trinkets from the great Mughal'.

James and the Company are both pleased with all that Sir Thomas has been up to in India; in time, he is off again as king's envoy to the Ottoman Porte at Constantinople. There, since old habits die hard and a mulish leopard cannot change its spots, he bickers incessantly with the French ambassador over precedence, over who, amongst four European envoys, for instance, will sign above, and who below, a joint letter to the Turkish government. It is a good moment to say goodbye to him, there at his desk, gazing at the letter that he has just signed in such a way that he has left absolutely no space for anyone to squeeze in a signature above his, gloating over the trick that he has played on that frog of an envoy from Paris, and exulting in diplomacy's simple pleasures.

But diplomacy's complex designs and history's intricate lessons, when does he reflect on those? He must, he is an intelligent man. Mooching about for four months in Surat for instance, waiting for a ship to load, or the tide to turn and a monsoon wind to take him away, of course he thinks incessantly of his three years on the sub-continent and what went right and what didn't. They have wandered over the Central Asian steppes and arrived by way of those mountain passes, this Mughal lot, they thrive on the great plains, they are landlubbers, what do they know of the sea? So be it, not to ignore the oceans is one lesson that history will not let them forget. That is, after they learn it. *If* they learn it. Four thousand seven hundred miles of coastline and not one of them—Gujarat, Bijapur, Calicut, Travancore, Vijaynagar, Golconda or the Mughals, most of all, the Mughals—maintain what can seriously be called a navy.

Thus, Pietro Della Vale, the Italian nobleman travelling through India, comments in 1624: 'The Mughal is a very great and wealthy king, whose revenues arise from his own lands and not from the sea; and one to whom that little which is to be had from the sea is nothing because it accrues rather to some small captain of his, as the governor of Surat, and the like, than to the king himself.'

But is it wise to leave the oceans to the Europeans, is it not dynastic hubris? They are merchants after all, the rest of them are not diplomats fretting over protocol. From Surat, within years of Sir Thomas's departure from these shores, the English move both westward to fight with and oust the Portuguese from the Persian Gulf, and south-eastward to barter and bicker with the Dutch in Bantam and Batavia. In the decades to come, as Surat declines, they found Calcutta, they grab Bengal. With the tenacity of termites, they make inroads wherever they can and then wait for the grand edifice to crumble, to fall. In a hundred years, it is all, all over.

Two last facets of that dynastic hubris before the end. One dates from November, 1644. Sir Thomas, obese and suffering dreadfully from gout, arthritis and depression, is on his deathbed. He cannot spare a thought for what Old Khurram is up to four thousand three hundred miles away in Agra. Well, Old Khurram is building a mausoleum, all in white marble, for his favourite queen. He has been at it for twelve years already, it will take another nine to be completed. (He's in there too. In 1658, his son pulls him off the throne so that he can sit in his place; he imprisons Daddy in Agra Fort till his death in 1666 and then buries him beside Madam Mumtaz. Pleased with himself, the son has already christened himself Alamgir,

Conqueror of the World.) The marble for the monument comes all the way from Makrana; in modern times, the mausoleum would have cost over fifty billion rupees to build. It now hosts some three million visitors a year. They come and gawk at what money and white marble can do.

In contrast, Sir Thomas's tomb in Woodford in Essex, England, cannot today be found.

This story began with a journal, it ends with a memoir, that of the *first* Conqueror of the World. So what does the emperor think of the ambassador? After all, the *Tuzuk-i-Jahangiri* has everything that one would want to know about the Mughal monarch who was so gracious to Sir Thomas—whom he liked, whom he promoted, whom he had whipped and killed, where he went, what he ate, who came to call on him, what gifts they brought, what he gave them in return, what his favourite foods, fruits and animals were, and what he thought of Kashmir, Agra, Ahmedabad, elephants, horses, and hunting trips. History it has—how ancient Cambay is and what it was called in the olden days—and politics—how one subdues the troublesome Ranas of Rajputana—geography—the pleasures of the gardens of Kabul—and diplomacy—the visit of the Persian ambassador is described and the letter from his boss, the Safavid Shah, is given in full.

Yes, the Tuzuk has *almost* everything, for it is odd, though, that of Sir Thomas, his embassy, his king and his country, in all those seven hundred pages, there is not a hint, not a whisper, not a *single word*.

Othello Sucks

This being at some moments a piece of non-fiction, at others a radio play and at yet others a comic strip in prose, Father, one of its four principal dramatis personae, feels that the title is incomplete without a colon. Othello Sucks, colon, and then an apposite phrase from Shakespeare's play.

The radio play starts with Younger Daughter at dinner spitting out the title without looking up from reading her mobile phone. No one responds. *Othello sucks* does not even register with either Mother or Elder Daughter.

Chomp chomp slurp slurp gas. Father is in four minds. He does not want to be distracted from his khichuri with meatballs or his meditations on his indigestion or his plans on what to take in his tiffin tomorrow. Yet not to respond to a cry for help would be churlish; Younger Daughter would then flounce back to her room and slam the door shut so hard on her family that it would bring down once more some plaster from the ceiling; in a chain reaction, the trembling of the entire building would in turn trigger off the frenzied barking of the three Great Danes in the apartment two floors above.

Thus Father, airily: Well, who doesn't, in this world?

Prompting from Younger Daughter a torrent: Well, if it's English, no one in class can follow it. 'Ay you did wish that I would make her turn. Sir, she can turn, and turn, and yet go on And turn again; and she can weep, sir, weep; And she's obedient; as you say, obedient, Very obedient—' The lines sound like gobbledygook so you read the notes and learn that 'turn' also means 'pursue sexual encounters' and 'obedient' also means 'sexually pliant'. So then the lines make sense but big deal it simply isn't worth the effort! And the boys go around saying 'Miss Miss make me your obedient servant.' You dig deep for all that meaning and all you come up with is a potato and I have a Class Test tomorrow on it and I'll fail and I won't get an Excellence Award this year!!

Noises of plaster falling while Mother, coldly: How competitive you've made them.

And Elder Daughter, in a daze, as though remembering September 11: *I* had *The Merchant of Venice.* In not more than five hundred words, explain which of the gold, silver and lead caskets you find the most screamingly boring. Compared to that, a retarded black guy who sucks is a rock concert.

Whose bright idea is it to subject the children in this day and age and clime and country to Shakespeare? is an issue that Father has raised at several Parent Teacher meetings. He'd thought that the school, being a good right-wing South Delhi Punjabi institution, would be receptive, but it has turned out to be as deaf as the regulars around the dining table at home. But he has persevered: Shakespeare is not in the Central Board exam syllabus. I mean, do we want them as adults to speak in iambic pentametre when they apply for internships to CNN-IBN? No. Grammatically correct and lucid English, that's what we want. Think Rex Harrison in *My Fair Lady.*

Indefatigable Mrs Dasgupta the Language Skills Teacher, in response, has suggested that he come and give a talk to the senior classes on *Which English Do We Want to Learn? The Relevance of Shakespeare to India in the Twenty-first Century.*

She is renowned, says Elder Daughter, for roping in parents to lessen her own work. She sucks.

At the thought of Father performing in front of her classmates, Younger Daughter stops going to school. No one notices. She also begins to be marked absent from the dining table. Her three-hour Karaoke sessions in the bathroom however continue. Father begins reading up for his lecture and is soon an irritable wreck.

For beneath his babble, he is actually shocked by how dull and dimwitted he finds Othello the personality to be. And pompous. Pompous and dull and dimwitted because he is black. How could any reader ignore that?

The bugger is as embarrassing, he tells the bathroom mirror while flossing, as Hurree Jamshet Ram Singh. And about as funny. But one is black and the other brown. Same thing. Noble princes both, one beggar merely duskier than the other. Or is it me? Am I just rereading the play at the wrong time and is it meant for younger people of another country?

O thou dull Moor. Am I sure I know exactly what a Moor is? Abibe Bikila isn't a Moor is he? And Anwar Sadat but not Kenneth Kaunda—is that it?

Berber! Mauretania! shrieks Younger Daughter in response over the music and through the shut doors of her bathroom *and* her bedroom. *Including Mauritania!*

No one reacts. The cat continues to doze on the tea cozy at the centre of the dining table and Mother to inspect the screen of her laptop and curse the Internet Service provider. After a moment, Elder Daughter elaborates with a smirk: There's a black guy in her class whom I think she has a crush on. That's how she knows the little that she knows.

Into the conversation at the dining table, enter Cheikh Luigi Fall.

He is seventeen, tall, dark and handsome, one half Mauritanian, a quarter Italian, a quarter Turk. He is perfectly bilingual in Italian and French and claims fluency in Arabic and English. He is popular amongst his classmates in part because his English is a rich source of amusement for them. They envy him because he is exempt from Hindi and wanders off to the computer lab to surf while their heads ache and rock and reel over Tulsidas and Chhayavaad and Nirala. In a school—and nation—obsessed with cricket, he is terrific at football. To break the ice, the girls ask him what he's doing there with them. He confusedly explains that he's there because they arrived at the wrong time of year, and that after some months he hopes to move to the American school.

He is completely tranquil, as meditative as the Gandhara Buddha, during *Othello*. Leave alone Shakespeare, he can't follow a word of Mrs Dasgupta's English.

Younger Daughter in fact is bemused to learn that for a large, underprivileged section of the globe, Shakespeare is not the first thing that comes to mind on hearing the word 'Othello'. Cheikh, for instance, on grasping that his class devotes one session per week to the play, is puzzled; his brow furrows—rather attractively, thinks Younger Daughter—as he asks: Verdi? Are we going to listen in class to Verdi?

Two days pass before Mother says: Enough is enough. Why have you stopped going to school?

Younger Daughter does not look up from her mobile phone but in the slouch of her shoulders can be detected the crouch of a cornered feline. Her elder sister, smirking out of nervousness, responds on her behalf: There's been a bit of an Incident.

Exactly how black is Othello, Ma'm? Would he be darker than you? is what Lamborghini has asked Mrs Dasgupta right at the beginning of class.

Everyone shut up. It was so silent, recounts Younger Daughter, that you could hear Lamborghini's Tag Heuer ticking.

Wow, says Father. I imagine that Bengal's sable daughter was not amused.

It was horrible, continues Younger Daughter happily. 'We are studying *Othello*,' said Mrs Dasgupta, 'because our own society is one of the most racist and skin-conscious in the world.' There were tears in her eyes.

He's horrible too, comments Mother, that Lamborghini. No one in our time would've *dared* to say that to a teacher even in his or her wildest imaginings.

Younger Daughter waves her mother's time and her imaginings into the chicken curry. She then looks down at her mobile phone for inspiration to compose a case for the defence. He's been overlooked for Head Boy and he's sure it's Mrs Dasgupta's fault. At the Teachers' Council meeting, apparently, it was she who said that there should be a Head Girl this year because we've had a Head Boy three years running.

Aha, exclaims Father, Hell hath no fury like a man overlooked. In fact, that's *exactly* what I'm going to say in my lecture. *Othello* is about Iago. He is unjustly overlooked for promotion and so something snaps in his head. He *has* to be surrounded by dullards so that he can work his revenge out in a couple of hours. The rest is...noise.

No one pays him any attention. The only thing nice about Lamborghini, muses Elder Daughter, is his wealth.

Lamborghini drives one even though he is underage. His family has no Indian car other than a Maruti Esteem that the servants use to go to the market. Younger Daughter's parents do not know his real name. They don't care. They become aware that such a being walks and drives on the face of the earth when a huge scarlet head-turning thing scrunches to a stop one evening outside the gates of the house. Younger Daughter, who has the hearing of a canine for things that matter, through the music and the two shut doors, registers the arrival of the car and within eighteen seconds is gliding out through the front door when:

Just where, asks Mother, do you think you're going wearing those clothes?

Mumble mumble, says Younger Daughter.

Is he playing the chauffeur in a getaway car that he can't come in to say hello to us?

Embarrassed, scowling and in a foul mood, Younger Daughter exits and re-enters some moments later accompanied by something large.

Mumble mumble, says Lamborghini.

The worser welcome! says Father. I have charged thee not to haunt about my doors. In honest plainness thou has heard me say My daughter is not for thee. And now, in madness, Being full of supper and distemp'ring draughts, Upon malicious knavery dost thou come To start my quiet.

No one reacts. The family members look horrified and Lamborghini frightened. Plaster falls as Younger Daughter, softly moaning in shame at having the parents she has, rushes off to change into something less revealing.

Lamborghini, who at the age of seventeen has made a reservation, is taking Younger Daughter out to dinner at the Taj Machaan.

The nerve. She has to have dinner at home. The maid's cooked. Carrot and beetroot soup. Full of vitamins. You want to stay too?

Mumble mumble.

Do lunch. Why don't the two of you do lunch outdoors on a sunny day? Vitamins. Our daughters are petrified of the sun for fear they'll turn black. You too?

Lamborghini is more pale yellow than fair, a shade that would look rather nice, notes Father, on an expensive car.

Mrs Dasgupta's complexion actually would look even nicer, like an advertisement for Belgian chocolate with 72% cacao in it. Only Cheikh though is thinking of all the chocolate that he can't find in India as the class holds its collective breath while waiting for Mrs Dasgupta to throw Lamborghini out for saying what he has just said.

She doesn't have to. Without even mumbling anything, Lamborghini himself stumbles out of the room, down the stairs, across Assembly Quadrangle, out the gates and into the waiting Toyota Lexus. The guards at the gate stop their game of cards to stand up and salute his wealth. They don't do that for every student.

He hasn't been back in class since, concludes Younger Daughter impressively.

And so? What does *his* lack of breeding have to do with *your* truancy?

Younger Daughter waves her mother's question into the sprouted moong dal and garlic fry. But that is not the only one left unanswered. No one in school has yet replied for instance to Lamborghini's question either. Exactly how black is Othello, Ma'm?

It is Cheikh who, surfing the Net in the computer lab, returns with the responses of history's well-known men.

Pretty black, is the answer and not particularly pretty, for it is not Othello's stupidity that disturbs Samuel Taylor Coleridge but his blackness. 'It would be something monstrous to conceive this beautiful Venetian girl falling in love with a veritable Negro.' Ditto Charles Lamb: 'There is something extremely revolting in the courtship and wedded caresses of Othello and Desdemona.' Neither critic is disturbed by the fundamental assumption of the play that Othello is dumb because he is black.

Nor is Elder Daughter. Desdemona is even dumber, she snorts. I mean, Desdemona *really* sucks. They're made for each other, so what's the problem? No one in fact is sorry to see her strangled. It does improve the play.

It is again Cheikh who points out in class that white audiences being disturbed by Othello's blackness was—is—will be—a global phenomenon. He quotes Stendhal recounting an incident that occurred in the August of 1822: 'Last year, the soldier standing guard at the interior of the theatre in Baltimore, seeing Othello who, in the fifth Act of the tragedy of that name, was going to kill Desdemona, cried out: "It will never be said that in my presence a damned black would kill a white woman." At that moment the soldier fired his gun and broke the arm of the actor who played Othello.'

Playing Othello therefore has proved dangerous for some whites even when they, for a protective shield, have painted themselves blacker than jet.

And exactly how black do *they* consider Othello to be? Here is Laurence Olivier in his autobiography dated 1986: 'Black all over my body, Max Factor 2880, then a lighter brown, then Negro No 2, a stronger brown. Brown on black to give a rich mahogany. Then the great trick: that glorious half-yard of chiffon with which I polished myself all over until I shone...The lips blue-berry, the tight curled wig, the white of the eyes whiter than ever and the black, black sheen that covered my flesh and bones, glistening in the dressing-room lights...I am Othello...'

Or Enid Blyton's Mr Golly. A tragic golliwog given to histrionics and hyperbole, an old black ram, a barbary horse who, gullible and garrulous, murders an innocent woman and then commits suicide. Well, why not? Even golliwogs have souls. Being black, a lot of soul.

Mrs Dasgupta unfortunately is not impressed with that line of argument. They bump into her when they are summoned to school to discuss with the Principal Younger Daughter's means of transport between home and school and back again. Discussions around the dining table at home—round in shape, it may be added—have revealed that for the past two months, in the mornings, Younger Daughter has been dutifully waving to Father and boarding the school bus but hopping off it before the first teacher gets on at the next stop; she however arrives in school in the Lamborghini well before the bus. It is a comfortable and powerful car and she can unwind in it properly over her morning cigarette.

If she gets thrown out, says Mother, I'm packing up, getting a transfer and taking them back with me and away from this foul city.

Father doesn't argue. They prefer to bicker in front of the children, firmly believing that hearing the verbal duels of their parents helps in their mental development, giving them metaphors and turns of phrase that they would otherwise have taken a decade to make their own. (Elder Daughter, for instance, ever since her second term in KG has peppered her exchanges with 'bootlicker' and 'asshole'.)

You want to go on ahead, asks Father, hoping against hope, and seduce the Principal while I chat to Madam Maa Kaali about my views on the Moor of Venice?

Father is annoyed to learn that Dasgupta has practically forgotten her invitation to him to talk to the senior classes about Shakespeare.

Oh...I didn't know you were *that* keen...we'll have to see about a slot...Saturday seems possible but I can see the children *not* being enthused at having to come in on a holiday to listen to your radical views on Othello...They *love* the play, you know...

Oh.

Suddenly they are surrounded by a dozen noisy children,

all at once overwhelmed by the youthfulness of youth. The students are expectedly all talking at the same time and squeaking excitedly about nothing of interest to anyone else. They turn out to be Younger Daughter's classmates on their way to an elocution class in the open air. Mother recognizes some of them. Good morning, Auntie! Hello, Uncle! The elders smile at their youth. It is infectious. One girl, with eyes more sparkling and a manner saucier than those of the others, asks Father: What happened at the Principal's, Uncle?

Father prepares to mumble a reply but is tongue-tied, suddenly, by how *old* he feels in their presence. The boys seem so lithe and...uncaring of their bodies and the girls so...so in bloom that he feels creaky, musty, disjointed, he feels as fragile and yellowed as a page of an unopened classic.

They don't fortunately need an answer, for just then, the tall North African boy at the back, realizing whose parents they are, greets Mother and Father with: Good morning, Mrs____ and Good morning, Mr____. His classmates, laughing and shrieking, pounce upon him with quotations from Othello: We don't say that here, you erring barbarian, we say Auntie and Uncle because all humanity is one hopelessly enormous Hindu joint family!

Villain, adds Father, half-recovering, that was most heathenish and most gross.

What you know, you know, sir, responds Cheikh in an accent that—like those of the others—falls far short of that imaginary Shakespearean ideal; a European accent his is—unlike those of the others—of one who has grown up in a world wherein English barely appeared on his radar, who has experienced it en passant as the language of Hollywood and North America.

From this time forth I never will speak word. And amidst

the laughter, O dear, says Father to himself, for he notes that the boy is green-eyed.

In his talk to the students that Mrs Dasgupta has not found the time for, Father has planned to devote some space to the green-eyed monster. For decades, he has known Act Three Scene Three—the great temptation scene—by heart and has recited chunks of it to himself the way his contemporaries sing Kishore Kumar and Blind Faith in the shower. O beware, my lord, of jealousy! It is the green-eyed monster, which doth mock The meat it feeds on. To Father, the *Othello* music is more melodious than the most irrepressibly peppy Hindi film hit or any epochal rock anthem.

But the intensity of his love for that euphony is secret, because he has always felt it to be freaky, absurd, so out of place as to be an embarrassment. Shakespeare is white and his audience is white, and don't you forget it. For two centuries he has been used as a whitening agent for the colonial mind—bleaching powder, if you will; read him as white, for the poet of all humanity is fiction and does not exist; black Othello sucks because the Bard behind him is white.

The Principal is fair, affable, huge, hairy. Mother is annoyed that he and Father spend the first quarter-hour chatting about the good old days at St Stephen's College. That is *not* what she has taken half a day's leave from office for. And then suddenly the googly.

And is your daughter ha ha smoking your brand of cigarette? Wills Navy Cut, wasn't it?

Ha ha *ha*, responds Father, not ready to be outdone, I don't know, we haven't smoked together yet.

The issue is complicated. Younger Daughter is in the running for Head Girl but they cannot have a Head Girl who smokes.

The issue is simple, argues Father at the dining table. Puff away to death *after* you've left school, what's the problem?

She can't stop smoking, slips in Elder Daughter, because Lamborghini has just gifted her an entire carton of Silk Cut as a *pre*-birthday present. When he kills her, he can then become Head Boy. It is much cooler though to smoke than to be Head Girl.

She doesn't want to waste the remaining two thousand cigarettes, adds Mother in a tone of ice. Those are *your* miserly genes.

In India, females who smoke are morally loose, you know that, returns Father to the attack. They smoke, they wear skirts and elope at midnight with some most unsuitable weirdo.

That's not me, counters Younger Daughter, shrieking, en route to slamming two doors and setting off once more the Great Danes in the building. *That's Desdemona!!!*

With whom all the girls of the class have a problem. They find Act One to be fun because here's this obviously kinky Venetian chick doing a moonlight flit with some old and ugly ram, some Army type. I mean, how freaky is that? To them, the real tragedy of the play is twofold: one, how Desdemona from kinky chick with a mind of her own so rapidly descends to become dumb dame, silly and passive and—oof!—so dull. And then secondly, it is simply dreadful how all those horrible males in the play continually refer to all the females as whores and Shakespeare does fuck-all to dispel that impression that Venice has of women. I'faith and Zounds, Ma'm, but the bard in *Othello* is an MCP.

To wind up then, a coda. Or in the words of Iago in Act Three Scene Three, Scan this thing no further, leave it to time.

And to wind up then, one by one the loose ends. Father gets so entangled in the Shakespeare industry, in the critical biographies, the scholarly monographs, textual variations, performance histories, the post-colonial discourses that he never finishes preparing his paper. At the dining table, he is appropriately embarrassed to learn from Younger Daughter that it has been two weeks since the class has finished *Othello* and moved on to *How to Win Friends and Influence People*; not surprisingly, the class as one has begun to pine for sweet Desdemona, the blacker devil and honest, honest Iago.

The loose ends continued. Snigdha is chosen Head Girl. She is a horrendous tart, elaborates an outraged Elder Daughter. Younger Daughter smokes thirty cigarettes in two days and stops all other activities except for breathing. This can't go on forever, says Mother's sms to her after two days.

Wait and see, responds Younger Daughter after another two days.

Nirbhaya Bhavah, advises Father, feeling multilingual. No one is sure whom the advice is for.

Leave it to time, says Iago. It is thus a week later that Father, in the car on the way back from work, hits upon the title for a paper that he will never deliver. Othello Sucks Colon The Pity of It Iago for It Is Your Play. Father is delighted; Shakespeare

however is obliterated from his head even before he has parked in front of the house. The lights in all the rooms are on and the music so loud that no passerby fails to glance up at the windows. The Great Danes, more attuned to post-modern rock'n rap, frenziedly bark their disapproval like fans booing at a concert. Father has the impression that the mad woman who owns them has placed before their muzzles the microphone of a public address system.

He cannot immediately place the music. That is not saying very much. At the front door, with some of the wonder of

Alexander Fleming examining his blue mould and its penicillin, he says to himself: But it's *opera*. He rings the doorbell fourteen times. He searches for his house keys. *Italian* opera.

Chi e la? Otello?

Father opens the door and is physically engulfed by sound. His eardrums hum and he can actually feel it tingling his skin. He is certain that Younger Daughter has hanged herself out of depression, her lack of vitamins and her love of bloody drama and Verdi is her way of saying arrivederci. Mother in front of her laptop and Elder Daughter before her Ipad are both at the dining table. Father is sure that they are asking Google what to do when a near and dear one hangs herself.

Elder Daughter sees him. She is beaming with joy and mischief. Communication is possible only by means of sms, email or sign language. She smses Father: Guess who gifted her the Verdi CD.

He couldn't care less. He smses back: Frankly my dear I don't give a damn. How can we stop the music?

Reading his mind, Younger Daughter presses a button in the bathroom. The silence is shocking; it feels like kilos of winter clothes being shed all at once, clouds lifting, like freedom, as though one could stretch one's limbs again in the warm sun. The dogs, flummoxed, remain open-mouthed and dumb for a whole day.

She wants to know, says Mother, if she can go out for dinner. I've said yes but she has to ask you too.

Father feels the presence of Younger Daughter behind him. He turns. He hasn't seen her for a day and a half. Beneath her bandanna, her face is radiant, almost unrecognizable.

It suits you, that rag on your head.

Cheikh wants to take me out to dinner. We've made a reservation. Younger Daughter is blushing with joy.

The bandanna is Cheikh's first gift, a silk handkerchief, spotted with strawberries; the silk is from Egypt.

Oh, says Father, so what is the plot for the evening? You lose the handkerchief, he goes on and on and on about monumental alabaster and Promethean heat; when you can't take it any more, Heaven have mercy on me, you moan, then he strangles you?

Your daughter has made arrangements for any eventuality, says Mother in a voice so dry that the cat on the tea cozy twitches her right ear in appreciation.

At least he doesn't smoke, points out Elder Daughter. And if they have children, their skins will have more melanin to better absorb ultraviolet light.

Sure, go ahead, have fun, says Father. But who's 'we' in 'made a reservation'?

Lamborghini of course. A threesome. She just loves that car.

The Killings in Madna

'Sub-Divisional Magistrate of Rameri, Sir, holding on.'

'Hmm.' Srivastav picked up the receiver, winced automatically as the click from the PA's phone blasted against his eardrum, and explored his nose for a while, waiting.

'Hello. Hello?'

'Yes, Shafique?'

'Sir, good morning sir. Reporting from Rameri sir. I went to the site just now sir. Couldn't go earlier because returned this morning only, sir, from tour, and learnt only this morning, sir, at eight—'

'Which site?' Srivastav frowned at the huge teak board on the right wall.

'Sir?'

'What site bhai?'

A startled pause. 'But the Police Superintendent must've reported, sir, he was there this morning too.'

'No he hasn't, you report now,' said Srivastav patiently. Then the telephone made some incredible noises. Srivastav waited. He hated the teak board; its size, the complete absence of grace and proportion in the painting of the names on it. Initially they had even misspelt his name, had written *RAPE* Srivastav. He hated the inevitability with which the board drew attention to itself. Some bores of Madna would perch on the edge of the chairs in the office, knees tight together, and say, 'DM saab, a very nice board sir, a slice of history, the names of all the District Magistrates of Madna over eighty years on one board, right from 1902, absolutely historical sir.'

'Sir.'

Srivastav yawned unexpectedly; his mind half-returned to his sub-divisional officer.

'Last night at about eleven, there were five killings on the Madna-Rameri road sir. Bad killings sir, beaten to death with stones and bamboo rods, we found three sticks of bamboo sir, with caked blood on them, brown and thick. No one is sure how many killers there were, about five or six sir, says the one survivor, their modus operandi was stepping onto the road from near the culvert—'Shafique paused here, to give Srivastav an opportunity to grumble and frown at his incoherence.

'Sir. Just after Gurdev's dhaba there's a big dip in the road, and a culvert sir, where the Forest Department has built that shelter to guard all that bamboo that's being cut. The killers waited by this culvert sir, quite close to the Forest hut, but the Forest guard heard nothing he says, no cries, no sound, odd. The SP saab even suspects some connection with bamboo piracy sir. In about half-an-hour they stopped six passers-by, four cyclists sir and two Sikh businessmen on a scooter. Must've stopped them by force sir, or some excuse. Then they dragged them off the road, no plan, indiscriminate murder, anyone who stopped. All victims identified sir, three residents of Rameri, two of Madna, one survivor also of Madna. Families notified sir. Very sad, two cyclists were returning home after dinner at their sister's, the businessmen had four thousand with them, their shop says. The others couldn't've had much, a few hundred in all.

'One cyclist escaped sir. They beat him too, must've thought he was dead. He saw them stop the Sikhs' scooter. They jumped onto the road and just swung a bamboo at the man in front.

So the scooter fell, spun round and round and crashed into the bamboo. Then they went for the businessmen. Then this cyclist, his name's Kapoor sir, crawled along the nala and round a bend in the road, about five hundred yards sir. Then he hid in the cut bamboo. He fainted once or twice sir, nights quite cold in that open area and they'd smashed his wrist and taken his watch, so he didn't know how long he waited. Finally he stumbled and crawled to Rameri, because by then less traffic sir, just a few trucks, and their drivers too drunk to stop for Kapoor. Tough fellow sir, went straight to the police station. The FIR says crime reported at 2.45, but the police reached the site at about seven sir. Kapoor says the police were quite unhelpful, but later they took him to hospital, wounds not so serious. Was discharged at about 10.30 and has already returned to Madna—sir?'

Srivastav simplified and repeated his question. He was trying to get at the implications of the killings, their reverberations; I am not a bloody policeman, he told himself, I am an administrator, I don't need these petty details.

'Yes sir, the news *has* spread all over Rameri. People as usual are complaining that the police can't do anything. *Could* be a law and order problem in a few days sir.'

'Okay. Remain at headquarters. And report immediately any tension of any kind.' Then Srivastav leaned back and looked blankly at his desk, wondering. He wiped his forearms with his pale yellow hand-towel. He hated his chair. It was orange, of some expensive artificial leather, squeaky and non-absorbent, hopelessly impractical for the heat of Madna. The world of the district was quieter and, Srivastav admitted, five murders on the state highway were more than sensational: the event was cataclysmic. He tried to visualize the killings on the orange decolam of his table and looked up when the connecting door between their offices opened slowly and Joshi, his Resident Deputy Collector, sidled in.

Joshi was fifty-four, excitable, delighted with any emergency the details of which he could exaggerate or at least distort; an ageing alarmist in a flapping grey safari suit.

'You've heard, Joshi saab, haven't you?'

It was unlikely that Joshi had not heard. 'Yes sir, about ten minutes ago. Kapoor's a teller in Union Bank, and his Manager's my neighbour, he told me just as I was getting into the jeep.'

The district was at his fingertips. He had been born in Madna. For decades he had had an ear to its ground. Srivastav was the outsider. Collectors in the district are birds of passage, transient decorous representatives of a remote government. Srivastav would leave as he had come, abruptly, on sudden orders of transfer, causing no ripple in Madna, his bequest one more name on the teak board. Joshi was a sharp contrast. Srivastav relied on him to get at what he called the pulse of Madna.

'A tough time for the police sir.' Joshi smiled delightedly. Two hundred thousand paans had tainted his teeth the colour of blood. 'The SP will probably be transferred.'

'He hasn't even phoned me yet, the SP, to report this, now that's both unexpected and irritating.'

'Sir,' said Joshi and no more. He could not criticize the Superintendent of Police to his Collector, not past a certain point.

'What does Madna say?'

'Much sympathy for Kapoor sir. He's loving all that attention, keeping open court at home today. The *Citizen's Voice* has already interviewed him for tomorrow.' Behind his brown spectacles, Joshi's eyes were round with excitement. His translucent, flabby cheeks almost quivered. 'Sir, the SP was in Rameri last evening. He had dinner with the General Manager at that paper mill. He returned at about eleven, he should've seen the killers on the road.' He beamed at his Collector.

An absurdity, but Srivastav allowed all kinds of stuff to come his way. He thought highly of his own discernment; later, in tranquillity, he would cautiously sift the evidence, explore, examine, and emerge in quiet triumph with premature, immature decisions. 'I see.'

'And sir, Rameri notified the SP at three in the morning, but the constable at his house said the SP was sleeping, he couldn't be disturbed.'

Now this was serious. Srivastav tucked it away in his mind and hoped to God that he would remember it at the right time. 'Joshi, if you could get your neighbour Manager to agree, you and he could visit Kapoor. Commiserate etcetera, and also make sure that he isn't talking too much. The more reporters and people he talks to, the stronger their reaction, and the tougher the job of the police.'

Joshi wiped off the sweat drops on his upper lip. In excited agreement he fluttered his pale hands, like butterflies. Then he hunched his shoulders and turned towards the door. The telephone rang. 'SP on the line sir.' Srivastav asked Joshi to stay. Joshi returned to his chair with flurrying limbs.

'Good morning DM saab.' The Superintendent's voice conjured him up quite accurately, short, obese, shrewd, well-matured in the study of iniquity.

'Morning Dhiraj. I expected your call much earlier. I was about to call you myself.'

'Oh yes uh yes—'

'I heard early this morning. Shafique phoned hours ago. He caught me just as I was going out for badminton.' This lie should hurt you, Fatboy, smiled Srivastav to himself.

'Ah. I met Shafique myself this morning at the place of the killings. I asked him whether he'd contacted you. He said yes. An efficient fellow, Shafique.'

Srivastav's face flushed a little at this nonchalant lie returned for his. Suddenly he wanted to snap, Section Six of your Police Act tells you I am your boss, you are answerable to me. But he said nothing. It is not good for a district, he reminded himself loftily, that its Collector and Superintendent of Police should quarrel. Then the Superintendent's face bobbed up in his mind, the small eyes encased in fat, the wispy moustache above the thin red lips, and Srivastav could curb himself no longer. 'You should still have called me immediately, Dhiraj. As a Superintendent of the district police, isn't it your duty to inform your Collector of such an important incident?' Srivastav smirked, leaned back in his uncomfortable chair and waited for the Superintendent to squirm.

He did, but indirectly, with much circumlocution. 'Yes... busy...had presumed...would have telephoned after some progress...Shafique...'

Srivastav sipped tepid water and held the telephone some distance from his ear. It was an easy way of expressing contempt for the policeman; for, face to face, he would have had to be moderate. Across the decolam, the obliquity of Srivastav's reprimand would have provided the policeman the chance to pretend that it, the reprimand, did not exist at all. Srivastav was not timid, but the relationship was intricate. He had to tread softly.

'Dhiraj, I hear that just after Kapoor reached the police station, Rameri telephoned your house, at three this morning, but the constable on duty did not wake you up. I can't believe this negligence.'

Kumar—Dhiraj—sighed faintly. 'Yes. I was shocked myself. I intend to suspend the constable.'

Srivastav's lips slid off his teeth mirthlessly. It was a very old story, one scapegoat, any scapegoat, as long as it looked as though the choice of scapegoat settled the issue. And sometimes even appearances did not matter. That constable got his orders from you, Fatty, to let you sleep like the innocent.

'Okay good, and what progress in the case?'

Kumar slid smoothly into the official, the professional mode. 'Oh we've begun. Combing the area, rounding up suspects, investigations proceeding. I find that Forest guard suspicious. You know Srivastav saab, there's a lot of bamboo being stolen from the area but the Forest Department never admits it. We are exploring that also, maybe a connection there. I've spoken to DIG saab about this of course. He's coming in very soon, will you join us for lunch? We could—'

Srivastav evaded lunch. '...But I'll look in in the afternoon. You'll be going to Rameri with Mr Makhija?'

'Yes, at about three.'

'I'll try and be there before that. Okay Dhiraj.' Srivastav leaned back again, arms behind his head, his thumbs idly manoeuvring his shirt collar to dry the sweat off his neck. He was surrounded by featureless high yellow walls. His office had two windows with those ridiculous half-curtains which irrationally reminded Srivastav of a woman's Occidental evening gown, satin or silk barely covering breasts, exposing large chunks of shoulder and upper thorax. Through the windows he could see two of the arches of the corridor and a semi-circle of merciless blue sky.

Did I manage Dhiraj well? He couldn't be certain. And now the district would really come alive. The Minister would call, long distance at some absurd hour at the end of a prolonged day. He would want to know, he would complain about fielding questions in the Legislative Assembly ('Why did this have to happen in the session, hayn?'), about the 'deteriorating law and order situation'. In a day or two he would arrive in Madna, the officials would scurry after him, his presence would quite overturn the placid chaos of district administration.

Then Vishwanath, the bald ex-MLA, a paan-spitting goonda, once a Sharma, who had left behind his Brahmin surname at some obscure bend in his political career, he would head a few noisy morchas, concoct new derisive slogans against the magistracy and the police. The local yellow papers ('of the shade of shit', the ex-Collector had called them, exhaling aromatic pipe smoke) would gorge on the killings, interview and publicize the most improbable people. The killings would be politicized; like the constable, a few others would be suspended or perhaps transferred. The killings themselves would drown under the weight of other tensions, desires, complexities.

Srivastav pressed the buzzer. His PA's head emerged from behind the curtain. 'Where is our dear SDM under training?' The head nodded and disappeared. All the curtains in the room had the reiterated pattern of a fat baby with a rose in his left hand laughing at a parrot just above his head.

When the PA returned, he was bespectacled and officious, examining with dignity an open file. 'He's with the District Treasury sir.'

'Oh a useless place. Send a message, ask him to be at my office at two. He'll go with me to meet the DIG.'

At five to two, Srivastav was attacking his sandwiches and ignoring the faint acidity behind his sternum. The curtain rippled a little and Agastya Sen slipped in. 'Good afternoon sir. Oh sorry sir, I didn't know you were at lunch.'

'No no, that's alright, come in. Here, have one.' Srivastav mumbled through a stuffed mouth and, waving away the genuine protests, forced a sandwich on his trainee sub-collector. Agastya ate slowly, with embarrassed face and closed mouth, avoiding his boss's eye, blankly examining the decolam.

It was an honour, Srivastav had once held, almost a privilege, to train a junior in the wiles of administration; when Government gave a Collector this responsibility, it clearly indicated that it thought highly of him. But Agastya Sen had brought disillusion. He irritated Srivastav by what Srivastav took to be his disinterest in the district.

Agastya was slim and tall, bearded and self-possessed. Across the table, Srivastav examined his carefully expressionless face with mild distaste. Slowly a silent deadly fart wafted up to Srivastav's nose. He sighed irritably and said, 'How's the Treasury?'

'Okay sir.'

'It shouldn't be. During my training it was a pain in the arse.' A bawdy idiom was unfamiliar to Srivastav but he used it with Sen to show that he was an informal, chummy boss, for the trainee's taciturnity unnerved him a little.

'You've heard of the killings near Rameri?'

'No sir.'

'Tch but you should have.' Srivastav was irritated with his own anger. 'You must be involved in the district Sen, if you want to be a good administrator.'

'Sir.'

Srivastav cooled a little. 'Anyway the killings will be a good chance to see how we mismanage a crisis, what happens with the police and the politicians, how the district reacts.'

In the car, Agastya got the details. The killings thrilled him. His disinterest in the district was really a longing for his old life, the irresponsibility of his university days and the attractions of his Eng Lit. But these killings enlivened Madna. They pushed aside for the moment the deathly monotony of revenue courts and Family Planning functions, the agonizing dullness of land acquisition and rural development. To Agastya, the killings somehow made Madna feel like his Delhi, where they would have appeared on page three of *The Statesman*, and where, over tea, in his hostel room, he would have commented on the sad confusing details, after which desultory lewd conversation would have concluded in the decision to skip the first two classes that day.

The police officers were in mufti, in expensive pale shirts

too tight for them, exposing ovals of fat flesh and hair at the great folds of their stomachs. Makhija, the Deputy Inspector General of a range of six districts, was in Kumar's seat behind the desk, on a swivel chair tilted dangerously. On a visitor's chair, Kumar swayed his vast buttocks from side to side, searching for a comfortable equilibrium, and mumbled threats against incompetence into the wireless. Srivastav introduced Agastya to Makhija. 'Aha, so we meet the Collector's understudy?' and Makhija laughed fully, with jiggling torso, startling everyone a little. He believed in the trappings of sophistication, in speaking softly and slowly, in smoking India Kings, carrying a gold Dunhill lighter. Kumar waddled into another room and ordered coffee.

'A terrible business, Ravi, here, look at these photographs.' Srivastav leafed through them, grimaced appropriately, and after a moment's hesitation, handed them to Agastya. Srivastav leaned back too; now he and Makhija looked like two antagonists separated by three feet of teak, bored and polite, disinterested in negotiation.

The photographs were of the size of postcards, black and harsh white in the dazzle of flash cameras. They enthralled Agastya. On uneven stubble ground, in that surreal glare, on its side, lay a naked body. Its hands were tied behind its back. There was no head on the neck, just a mash of blood and bone, brain and ripped flesh. The one visible ear was untouched, well-formed, distinct. The hair was ruffled, as though in affection. The rest was pulp, batter for a pudding. They had bludgeoned on and on, in photograph after photograph, till the blood in the gullet had turned the shrieks to blubber. Agastya's eyes flicked guiltily to the loins of one body; they were ruined too, dark, ravaged, unrecognizable, blobs of matter waiting for some creator's hand. God, he trembled involuntarily, how could one of us do this to another?

Makhija tapped an India Kings on the table and lit it. 'There was a similar case in Madhya Pradesh last month, we suspect the same gang. We've sent for a report.'

'It must've been quite easy for them, to kill and escape on the criminal line, you know, that slow passenger train from Rameri to Mariagarh. Full of bloody criminals, very popular with them.' Kumar's fat fingers played dexterously with a paperweight, distracting everyone. He began abruptly again, still looking at the table. 'That ex MLA will create trouble. I think he'll use Kapoor, that victim. I wish I could send a man to Kapoor. Tell him not to act funny, we'd put him back in a hospital bed.'

Srivastav asked, 'This bamboo stealing, is there any connection?'

'That's a long shot,' said Makhija airily, 'but we try and keep many things in mind. It helps to keep us confused.' Everyone laughed.

Then they fell silent, as though the laughter had been sacrilegious. Makhija sighed. 'This case will take its toll. There'll be one or two meaningless transfers, constable, sub-inspector, SP, DIG.' He shrugged. 'Perhaps Dhiraj and I will come in for a little drubbing.' His fingers turned the Dunhill on its head. It clattered onto the teak. He smiled a little. 'You know Ravi, the police and the magistracy are *both* representatives of Government, don't people see this?'

Srivastav laughed. 'But we get our morchas too, you know that.'

Coffee came in then, with much ceremony, shuffling of feet, and orders hissed in panic. Srivastav took a noisy sip and continued, 'But investigation is *your* business sir.'

'Oh yes of course.' But Makhija had turned listless, as though he had wished to convey the incommunicable, and had now ceased to hope.

Srivastav handed his cup to a nervous constable and asked Kumar, 'Rameri is one of our problem police stations no?'

Kumar furrowed his brow and pursed his lips. 'Well it has its drunkards and its corrupt, inefficient, lazy, ignorant fellows. We all have to manage with what we have. You've met the Deputy at Rameri, Pathak?'

Srivastav grinned. 'Oh yes, I'm told he and Shafique drink themselves senseless every night.'

'Clever men, they use their past records as convenient excuses.' They all laughed. Srivastav declined an invitation to accompany the policemen to Rameri. He and Agastya left soon after.

In the car Srivastav cheerfully asked, 'Well, what did you think of them? Did you learn anything?'

The question nonplussed Agastya. 'Sir?'

Srivastav was expansive. 'Do you see the interdependence, the intricate connections in the district? From a constable to a Collector?' He vigorously explored one ear with a forefinger. 'A crisis like these killings makes these connections so clear. The success of a Collector, a DIG, an SP, depends on the acts of some obscure lower functionary somewhere.' He shook his head in a kind of awe.

So what, asked Agastya silently. That happens everywhere, stupid.

The public reaction to the killings in Madna was, as is usual, varied. The cook at the Circuit House told the chowkidar that when the Minister had come, he had almost shouted at the Police Superintendent. Kapoor's father, an old resident, was pleased that the killings had got for Madna two inches of the front page in two national dailies, but was indignant that neither newspaper had mentioned his son. At the Madna Club the Additional Sessions Judge declared at the bridge table that those truckers were to blame. Vishwanath, the ex-MLA, fulfilled all expectations by organizing two morchas in one week, memorable for their gaiety and bluster. Some students of the Graduate College haphazardly and half-heartedly tried for a holiday. The Union Bank Manager told Joshi over the wall that after sunset these days no one ever went to or came from Rameri. Except the trucks, cackled Joshi. One Assistant Conservator of Forests, pale and enthusiastic, was outraged at the suggestion that the dacoits were robbers of bamboo who had been surprised in their piracy. Vasant Krishna, the Minister, arrived, bustled about, tut-tutted, and left. Monga, the proprietor of Hotel Madna, said that at least two hundred goondas in Rameri itself were single-handedly capable of such an act. And at least five hundred in Madna town, added Sahni of Ajanta Bar and Restaurant. And some of the workers on daily wages in the paper mills, who heard a rumour that a few among them had killed those men, did not probe.

Four mornings after, on Srivastav's instructions, Agastya turned up at the Circuit House at ten. The Minister, the Collector, the Superintendent of Police and the Minister's satellites were to visit the site. The verandah of the Circuit House was crowded. Agastya abstractedly hunted for a familiar face. Five white Ambassadors formed the motorcade. He recognized the Collector's and the Superintendent's cars. In the district, he remembered the joke, a Government official was known by his vehicle and his promotion in the bureaucracy was a move up from the Jeepocracy to the White Ambassadocracy.

Agastya wandered past the faces into the equally crowded drawing room. Sycophants in khadi perched on all available perching spots. Agastya tried to catch Srivastav's eye. Srivastav was laughing madly at the Minister's joke. On cue, the rest of the drawing room was laughing madly too. Joshi flitted among the sofas, eyes agleam. The Minister removed his cap, scratched the centre of his bald head, and idly looked around. 'So Sen saab?' said a man in white sitting closest to the door: the owner of a local cinema hall, he was often seen at the Collectorate. 'So DM saab?' said the Minister, and heaved himself up. On cue, the drawing room broke up.

Outside the sycophants fluttered, the petitioners unconsciously cringed and tensed, Joshi flitted, the policemen stood to attention, their paunches collapsing all over their belts, Kumar joked with a group around him, the children stared faintly critically at the bustle, chased one another across the wasteland of a lawn, waved madly when the motorcade moved and raced the cars to the gate.

Agastya was with the Superintendent of Police. 'You come with me,' Kumar had said. He crossed his fat legs, leaned back on the maroon corduroy upholstery, and adjusted his khaki shirt over his lard. In his uniform, he looked like a policeman in a TV comedy serial.

The cars raced through the narrow unplanned streets of the town, honking indiscriminately. Cyclists got off and stared. The cars screeched for impeding cattle, tongas, rickshaws, carts, vendors, pedestrians.

'So Sen, how are things?'

Sen smiled and mumbled.

The cars shook off the shacks on the edge of town, its stragglers, as it were. Red earth bordered the grey battered state highway. The washed sky of autumn, a sharp but pleasant heat, green and brown scrub on red cracked earth till the unnervingly flat horizon; young ugly banyan trees sporadically unsettling the monotony, an isolated rice field as though ostracized by its community, a rash of red roofs in the middle distance, dark tribals with lacklustre eyes, more tough mulish scrub, some bare reed patches awaiting rain, abruptly two roadside shacks, dhabas for the truckers, then a dip in the road, a culvert, a furlong or two of stacked bamboo, a big Forest Department hut. They were there.

The satellites scrambled out, adjusting caps and Nehru jackets. Srivastav was with Krishna. Both looked around slowly, like explorers in a new world. Kumar waddled away towards the Nehru jackets. A jeep screeched. Pathak, wheatish, saturnine, the Deputy Superintendent of Police at Rameri, popped out, joined them and saluted. Dark rumours surrounded his private life like flies around faeces. From a distance, Agastya watched the entire troupe hop from spot to spot on their guided tour, the whole dumb-show, the half-turns from the waist, the gestures toward the horizon.

The place unnerved Agastya; it was so appallingly ordinary. He couldn't connect the cracked uneven ground beside his tennis shoes with the photographs he had trembled at. He kicked the ground tentatively. He looked away. Alongside the forest hut squatted a woman looking their way. A pot squatted on a wood fire next to her. He had believed that the visit to the site would be illuminating, that he would return with greater interest in at least one incident in the district. But this spot refused to support any preconceived idea; this was just bamboo, scrub, and sky up to the world's end.

Just a few months ago, he had been the bunker of classes; now in a few months, he would be answerable for a sub-division where such a monstrosity could occur. At this spot, both past and future turned unreal. The world had become inexplicable, bizarre, a place of bewildering incongruities, where a shrewd policeman could look like a comedian, where *those* photographs could emerge out of *this* ground, where such violence could leave so dreary a place so unchanged.

He strolled along, casually following the pantomime ahead. Just—how many days was it?—just five days ago, they had turned heads to pulp here. And there was the nala. Kapoor had stumbled and crawled along that, with his smashed wrist, under the bright light of a white moon. And now the sun warmed his, Asastya's, shoulder blades.

On the return, he was again with the Superintendent. Kumar wriggled until his shoulders found comfort against the maroon corduroy. Then he grumbled, 'How can I solve this case with such inefficient buggers? I told them comb this entire area well, search every foot. It should've taken them at least a week, they say they finished it three days ago.'

A week passed. At the Ladies' Evening, Mrs Kumar told Mrs Srivastav that Kumar saab was suffering a very high fever, must be viral, but he was still spending practically days and nights at Rameri over the case: he only returned to shave, bathe, and eat an occasional breakfast. Mrs Srivastav duly reported this to her husband and Srivastav duly hoped that it would at least reduce Kumar's weight. In the *Citizen's Voice*, Vishwanath shouted some more. In the Assembly, legislators noisily asked questions to the answers of which they paid no attention. Srivastav telephoned Shafique and shouted at him for not reporting progress. Shafique's defence was that Rameri had been reasonably quiet.

Four days after, the police said that they had solved the case. In their lingo, they had apprehended one murderer and the other four were absconding. This time, in the middle of the buzz and the excitement, Kumar himself telephoned Srivastav to give the details. The killers were all workers on daily wages at the paper mills near Rameri.

'Last night a man stole another's bicycle near the railway station. The owner had got off the cycle to piss. He saw the thief, chased him, caught him. Beat him up well, a few passers-by also helped. The thief was small, weak, half-mad with hunger and some illness. Then they took him to the Rameri police station. Of course these days we ask *everybody* about the killings. So they asked him, he said he was one killer, and he named the others. He said they all stayed in Ram Kund, that slum near the tank in Rameri, you know na which one I mean, where all these daily wages workers are. We checked for those four fellows. Missing since the night of the killing. Their wives were, you know, scared, or sullen, or innocent, wide-eyed types. Said they didn't know. One said her husband had run away with some woman.

'Our bicycle thief,' and Kumar chuckled softly, 'is a cousin or a relative of one of the others. They're all from Bastar. He came here half-dead about a month ago to look for work. He says his cousin had promised him some at the paper mill. But he didn't get anything regular, and when they planned the killings, he was quite eager. That night he killed too.

'They got about four thousand, he doesn't remember exactly how much. Then they wouldn't give him any cut, pushed him away, beat him up a little. After that, he walked the road to Rameri, like Kapoor. He went back to his cousin's shack, but the wife threw him out. Said she had no food. She sounds a real toughie.

'Since then he's been at the railway station, eating with the dogs, he says. He had nowhere to go. Sat on the tracks, trying for a return train to Bastar, but he didn't know which one, he didn't know whom to ask, he didn't have any money at all. So he stole the cycle. He was almost insane by then. He says he was just going to follow the rail tracks to Bastar on that cycle and then sell it and then eat. Mad no? I think he knows where the others are, or where they might be, but isn't telling because he fears he's talked too much. They always think that after we feed them. And a little scared too. After all the police. But we'll get the information from him, DM saab.'

Srivastav gulped down the expected uprush of envy, anger,

depression and congratulated Kumar. Then he looked up from his table, for a moment, at the sad eyes of Joshi.

Kumar waddled all evening through the bridge room at the Madna Club, disturbing every table with the details. The diehards from the State Electricity Board scowled at the interruption, they were beyond murders, some others congratulated him. Srivastav faced everything, from a Seven No Trumps to the distant shouts from the Tombola, with a fixed half-smile. 'I still have fever,' Kumar said to every quartet, 'look, feel,' and thrust out an obese, hairless forearm.

The deaths in Madna, however, continued. At about five the next evening, Shafique telephoned Srivastav from Rameri. 'Good evening sir. Bad news sir. That killer died about an hour ago, in police custody. '

Srivastav looked at the teak board, conscious vaguely of a faint tingling on his skin. 'Oh.'

'Yes sir.'

Srivastav sighed absentmindedly, searching again for the reverberations of the act. 'There'll have to be an inquest. You'll have to do it. '

'Yes sir.'

'Have you done any?'

'Yes sir. Once.'

'I'm sure the SP'll be there for the inquest. He'll force his suggestions on you. Ignore them. No bowing to any pressure, Shaflque.'

'No sir.'

'What about witnesses?'

'We're getting our own, sir.'

'Yes. The SP will get some. Don't accept them.'

'Yes sir.'

Srivastav bit his lip and thought some more. 'When do you start?'

'As soon as the witnesses arrive, sir.'

'No one, *no one* is to know of this, Shafique. This could be dangerous.' Srivastav thought fleetingly of Vishwanath.

'Yes sir.'

But murder will out, thought Srivastav. He began to feel a little sorry for Kumar. An hour later, over tea at home, he himself told Mrs Srivastav and Agastya. 'One more killing in Madna,' he said.

'My police attachment begins tomorrow, sir,' said Agastya.

'Would you like it at Rameri? It could be an interesting place.'

'Yes sir.' Agastya could think of no other answer.

'Then you should leave now. See how an SDM conducts an inquest.'

Agastya's mind was quiescent, at rest after a deep afternoon sleep. In the jumpy jeep, the wind from the horizon was cool and dusty. In that twilight, his mind was in the past, thinking of happier times. When they passed the dhabas and the stacked bamboo, he was remembering the hilarious letter he had received that afternoon from a batchmate in Assam, delightfully vitriolic in its description of that trainee's district and Collector.

Shafique was in the verandah at Rameri Police Station. 'Evening sir.' A few constables saluted.

'Hallo Mr Khan.' Agastya tried to get out of the jeep with both agility and dignity. He shook hands with Shafique. Shafique was fortyish, tall, quiet, good-looking. Three years before, he had been almost suspended for being drunk at a meeting called by his Collector.

The police station verandah was long and a hideous blue, lit by tubelights. At one end was the Deputy Superintendent's office, at the other end the lock-ups. Occasional wafts of urine entered the Deputy's office, where Agastya found Kumar. 'Good evening sir.'

'Arrey Sen, pleasant surprise.' The obese forearm waved him to a chair. 'So you're here as the DM's spy, to see whether the police behave?' Kumar jiggled his chest and laughed.

The suggestion startled Agastya. 'No sir. Mr Srivastav wanted me to attend an inquest. He said it was rare and would be good for my training.'

'Of course of course.' Shafique stepped in. 'Yes Shafique?'

'Shall we start sir? The last witness has just come in.'

'Arrey you don't have to ask me when to start,' Kumar smiled conspiratorially at Agastya. 'I'm here just as an observer.' He struggled out of his chair and straightened his tight clothes. He put his arm around Agastya. Shafique led the way into the strong room.

A corpse in loincloth on the floor. Again the tubelights faintly reflected in the hideous blue walls. Three or four men beside the table, a constable or two. Pathak, rearranging the men at their entry. The corpse was straight. The eyes were closed. On the table, a very fat Code of Criminal Procedure. Beside it, some roti, and dal in a tin mug. A concave stomach, as though the corpse had pulled it in and was holding its breath. A shallow navel. One closed wooden door. One iron door to the Armoury. A thick stubble on chin and cheek. The rib cage skeletal, out of an Anatomy book. The red unblinking eyes of one swarthy constable. In the air the rancid smell of urine. A brown loincloth. Large feet and knees. Thighs thin, loose wrinkled skin. He looked it, once a half-dead man who hadn't even got work on bloody daily wages.

Shafique picked up the fat Code and began his inquest. Kumar went and leaned against the table and scratched himself. The witnesses followed Shafique around the room. Pathak periodically pointed out what he thought Shafique should note.

'Died at 4.50, suddenly, while he was eating.' 'Of course the roti and dal to be sealed and sent for examination.' 'He just fell down from his chair.' 'We thought he had fainted out of weakness.' 'See, no external marks of injury.' 'No, no visible marks at all.' 'Turn him over. Let's see the back.'

A constable held an arm and leg and turned the corpse over. Rigor mortis had set in. The corpse was hard, like a biscuit. It went over like a cricket bat, its skull and knees cracking on the floor. With the corpse on its stomach, the air turned faintly malodorous. There seemed in it a hint of carrion. The witnesses stepped back in unison, exclaimed, turned their faces away and held their noses.

'Tch that's faeces bhai, not rotting flesh,' said Kumar with a smile. 'It's too early for the body to rot. See the damp patch around the anus.' Everyone looked at the patch on the loincloth. Shafique noted it down. 'The sphincter relaxes after death. '

'No marks of injury on the back,' said Shafique. Despite the presence of Kumar, Shafique was being thorough in his examination, or so it seemed to Agastya.

'No, none,' said the witnesses, looking at one another.

Agastya suddenly said, in a high voice, 'They say if you beat the body with rods with towels around them, then there are no marks.'

'So you read thriller books, Sen?' chuckled Kumar. 'No, even those marks show up, like blotches, after rigor mortis.'

The witnesses again looked at one another. Pathak smiled.

Agastya wanted to say, Shafique-jee, take off his loincloth. They could've smashed his testicles. But he kept quiet. He was inhibited not by Kumar, but by a sudden recollection of the photographs. Again he was assailed by a sense of the unreal, that this *thing* on the floor, as hard as furniture, could have turned someone *else's* testicles to pulp.

Shafique looked his notes over slowly, then at the corpse, around the room, at the witnesses, again at his notes, then nodded uncertainly. The constable turned the corpse over again.

Shafique took the witnesses out. Kumar summoned Pathak and whispered secrets to him. Then he and Agastya returned to the office. In a corner sat the witnesses. Shafique was writing at the table. At Kumar's entry, the witnesses left, despite his false protests, to sit in the verandah. Someone brought in thick sweet tea.

'Now what, sir?' asked Agastya.

'Now what? Now Shafique writes his report and the witnesses sign. Then we send the body to the hospital for a post-mortem. Then we wait for the report to see the cause of death. Then we inform the next of kin of the deceased of his death. Then we dispose of the body. All tonight.'

'That sounds like a long night.'

'Yes. But you have to get used to it, at least in your police attachment.' Kumar now sounded humourless, tired and sick.

So it happened. Agastya, Shafique, Pathak and a silent Kumar moved to the Rest House to wait for the post-mortem report.

Kumar and Agastya sat out in the driveway. Shafique and Pathak flitted from light to shadow on mundane business. Kumar and Agastya scratched their mosquito bites, watched the domesticated stray dogs and the fireflies. Occasionally a train screeched past on its way to Delhi.

'Sir, did the police kill him?'

'Of course not. The inquest report doesn't say so. Neither will the post-mortem. He probably died of his illness. What that is will soon be clear. '

Pathak stepped up, enquired about dinner, and disappeared. Kumar sighed. 'This is real bad luck. We solve a case and this man dies in custody. No one will believe that the police are innocent. Hence, Sen, all this work by night.' He waved his hand against the dark. 'We must behave as though we are guilty. Must get rid of the body fast. It's damning evidence.' He changed his tone. 'Have you ever been to Ram Kund?'

'That slum? No sir.'

'A dangerous place. Knifings, gang trouble, drunkards, gambling dens, illicit liquor thekas. Very little money among too many people. Criminals breed there like rats. I'll take you there on a round sometime during this police attachment.'

Someone came up with thick sweet tea. 'What was your discipline, Sen?'

'Mine? English sir.'

Kumar raised his eyebrows in a perfunctory gesture of praise. 'I was a student of History. It amazes me now. The police is a terribly brutalizing job.' He was not in any confessional mood; he had three, or perhaps four, hours to pass, and he had the ability to appear to relax and talk desultorily of interesting matters while his mind ticked away furiously.

Dinner was varied and uniformly badly cooked. 'Tomorrow Sen, you'll learn the procedure at the police station. Look at all the registers, the strong room, note how the FIR is written. When this pressure eases, I'll map out your training programme properly.'

After dinner, Kumar telephoned Srivastav. Then he returned to the driveway. Agastya went to bed after about two hours and slept through all the mosquito attacks.

In the morning he went out to the verandah for tea. He was surprised to find no one there. 'Where's SP saab?'

'They all left early this morning saab, at about five,' said the chowkidar. 'At Jompanna last night some men were killed on the road. Exactly like the last case. They're saying, same goondas. They've all gone, SP saab, SDM saab, DSP saab.' In an unsure, slightly dazed state, Agastya bathed, dressed, ate, and telephoned the police station for a jeep.

In the daylight the courtyard of the police station looked smaller and more barren. The hanging roots of an ageing banyan clutched at the front wall. In the verandah waited an Inspector and some constables. Everyone saluted.

To cloak his embarrassment, Agastya turned immediately to business. 'What news from Jompanna?'

'Exact details not yet known sir. But sounds like the earlier killings. SP saab has gone there sir.'

Agastya looked around for subject-matter. 'The corpse disposed of okay?'

'Yes sir. Just this morning we gave the body to the wife of a cousin in Ram Kund.'

Agastya's head jerked up. 'Was the SP here then?'

'No sir. He had left for Jompanna.' The Inspector had a placid face and red eyes.

'But did anyone tell you to do that? You were to *inform* the next of kin and then burn the body yourself.'

The Inspector's expression did not change. The years had brutalized him too. He was not used to making his own decisions; he had grown old in hearing both orders and abuse from above. Now he switched off his mind and settled down to Agastya's agitation.

'How could you've done this?' Agastya was a little surprised, and a little pleased, at his own anger.

'The cousin's wife wanted the body for some last rites sir.'

'Now they have the body *and* they believe that the police killed him. Don't you see how dangerous that is?'

'Nothing will happen sir.'

Agastya went to the Deputy's office. Someone brought in thick sweet tea. He asked for the FIR register and tried to decipher some constable's handwriting in the report on Kapoor. His mind flitted continually from Jompanna to the corpse flipping over with the clatter of a cricket bat to Kumar's hairless, obese forearms.

Abruptly there were a few exclamations on the verandah. Agastya went outside.

A silent crowd was entering the courtyard. Leading it

were four men carrying a body swathed in white. The body was carefully placed at the foot of the stairs of the verandah. There would have been about thirty men, a few women, a few stragglers and the ubiquitous urchins. Most looked dark and poor. Most were in white. They filled the courtyard.

Agastya was suddenly nervous. He sat down beside a pillar. 'What nonsense is this?' asked the Inspector.

No one answered. More than thirty faces squinted up at the verandah. One man moved a little closer to the body, adjusted the towel around his shoulders, and said, 'You've killed this man and are saying that he died just like that. You cannot protect anyone from murders on the roads. You even say that some of us are killers just because we are poor. We have had enough.' He adjusted his towel again.

'Don't talk nonsense.' The Inspector's face did not change. 'We'll show you the post-mortem report. He died of an ulcer.'

'We don't believe your report. You've lied in it.' A sparrow flew out of the eaves of the verandah, startling Agastya.

'Come back when the DSP saab comes.'

The man said nothing. The Inspector was no orator. He looked around, a little helplessly, perhaps hoping to spot a superior police officer somewhere.

'We're going to burn the police station.' The crowd rippled a little.

'Here,' the Inspector turned to a constable, 'get me a gun.'

Later, Agastya remembered, against the backdrop of the banyan tree and the autumn sky, each move quite distinctly. He himself felt secure beside his pillar because he still sensed that he came from another world. The Inspector held up his rifle and asked the spokesman of the crowd to be sensible and go away. The spokesman moved forward a foot.The Inspector told the spokesman not to take even one more step. He did. At a distance of two yards the bullet blasted his face and threw him into the crowd. The Inspector shouted that he was very, very serious. The crowd, a little uncertainly, moved closer to the steps. But this is not happening to me, Agastya tremblingly tried to reassure himself, as he waited, one way or the other, for some more deaths.

Bombay, 1984

The slow train stopped yet again. Jamun had read in a plaintive article somewhere that in the suburbs, many commuters, when near their houses, pulled the alarm chains to stop the trains. Then they scuttled across the tracks to their hovels in grey concrete blocks. Beyond the train window, two feet away, stood a sheet of corrugated iron. A hole had been torn in it. He could see the back of a mirror at the base of the hole, and around the mirror a man's sagging, etiolated chest, with nipples dark pink, like suppurative insect bites. A bit of his right arm moved rhythmically beside the mirror. He was shaving. Here by the tracks, sharing an iron box with the rats of Bombay, surrounded by defecation, it was absurd, it seemed to Jamun, that this man was shaving. With his smooth cheeks and chin, he must keep up appearances; Jamun half-smiled at that thought. Once that man must've been new to the city, long before it made him its denizen. Work might've wrenched him away from home too, and dumped him here, one more inhabitant of one more city of encroachments and unauthorized constructions, where his glimpses of the sun were dependent on his shaving mirror and the unscheduled halts of trains. The train started again, but the desolation remained.

Jamun felt completely empty and remote. He looked down at the dried mudprints of slippers on the compartment floor. This arrival in an alien, unknown place was inevitable, like birth or death, this weaning away from home, inescapable, a second severed umbilical cord. He leaned his head against the window stains and watched the passing poles and wires and blocks of concrete. There is not a blade of grass in Bombay, Anand had said. Except the scrub rising out of the excrement by the tracks. God, the agonies one suffered just to stay sad and half-alive. Again Jamun half-smiled at his self-pity.

Across from him, Sheela uncrossed her legs and continued to stare out. Jamun looked at her gross, seductive face. Abruptly she said, 'Booblu, you should know something.' Jamun hated her pet name for him but Sheela thought it cute. 'I might be pregnant.' The train was slowing down again. She looked at him a little tensely, as though prepared for almost any reaction.

How can anyone called Booblu make a girl pregnant, thought Jamun fleetingly. 'You're sure?'

'I think so. I'm always regular, now I'm ten days overdue.'

Like a library book, thought Jamun's disordered mind. They watched the train move into the pandemonium of Bombay Central. Hot coolies with large sweat patches and loud voices surged through the train. Jamun and Sheela got off. He saw the queues at the ticket counter and the anxious, unseeing railway-station faces and still wanted a ticket home.

Outside they battled the rabble of hotel-and taxi-pimps. In the cab, Jamun said loudly, to beat the million horns, 'Have you done anything about this?'

'I thought you should know first.'

Jamun looked at her, her profile, at the dandruff in her hair. He patted Sheela's thigh and said, 'I'm sure everything'll be okay.' She nodded. The taxi turned into a gate. 'That wasn't long,' said Jamun.

The Training Institute was shabby and one-storeyed. There was green slime on some of the many damp patches on the walls and an iron grille instead of a door into the lobby. A faint smell of dead rats and smegma which, in later years, Jamun would always associate with that year in Bombay. Just behind the grille sat a thin genial man in an office chair, happily and loudly sucking in his tea from a saucer. 'I'll need help with my luggage,' said Jamun.

'Oye Moriya!' yelled the man into the corridor behind the water cooler. He turned back to Jamun. 'You've come for the training sir?'

Jamun and the taximan took his luggage off. Sheela remained in the back seat. 'Don't know how long settling in will take. I'll come over as soon as I'm free. Should I telephone first?'

'It's just here.' Sheela gestured over her head. 'Off Marine Drive itself. A lovely flat, you can almost walk it from here.' Jamun looked at her wide purple lips and heavy jowl. They nodded and smiled awkwardly at each other. The taxi left. Jamun remembered the June afternoon when he had suggested that they bathe together. Sheela had been shy and reluctant beneath her flippancy. Her banter had irritated him. Even when he had desired her he had felt alone.

Moriya was sitting on Jamun's blue suitcase. He was a small powerful man. 'Where's the office?' asked Jamun. In reply Moriya pushed his chin out towards the grille. He, the thin man and Jamun shared the luggage. The thin man talked a lot.

The hostel room was instantly depressing. A broken cement floor, with small craters. Jamun stumbled over one. Old pink walls, two windows. One looked out onto a small field where some urchins played at cricket with a stick and an indistinguishable grey blob for a ball. Behind the field the rest of the universe was stopped by the nether floors of a skyscraper. Countless airconditioners and some jagged holes in window panes. Beyond the other window Jamun saw a bare narrow patch, a wire fence, then some sweating men in loincloths. 'Who are they?'

'The Youth Club sir. People come for exercise,' said the thin man.

'This room's dirty. Could you arrange for a sweeper?'

Jamun followed the thin man out and asked for the office. The open corridor looked onto a large cement courtyard. On the cement were the fading lines of a badminton court. The office lay beyond the courtyard.

Its first room had an old desk and behind it a short fat bald bespectacled and extremely unhelpful man. His breath seemed somehow to smell of farts. Jamun said, 'What are the joining formalities? I have to sign in.'

Looking down on the bald head with its strands sprouting up above the left ear and stretching heroically across to the right, Jamun wondered at himself. Here, in a strange building, in an unknown city, alone, signing up for a job I'm not interested in, having made a girl pregnant, what am I doing? He wanted to peel off the bald man's strands and let them hang beside his ear. They could reach, he thought, the pens in the shirt pocket, or they could gag his mouth and lessen its stench. In this daze he met the Director of the Institute and then returned to his room.

While settling in he thought disconnectedly of home and Sheela. In his dislocation he remembered the afternoon when, to lunch-hour music from the radio, he had taught Sheela how to inhale smoke. Earlier she used to puff away at cigarettes without inhaling. How dizzy and sick she had felt.

At lunch Jamun met a Mrs Karve, the other trainee. 'Normally a batch of three or four, but this year you are small, just the two of you,' smiled the Director. Mrs Karve was from some obscure Maharashtrian town. She had two children. Jamun was immediately prepared to be disinterested in her. She was short and a little squat. Mr Karve was something in the State Bank.

In the late afternoon, before leaving to meet Sheela, Jamun

wrote a letter home. For a moment, he was tempted to write, 'Ma, Sheela is pregnant. Maybe she's lying to get me to marry her.'

Sheela was staying with her sister and brother-in-law in a huge old flat just off Marine Drive. According to Sheela her brother-in-law had often been offered unimaginable prices for it. She used to talk nonstop of her holidays in Bombay.

Her sister Alka seemed friendly. 'I can't believe this is your first visit to Bombay. I mean, *everyone* has been to Bombay.'

'He's absolutely rural yaar,' laughed Sheela. Jamun was surprised at what he took to be her false gaiety. Compared to her sister's, Sheela's voice was even more loud and jarring.

Alka left for the kitchen to organize coffee. Jamun moved out to the verandah. Sheela followed. The bright sun on a sea of rippled glass, the sea endless and oblivious, and below, the distant toys bustling on Marine Drive. 'Your sister's very pretty,' said Jamun.

'It runs in the family,' smiled Sheela.

On the breeze drifted in the nauseating smell of the sea. At last Jamun said, 'You have to get an abortion, no?'

'Let's discuss that later.'

Jamun was surprised. He moved closer, but she pulled away. 'We've never discussed marriage but this shouldn't force us into it.'

'Later.' Sheela was loud all evening. She played raucously with her nephew, an eight-month-old bore who resembled Winston Churchill. He urinated on her and she pressed her face into his stomach. Jamun was by turns bored, irritated and worried. 'How dull you are not to like children,' said Sheela. Jamun wondered whether she had told her sister about her pregnancy.

Satish the brother-in-law arrived, tall, soft and fat, something in some ad agency. His spectacles were tinted and he looked like a maker of hard porn. He fixed Jamun a whisky. They pulled chairs out to the verandah and watched Sheela change the piddler's nappy. 'You married?' asked Satish.

'No.'

Satish nodded several times. Jamun stayed to dinner. While Sheela distracted the child, he helped Alka lay the table. He noticed the thin wrinkled skin on the back of her hands, it looked almost brittle. He wouldn't have associated that skin with the adhesive heat of Bombay.

'Sheela's good with the child.'

'Yeah, she's too stupid to be anything more in life than an ayah,' laughed Alka. The two sisters got on well and seemed to like each other.

Sheela drove him back in the Maruti. 'You drive very badly. You're really rash and blind,' said Jamun.

'But I love driving. With my father I never get to touch the car. Here with my sister I can do what I like and Satish is very nice. He taught me driving when I was here four years ago. My parents are boring yaar compared to my sister.' Sheela talked on, unnecessarily.

Jamun had often told her that she spoke so loudly because she was a little deaf, and that was because she always listened to her cassettes on the headphones of her Walkman. At the pizza parlour near her hostel, she had as usual closed her eyes and begun nodding her head to her monotonous rock music. Then Micky had picked up the Walkman and whispered into it. Her beatific smiles had then turned genuine. Later Micky had said, 'I said some sexy stuff into that stupid machine. She wants it bad. I'll hump her, you joker, before you even get close enough to smell her skin.'

'When should we discuss the pregnancy?' Jamun interrupted Sheela.

She said nothing, but took a right turn at great speed.

He also kept quiet. His sense of desolation made him passive, quiescent in front of any outrage or complication that might involve him.

At the gate of the Training Institute she asked, 'Coming home tomorrow?'

He poked his head in through the window. 'What about your pregnancy?' The word sounded alien.

'So?' Her tone was aggressive even though she was looking away.

'We've to get a pregnancy test. Do you know anyone in Bombay?'

'No.'

'Should we tell your sister?'

'Are you nuts?'

Jamun got back into the car, reluctantly prepared for a long discussion. 'We'll have to return to Delhi as soon as we can.' Any reason, he thought, to get home, even an unwanted pregnancy.

Sheela said nothing. The silence was almost hostile.

Jamun returned to his room and wrote a letter to a friend in Delhi. 'Anand, an emergency. Send me a telegram saying, *Ma in hospital after heart attack. Come*. Sign it *Papa*. No jokes. Send it immediately, and Lightning. I'll explain why when we meet. Otherwise things are okay. This place promises to be really dull, maybe Madras and Jabalpur will be better. I'm training with a female called Karve. But send the telegram.'

He went out right then, at midnight, to post the letter at the box by the gate. His letter of appointment to the job had said unequivocally that leave during training was impossible.

The cement courtyard was bright with moonlight and the surrounding corridors black and faintly menacing. Jamun could hear distantly the eternal noise of the city. The corridors and courtyard reminded him of some ancient ancestral house, perhaps in Lucknow, where an unending, unmanageable and impoverished family would have lived and quarrelled together, twice a week, on Mondays and Thursdays, for four years in a TV serial.

The fake telegram was an old and trusted ploy, but he wasn't particularly interested in its success. Nothing seemed to matter. He returned to his room, switched off the light and got into bed. With the darkness came desire. Once, just seven months ago, on an impulse, he had sent a telegram to Sheela at her hostel. The telegram had merely read *I lust you very much*. To Jamun the act had been exhilarating but Sheela had been touched, amused, embarrassed and annoyed. For in the hostel all telegrams were put up on the Mess Notice Board, open, their secrets unprotected. Everyone had read his message. How silly it had then seemed.

He had tried to explain to Sheela once how he felt, that love was a euphemism, that what everyone felt and eulogized was actually lust and the sense of possession. There were these phases in one's life, late teenage, or the middle twenties, when one expected of oneself to fall in love, when one was expected to be seen with a girl, attending seminars, catching buses, seeing movies in large outwardly happy groups. But lust was different, and not as transient. It was a biological necessity, a part of one's metabolism. Then the personality and wishes of the object of lust didn't matter, and lust was somehow linked to the loneliness, which was infinitely more fundamental and long-lasting.

Sheela had been offended, hadn't shown it, but had scoffed at his theorizing. She had said, 'You think it's very, what's the word, macho? To say you feel lust and no love and all that rubbish, because admitting to love you think will be sentimental. You're just shit scared of your bloody emotions.'

Jamun had had no wish to explain further because he had a core he found impossible to unveil. But he had disliked her for her assurance and the confidence with which she claimed him. I'm precious too, he had wanted to tell her, and I want to be alone and free; he had seen her as a threat to his dreams of dispossession.

He woke to the clink of metal. The room looked less ugly in the soft early-morning light. On the wall a patch of yellow showed up where the caked pink limewash had fallen off. The patch was shaped vaguely like Australia. Jamun watched it unthinkingly.

The sounds were from the Youth Club beyond the window. After a while someone hammered at the door. Tea. He went over to the window. The tea was hot, sweet and sickening. A few feet away stood a sweating torso on pale, trembling pencil legs. With his mind elsewhere Jamun watched the disproportionate figure tug at a barbell.

At Lucknow station, over a year ago, he had seen Sheela perfectly, it seemed to him, the oval head jigging with laughter at Micky's joke, surrounded by suitcases, leaning against a pillar proclaiming a new Hindi film. Dipping his stale rusk in his tea, with the roar of the chaiwala's gas stove in his ears, he had remembered then that Micky

had said, she's from Calcutta yaar, all these Cal females are as loose as pyjamas, you can make her anytime. In the following months the confused Jamun had often felt that if Sheela had been more affected, less open and friendly somehow, then he would have apologized for the grossness of his emotions.

At breakfast he sat beside Mrs Karve. Her sari was an eyeblinding green. 'It's sad that there are only two of us. If there had been more, then we could've written letters in class without their ever noticing us.'

Mrs Karve smiled politely. 'You're from Delhi?' Her Maharashtrian accent was strong.

'Yes.' Pause. 'How old are your children?'

'Dattatreya is five and Dinkar will be three this month. I am going to miss his birthday.'

'Tch tch.' They laughed at that.

The introductory lectures were excruciatmg. Before leaving for Bombay, Jamun had heard his father yet again on marriage and loneliness. 'I didn't want to marry your mother, you know that. On the day of the registration, in a borrowed car in Behala but you have no idea of that part of Calcutta—we were going to the Alipur courts, I said to her in the car, we shouldn't marry because I'm not the right person to marry. That wasn't a nice thing to say—and neither an original line nor thought—but I meant it, I was so panic-stricken and depressed. She was crying, she cried right through the responses and the signing, those tears were what our witnesses observed and remembered. And over the years, you've heard her say a thousand times, haven't you, that she would've killed herself long ago had it not been for leaving behind on the children the stigma of a mother's suicide.'

After the afternoon session Jamun automatically got into a taxi to go to Alka's flat. He didn't particularly want to meet Sheela, but he felt an obscure obligation. He again settled down in an armchair and watched her with her nephew who again wet himself. 'Does he have diabetes you think? The amount he piddles.' The sisters laughed.

Later he asked Sheela for a walk down Marine Drive. 'Forget it yaar,' she said, 'feeling too lazy.'

He was irritated and said, 'I've written to Anand to send a telegram to me. As soon as it comes we should go back to Delhi and work out your pregnancy.' He immediately thought, I should've said *the* pregnancy, or perhaps *our* pregnancy. Sheela said nothing and cooed to the child.

Jamun went out to the verandah to look at the sea, immense and impersonal. Once he had been excited about Bombay. He had thought of nights with Sheela away from her confining hostel and its Auschwitzean rules. But here with her sister and nephew she was another person, strange. He had considered himself a successful strategist when she used to lie to her warden and come away with him. Now those once-exquisite assignations in borrowed rooms, the lying together with minds at rest, and gauging the passage of the hours by the glow of the sun on the pink bougainvillea by the window, all that seemed remote, sometimes a little sordid.

Sheela came out. Jamun said, 'As soon as I get the telegram I'll ask the Director for leave. Then you say you forgot to submit your exam forms. If you like I'll telephone you from somewhere, and you pretend it's someone from Delhi, a classmate or something, say Raman, who's calling about the exam forms. And the last date is imminent et cetera so you have to return.' Jamun stopped listlessly. 'Why didn't you tell me this in Delhi, before we left?'

'I didn't want to spoil anything. I was scared.'

Jamun didn't want to accuse or to hurt, not just then anyway. But he did want to escape the fetters of guilt. Yet away from her there seemed to be only desolation and lust; and with her there wasn't much else. He had always enjoyed being alone, but it seemed to him that Sheela had brought him a kind of emptiness. It couldn't be true, yet their moments of joy now seemed so remote. He picked up a cushion from the verandah floor and threw it onto the rocking chair. The chair began to move. To its creak, Sheela said, 'I'm still scared because I don't know what's going to happen.'

'You were very regular, no?'

'As regular as the bloody moon.'

Jamun smiled at her reply and turned to her. But Sheela, with eyes closed, had lifted up her face to the warm sea breeze. He spoke to her profile. 'Maybe it's just delayed or something. But we'll feel more secure in Delhi, won't we? We know people there, we know...the city. Here—'he gestured helplessly at the skyline. Sheela was in her tight orange corduroys. He felt faintly the stirrings of desire. In school they had been made to study a poem called 'My Last Duchess' by Robert Browning. The poem had been about a Duke who kills his wife, or something like that. Jamun had liked one bit,

Oh sir, she smiled, no doubt,
Whene'er I passed her; but who passed without
Much the same smile?

In school the lines had seemed to apply to Mrs Gonsalves, his Physics teacher. Later Jamun saw Sheela also as absolutely undiscriminating in her friendships;

'...at least holding hands
with anything in pants,'
Micky had once said.

Jamun had not been in the least keen that his parents and Sheela ever meet. But they did, inadvertently, one July afternoon when she dropped in unannounced to borrow some money to pay the auto-rickshaw and foist on him *The Best of John Denver.* After she'd left, Jamun's mother had summed her up as cheap and vulgar. 'Lust,' she had said, clinking her bangles while she poured out the tea, 'is making you see her as good company. She has a good body, and a good skin, and a vulgar attractive face. You two have nothing in common. You're not serious about her, I hope?'

'I've told you so often Ma, I can only be serious about poor divorced Muslim transvestite whores.'

'Well, which of those is she not?'

Jamun's mother was intermittently inquisitive about her son. She used to snoop around in his room, and had once unearthed a book called *Misconceptions about Contraception.*

As a joke Jamun had bought it for Sheela and had written in it, *'So that in the years to come, my lust, you, irrepressibly witty that you are, can say that I had just about as much foresight as foreskin.'* Sheela'd taken one look at the cover, murmured, 'This is just the kind of crap that'll get me thrown out of this shithole' and gifted it right back to him. Then his mother, glancing at the title, had sniffed before putting the book back, not in the shelf but on his table so that he'd know that she'd been around that afternoon.

The shriek of slammed brakes drifted up from Marine Drive. From their verandah, as from an eyrie, they watched the distant tableau. A white Fiat askew, the disturbed traffic, the crowd forming, and in the background, as always, the hush of the uncaring sea. 'We always used condoms. I mean I always did. How did it happen?'

'One must have had a hole in it. Remember that joke about a bastard perforating condoms in revenge?'

'Is it an accident or isn't it?' From that height they couldn't quite make out.

'Which do you mean?' They both laughed, a little startled by the unexpected cordiality.

The cars began to snarl up. At the corner, the cleverer drivers, the old hands who knew the traffic muddles of Bombay, were turning off Marine Drive into the street with the ice-cream shop Sheela had raved about the night before. She said, 'How's training?'

'As boring. I sat in class and dreamed about my PhD at Brown.'

'How are the others?' Sheela interrupted him. She had often suffered his dreams of studying at some prestigious foreign university.

'There's only one other. She's okay. Prabha Karve. A mother of many children with unpronounceable names. She's short and has tufts of black hair around her midriff. Not just down, but thick wavy hair.'

'Again you judge by appearances. I've often told you, behind my sexy face lies a heart of gold.'

'That has never been in doubt.' But Sheela did not laugh at that. She looked down at the traffic. Jamun felt foolish and continued speaking to cloak his awkwardness. 'Mrs Karve's familiar with Jabalpur. She said it's quite a nice place. I said I was petrified of going there for the training later. One more unknown town in this vast hinterland. Just Karve and me, it's going to be really tough and lonely.'

'You can always make her pregnant.'

'Bitch.' They laughed.

'You'll get leave?'

'I'll lie, shouldn't be difficult.' He paused and moved closer to Sheela. He looked back into the room. Alka couldn't be seen. He bent down and gently kissed Sheela's shoulder. She shifted a little. 'I like your smell,' he said.

As though to break things up, Alka appeared with coffee. They spoke of the weather and the traffic jam. 'How's the training?' she asked Jamun.

'Teething troubles, that's this child's problem,' laughed Sheela. 'Can't grow into his new job. He once dreamed of a PhD and now can't wake up. But I think he will soon, poor boy, misses his mama's lap.'

Two days later the telegram arrived while Jamun was in a lecture, absentmindedly eyeing Mrs Karve's midriff. It read, *'Ma in uppal with fart attack. Come.'* The vulpine Director, a sort of pimp for Big Brother, asked Jamun to ring up Delhi from his office. 'We have STD, go ahead.'

Silently cursing the pimpness with which the Director crosschecked the telegram, Jamun dialled Alka's house, and then dialled three digits at random after the phone began to ring. 'Amazing,' he beamed at the Director, his fist clutching the receiver, 'got through to Delhi first try.'

A woman's voice answered. Jamun hoped that it wasn't Alka and began in a high loud voice. 'Hallo, is that Delhi? Hallo? Is that Baba? Baba, it's me from Bombay!'

'Just who—'

'Hallo, Baba, I just got the telegram—'

'Oh hi Raman! Hi! What, from Delhi? How did you get my number?'

Jamun turned his back to the Director to hide his suppressed giggles. But he couldn't contain the heaving of his stomach. A warmth at Sheela's quick uptake suffused him. 'How serious is it?'

'Oh yes, obviously. You always ring up for some boring reason or other. '

'Oh poor Ma, I'll get leave from here, I'll catch the first available flight home.'

'Ohhhh! Of course, how horrible, ohhh now what do I do, huh Raman, please?'

'No don't bother about the airport, I'll just take a taxi or something.'

'Yes that's the only thing, but how disgusting of me to forget. Yes I suppose that'll be the thing to do.'

'Don't worry, Baba, I'm coming.'

'Thanks a lot for calling Raman, you're a real friend, and just tell that bastard Maheshwari I'll get him the forms in time.'

'Okay, Baba, bye, and see you very soon.'

'Yes I'll do just that, thanks once again, bye, be seeing you soon.'

Jamun turned to the Director and said, 'A heart attack sir. My mother's back home now, but she wants to meet me very much. Thank you sir, for the phone.'

With one wave, the Director sent Jamun's gratitude to the ceiling. 'You should leave as quickly as you can.'

'Thank you, sir. I'll go and check about the tickets.'

Again the taxi for Sheela's. He was galled even by this ritual, this meaningless daily seventeen rupees. The taxi stopped at a light near some massive telecommunications tower. He remembered, ages ago it seemed, the first film that he and Sheela had seen together, an insane Hindi extravaganza in a huge new hall in Lucknow. They had enjoyed the trash so much just because they had been together, knee touching knee, fingertips occasionally on forearm. She had laughed helplessly when he had breathed into her ear that the vamp in the film looked amazingly like her. He remembered fragments of their common past in abrupt flashes, and most of these memories confused him, because their magic seemed irretrievable.

Sheela opened the cream front door. Her face glowed with conspiracy. 'I've to return to Delhi immediately. I forgot to fill up those bloody examination forms.' She stank of tobacco and her perfume. He had told her often how much he liked its smell. 'It's much simplier than bathing, yaar,' she had once said.

'You got leave? Talk,' she whispered, and gently patted his stomach.

'Be careful. There's a baby in there.'

'Bastard.' They laughed. Again between them a flicker.

'This stupid girl,' said Alka over tea, 'takes off on a holiday without bothering to find out whether she has anything important to do before leaving.'

'Absolutely right,' said Jamun. 'It's the best way to travel.'

'It's just an exam form,' laughed Sheela, 'I can always stay here and fill up my forms next year. '

'I might be going too,' said Jamun. 'Three or four holidays coming up, some Marathi hero died or was born or something.' He had always concocted with ease. 'We could go together, but how do we get train tickets?'

'Oh Satish will get that done.'

The globular, lemon-green shade that hung from the ceiling danced in the salt breeze from the windows. 'I think we should leave tomorrow,' said Sheela, 'but how'll we ever get tickets for tomorrow!'

Jamun again registered her loud voice. His Second Standard Class Teacher always used to say, 'Learn to speak softly. That is good manners.' He suddenly wanted to say so to Sheela, to jolt her out of her happiness. Then Churchill started shrieking from the bedroom. 'Time for the bastard's feed,' said Sheela.

Satish proved inquisitive. 'Which Marathi hero? I don't think there's any holiday this week.'

How do people ever plan things like murders with nosy types like Satish around, thought Jamun irritably, and said, 'The Institute is closed for two or three days. Thought it must be a Marathi hero. Never bothered to find out why, just in case it was a mistake and they opened up again.'

A valedictory dinner that night. They all drank a little and laughed a lot. Jamun saw Sheela's head jerk back. When she laughed, when her lips split and her belly shook, the sound followed later and sometimes never. She doesn't know the implications of pregnancy, thought Jamun, the child.

Two mornings later, again the nondescript ugliness of Bombay Central. Jamun watched the insane bustle on the local trains on another platform. The human mass at the mouths of coaches resembled fish eggs. Small dark agile men leaped into them with cane baskets and disappeared, like frogs into mud. Their train glided out on time. They waved to Alka and the child. Jamun again noticed how much prettier than Sheela she was and felt vaguely guilty. From the window, passing glimpses of Bombay's suburban stations, with their odd attractive names; each name had character, with its strong regional tang. There seemed a clot in his stomach, like a lump of blood, at the thought of returning home. When he had arrived in Bombay he had felt that home had been lost forever. Now even though he was returning, he still thought it inaccessible; it had now withered into the destination of clandestine visits that had been arranged with endless petty lies, a place of abortions. Just for three or four days; he knew that the ecstasy of arrival would not compensate for the emptiness of departure.

He looked out at the ugliness, the absolute desolation of the city. Ten-storeyed grey box flats with slime climbing up the pipes that took the shit away, box verandahs of bored lonely women and men blankly surveying the deformed world while waiting all day for TV to start. He looked across at Sheela, at her oddly magnetic face, now a little unsure.

'Come and sit here.' She did. They were alone in their compartment. 'How should we begin in Delhi?'

'I don't know.'

'First by getting into bed.'

She tried to smile. 'I've no idea what's going to happen.'

He could say nothing. He put his arm around her. In Lucknow, at their last parting, she had cried much, silently. He had been surprised and guilty at the absence of any comparable sorrow in himself. 'We'll hunt around tomorrow itself.'

'Bombay was so nice.'

'You mustn't worry. This abortion thing will get over really fast.'

Sheela looked up into Jamun's face. 'Yesterday I caught a local train to Bandra to meet an old friend, Anjali, have you ever met her, she's pretty boring. In the compartment, just above the last row of seats, there was a small board, an ad for a clinic, it said abortions for only seventy.'

'But we couldn't've gone to some unknown dirty place.' There would've been grime and guilt in a small harshly-lit waiting room, the lovelessness and anxiety in the faces of other fathers-by-error, and a dusty telephone that wouldn't have worked. Outside the world would have continued to move like the sea at Bombay, an unending purposeless ebb and flow, totally heedless of the anguish of men. 'There are also some Marie Stopes Clinics.'

'Who was Marie Stopes?'

'I don't know, some do-gooder.'

Their conversation was staccato throughout the journey. The expressions of tenderness and concern were awkward, almost false. The silences seemed eternal, the depression insidious. When they caught themselves looking at each other, their mouths would contort, as though bitter with remembrances. The hours moved, the landscape changed, and the skies, Surat, Baroda, Ratlam, Kota, fleeting fugitive visions of the hinterland; for Jamun the cloud heaved a little only when he saw the polluted morning sky in the near distance over Delhi.

They went to the hostel first. Even Sheela looked more cheerful in the familiar surroundings. 'Ugly as ever,' she said happily.

'I'll look in at about five.' Jamun went home. His parents were surprised and pleased. 'Some Marathi hero was born or died or something. Just a few days off. I couldn't get through on the phone from Bombay, horrible lines, so I just turned up.'

Almost immediately he telephoned Anand at his office. His mother grumbled, 'Not even a-quarter-of-an-hour at home and you want to meet your friends. Especially that Anand.'

'I'll be back for lunch, Ma.'

'We are honoured.'

Jamun took the car keys from the table in his father's room. He felt happy to be driving again on Delhi's wide roads. Delhi was not particularly lovable, but it was familiar. For him happiness had always been fragile and unexpected, even unsettling, like a time bomb. Birth, education, a job, marriage, the petty adjustments of domesticity, a home of one's own, the breeding of children—he found the conventions of this circle meaningless, and the obtuseness of the world that arranged this enervating succession galled him. He had grown up in one spot, had grown accustomed to it, like a finger to stroking a scar, and then had been wrenched away to an alien place. Rootlessness was agonizing enough within, yet the conventions of existence externalized it, and buttressed the agony with objective symbols for the eye.

Anand was an architect. His office was the size of a lavatory. He shared it with four other bright young urban planner types. Their tables were six-inch ledges of some black synthetic thing. Everything was built in or so recessed that one banged elbow or skull against metal or wood each time one stretched to take a deep breath. Each architect earned fabulous sums.

'Let's go out for coffee somewhere.' The cafe they chose smelt of chhole and sour milk. Grease and forearms had dulled the scarlet decolam of the table.

'So you couldn't bear your training or what?'

'Your telegram read, Ma in uppal with fart attack. Was that intentional? '

Anand laughed. 'It was a phonogram. Be happy it reached.'

'Sheela's pregnant, she thinks.' Anand's smile disappeared. 'We didn't know where to go in Bombay. You once said you knew some decent places.'

'Not places. Just one place. That's bad news.' Anand looked away for a while, out to the hive of offices across the dry fountain. 'Poor thing.'

'Yes.'

'I know one good place,' he repeated. 'Costs about fifteen hundred, all told, air-conditioned and so on. You want to go tomorrow? I'll ring her up from office, for, what, eleven tomorrow morning?'

'What's her name?'

'Dr Singh. I call her Aarti. She's quite nice. Has a degree or two from Basle. Is that in Germany or Switzerland?'

'Anyone you know has been to her?'

'My sister. Twice. Can you imagine?'

'Fifteen hundred is quite a lot.'

'You must pay for your sins.'

The dulled waiter brought coffee. Anand said, 'I feel sorry for Sheela, though I never really liked her.'

'Yes. When you first met her,' Jamun smiled though he suddenly felt almost nauseous with depression, 'you'd hoped I wasn't serious about her. You'd said—remember that late-late-night coffee at the Machaan?—that "she's mentally just not in your class, boy. A silly girl without a thought in her head whom you seduce and deflower to win a bet."'

'You've got it wrong. Why d'you get everything wrong? It rhymed, I remember, it was a sort of couplet, either "head" and "bed" or "net" and "bet".' He laughed. It sounded like an outraged yelp. 'She's a sort of cute disaster.' They were both conscious of the baseness of their remarks, but also that there was no one else to hear them. Anand continued, 'She'd do very well for Micky'.

'He isn't even cute.' Anand laughed again because it was expected of him. He was an old friend. Jamun continued, 'Micky's very violent and...aggressive...in his...expressions of love. In Lucknow sometimes he'd dash off to some bush just to pluck a flower for her. An exhibitionist.' Which Sheela had seemed to like, he thought.

Anand lit a cigarette. 'She's very young. And for most girls in our world, sex is not casual. Did you mislead her perhaps?' He looked away at the man behind the coffee percolator. 'Perhaps she assumed, or expected, marriage.'

'I don't know. We were always flippant.' Except that time

in Lucknow, when she had wept. Most of the time she had been so happy, and so appealing in her sunniness, that Jamun had sometimes wanted to cause her pain, subtle and complex, to bewilder her so that she could descend, even for a while, to his emptiness.

Anand exhaled luxuriously. 'But good. Get this operation over with and then sit back and think.'

To Jamun, that sounded like an epitaph for Sheela, she seemed to have moved to the country of the dead. He lit a cigarette too, though he rarely smoked.

10.50 next morning. The opulence of the clinic was intimidating. It was in one of Maharani Bagh's new mansions, vast and vulgar. Unsure of themselves, Sheela and Jamun walked from the car close together, subtly touching each other in what would once have been erotic, back of hand against outside of thigh, breast against tricep. A large unweeded garden, a carved wooden door with a one-foot Khajuraho woman for a handle, the chill of effective air-conditioning, a cold hard woman at a white desk. Jamun inhaled deeply to down the bobbing nervousness.

'We have an appointment with Dr Singh.'

The woman pushed her huge spectacles up and consulted two diaries. Sheela vanished through another door. Jamun mumbled 'Good luck,' but she didn't acknowledge in any way, perhaps she hadn't heard. She was in her bright yellow salwaar kameez. Leafing through glossies on the coffee table he waited and wondered. Couldn't they tell from the urine these days that a girl was pregnant? He and Sheela were so ignorant. Then his mind wandered, pregnant women actually piddled out babies the size of cells, and pregnancy could be checked by examining piss under a microscope for these babies, who, wallowing happily in maternal urine but stifled under glass, waved at the monstrously distorted human eye above them.

With each pregnancy actually a million babies were born but they all died when their heads exploded against the porcelain of the commode. The one who survived hung onto the moist walls of the womb with its claws.

Sheela emerged, expressionless. Jamun stood up, but she didn't look at anybody. She said something to the cold hard woman, then they moved out, stopped outside at the Khajuraho handle. 'Well, what happened?' But he didn't want to know. He wanted to be rude and then go away, to say, maybe Dr Singh cooed to you and skilfully slipped in two fingers and pulled out a foetus with Micky's mind and Satish's face.

'We'll have to come back tomorrow to meet Dr Singh, she's only in in the mornings, but the report itself will be ready by about four this evening.'

That seemed to leave Jamun in limbo. 'Perhaps we should go and have coffee somewhere,' he suggested, 'and get into bed or something, I don't know.'

Sheela said nothing. While driving he looked at her often. Cocooned in himself, he had never considered her loneliness or her wishes. 'You like babies a lot, don't you? All that cooing and nephew's piddle. You'd have liked this child.' Sheela continued to look away. 'But marriage wouldn't have been possible, it's far too early, we'd have ended up like my parents.' He stopped, out of a kind of helplessness at touching upon the unspeakable.

After a while she said, 'Do they, do your parents know about all this?'

'No, of course not.'

'I want to tell them. That you made me pregnant and that you want me to abort.'

'Okay, sure. And remember to tell yours too.' He parked badly under the derisive eye of the parking attendant. The cafe seemed to be full of schoolgirls. 'Your telling them will hurt them, that's all, perhaps confuse them a little.'

'So?' Sheela lit a cigarette.

'Remember how I taught you to inhale?'

She exhaled into his face.

He felt faintly aroused, and continued, 'Abortion is the fruit of lust. Now who could've said that? Maybe me. If we had been in love, then we'd have had the baby. And if we hadn't lusted then we wouldn't have slept together.' She closed her eyes and leaned back, her hair disturbing the leaves of some potted shrub behind her. She stretched her legs out and continued to exhale in the direction of his face. Her cold face could've been tired or disinterested; or a mask hiding her glacial dislike. He again saw her perfectly, like he had once at Lucknow station, the brown throat, the firm, almost hard, upper arms. Ideally he wanted a sort of djinn or familiar, who would appear when required, in the guise that Jamun desired, glut each of his sexual caprices, and then leave him absolutely alone; he would never impose himself on Jamun; when not needed, he wouldn't even exist. Wanting to hurt and be hurt, he picked up Sheela's leg by her calf, pushed off her sandal, pinched her skin hard through her salwaar. He rested her foot on his chair, pressed his crotch tense against her heel, his knees stubborn against her leg, and bent down and kissed, and bit, her

unclean toes. Only such an act could silence the schoolgirls at the next table. Her eyes were still shut, but Sheela was smiling.

Of course they left instantly. They were laughing excitedly on the way to the car. Jamun stopped for bananas. 'Here, have some phallic symbols.' They giggled and gobbled two each. This was an amazing way to end, he thought, of course it was ending, no more threats to those dreams of dispossession. In the car he licked the salt off Sheela's neck and felt her warm stomach beneath the kameez. 'Shall we name the foetus before they kill it? Let's call it Booblu Minor.'

Sheela said, 'If I'd kept my thighs crossed, I'd have had you begging for marriage from Day One.'

'Why, I'll still beg in front of you, not for anything, just whimper and beg.'

'Then beg in front of me while I tell your wonderful mother about the mess you've got me into.' But this kind of conversation always ended up embarrassing her.

'Why don't we go to Anand's flat? Now we don't even need condoms.' Jamun got out of the car to look for a 'phone. One chemist lied and said that his phone wasn't working, one huge general store simply refused. Jamun succeeded at a bookshop run by a mother and her daughter. 'Anand, speaking from Khan Market. Went there this morning. They'll give us the report at four or so. I say, is the key to your flat still under that brass thing?'

'You'll never learn.'

'Now we don't even need condoms.'

'My sister's been staying with me for weeks. She left her Hyderabad job and is now looking for another.'

'God, she can have mine, anytime.'

'She might be out, in which case she'd have taken the key.'

'Any other place you can think of?'

'Your ugly Ambassador, you monkey.'

'Tch, bye now. I'll call again.'

'Good luck.'

When he returned to Sheela, she had changed, Again a wan dying face, eyes crinkling in the cigarette smoke.

'I see that you're not on heat anymore?'

'I want to go back to the hostel.'

'Okay.' He moved the car out. Even the demands of lust are enervating, he thought; he would make no claims beyond them. 'When shall we go for the report? Tomorrow morning? Then we can even meet nice Aarti.'

'Okay.'

Jamun returned home. 'See, I told you I'd be back for lunch,' he told his mother. At the table, his father asked, 'How's the job?'

'Dull and meaningless, but I expected nothing else.'

'It's important to like your job. If you really don't like the one you have, you should think again about your PhD.'

'Yes, let's see.' After lunch, Jamun and his father played two games of chess. Then he wandered from room to room, opening cupboards and unlocking memories; a bewildering afternoon in which he often thought that he in his past had been happy, and then wondered whether he thought so just because it, the past, was irretrievable. In the evening he watched TV with his parents. He looked at them steadily gazing at the screen without registering any of its belches, and wondered about their youth. Perhaps they had been like him, perhaps he would finish up like them, in front of a TV, and at the point of his surrender to that uncaring sea, its hush would become a roar.

At the clinic the next morning the report said that Sheela was not pregnant. Dr Singh turned out to be fortyish, prim and revolting.

'Definitely not a pregnancy. Your period could be delayed for a variety of reasons. Stress or some illness. Get yourself a thorough check up. No, payment outside please.'

Outside the clinic they paused uncertainly beneath a jacaranda in bloom. 'So are you ill, or what're you so stressed about?' Jamun smiled.

Sheela bit her lip. 'It's really odd. I suppose this test was foolproof? Maybe I should really get that check-up.' In the car she said, 'I feel weird. All that tension for nothing.'

'Coffee somewhere I think. But not yesterday's cafe perhaps.'

Sheela laughed. 'No, let's go there and nowhere else.' They moved off. Jamun was content to let things be. She repeated, half to herself, 'It's strange.' They chose the same table. He asked, 'Do you want to go to Bombay again?'

She looked away. 'No, that would be very funny. I just want to sort of stay here and unwind for a bit. Then I'll see.' They had very little to say to each other, there seemed no cause for celebration. After coffee they had nowhere to go, so he dropped her back at the hostel. 'I'll probably go back tomorrow, I'll write from Bombay.'

'Stay a day or two more?' Sheela asked unconvincingly.

'No, we'd better leave each other alone for while, to recover from Booblu Minor.'

She laughed, waved and went lightly up the stairs.

On the train to Bombay, returning to the unknown city and an empty future, Jamun again felt ill with depression. He curled up in his berth and was assaulted by savage masochistic images of, among others, Mrs Karve. He wanted to be beaten senseless, to be deprived of his mind so that he didn't have to think.

Eight empty days in Bombay, the city of dead rats and smegma; on a few evenings rummy with Mrs Karve, on a few others watching the patch of Australia on the wall from his bed and absorbing the grunts and clinks from the Youth Club next door. Then, for their next phase of training, Jamun and Mrs Karve moved to Madras.

Madras was humid and alien-tongued. The new Training Institute there was on the edge of the city, close to the beach, girdled by fishermen. A small clean featureless room, the same classes, in the evenings slow walks in the compound, watching disinterested gardeners trying to create a lawn out of rubble. Jamun contacted dengue. The fever ravaged him for seven days. While Mrs Karve attended class, he lay alone watching the sanatorium-white ceiling, juggling with bitter-sweet images of his past. In the evenings Mrs Karve brought company and chatter because she had nowhere else to go. The fever procured an insidious intimacy between them. They listened to the delightful hyperboles of Urdu ghazals on her recorder and watched the evening pass the window. The songs spoke of loss and despair, the best of them creating a fleeting grace out of these ashes.

When I first saw you
the world moved on but I halted;
I haven't moved on since then,
waiting, still waiting
for you to move
with me.

At moments, the music and Mrs Karve combined to stir him gently, like the memory, or the shadow, of another desire.

At the end of that week, they had some days off. Mr Karve emerged out of the hinterland, good-looking, dull. Mrs Karve disappeared with him. One Sunday at twilight they took Jamun to the Marina in a noisy smelly taxi. Bleeding Madras, Micky always called the city after having spent five years at its IIT.

Jamun sat timid and bent on a bench, like an invalid, knees together. The sea breeze revived his feverishness, the late-evening sky was a mess of black and gold. Behind him, the Karves joined the babble of children around the chips and ice-cream walas. Here the sea was louder than at Bombay; it did not whisper, but roared its unconcern. In his exhaustion, Jamun half-smiled and prayed for the decline of all desire.

Three-seven-seven and the Blue Gay Gene

Simplest if one imagines all the world to be a stage—it's been done before—upon which unfolds a hundred-and-fifty-*year*-long absurd play.

Upon that stage, out of the darkness of her life appears Manjula, aged forty-five, ravaged but charming. The spotlight is on her loneliness.She speaks aloud her thoughts to her husband. He is not fit to be seen.

'If I took you to court, I could be famous and have a case named after me and be cited for decades hereafter in lawsuits and classrooms and legal forums all over the land. *Manjula versus the Union of India*. Section 377. I have a dream.'

Section 377 of the Indian Penal Code—which is what Manjula dreams about, a phallic article indeed—reads as follows:

377: Unnatural offences: Whoever voluntarily has carnal intercourse against the order of nature with any man, woman or animal, shall be punished with imprisonment for life, or with imprisonment of either description for a term which may extend to ten years, and shall also be liable to fine.

Explanation: Penetration is sufficient to constitute the carnal intercourse necessary to the offence described in this Section.

'What does it *mean*? For starters, what does "against the order of nature" mean?'

The questions are posed to the world from a stage just as wide but Manjula does not hear any of the answers that have been framed over a hundred and fifty years of confusion on the subject. Her mind is too full of her son, still in hospital, and her husband who unfortunately is not going anywhere.

'I'm going to ask Samarpan to translate 377 for me into modern Indian English.'

Always ready to help his mother, the only woman he adores, Samarpan takes an entire weekend in his hospital bed to come up with:

'377: Unnatural offences: As per existing law, a penis can only fuck a vagina. And only to make babies. If a male pokes any organ of his body into any hole of any other living being, or even if he uses a condom, boy, will he get buggered. A mother poking her infant's mouth with her nipple and loving the sensation even though her dugs are dry is liable to be imprisoned for life.

'Explanation: Penetration means fuck. And bugger bugger.'

That was much clearer. The boy's language was absurd, offensive and obscene but so was the original. Manjula thanked her son and, armed with his exegesis, returned to her contemplation of the different lines of argument that she could educe in a crowded court room in the case that would make her immortal.

'Milord, my husband—who is also my lord—has been buggering me, two or three times a month, for the last twenty years of our marriage. We are happily married. We have one son. He almost died last month. But since he didn't, we are still happily married. I'm not sure what his death would have done to our conjugal relations. I initially found being buggered quite distasteful and demeaning. But because my husband, my lord, also massages my vagina with his left hand and mauls my breasts with his right at the same time as he is pounding me from the rear, I began with time to quite like the experience of being buggered. We use mustard oil. So when we have sex, I am reminded of my grandmother and her cooking. My husband is a nice man, a Brahmin, a gentleman. For starters, he ought to be imprisoned for life under 377.

For starters, in the beginning was the word of Thomas Babington Macaulay.

'The Penal Code, Manjula, was a hundred years old *before* you were born.' So Manjula's mother, a retired judge and no mean busybody herself, edifies her daughter. 'It is the work of a genius—incestuous, smug—but a genius. I do not use the word loosely.'

'Which word do you not use loosely—smug or incestuous or genius? I don't know, Samarpan considers himself to be a genius.'

Unlike Macaulay, Samarpan is not incestuous. He is gay. He *is* smug, though, and just a wee bit annoying, and shall be left in hospital for one more week.

While, in the far corner of that revolving stage that has a life of its own, Thomas Babington Macaulay is at breakfast in Calcutta's Government House. It is April 8, 1838 and he is, if possible, even more pleased with himself than usual because he has at last finished with the Indian Penal Code. It has been sent off and is now merely waiting for Hobhouse and MacLeod to wake up to their responsibilities, to have it examined and promulgated as law. That is going to take a mere twenty-four years but Thomas doesn't know it yet; he feels it to be one bloody good step taken towards civilizing those dusky beggars who surround the island that is Government House.

Some of them of course have infiltrated Thomas's establishment as well and actually make his existence quite pleasurable. He wouldn't know what to do without them.

Muzammil, for example, who at that very moment has brought in fresh muffins and a nice new pot of Chinese tea, is quite, Thomas feels, the perfect second khansamah, discreet, silent, restful. The Indian Penal Code would do him a world of good.

Ah, but if Thomas only knew how on the contrary the perfect second khansamah would be simply appalled by the Code's obtuseness. For the discreet and dusky Muzammil is bisexual. They are everywhere, to be found wherever life is. He is sort of homosexual, part time, so to speak. He and Lalji, the storekeeper's assistant, find living to be more pleasurable when they can couple twice a week. They are both happily married and between them have six wives, seven sons and eight daughters. Their special relationship too is discreet and dusky; their world sees them as good friends—rare bum-chums, if you will. They would not have it otherwise—indeed, if probed, would deeply wonder if there *could* be an otherwise. As a caste Hindu, Lalji is defiled by the mere touch of Muzammil's little finger; the khansamah's circumcised member in fact sends him every time, for seven generations, to Talatala, the profoundest Hindu hell, from where the correctly-intoned incantation and rightly-performed ritual bath do not fail, on every occasion, to tug him back at six in the evening, well in time to cook the books of Government House.

A tale of true love their story is; it is part of the pre-history of 377. Lalji for instance truly loves his second wife, his two youngest sons and all his daughters. And Muzammil. Whom Lalji loves most at any one given point depends of course, amongst other things, on how perky his gay gene is feeling at that moment, that is to say, on how the blood is coursing at that instant in his veins, which in turn depends on the hour of the day, the day of the week, the season of the year, the phase of the moon and the position of Saturn in the heavens. Ditto Muzammil. True love has been ordained for them; what they do on sweltering afternoons amongst the serene cows in the cattle shed is their destiny, their joy, their secret and none of the world's business. They themselves would do nothing to rock the boat but if things do turn sour, that too of course would be their karma.

'They are wise,' comments Hiranmaya to his son Samarpan, 'in wanting to be left alone. Unlike someone we know.'

In response, Samarpan shuts his eyes, and with difficulty turns over in his hospital bed so that his back is to his father. He loves his parents but does wish at times that they would leave him be. Pay the hospital charges of course and thereafter, for a while, just let him alone.

Those charges. For a stay of six weeks in a shared room, the South Delhi hospital presents Samarpan with a bill of a little under nine lakh rupees. He riffles through the sheaves, understands almost nothing, wonders why the language of science is so arcane and passes them on to his father. The treatment covers one fractured rib, a perforated lung, one broken femur, abdominal trauma resulting in rupture of the spleen and liver, acute haematemesis, anal rupture and bleeding, anal sphincter tear, tearing of the penile shaft, one broken collarbone, a perforated eardrum and severe abrasions and lacerations of the skin. A photo of his, of untraceable origin, is all over the Net. It is a closeup of his face; he is unconscious, his lips, nose and eyelids are livid and swollen, not much else can be made out of his face for the blood. He is gagging on someone's penis. Samarpan is eighteen going on twelve. His body will never fully recover but within four months will be ripe and ready enough for further damage.

'That's not true and you know that. We too want to be left alone but it's the cops and people like Pramod Swineflu who just won't let us be,' is what he *wants* to say in response to his father but that would trigger off a heart-to-heart that he's *so* not in the mood for; so he keeps quiet and instead pretends to nod off so that he can daydream about that ward boy taking off his uniform. It is the surest sign of Samarpan's recovery.

He is a genius and a virgin, Samarpan. He is also a bit of a fool. He has never either buggered or been buggered, so 377, he believes, cannot touch him for, in the absence of a telltale bruised sphincter, where is the proof? Unless he's caught with his pants down, so to speak, and his mouth open, with another male, also with his pants down. Which is more or less what happens under the Kotla Mubarakpur flyover on the night of July 3, 2009.

That evening begins with Samarpan cruising at Defence Colony Market. His parents are away for the weekend, celebrating Pramod Swineflu's sixtieth birthday at Neemrana. Getting them to go has been sort of touch and go; Samarpan clinches it by telling his father to agree for his mother's sake and his mother for her own.

'You need a break, Ma.'

'Most of all from your father, I should think. The one thing nice about this weekend is that Swineflu will only join us there tomorrow morning. At least one evening free of his presence. He says he's going to Alwar this afternoon to pick up and escort his elder sister to Neemrana. Her wealth explains his fraternal devotion.'

Their host for the weekend makes Manjula uneasy; Hiranmaya finds him revolting. Pramod Kumar is an ex-policeman, Chairman of the Residents' Welfare Association, an authority, a gabbler, on how to contain the swineflu, an aficionado of middle-history Hindi film songs, of which he has a thousand on his mobile phone, each of which, depending on the appositeness of its lilt and theme, he has assigned as ring tone to a contact phone number; he is also a fund of tiresome, risqué jokes with which he has for months been trying to cosy up to Samarpan. Samarpan believes that a few more men like Pramod Swineflu would turn the whole world permanently heterosexual.

He has cruised before, Samarpan. There have been times when he has wondered whether he's doing it correctly. His being witty and shy is no doubt the reason why it has never ended up in the earth moving for him—with an unknown somewhere, under a flyover or in a park or a ghastly public toilet. But he's quite content, to sit on a bench in a fine drizzle, smoke cigarettes under a menacing sky, make eyes at an autorickshaw-driver while the latter scratches his balls and expectorates some paan before driving off with a couple of chattering female customers. For Samarpan, it's a thrill even to exhibit his intent to himself.

On the evening of July 3, 2009, he is terribly excited. He has felt all day that he *ought* to be celebrating, making merry, letting himself go. For the day before, the Delhi High Court has declared that Section 377 of the Indian Penal Code, insofar as it criminalises the consensual sexual acts of adults in private, is violative of Articles 21, 14 and 15 of the Indian Constitution. Samarpan rushes downstairs to find out what that means. It is impossible though to get at the grandmother's bookshelves without first having to deal with her.

'No, just looking, you know, General Knowledge, just in case I'm waylaid in the street by a TV channel or something. Your grandson after all. Shouldn't come across as *too much* of a fool.'

The TV channels in fact show the gays of Delhi painted up and parading at India Gate in celebration of the judgement. The grandmother watches, fascinated. Where did they all spring from? Samarpan watches too, half-repelled. They don't look sexy at all. And the policemen on the scene with their staffs of bamboo, when the TV camera doesn't catch their eye, all look ready to bugger the whole lot.

They are depressed, the cops. By declaring 377 unconstitutional, the Delhi High Court has taken some of the fun out of their lives. It was good, 377 was, for arbitrary detention, brutal harassment, torture, forced sex, male rape, eunuch rape, extortion, blackmail and general extreme mental and physical abuse. It was good because it was so slippery, it worked so well in tandem with some of the other Sections of a Code so acknowledged for its slipperiness—293, 294, 142, 147, 268, 292, 309, 174—the list is as long as the volume.

Take Madras in May 2006; just one example out of twenty thousand. The police booked one Pandian under 420 for theft and sexually abused him in jail for a fortnight. So what's new? He was a eunuch, a human being against the order of nature and, under 377, perfect fodder meat for them. He was released on bail on May 19, 2006 on condition that he should report every day to Vyasarpadi Police Station at ten a.m. In fact, one police constable would come to his house to take him away every morning at eight and deposit him at home, exhausted, glum, unable to eat, at eleven at night. All day, a dozen policemen raped him in the mouth and poked those staffs of bamboo up his anus. On June 12, Pandian set himself on fire outside that same police station. While he was dying in hospital, the cops filed a case against him under 309 for attempted suicide; when he died, they switched to 174 for failure to obey the orders of a public servant.

How slippery 377 is. The cops use it against almost everybody—beggars, eunuchs, unemployable idlers at a busstop, AIDS outreach workers, coolies, cycle-rickshaw-walas, joggers in the park—to establish, even though it can never be in doubt, their almost limitless power to abuse their power; at the same time, partly because it is *so* slippery, they rarely bring up charges under that Section of the Code. They can then say—they then *do* say—that 377 is a benign provision, a rarely used statute, why repeal a law that is so dormant, such a sleeping beauty.

Leaving the police at India Gate to ponder over a life without 377, Samarpan selects Durgadas Basu from his grandmother's bookshelf, it being the fattest, most vellum-bound tome, a sadomasochist's delight in its flaunting of gilt and leather, and is carrying it to the dining table when she decrees to the TV screen, 'They should be able to have it struck down by the Supreme Court. Out of that present lot, I don't see anyone who would want to be remembered as the judge who legally brought homosexuality out on to the streets in India.'

So there he is, young Samarpan, sitting on a bench in Defence Colony Market, smoking his third cigarette despite feeling dizzy after the first two, watching that cute hulk in tight white pants buying stuff at the paanwala's and thinking of this and that. Of his schoolmates saying that you could tell a gay by his inability to whistle, by his womanish hips being broader than his chest, by how as a baby he couldn't stop sucking his thumb and so before long had begun sucking something else. Samarpan wondering at the possibility, at long last, of freedom from all that.

'You have matches?'

The hulk is beside him on the bench, smiling. He has dimples. Fucking *dimples.*

How old is oral sex in India? History is silent on that crucial point. No archaeologist has ever suggested for instance that the vivid Harappa Head of the priest-king, bearded, with its eyes half-closed, captures memorably in stone the expression of a man enjoying being blown. Though of course in the three thousand five hundred years after Harappa, fellatio becomes respectable enough to be performed in relief, in stone, in public, indeed, in a religious place—mystifying blowjob upon blowjob on temple walls celebrate men—and women—taking time off for sex with men en route to laying down their souls, in the sanctum sanctorum, at the feet of Shiva or one of his comrades in the pantheon. At Khajuraho and Konarak and a dozen other temples, blowjobs and buggery adorn the walls of the abodes of gods most wise and understanding; those acts visibly are part of the order of supernature. Once upon a time, the law in India, in the golden age before Macaulay, was almost as wise.

As can be witnessed from the true love of Lalji and Muzammil. Remember them? When last seen, they were frolicking amongst the cows in a shed in Calcutta not far from where the Nakhoda Mosque will come up almost a hundred years later, five hundred kilometers north-east of—and six hundred years after—Konarak, serene in their karma while waiting for the afternoon to wane. Even though Thomas Babington is, so to speak, ready in the wings with Section 377, the lovers are discreet and for the time being nothing can touch them. For the Penal Code is not yet in force and acts against the order of nature, at least for the next twenty years, cannot be punished with imprisonment for life. So what could go wrong with their true love?

Enter a complainant.

You would need one, an outraged busybody with a medieval mind or a disgusted father-in-law on behalf of his forlorn daughter or a missionary in position, some non-C.F. Andrews type. But the complainant, whoever it is, soon discovers that the wise law, like an anxious god worried for his devotees, has placed some nice hurdles in his quest to bugger the cause of true love.

For one, it is quite possible that Lalji and Muzammil—for

the crime, it may be reiterated, of imitating in private life the act of desire sculpted on a temple wall—cannot be tried in the same court or indeed by the same law. True justice, being wise and tending to prefer, in every epoch and all over the world, shades of grey to black and white, might just send that offended complainant to *parallel* systems of redressal—in effect, into a spin. For Muzammil is Muslim, a good godfearing Sunni, and only Mughal law—the Sadar Nizamat Adalat—would apply in his case. Under that law, the usual discretionary punishment that is meted out for sodomy is a free ride on an ass and on occasion, a whipping—an ordeal, may it be noted, that would turn to pleasure were Lalji to wield the whip. And against Muzammil the testimony of Lalji himself might be invalid because, depending on the circumstances, that same law, before Thomas Babington stepped in, might not have permitted Muslims to be prosecuted on the evidence of non-Muslims.

Against a hostile world, Lalji is equally well-protected both by his law and his religion. In 1838—in fact, ever since the dawn of justice (and desire, and sodomy), that law has flourished under the banyan tree of the *Manu Smriti*. As in everything else about Hindu practices, it is complicated; and homosexuality, like a thousand other matters, is inextricably linked with ritual, erotics, the occult and other such distracting stuff. Buggery, or adhorata, 'under-love'—Lalji will animatedly explain when pressed—either between males or between sexes, is one of the principal means of awakening the potencies of the rectal centre, the animation of which energizes the artistic, creative and mystical faculties. Perversion? Against the order of nature? *Chhut!* Why, the anus is one of the most important chakras of the body and constricting it, concentrating on it, stimulating it, inserting things—a plug, digit or member—into it are standard yogic-tantric disciplines based on the occult correspondence between it and the higher centres of the subtler human body.

The court though, Lalji suspects, just might not be impressed with the argument that Muzammil buggers his fellow employee for religious reasons. Yet that does not unduly worry the storekeeper's assistant. If the judge at the Fort William courthouse, reasons he, is a caste Hindu with some knowledge of the classic law texts, of *Manu* and the *Arthashastra*, with luck he would also be imbued with the perspective, the wisdom, of the ancient legal codes; would, for instance, find heinous the crime of *heterosexual* adultery—punishable with death—and in contrast see the sport in contingent homosexual fun—to be chastised with just a fine or loss of caste or a ritual bath. The last two punishments in any case Lalji has lived with ever since he has (wink wink) known Muzammil.

So the days pass with the two buggers worrying more—and with reason—about drought and famine and smallpox and cholera, and finding employment for their unemployable sons and husbands and dowries for their daughters. Fittingly, they are much less anxious about the likelihood of some of their progeny or their extended families being gay; about, say, the illegitimate son of an aunt's third cousin who shares with them both the proclivity and the knack of being discreet. These things happen, they run in the blood, they would say; thus, after the manner of a future generation, they would attribute his conduct to their common genes.

And then one fine day in 1861, the whites bring in a white and utterly alien morality to overwhelm the law courts of the land.

'The Penal Code,' says Manjula's mother when she feels that no one has paid her any attention for quite a while, 'according to Macaulay was not a body of ethics. It must content itself, he wrote, with keeping men from doing positive harm, and must leave to public opinion and to teachers of morality and religion the office of furnishing men with motives for doing positive good.' They are all at her dining table on the ground floor. They have just discovered that climbing the stairs hurts Samarpan a fair bit in the lower abdomen. No one is paying Manjula's mother any attention because they have better things to do. More specifically, they are taken up with being appalled at the thought of perhaps having to fix up a room for the boy on the ground floor, well within the grandmotherly orbit. How will he ever recover in the absence of any mental peace? But Manjula's mother has been a judge of the High Court and the inattentiveness of her audience has never deterred her. So she continues, pensive and beady-eyed, to compel the walls to incline to her point of view. 'But the more I think of it, the more certain I am that the Penal Code was part of the Macaulay strategy—stratagem—to alienate the people from their world, thereby making them easier to govern.'

'If you don't want that tea, don't drink it. Then I'll help you up the stairs.'

That pain in his son's abdomen, hopes Hiranmaya, is not some hitherto undetected damage to his kidneys. The last ultrasound at the hospital at least seemed to have indicated an all-clear. Hiranmaya is due to go off to Europe for a couple of weeks—Brussels, Oslo, Amsterdam—on a professional junket but is scared to leave his son. The boy's face is an open book of gay porn. The clearest evidence of his mental recovery, feels his father, is that on it can be read his impatience with the elders of his family, his eagerness to be alone so that he can connect once more with the world from which had emerged the decoy who had had him beaten up almost to death. They need to get him upstairs before he discovers that his mother has hidden his second mobile phone.

She might not even remember where she has stashed it away. For in the last six weeks she has been more incapable than ever of focusing on anything for more than a few seconds at a time. How to establish that her son's gayness is not the fallout of his love for her but the fault of his father's genes? That is what has been buzzing around day and night in her head. She is as certain of it as of her motherhood, but how to prove it in a crowded courtroom? And submerged in all that welter in her skull, bobbing up every now and then like a ping pong ball, is the thought that it is no great matter, that why he is how he is is a mere distraction in the game.

Father helps son up the stairs. Samarpan's body feels thin and fragile, smells of ill-health. He is delighted to be back home and, humming to himself, rushes (slowly) to his laptop. He is instantly annoyed to find that it isn't working. 'Have we cut off the Internet as a security measure?' he demands waspishly of his mother.

She doesn't respond, because most things entering her skull in one ear exit at once through some other aperture, usually a nostril, and leave behind no trace save for a dim, not unpleasant, humming. It is how she has survived, since the age of two, the conversation of her mother. 'The hospital clearly said that you shouldn't go out for some days but I'm sure your friends could visit you here.'

'Better to talk to them in the flesh than on a screen,' adds her husband. Oh, perhaps shouldn't've said in the flesh. Sure to send the thoughts of this wretched boy careering off in the direction of the Kotla Mubarakpur flyover.

Actually, the one person that Samarpan aches most to meet at that moment he can't invite home. For one, he doesn't know either his name or where he stays. All he has for him is a phone number—Samarpan's own, because the other stole it—and the nickname that Samarpan thinks of him by, Dimples. Within the first hour of his getting home, from his grandmother's phone, he's called his old number twenty-two times. Out of coverage area, says a robotic, slightly retarded, female voice. *Please send me the photo,* he next texts him. And then repeatedly, fearing that he has used far too many words, *Send photo. Send photo.*'

Parents and son have not discussed the events of the night of July 3, 2009. Attacked by miscreants, Samarpan manfully resists, they steal his wallet and mobile phone and enraged, teach him a lesson for trying to be manly, so goes the official version. The parents hope that by not talking it over, they will help it to recede into the depths; that with each passing day, the boy will slough off his gay skin to emerge a happy, handsome heterosexual.

But suddenly they are everywhere, gays. No doubt the outcome of the High Court judgement, they begin to take up large amounts of airtime on TV.

'According to the estimates of 2006,' says a painted face to the family assembled around the ground-floor dining table, feasting on Pramod Swineflu's welcome-home carrot halwa, 'there are twenty-five lakh gays in India. But, at a conservative one per cent of the population, the actual number who have had homosexual experiences will be over ten million. Because of that imbecile 377, how can you call ten million fellow citizens criminals?' At that point, the camera, no doubt unable to bear the excitement goggling out of the eyes above the paint, pans to a crush of fancy dresses, peacock feathers and V for Victories. 'They are farmers, lawyers, academics, civil servants, CEOs of enterprises, actors, dancers, writers, doctors, sportsmen, politicians, priests of various hues, sweepers, TV anchors, bus drivers, police constables, shopkeepers, jewellers, school teachers, fashion designers, hotel managers, pilots, engineers, tourists, terrorists, godmen, students, judges, drug addicts, guards, cooks, sailors, Army jawans—'

'Okay okay I get the point, Paintbox.' Hiranmaya to the TV.

'—Are we lesser human beings? We don't make bombs, we

don't behead people on YouTube, we just want to be left alone to express our love. It *is* love. And you call yourself a Welfare State?'

What's in a name, Paintbox, is the correct response to be made at this juncture. Nobody says so but everyone around the dining table more or less thinks it. The elders are all horribly relieved that Samarpan is not in fancy dress and declaiming on TV. Manjula in particular is even more distracted than usual at the sight of such a large congregation of homosexuals. What an impressive concentration of the gay gene, says she to herself as she watches a set of painted lips lock into another.

But is there really one, a gay gene, that is, is what she has so often enquired of the world. She asks it again of the clothes and reports and medication that have returned with her son from the hospital; and if so, am I, the mother, its carrier? Nothing is certain. In the weeks that Samarpan's been away convalescing, she's been reading up; she's looked up stuff on the Net and like a thief, riffled through the shelves in his room for illumination. They are quick, she and her husband; guessing his password—gayatrimantra—and hacking his laptop open takes them three minutes and seventeen seconds. She is appalled—and Hiranmaya vaguely titillated—by the gay porn sites that their son has been visiting for years. 'How absolutely disgusting. We shouldn't be doing this, you know,' says he, furiously clicking away at one link after another to glimpse as much as he can of a new world before the spell is broken and she asks him to stop.

It puzzles, annoys and depresses her to read so much and yet learn nothing about the gay gene. No one is certain whether it even exists and if it does, how it is transmitted. No one knows for sure whether homosexuality is genetic or the result of environmental factors or some unfathomable combination of the two. Penguins and bonobo chimpanzees—in fact, over *four hundred* species of animals—engage in homosexual behavior and yet no one can definitely aver that gayness in the animal world is an expression of true sexual desire and not of a need to establish dominion.

'That does sound,' murmurs Hiranmaya to himself, 'like the British in India.'

Manjula relearns en passant that the cootchie-cooing of one male baboon to another is, even while being natural, an act against the order of nature because they are making love without making babies. Then she is distracted from her pursuit of she no longer remembers what—ah yes, the gay gene—by the nugget of information that human *females* tend more towards bisexuality than males and furthermore, change their sexual orientation during their lives more often than men. How odd. And then, what the hell.

She is next diverted from the bisexuality of the human female by the fickleness of the fruit fly. It switches from heterosexual to homosexual when a single gene in it is altered. Further, when the ambient temperature is raised to 30 degrees Celsius plus, modified male fruit flies lose interest in females and become even more receptive to other males.

'*Which* single gene? Do human beings have it?'

Hiranmaya has no idea what she's talking about. Men are so obtuse. She explains. He takes aeons to follow.

'If they were ever to isolate the gay gene, Manjula, foeticide in India would go up a thousand fold. Doctor saab, is my foetus gay? Hey Ram and tauba tauba. Then inter the bugger hugger mugger.'

From Samarpan's storehouse, Manjula gleans enough to be permanently confused not only about the gay gene but also about 377.

His parents note with bemused tenderness that the boy has converted his old class XII geography exercise copy into a scrapbook of the history of that Section of the Penal Code. They pore over it for an entire Sunday. 377 is bewildering. It is small consolation to them to learn that for over a hundred and fifty years, it has perplexed *everyone* whom it has touched.

'I wish you'd stop laughing. Really.'

'Yes I really should. It is so against the order of nature.'

Hiranmaya's sniggering is in fact a sort of nervous reaction. He is not so much amused as appalled at what the courts discuss. At first glance—even at second—it is hard to distinguish between their subject matter and that of Samarpan's gay porn sites; he has the impression that a second set of actors, wearing penguin robes and judges' wigs, has emerged on to that stage as wide as the world, has surrounded the players on the gay sites to analyse and pass judgement on their activities.

It is from them that he learns that in 1884, for instance, the court of the Session Judge of Mysore decreed that a blowjob was not buggery.

The act charged against the accused, of having opened (another's) mouth, put in his private parts and completed his lust, does not constitute the offence of sodomy, as it does not constitute carnal intercourse with penetration, under the section.

Ergo, at least in 1884, in Mysore, one could fellate and not be imprisoned for life under 377.

'I do not understand, my lord.' Manjula is still spotlit in the loneliness of that stage of her life. 'The history of 377 is revolting and unremittingly obscene. It is an endless and abominable narrative of gratification without consent, of rape and the sexual assault of minors. It has *nothing* to do with homosexual love between consenting adults, with the temperament of my son. It just provides amusement to people like my husband. And I see from my son's scrapbook that over the decades, different courts have interpreted 377 in such a manner that it has now come to prohibit *only* those acts engaged in by homosexuals. Perhaps with evolution some men will grow vaginas and at last their coupling will not go against the order of nature.' She pauses to sigh heavily. 'If Macaulay was a genius, then why are things so confused?'

Well, one can't really blame one short, fat Englishman for everything, she realizes that. But one can try. Because it is not poor Manjula alone; *everyone* is confused.

In 1925, for instance, the High Court of Sind, disagreeing with the conclusion reached by Mysore in 1884, begins to draw in the noose for poor gays. It decides that no, 377 *does* cover oral sex, that carnal intercourse against the order of nature *includes* fellatio which—the judgement thunders—is 'the sin of Gomorrah,' 'a vice,' according to Justices Kincaid and Kennedy, 'less pernicious than the sin of Sodom.'

'Oh to spend,' murmurs Hiranmaya to his son's scrapbook, 'six months of the year in Sodom and the other half in Gomorrah and bollocks to the parting of the Red Sea.'

377, it has been noted by a thousand wise men over the years, speaks only of certain vague and ill-defined acts but succeeding judgements across the decades have narrowed its impact down to menace only a specific group of people, those poor sods, gays. So in 1992, for instance, the Madras High Court decreed that Brother John Anthony, the sub-warden of the Boarding Home attached to St Mary's Higher Secondary School, Tuticorin, was guilty under 377 because he used to get the boys of that hostel to jerk him off; he could in theory (and should in practice) have been put away for a hundred years. Instead, the effect of the activities of Brother Fagin has been that after 1992, one cannot in private, out of love, stroke and give pleasure to a lover without running the risk of being jailed for life.

And in the same year, the Gujarat High Court said that coming between someone's *thighs* too was in principle punishable with life imprisonment. The language of that judgement is, well, unambiguous.

In intercourse between the thighs, the visiting male organ is enveloped at least partially by the thighs when the thighs are kept together and tight. As can be seen from the dictionary meaning the word 'penetrate' means 'find access into or through, pass through'. When the male organ is inserted between the thighs kept together and tight, is there no penetration? The word 'insert' means 'place, fit, thrusts'. Therefore, if the male organ is 'inserted' or 'thrust' between the thighs, there is 'penetration' to constitute unnatural offence.

Since the statute does not specify any particular opening into which penetration can be made, penetration into any orifice of one's body, except the vaginal opening of a female, is sufficient for establishment of the crime.

This is Samarpan's world. What in the scrapbook transfixes the parents and hinders them from facing for any length of time the catastrophe that has befallen him is the gusto, the relish, with which the courts wade into the violence that is the lifeblood, the sap, of that netherworld that he has so happily entered.

'Pramod Swineflu is here. For the last half-an hour, he's been discussing 377 and the High Court judgement with your grandmother. And how to have it repealed in the Supreme Court.'

'That freak. He looks like someone who's just eaten your mom. I'm resting and simply cannot be disturbed. And if he comes up, Papa, I'm going to dress up in some wedding finery and jump off the roof, is that understood?'

'I'm going down to tell them that you've already done so.

Then when they rush out, you jump and land on his head. How about that, is *that* understood?'

The two downstairs have been so intent on impressing each other with their acuity of thought that it is unlikely that they would have rushed out for a teenager in a nosedive. 'Deleting 377,' Pramod Swineflu has said for forty minutes in twenty-eight different ways, 'will be misconstrued as providing unfettered licence to homosexuality. As it stands, it in fact prevents the spread of HIV. Indian society by and large loathes gays coming out. Purdah must be maintained. The state must protect public health and morality. Gays spread disease and should be punished under 269 and 270 of the Penal Code. I am entirely in agreement with a certain Mr Radhakrishnan when he argued in court that criminal laws are necessary to prevent social degeneration. Every organ of the body has a designated function. The mouth is used for eating and for making sound. The anus is used for the excretion of waste. The body requires—'

'The anus is also used for making sound,' points out the grandmother's fine legal brain.

'—its different parts to work in tandem, each organ performing the functions preordained by nature. The use of the anus or the mouth for sexual activity goes against the normal functions of the human body and the order of nature; society will put its foot down and stamp out such abuse.'

Pramod Swineflu roams around the country doing a fair amount of that stamping himself. Six months later, for instance, he is going to rush off to Aligarh to crusade against Shriniwas Ramchandra Siras.

All eyes are to turn now to that stage as wide as the world to behold the tragedy, the replay, of the individual at odds with his society. The hero is small, bearded, a sixty-four-year-old Reader in Modern Indian Languages at Aligarh Muslim University;

he steps into the spotlight in a jacket and tie. His hubris is his self-confidence in proclaiming to the wide world his gayness; he announces, 'I love males. You want to make something out of it?'

The world does. On February 8, 2010, it, in the form of some media riffraff and some Pramod Swineflu clones, storms into his apartment on campus and catches Siras in flagrante with another male, a poor sod of a rickshaw-puller. They click and film the couple and distribute the photographs and video clips to the newspapers and TV channels, Aligarh goes ballistic, its outrage however fuelled not by *them* but by Siras! He loses his job and is asked by the university to vacate his apartment.

He goes to court against being fired. Meanwhile, crowds of Pramod Swineflu clones jeer and abuse him all day, demonstrate against him, organize processions that foulmouth, revile and thunder against what he represents. The scum have a great time. He moves to another part of town. They follow him. He speaks of migrating to the United States, the land of the equal and the free where he says that he will not be persecuted.

Instead, on April 7 of the same year, he is found dead in his new flat. Poisoned. By person or persons unknown. Perhaps himself.

So what's new?

Injustice and tragedy are older than the hills. Samarpan's grandmother has not been impressed with anything that the ex-policeman spouts, and with hard-luck stories even less than with medieval-minded crusaders. The public comprises obtuse and dangerous individuals like Swineflu, it cannot be entrusted with anything, thank God for the courts and their enlightened judges, who must never be made to retire and instead should be rewarded with even higher salaries and grander colonial bungalows—that is her view.

Oddly enough, it is a funny-mirror image of the opinion

held by many involved in the struggle against 377. They believe that the cops will never let go of that Section of the Code out of the love of a cowherd for a lactating cow; the police is a merciless, occasionally malevolent and immensely powerful beast. It can only be subdued by another even more so. Hence the recourse to the courts.

'Looks like our patient is not going to come down. I'll go up to look in on him.'

For an ex-policeman—or perhaps because he was till recently active in the force—Pramod Swineflu is in poor health. He is short of breath after taking the stairs to the first floor. Samarpan is nowhere to be seen. That doesn't deter the ex-policeman from snooping around in the boy's room. Hiranmaya, intrigued, observes him from behind the screen door to the terrace where his stress has taken him to smoke one of Samarpan's cigarettes. Samarpan himself, alarmed, watches the intruder through the one centimeter available between bathroom door and door-frame. Manjula is just outside the room, about to enter to replace her son's scrapbook on his table.

Pramod Swineflu's mobile phone goes off in his pocket. Its loudness startles them all.

'Aadmi hoon aadmi se pyaar karta hoon...' belts out Mukesh from within Pramod Swineflu's pocket. He takes out his phone but doesn't answer it, doesn't even look to see who it is but long before he can switch it off, Manjula, entering, exclaims, 'But that's so familiar! Where's it from?'

'*Pehchaan,*' elucidates Pramod Swineflu, grinning ferally at her, 'Filmfare award, 1970. Manoj Kumar, Babita, Balraj Sahni.' He raises a hand in a limp farewell and begins to back out of the room. 'Music by Shankar Jaikishan. Have to go. Forgotten my insulin.' He is on the stairs when the phone rings again.

He takes it out, it seems to slip out of his hand, for they hear it clattering on the steps, next him cursing and the song happily continuing, several bars of it and, long after he passes out of earshot, somehow even hanging back in the air, lingering like guilt.

'What an oddball.' So inaugurates Hiranmaya a rare—and brief—family conference in his son's room. It is only typical that neither parent speaks of what is uppermost in his, her mind, namely, that it seems to them that Swineflu in his phone had allotted that Mukesh song to Samarpan; the call therefore that the ex-policeman was so reluctant to take could only have been made from the teenager's mobile that had been taken from him on the night of July 4. Then they see from their son's eyes that he has known that fact all along.

Those mobile phones play an important part in the story. Their text messages in December 2008 in fact begin it.

No matter how empty your life is, you can fill it with meaning by first being thankful that you still have one. Good morning! Have a great Monday! Your P.

Are your troubles weighing you down? Shrug them off, pick up some new ones! Take care, I am there! Good morning, young man! Your P.

Friendship is the dew drop trembling on the petal of a tulip. You and I can take it forward. Rise and shine and taste that drop, young fellow! Your P.

The essentials of life are something to do, someone to love and something to hope for. Which of these is missing in your life? Don't worry, I am here, there and everywhere! Good morning and have a great Thursday! Your P.

You are nature's red red rose. But who is your gardener? He is waiting for you. Your P.

At last, on Saturday at 5.45 a.m., Samarpan responded, *'Just who the fuck is this, exactly?'*

His P—whose success rate in the course of a long and distinguished career in lust, with boy, girl and beast, has been one hundred percent—in seven months makes no headway with Samarpan. He offers the teenager an Apple iPhone 3G. Samarpan accepts it gratefully and gives the old phone, gift-wrapped, to his father on his birthday. Swineflu calls his heart's desire fourteen times a day. Heart's Desire almost always lets the phone ring; once or twice he picks up only to pretend to be someone else. 'Hi. I think he's masturbating in the toilet. May I take a message?'

Undeterred, Swineflu proposes that he escort Samarpan to a first-rate psychologist-sexologist in Pune whom he knows well. 'A good sexy lady. She tells you to focus on women. She shows you photographs of Katrina Kaif and then some nudes and she talks sexy too. She offers you injections of sildenafil, trimix, papaverine, tadanafil. So in our second session, I just asked her to fuck me. She called the police. Set a thief to catch a thief. Let me get an appointment for us.'

Incapable of hearing no for an answer and even though he can't swim, Swineflu takes to hanging about in the changing rooms of the Club on the days when Samarpan does his thirty lengths. He fits in well with all those middle-aged men, the gays in denial, who are in the nude animatedly chatting politics while discreetly eyeing wang sizes. Swineflu is incensed that demure Samarpan changes in a cubicle *and* with a towel about his waist.

Unfazed, Swineflu asks him what size undies he wears and showers him with Tommy Hilfiger and Calvin Klein. The undies are really very nice and each time that he is wearing one of them, in return all that Samarpan is required to do is to wink at his benefactor. He does so but with a knowing, patronizing leer that has nothing in it of reciprocated desire.

He is to learn that Hell hath no fury like a messed-up, closet bisexual scorned.

The bait that Pramod Swineflu chooses is a lad from his village, gorgeous, mindless, at heart a good soul, in awe of people who can read and write, happy to fuck anything that moves. They had first met in 2004 on the policeman's last visit to his grandfather; the lad had escorted him to the cattle shed and, glowingly proud to be a mentor, shown him how to mount a calf.

Unknown to the lad, a forefather of his, Khandu by name, is in fact in Samarpan's scrapbook. In 1933, to cite the judgement of the First Class Magistrate of Multan, *'Khandu was seen having carnal intercourse against the order of nature by placing his penis inside the nostril of a bullock tied to a tree.'* Spanning the generations, Khandu's genes have surfaced once more both in the lad's love of cattle and his dimples. For him, the world is divided into the herders and the herded and Pramod Swineflu is so clearly one of the former; his own duty is to please as many of the other beasts as he can and when required, of course the herder himself.

On the evening of July 3, 2009, he does not quite know what is expected of him. All to the good; too many instructions and Dimples, perennially looking around to see who wants it bad, forgets all of them. Oblivious of the drizzle, the lightning and thunder, he walks with Samarpan from Defence Colony Market to the Kotla Mubarakpur flyover; he is pleased at the look of nervous, rapturous desire on the teenager's face, there's a rich cow to be milked here, boy.

His expectations from the evening do not include the goons waiting under the flyover. He takes them on, he loves a brawl.

From the shadows, Swineflu hisses at him to back off; Samarpan recognizes that voice. That is not part of the plan at all. 'Take a photo, *take a photo,*' sputters Samarpan to Dimples. Incensed at how Dimples has made a hash of it, Swineflu joins the goons in attacking the boy. Trembling, Dimples fiddles with the boy's phone, fortuitously clicks during the next flash of lightning, then pockets it; it is a nice model, an Apple iPhone 3G. Aghast, he watches Swineflu sit on the unconscious boy's chest to take the photographs of that battered face that he later is to dispatch all over the Net.

'You fuck off. I don't want to see you again either here or in the village. You hear?'

'Yes sir. But how will I join the government job that you promised me?'

'First I'm going to bugger your wife for a whole year while you sit and watch. Then we'll see.'

'Yes sir.'

Depressed, alone with the fractured and bleeding body, Dimples searches for numbers on the Apple 3G, takes fifteen seconds to read 'Papa' and calls.

'A hit and run. No me, I'm a passerby. My name?...Musafir.'

He is nonplussed that the parents are at Neemrana and will take three hours to arrive. Reluctant, apprehensive, he nevertheless follows Hiranmaya's shrieked-out instructions, speaks to the doctors whom the father calls, takes the son to hospital. He does save the boy's life.

And help take Swineflu's.

It takes Dimples some hours though to read the two text messages that Samarpan sends him on returning home from hospital, half a day to be certain that they mean the same thing and a full week to locate in the mobile phone the photograph that they refer to. Its beauty stirs, dimly, some emotions even in Dimples's skull. In the perfect white light of that flash of lightning, the camera has caught Swineflu with upraised arm, a bicycle chain wrapped around his fist, about to strike a cowering Samarpan held fast by a couple of goons. Dimples takes a day to work out how to send the photo and then, delighted with modern technology, sends it thirty-one times. Adding a text, Samarpan conveys it to his parents: *'What more evidence do we need?'* Hiranmaya's uncontrollable first reaction is sorrow that neither wife nor son will ever recognize that message to be a quotation from *Jesus Christ Superstar.*

Over the next few months, leisurely, meticulously, without exchanging a single phrase that refers directly to the subject, the family together conspires to kill Swineflu.

Hiranmaya to Manjula: 'We should return Swineflu's bowl. Doesn't look nice. The one in which he'd sent us that fabulous carrot halwa god knows how many weeks ago.'

Samarpan to Manjula: 'You can't return the bowl just like that. Doesn't look nice. Cook him something.'

Manjula to Samarpan: 'I'll make him some moong dal halwa. It's his favourite.'

Manjula to Hiranmaya: 'You'd have to help me get the best ingredients.'

From his pharmaceutical world, Hiranmaya brings her the anti-depressant Dothiepin and leaves the pills in the kitchen next to the gas burner. Manjula puts enough of it in the halwa to kill an entire cricket team. She is patriotic and does have the Indian team in mind. Just to make sure, she adds extra dollops of ghee, sugar and crushed almonds to the halwa.

Husband and wife take it across to C Block in the afternoon of February 24, 2010. India is playing a one-day cricket match in Gwalior against South Africa and nubile naked women could perform cartwheels in the streets and no one would notice. Swineflu too is in front of his TV and not too happy to be distracted from it even by the halwa. To immediately get rid of its bearers, he begins to wolf it down without taking his eyes off the screen, absent-mindedly, every now and then, going 'wah-wah!' in appreciation of its taste. His guests sit with him to wait for the Dothiepin to take effect.

'Excuse me,' says Hiranmaya to a dying Swineflu and, using his handkerchief, extracts from the other's pocket his mobile phone. He checks to see whether the incriminating photograph is in place all over the Net and then carefully sends a text message to Swineflu's thousand contact numbers: *I am sorry. I see no other way of saying so.* They leave discreetly, in passing noting with pride the jingoistic hysteria on the screen.

Manjula needs to have the last word. She is blue and must speak to someone; but she is in fact so blue that under the spotlight she remains tongue-tied, soundlessly weeping.

She knows not why she is so sad.

She is partly blue, she realizes, because her dreams of becoming immortal by means of a court case have receded into the blue. In her son's scrapbook, she has encountered her alter-ego, Grace Jayamani, who in 1980 told the Karnataka High Court that she wanted a divorce because she was sick to death of her husband buggering her. She got it. But Manjula doesn't want a divorce; she just wants to be famous. Besides, Hiranmaya has changed.

He wants to be buggered. He is gloomier than ever. From his conference in Brussels, he has morosely returned with an expensive dildo that he bought in a dark mood in Rembrandtplein. 'For too long have I lived divorced from the real world,' he dejectedly tells his wife, 'and now it is time to feel that ivory tower in my colon. You must help me, be my Macaulay, the Raj, the late Swineflu, the police force, 377 and the entire Penal Code.'

Then again, both husband and wife are blue because that wretched 377 will never go away. Even when it has dropped out of the statute book—which it will, one day in 2019 or in the year 2525—it will wriggle out of there only to worm its way back to where it came from, the skulls of the Pramod Swineflu clones; it will settle down there once more, curl up and wait for the resurgence of the right, intolerant, bigoted moment. Both the parents believe, individually and separately, that one possible answer to the worm would be to catch them young, the school children—at the age of nine or so—and teach them to be gay.

And finally, the mother is blue because the wretched son is blue. Even at the sunny Lodi Road crematorium during the last rites for Pramod Swineflu, where no one looks as though he's been wasting his time weeping and the moustached middle-aged men are chatting about politics, where Samarpan makes eye contact with Dimples four hundred and six times in twenty-one minutes, the teenager is so thrilled that he becomes depressed: is this *all?* This tingling, this longing for the postponement of the fulfillment of desire, in the decades to come, is this all that I can look forward to? Sitting in the sun and that fragrant woodsmoke, he sinks slowly into gloom, he can see his father telling him that he is blue because it runs in the family.

Sparrows

On the twentieth of March, at five seventeen in the morning, a single male sparrow is astonished to find the verandah outside Jamun's bedroom all windowed-up and glassed in. Those panes preventing ingress hadn't been in place in October; changes being challenges, sparrows dislike them. Who doesn't?

To help him to stay aloft in that one position outside the shut, central window, his wings beat over fifty times per minute. Because his bones are hollow, his heart can bear that exertion but not for long; and flying being less strenuous than standing upright in mid-air, after a couple of seconds, he glides to the left window to tap with his beak his compelling urgency.

Between breaths, he also chirps away.

Sparrows inhale more than fifty times a minute. Their exhalations, though more extended, are not particularly musical. They couldn't care less. They make do with a vocal frequency that stretches from 3500 to 7500 Hertz. That range is much higher than that of whales, for instance, at 15 to 25 Hertz and of humans at 65 to 1300 Hertz. But homo sapiens of course produces the widest variety of sounds from his throat; in the animal world, only homo sapiens feels wise about that sort of thing.

The sounds though that sparrows emit within those frequencies can adequately express love, desire, fear, anger, annoyance, envy, joy, pride, sunniness, angst and to be or not to be. Just because human beings do not pay attention does not mean that sparrows don't say it. At the moment, the excited squeaking of the male bird conveys to his spouse alarm, exasperation and a hint of an apology.

Jamun too would have said sorry had he been awake and feeling alive. Enclosing verandahs in glass, and thereby circumscribing a house, rendering it as it were blind, is—even genetically—just not his thing. Like his late parents and his elder brother, he has always tended to prefer airy living spaces, rooms the doors and windows of which have remained open to wind and gusts of rain, welcoming, in ascending order, dust, mosquitoes, flies, wasps, geckos, sparrows, pigeons, neighbourhood cats and the occasional observant thief. He in fact does not like in the *least* the apartment recently allotted to him by his office.

'The Father of the Nation disliked windowed-up verandahs,' Jamun addresses the back of the bald head of Brajkishore the taciturn caretaker as he, a statue before the locked front door, examines without expression the forty keys on the ring in his hand. '"I do not want my house," said he, "to be walled in on all sides and my windows to be stuffed. I want the cultures of all lands to be blown about my house as freely as possible. But I refuse to be blown off my feet by any."'

The bald head twitches—as though tapped—at 'blown off' and then after a pause turns only forty degrees in Jamun's direction to murmur obscurely, 'Not bombs but air-conditioning sir...Mahajani Saab—the previous occupant—had windows fixed in all three verandahs...there's a certain...status, you know, in these new split acs...Then he put in a generator because he feared the four-hour power cuts of east Delhi here in south Bombay...' Having decided on a key, the caretaker crouches over the lock.

Mahajani is Jamun's immediate superior at work; Jamun

in fact has arrived on transfer to the post that Mahajani has vacated on promotion. It is not easy to fill the shoes of a man so pleased with himself that he floats; his feet, barely touching the ground, twinkle when he walks.

Mahajani's air-conditioners put off the sparrows in several different ways. Because of them, just as the verandahs have to be glassed in, the windows have to remain permanently shut, and the ceremonial entrances and clandestine exits of the birds have yet one more route denied them. Like humankind, sparrows like to feel both snug and not hemmed in. Then again, it is because of the new air-conditioners that a sibling of the male sparrow tapping at Jamun's window is constrained to build his nest in one of the compressor units atop a window ledge outside the flat; one fine November morning, he loses his entire family of four fledglings to Bendre's cat. In the unmusical chirruping thereafter of all the sparrows of Grant Road can be heard—but only by the attuned ear—a lament for what air-conditioners and other mod cons are doing to the death rate amongst them.

Jamun in fact is dreaming about them that morning. He dreams often of the dead and the dying. His ears are not as deaf as those of other humans and the tapping, whirring and chirping at the window have percolated into his vivid, subconscious memory of tea on a typical Sunday morning, over twenty years ago, with his parents in the open, airy verandah of a house that doesn't exist anymore. With Urmila his mother and Shyamanand his father, there are at tea, uninvited, a dozen sparrows.

On the circular cane table stand three different pots of tea for three different personalities. Jamun drinks his Assam Gold strong, almost bitter, with a hint of milk. Shyamanand has an expensive, palely golden Makaibari First Flush. Urmila doesn't care what she drinks as long as it is not what her husband is having. The sparrows have been given, on the verandah ledge, a large earthenware bowl of tap water.

Tea takes long on Sunday morning and ends in fact only with the departure of the birds. Even though they have not been invited, alongside the bowl of water on the verandah ledge await them crumbs of milk rusk in a steel plate. They eat, drink and make merry. Life is short.

The milk rusks give them carbohydrates, protein, sugar and sodium. The sugar and sodium they don't need, not in those proportions. They know it too and actually prefer the grains of ration-shop rice that they get on the days on which Ramdev the servant, feeling hungrier than usual, has finished the rusks with *his* tea. 'Rice rather than milk rusk,' says Shyamanand, whooshing into his beard, 'is healthy even for the Indian economy.' Between pecks, the sparrows nod.

Talking to birds is therapeutic. Everyone benefits. And the smaller the bird, the more sparkling the conversation. Medieval Italian saints have preached to them and in Indian folktale, they have imparted to princes the science of statecraft and an understanding of human nature. Shyamanand exchanges his views with them in Bengali. It is the language spoken by two hundred million people around the world. They don't get its music, they don't mind. Their ears feel the vibrations of sound, they are not threatening, they get on with their hopping and pecking, nodding and chirruping and, drawn by the crumbs of toast, at last land on the cane table.

The family becomes even more still and silent than usual. For a month of Sundays, Shyamanand has been trying to get the sparrows to alight on his paralysed left arm. Why is not wholly clear; perhaps life hopping about on it will give his own existence a hint of meaning. The moment they alight on the table, he, laboriously, with his right arm, turns his left over in his lap and places in its palm the crumbs and grains of the meal of the day.

There are four birds hopping around the table; the two males are larger, more puffed-up and full of themselves—

naturally—with black bibs, reddish-brown heads and pale cheeks. The two females are mousy brown in colour and more self-effacingly non-descript. They are all related. Fourteen months previously, two of them hatched in the same nest within three days of each other; two others share the same mother. She is there too. Despite her general mousiness, she changes male partners like a manic depressive his moods. Her present consort is her son from the previous year. Incest is cool.

A male sparrow hops to the edge of the table and burrows his beak in the warp and weft of its cane. He is a mere twenty centimeters away from that paralysed left arm. His proximity makes Shyamanand lose the thread of his therapeutic babble, slow down his delivery to the incoherence of a 45 rpm played at 331/3. All of a sudden, a female, the incestuous mother, rises aloft in an agitation of white wings and, dislodging a feather that floats down into Urmila's teacup, returns, for reasons unclear, to the verandah ledge. Urmila squeaks sharply in disgust and protest.

'Oof, I've to change my teacup. They carry a million diseases.'

Sparrows don't *like* sharp squeaks. So the other three take wing too. One circles the ceiling fan twice before settling down on a branch of the bougainvillea. Two rush off indoors into Jamun's room. Shyamanand is crestfallen and cannot prevent his thoughts from returning to their favourite texts, namely, one, the pleasures of his married life—'See, they left because of your screaming. Not even birds can stand it.'—and two, the most painless and dignified way of killing himself—'I can only slash my left wrist but will the blood flow freely from these paralysed veins?'

'I think it should,' murmurs Urmila absentmindedly and to herself, not fully distracted by the theme of death self-inflicted from that of death by contagion.

But of the million diseases that she fears that birds can give her, she in fact knows very little.

Sparrows are commensal with human beings; it is inevitable therefore that with time they become vectors for several pathogens and parasites. Organisms such as salmonella, Escherichia, Cryptococcus, toxoplasma and intestinal worms could possibly enter the human body system largely by way of the droppings of those birds plopping down into the foods that men eat. As far as Urmila is aware, that hasn't happened yet to her tea. Though she can't speak for the rest of what they ingest. After all she has caught Ramdev in the kitchen making himself a sizable omelette of some fifteen sparrows' eggs that he has filched at a go from the several nests dotted all over the house.

Jamun returns from the kitchen with a clean teacup for his mother, then repositions his and her chairs so that they are all facing the verandah ledge. They will sit there for at least half an hour more, till the sun glides out from behind the east wall and begins to burn them and their desires. They have time till then to enjoy, on the ledge, with its aerial entrances and exits, its high-tension dialogue, its rapidfire changes of mood, its menacing postures and dramatic raving and ranting, its bedroom farce, savage duels and charming courtship, their favourite, biogenic, eco-friendly, in-the-flesh, Sunday morning TV soap.

It is a pleasure, in that half-hour, to discern a pattern in the movements, the restlessness, of the birds.

'You see that fat guy? He flew off mysteriously in the direction of Sagar's house but when he returned, he was followed by that female and the younger one who are now gorging on those crumbs. Did you see? That's Darwin. Altruism for the sake of the species. Would *we* do that? When the world ends and Sagar unearths the mustard oil and rice that he's been hoarding, I don't see him rushing here to invite us.'

'What can I catch from the feather of a sparrow?'

'I've just brought you a new teacup.'

'I'm just asking.'

Well, apart from the organisms in their droppings, sparrows, by means of their feathers, can gift to humans several of the parasites—such as ticks and fleas—that all those animals that share a habitat with homo sapiens carry. It is part of the give and take of commensality. I take your grain, I give you some bloodsuckers. You give me a roof, I help to save your life. But you don't, you never save mine.

You didn't, for instance, in Calcutta, in 1898.

Her Majesty's Surgeon Major Ronald Ross is in his laboratory at Fort William, contemplating, supine on his work table, a sad silent sparrow. He picks it up in his hand; docile, it does not even ruffle its feathers in protest. Its body is unhealthily warm, hot even, and its eyes lack lustre and seem to see nothing. Carrying it snug in his palm, Ross walks across to a side table atop which sits its cage. He opens its door, quickly pushes his hand in, gently deposits the bird amidst its mates and latches the door shut. He turns and hollers for Mohammed Baksh to take the cage away. None of the dozen sparrows in it stirs.

Mohammed Baksh has been dealing with sparrows in cages for months. In choosing him as assistant out of some twenty applicants, Ross is governed largely by appearances. MB looks the most rascally of the lot and is therefore, notes his future master, likely to have considerable intelligence. Ross's assessment is correct. MB's single fault, his master learns later, is that he gets stoned far too often on cannabis.

He needs to, for the work he does for Ross. Amongst other things, at night, while the Surgeon Major returns to Harrington Street to write his poems and his letters and bicker with the Italians over who has discovered what in the race for the Nobel Prize, Baksh, back in Dr Cunningham's laboratory in Fort William, first smokes a pipe. He then ties mosquito nets over the two decrepit hospital beds in the verandah and shakes loose under them, from their boxes of wire mesh, several dozen mosquitoes that have been bred from larvae in the laboratory. He next places on the beds and under the nets—careful not to leave in the latter the smallest gap as a means of escape for the insects—a couple of cages of sparrows. Finally, he himself settles down for the night on the floor between the beds. Any sudden squeaking and flapping from the birds is to wake him up to warn him that the laboratory cats are on the prowl and need to be shooed away. Those sparrows are important for the future health of mankind; with the cats is not how they are meant to go.

When nicely stoned, MB gives the sparrows—*and* the mosquitoes—names. Gul and Noor and Mumtaz, Latifa, Abdul, Sarfaraz. Differentiating between the birds is simple but the insects? But Mohammed can not only tell a dapper-winged from a barred-back—that too is easy—but one female culex from another. Further, he can make a mosquito do just about anything, dance to his tune, persuade it to bite a patient even in the daytime simply by murmuring some encouraging words of Urdu while holding the mouth of its test tube against the skin of the victim.

That ability of the assistant impresses Ross; he however is just not interested in Mohammed's naming ceremonies for sparrow and mosquito. He, Ross, must concentrate. He is therefore delighted instead every morning only to see that the insects, without fail, have during the night crept under the feathers of the sleeping birds and gorged themselves on their blood.

'Get me more birds, Bux. There are enough sparrows in this city to outnumber humanity.'

Well, yes and no. Mohammed Baksh reports that the plague

scare in Calcutta has prompted the bird catchers to flee the city and so perhaps they might have to procure the sparrows from elsewhere. Undeterred, they do. Only incidentally to catch up with his family, Ross takes the train to Darjeeling. But the hill station turns out to be full of sparrows that cannot be caught. The Surgeon Major records that the local Butias, Baksh and he fail to do so, and so he sets the police and the District Magistrate to the task. The Superintendent of Police assures Ross that if they can catch dacoits, they can catch sparrows. We, adds Ross to himself, shall see.

To the disinterest of the district officialdom and the elusiveness of the hill sparrow is added the plague scare that follows Ross like a curse from the plains. All across the tea gardens, the coolies who double up as bird catchers bolt into the blue whenever they sense the approach of the redoubtable pair from Calcutta. For it has been bruited about that the doctor's mission in Darjeeling is *forcibly* to inoculate everyone against the plague. It doesn't help at all that a second rumour then insists that Ross has been assigned the task of inoculating all the natives *with* the plague.

Eventually, of course, Ross, doughty that he is, gets the birds just as he gets everything else—enough larvae, coccidia, proteosoma, gymnosporidia and halteridium for his experiments on the one hand and home leave, global recognition and international awards on the other. He brings the sparrows back to Calcutta in dozens of cages, attracting not a little attention on the train. He loves it. Almost all the birds are dead on arrival. Sparrows hate dislocation.

As undeterred as his employer, Mohammed Baksh procures more birds in cages from Bow Bazaar and helps Ross to extract their blood to confirm under the microscope that they are indeed free of infection. Meticulously, they also check the mosquitoes that have fed themselves all night on the feverish sparrows and are thrilled to find, growing against their stomach walls, the plasmodium parasite. Next, in a marriage made in hell, the two, vector mosquito and healthy sparrow, spend the night together under the nets. In a couple of days, each and every one of the healthy sparrows is unhealthily warm, hot even; their eyes lack lustre and seem to see nothing.

But there is not enough malaria in Calcutta, at the same time complains Ross, to himself and in his letters to London, not enough for his experiments, neither amongst humans nor birds. In intermittent despair, he has even asked Surgeon General Harvey for permission to travel to more malarious regions in search of specimens. He is told that the sanction of the Government of India in Simla, eighteen hundred kilometres away, would have to be obtained. He frets. He wants faster results, he is not one to give up. This is a hand-to-hand fight with nature, notes he in his letters home, she always has a trick to evade me just as I am getting hold of her. But we will have it all out in a short time.

'I've been wondering,' says Jamun to his parents in a lull in their Sunday morning TV soap, 'how many sparrows Ronald Ross must have killed in his search for the means of transmission of the malaria parasite.'

Neither elder responds. Urmila pensively examines the untasted tea in her new cup and Shyamanand replaces on his plate, crumb by crumb, from several strategic spots on his left arm, the bait for the birds. Jamun correctly takes their silence to be breathless disinterest in what he is saying and sadly concludes, 'Better them than us, I guess.'

With the sparrows on his side, Ross continues the good fight for over two years. Casualties are close to a hundred per cent. From Ultodanga, Bow Bazaar and from as far away as Howrah,

Mohammed Baksh brings him, on the average, two dozen sparrows a week, of which only a handful escape to take up residence in the rafters of the laboratory; of the balance, Baksh himself every now and then takes a few home, the cats get several and Ross successfully infects the rest.

From the body of each ailing sparrow, he extracts just a few drops of blood, the minimum necessary to confirm under the microscope the presence of the transferred plasmodium parasite. Baksh then returns the bird to its cage to await developments; in two days, its corpse is dumped in the laboratory waste bin. Cats do not eat the cadavers of infected birds; their feathers exude a smell of the disease. It is the way of nature.

Every three or four days, in the backyard of the laboratory, Mohammed Baksh burns their dead bodies along with the rest of the hospital refuse. The Haris who cover Harrington Street, scavengers by caste, are paid a quarter of a rupee a month to dump the ashes and burnt and blackened waste, by hand cart, into the holy Hooghly.

Life and death and in between a brief, distraught struggle like a frenzied fluttering of wings; like man, like sparrow. Each of the sparrows weighs on the average some thirty grams—Jamun in contrast feels *so* gross—and lives for about three years. Unless interrupted. That brevity depresses him. Of course, almost everything does. What had *he* done for three years except drink tea and defecate. But there are things about them that he approves of. They *don't* like travel, they *don't* want to see the world; in their entire lives, when left to themselves, they do not venture beyond an area larger than ten square kilometers. He likes that. There is enough to see and experience in a verandah on a Sunday morning just as in a lifetime in Walden. And their singing is awful but they don't care. They are madly promiscuous; food and sex and ghastly singalong music, what else is there to life? And they lay four to six clutches a year because they live so dangerously and die so young. And they are *so* content in their plain ordinariness. That Jamun feels he should sit with and do a Francis of Assisi chat with them about, he who is so exhausted by his own mediocrity.

From what Ronald Ross learns from killing a dozen sparrows a week over several months, mankind benefits eternally, and he is awarded the Nobel Prize for medicine in 1902. That same year, sixteen hundred kilometres away, right across the subcontinent in Khetwadi, Bombay, Salim Ali, India's foremost ornithologist-to-be, turns six.

That morning of the twentieth of March, 2013, Jamun wakes up in Khetwadi at six thirty feeling as usual like a patient in coma. The birds have flown, both from his dream and from outside his window. He does not know that the United Nations has proclaimed that day to be World House Sparrow Day. Neither do the birds. Or that the federal government of Delhi has declared the sparrow to be its State Bird. Is it possible at all to live without knowing these important facts? Like the sparrows, Jamun manages after a fashion. His feet scrabble about like spiders to find his slippers, they fail, he walks barefoot to the kitchen to start the process of tea. Against the soles of his feet, the cement floor feels moist and unclean.

The grimy kitchen window, insignificant enough to have escaped Mahajani's air-conditioning zeal, is open. Jamun puts the kettle on and gazes unseeingly out at a tree on Dr Wilson Street. Three spoons of tea to half a litre of water taken off the hob at the first glimpse of the first wisp of steam like smoke from an idling cigarette. A teapot emptied of its dregs and left upturned all night without ever being rinsed. The tea is still Assam Gold and hasn't changed in twenty years. Things appear to be the same but of course they are not. There is a bird at the window but it is not a sparrow.

Beyond the kitchen window lies a ledge of iron slats that dates from Mahajani's occupancy and looks suspiciously wide and sturdy enough to accept an air-conditioner. Within a fortnight of moving in, Jamun has arranged on it the first pots of Chinese oranges, coriander, marigold and mint. Watering them involves some sustained yogic stretching through the window. They don't get enough sun but he thinks that they will survive. He is then sure of it when suddenly, early on Tuesday morning in the second week, the birds swoop down on them. They wouldn't have on the dying.

''Morning, fatsoes. Would you mind not screeching that much so early in the day?'

The birds do not respond. There are six of them amidst the pots and on the window sill, dull brown in colour, much larger, fatter, more aggressive and garrulous than sparrows. They hop from money plant to coriander to marigold, each swivelling continually to see what the other five are up to; they screech at one another without pause and ignore Jamun completely. It is not relaxing that early in the morning to be surrounded by personalities who are at the same time so fat and so restless.

'You'd want to shut up for a bit. And we haven't met before, have we? You have names? Are you babblers?'

The three verandahs of the flat being enclosed, Jamun has his tea at the tiny table in the kitchen. Toast, butter, honey, the stronger liquor of the second and third cups; the ritual helps his heart to stop fluttering and calm down at the thought of the struggle of going through another day. More at ease now that the tea seems to have come out just right, he is watching that one fat bird on the sill, dimly noting, with a distant part of his mind, how much larger and less attractive it is than a sparrow, how much more space and attention it takes up, when slowly but implacably, like a groundswell behind his ribs, he realizes, with a strange sensation of the floor rapidly receding from under him, leaving him breathless in mid-air, that he can't in the least remember the day or the moment when he *last* saw a sparrow.

When was it, why can't he remember? The thought harrows him all day, all week; it in fact festers within him, there beneath the layers, like some guilty secret, forever. While shaving, or gazing out of the window of the chartered office bus, or in his boss's room being buffeted by that snake's wit, at lunch gazing at the tiffin that he himself has packed and wondering how anyone could eat that shit, all that day on the twentieth of March, he worries and frets and gnaws at remembrance, Where are the sparrows? Surely they couldn't all be dead without my even noticing?

While the obese snake hisses on and on—but wittily, as always—about arbitration cases, performance guarantees and the perfidiousness of foreign banks, Jamun shuts his eyes to shut him out. It is of little use. Memory is as slippery as hands with blood on them. He recalls with ease a childhood spotted with sparrows—nesting in the cup above the ceiling fan, zipping around in dizzying loop-the-loops in the drawing room on drowsy summer afternoons; and an early adolescence too, Burfi and he at intense tennis-ball cricket in the verandah, totally uncaring about window panes and passing cars and yet so attentive to the pelmet that housed the nest of fledglings that a hit to the entire wall above the switchboard was considered to be out. And then there'd been tea on Sunday mornings with his parents and the sparrows; as a middle-aged young man, he had enjoyed those—a rare family togetherness, and those birds as evidence of life. When Urmila went to hospital and failed to return home, father and son, by silent, mutual consent, simply stopped the weekly tea ceremony. It was impossible to sit beside or face that distressing empty chair; what was extraordinary was that in all their hopping about, the sparrows too left it alone.

They met up with her once more, though, at the crematorium. Jamun remembers that in that cavernous hall black with burning, along with the pigeons, there had been sparrows fluttering about while Urmila burnt.

'You aren't paying attention, I say!...You have to represent us in Milan at the court hearing! Do you have a valid Schengen visa?...What did I say just now! Repeat after me!'

The birds are dying out because of the new architecture of the cities. They are avoiding me, Jamun, because of my mediocrity. They are being gobbled up by the world's carnivores. And me, where did I stand in my life when they began to shy away from it?

'When are you off to Colombo to visit your brother, I say? Do you have a valid Sri Lankan visa? If the dates clash, then you know which of the two you have to drop!'

Step by step, like a man of reason in revolt, Jamun aims for direction in his daily routine. On Friday the 22nd of March, he skips office, descends to the caretaker's cabin to ask Brajkishore how long it would take to have the glass of the three verandahs of his flat removed.

'*Removed?*...Oh...well, after you formally apply to Administration—they would have to have a look at this year's budget and the work orders already issued for March and April...' A five-hundred-rupee note glides like grease from Jamun's pocket to the caretaker's palm. Work on the verandahs starts at twelve noon that day.

The dust and roar of Bombay rush in with the removal of each pane. Jamun looks out at the pedestrians and traffic on Dr Wilson Street and inhales deeply the methane and black carbon particles in the exhaust fumes. At three in the afternoon, leaving the workers smoking and murmuring and labouring away at the rate of two panes a week, he goes out to walk through Khetwadi, past CP Tank and Mumbadevi Temple, across the bazaars Bhuleshwar, Zaveri and Mangaldas, to finally reach Crawford Market.

Guidebooks speak of its Norman and Flemish architectural styles but the Market is simply a shed spread across twenty thousand square metres. Under its cavernous dome bubbles primeval chaos. Jamun threads his way through the Saturday afternoon crowds and past the neverending stalls of vegetable, fruit and grocery, the shops selling furniture, plumbing, ironmonger's wares, saris, textiles, lampshades, locally-made foreign cosmetics, bathroom tiles and wcs of Italian design, to finally arrive at the pets' section, a sort of Noah's ark. Amongst the dogs, rabbits, goats, monkeys, langurs, cats, rats, mongooses, snakes and white mice are the birds; and amidst the roosters, owls, bulbuls, larks, crows, peacocks, ducks, geese, pigeons, parakeets and lovebirds, he at last spots the sparrows.

They are catatonic—malarious perhaps, who knows?—completely immobile on their perches, ten to a large cage, Jamun spots four such. Unlike the larger fauna, sparrows do not need Diazepam or Midazolam to be rendered docile. They have been brought to Crawford Market from Deonar, twenty kilometres away. Violent dislocation at times is enough to immobilize and slowly kill them.

The man amidst the cages is Mohammed Baksh. Jamun, shivering at the symbolic resonance of the coincidence—it must surely mean *something*—grins warmly at the vendor. Baksh, young, barely moustached, a man of the world nevertheless, hardly glances up from his mobile phone.

'Foreign you want? Uzbek? Chinese?'

'Uzbek,' responds Jamun automatically in the millisecond before realizing that what are being offered are not prostitutes but sparrows. 'No, no, Indian. How much?'

'Passer indica? Passer rutilans? What purpose? Shooting training? Medicinal blood massage? Eating? Curry? Fry? Omelette?'

'Salim Ali, our famous birdman, more than a hundred years ago, used to buy his sparrows from here, Crawford Market. He would fry them in ghee and eat them.'

'Second lane behind, seventh shop, Salim Ali.' Baksh, to indicate direction, swivels his head, once, a few inches to the right, without however taking his eyes off the screen of his phone. Either porn, concludes Jamun, or the stock market. 'He isn't back from his jumma, I think.'

'And what's so special about foreign sparrows?'

'China,' Baksh for a moment raises both limp hands to Heaven in speechless worship of the potency of the superpower, '*illegally* exports over six *million* sparrows a *year* to Belgium for the restaurants and markets of Italy, Spain and Portugal.' He briefly looks about him at his cages to mark the sad contrast. 'Now *that* is business. China is an inexhaustible country. Nothing endangered. How many sparrows do you want and why?'

'They fall. They die. They're dying out as a species, you know, even while we chatter. No one cares. No one studies them. Not in the numbers in which they study owls and shrikes and buzzards and cormorants and falcons and flamingoes. And what is the point of studying them if you aren't preventing them from dying out? Even as we talk.'

It is for that reason perhaps that Baksh abruptly winds up the exchange with, 'Take a couple. Two hundred rupees a pair.'

Jamun walks back home carrying the cage with its two sparrows. He attracts almost as much amused attention as Ronald Ross in the train to Calcutta from Darjeeling. Five minutes into the walk, the noise and press of the city begin to enervate him in the manner in which he imagines it to tell upon his burden. The cage sways wildly with each step, so do the sparrows, completely immobile, quietly inhaling the nitrogen oxides and hydrocarbons emitted by passing traffic. Jamun, feeling symbolic, tragic, has already named them: Ronald Ross and Edith Piaf.

A scare outside the Bhuleshwar flower market. Even in that congestion, he is unmanned by a sudden, great flurry of wings around his ears, like a ceiling fan gone haywire inches above his head. He crouches, cries out, almost drops the cage. The hawk majestically soars away to the top of a roof to plan his next attack. The fright though seems to imbue Edith and Ronald with some of the warmth of life. They both hop about in the cage the rest of the way home.

Only to attract, at the foot of the stairs, the attention of Bendre's grey tomcat. Greedy, vicious, stupid, he, seething with excitement, miaows without pause, round and round the cage, all the way up to the second floor.

This is not a good idea, says Jamun to himself as he shuts the front door in the tom's face. The flat is airy, noisy, luminous in the late-afternoon light from the open verandahs, ready to welcome dust, mosquitoes, flies, wasps, geckos, babblers, pigeons, neighbourhood cats and the occasional observant thief. The workers have left with the panes of glass, sweeping into tiny pyramids in each corner the rubble that is all that remains of their efforts. He puts the cage on the kitchen table, opens its door and waits for the birds to exit. He places next to the cage a cup of water and on its companion saucer some grains of expensive brown rice.

He sleeps fitfully that night, disturbed less by the city invading his apartment than by the certainty of his having lost the battle even before he has taken up arms. At five seventeen next morning, he is awake after a fashion, alert enough to see the casualties. The birds, seemingly acclimatized at last, have left their cage. Ronald is on the pelmet above the window and Edith on the stem of the wall lamp. One takes off, the other follows, the whirring ceiling fan gets both. Ronald lands on the mound of rubble beside the door, Edith at the foot of the bed table. Jamun struggles up, his feet scrabble about like spiders to find his slippers, they fail. He walks barefoot to the corpses, picks them up, trembles at their warmth. So small.

Once our men of science killed them to unlock nature's other secrets. Now they die in front of us and we don't see what their deaths are saying about what is killing them. Futile, thinks he, are these nature's warnings to the heedless, these providential ways in which sparrows choose to fall.

Can't Take This Shit Anymore

'School's declared Saturday as Untouchability Awareness Day,' announces Elder Daughter at the dinner table, 'and at a Special Assembly, the school behans are going to talk to us about themselves. I mean, that's *so* weird.'

Father—reluctantly—looks up from his pork vindaloo to play the sage. 'Untouchability, for starters, is politically incorrect, I think,' replies he. 'We say Dalit nowadays.'

'As long as the school buses run on Saturday,' adds Mother, her expression glum because certain that they won't, 'and I don't have to spend an entire holiday dropping and picking you up.'

On Saturday at dinner, Elder Daughter is pale and distraught and can't look at any food. 'This morning, Karishmaben—she's the one who helps the dumber KG kids in the loo and everything—spoke to us about herself. She belongs to the Valmiki caste. They are shit-lifters, she said. That is what her family has been doing for generations for a living. For years she used to carry baskets of other people's shit on her head. How can you continue to eat while I'm telling you all this?'

Four months ago, on another planet some eight hundred kilometres away from New Delhi, Devji to his mother:

'Ma, I don't want to go to school today. Or ever again.'

'Wonderful. Follow in the footsteps of your illustrious sister.

Remain with her in this cesspit wallowing up to your neck in the shit of others till merciful Death pushes your head in.'

The conversation between mother and child takes place in the mother tongue, at six in the morning on a monsoon day in 2016, in the village of Petwada.

Heena the sister butts in. 'Don't force him, Ma. At least the shit at home is our daily bread. In school, it's that of his horrid classmates.'

'You're a girl. Shit is your *element.* You keep your head out of this.'

'He's not even bright. And that stupid school will fill him up with even more of it.'

That stupid school is two kilometres away. But that twenty-five minute walk to it is fraught; it feels like crossing a minefield in which each exploding bomb tears off and pulverizes, not the head or a limb but the child's spirit, his self-esteem; and at the end of that walk awaits him his routine school day.

'Nothing doing,' retorts Mainaben the mother. 'You *are* going. Even if all that you learn in ten years is to write your name in shit.' In more contempt than sorrow, she jerks her head towards an insensate, alcoholic heap in the corner. 'I don't want you to end up like your father.'

In response, Amritbhai ceases to be insensate. He sighs, rolls over, sighs again, sits up and demands sleepily in his stupor, 'And what is wrong with the father? All he wants on this wonderful day is some tea.'

It *is* a wonderful day—though the family would be hard-pressed to understand why. A red-letter day it is, being the one hundred-and-fortieth anniversary of the foundation of the first brick sewerage system in the country—far away from Petwada though, some fifteen hundred kilometres to the east in Calcutta. 1876. What a year. Unknown to Mainaben and her kin, several other special anniversaries are virtually round the corner, to be celebrated, if they so wish, with the fanfare of a Hindu festival, each marking the day on which, over the decades, modern sewerage hobbled, at the Hindu rate of movement, closer and closer to their village. 1881, Bombay, eight hundred kilometres to the west-south-west. 1892, Delhi, a full thousand to the north. And 1938, Hyderabad, six hundred to the south. If God is kind—but He's *always* kind!—if God is *kinder*—then perhaps in the lifetime of Devji's children's children's children, that toilet and its pipes, that marvel of an ensemble, will rise from some vicinal city on a fabled eagle's wings and land with a divine clang and clatter at the foot of the statue of Gandhi, there in the centre of Petwada. They would worship it too, of course.

A contented silence while the family breakfasts. Devji is about to speak, to take up again with his fearsome mother the matter of his proposed truancy; he is silenced however by a look from Heena. Breakfast for all is black tea, gur and the dried-up, hard-as-slate rotis left over from the wages of the day before.

'We know why you don't want to go to school today.' Mainaben's voice is kinder now. 'You want to wear your new dark glasses and roam around and show off in the neighbourhood all day.' She peers into the tin pan to gauge the amount of tea left. 'You get ready now. Then you put on those glasses and go to school and Heena'll accompany you to Bavla Mod and take them back from you there. We don't want you wearing them where they'll cause trouble.'

'But trouble is more welcome than shit,' burps and chuckles Amritbhai into his tin mug.

'Yes, trouble is more welcome than shit!' exults Devji, delighted at his mother's munificence, 'Heenadidi and Ma are our experts on trouble, our leaders in trouble!'

The family leads lives—as a bewildered Elder Daughter comes to learn in the weeks that follow—that would be a little tricky to explain to the outside world. Their existence is circumscribed, governed and *defined* by the excrement of others. They carry human shit on their heads from Point A—more accurately, from Points A1, A2, A3, A4, A5, A6 and A7—to Point B and that is how they make a living. Difficult to explain. That that too is living.

Precisely speaking, it is the mother who carries the shit of others on her head. Even more accurately, it *used* to be. She has rebelled, thrown off the yoke and is now jobless, near-penniless. Her husband finds her work demeaning and would never be able to bring himself to do it; it is all right for women though, one has to live. *He* makes his living by descending every fortnight into a tank filled with the excrement of the vicinal municipality of Botadpuri. Cleaning it non-stop occupies him for six to eight hours. If he takes a break, he finds that he is unable to resume. It is not possible for him therefore to enter that tank without first getting absolutely drunk. The first time he did it some fifteen years ago, it was without alcohol, he puked eight times in the initial twenty minutes and couldn't go on; of course, he wasn't paid anything that day.

In the village, Bawla Mod marks one boundary of the residential quarter of the Valmikis. There, the potholed alley—largely dust when dry and mud when wet—turns once to make room for the modest graveyard of the Hela Muslims and then skirts the six shops-in-shacks of the Kadbi Patels before snaking its way in between the outlying, poorer houses of the Korama community of pigkeepers.

'Hurry up, I've my rounds to do,' snaps Heena at her younger brother. He walks slowly, with his head tilted back to keep the dark glasses from slipping off his nose. 'Anyway, you can't see a thing in those.'

'I *can*. Everything seems further away and I feel...' *Protected* is what he wishes to say but his voice trails off because he doesn't want his sister scoffing at him. Either snapping or scoffing, that's what she's always doing.

It is early in the day, not yet seven, and the two pass several Valmiki mothers carrying their scoops, brooms and buckets on their way to work. 'Jai Bheem!' Heena greets mainly those whom her mother gets along with; that number, over the last few months, has been slowly—pitifully slowly—increasing.

'Jai Bheem!' they respond, smiling, still a little self-conscious about their new way of saying hello.

It isn't much fun; no adult seems to see—leave alone admire—Devji in his dark glasses. And it's too early; none of his compeers is on his way to school yet. 'Didi, can't we walk on to the PHC dispensary and you go back from there?'

'Don't be a fool. You want to be beaten up by Chirag Marar or Manish Rana or one of those Banajiga brothers? And your silly glasses taken away?'

'They won't take them away if I tell them that I found them on an abandoned corpse.' He glances at his sister's scowling face but nevertheless adds because he's in a great mood, 'Besides, you're there to protect me. They wouldn't dare touch you.'

'I hate them.'

'They'll just call us names. But we're used to that.'

Only in a manner of speaking are sister and brother used to that, to what they hear from some of the youth of the other castes a dozen times a day, every day of their lives. 'Hey slut. Come and clean my shit. My arse is bursting.'

The children of shit-cleaners are themselves shit-cleaners. Shit-cleaners they will forever remain. Outside the confines of their own residential quarter, without upsetting a lot of people, they simply cannot wear ornaments or ride bicycles or tuck their shirts in or touch things in a shop or smoke upwind from anyone of another caste or let their shadows fall on anybody else or enter temples or sport dark glasses or drink tea from cups not set aside for them at public tea stalls or carry a bottle of water to school or keep sitting in a public bus if someone from another caste hasn't found a place or of course draw water themselves from the village well because they, in imitating the other castes, would be getting above themselves.

Sure enough, that very morning, en route to school, just after his sister has turned back—with the dark glasses—at the PHC dispensary, unmindful because glum again at the very thought of the day ahead, the boy Devji is rebuked by Ganjam Osthama the Elder. 'Watch where your shadow falls, you piece of dogshit.' To which adds Smriti Kumari his daughter, 'Announce your presence in advance, shit-cleaner, if you want to stay on in this village.' She is fourteen years old and three classes ahead of Devji in the same school.

Back home, Heena begins to prepare to start her day. For the last few weeks, after her rounds, she's been helping her mother sell tea at the Food Corporation Godown busstop on National Highway 47. That is a good three kilometres from their village. They will walk to work carrying what they need—a stove, a can of kerosene, a kettle, tea dust, sugar, plastic cups, rusk biscuits, matches, their lunch—yesterday's potatoes and rotis from the day before that—wrapped in newspapers. They earn almost nothing per day and each morning seems strange because they are happy.

Amritbhai watches them leave. Mother and daughter walking upright, in their new way, carrying not basket and broom but stuff for the other end of the alimentary canal. That is a phrase that came to him unbidden soon after his wife's rebellion; he uses it some fifteen times a day. My woman now occupies herself with the other end of the alimentary canal. It has brought down walls in his mind, that revolt of hers, he can barely acknowledge it to himself. They turn the corner; 'Ram Ram'—he greets Tola Pat his neighbour gargling and expectorating at his doorstep—Amritbhai has not yet been able to get around to using 'Jai Bheem'—and then, out of habit, searches the confined, ill-lit space that they call home to see if, by oversight, his wife has left behind a rupee or two. No such luck. And even if she had, his daughter would have double-checked.

Without further mishap, his son meanwhile has reached his destination.

School is a large shed in the strip of wasteland between the Saka Devi temple and a wide, filthy and entirely stagnant, open drain. The shed is divided into three rooms, each of which opens onto a verandah that runs along its length. Each room has a doorway (without a door) and a window without panes. The senior classes sit inside, Devji's class usually takes place in the verandah.

Amongst the children whom he studies with, there are two other boys of his caste, one of whom, Chikka, has been absent for close to a year. Devji looks about for Ragi the other, doesn't see either him or his bag, then puts his own down on the ground against the shed wall, well away from those of the children of the other castes; those satchels are all piled up pell-mell in a corner of the verandah itself.

Devji's bag is largely symbolic. He hasn't opened it in months, he is not certain what it contains, a couple of broken pencils, a splintered and effaced footruler, last year's Hindi textbook. He stands still and alone in the sun and waits for Ragi. The others are in groups, horsing around, chatting away. No one greets him, he greets nobody.

Despite the dark glasses, his day hasn't begun well. His stomach is rumbling, he might have to move his bowels again;

that would mean trudging back towards home and relieving himself in the bushes abutting the reed tank. The school does have a toilet but it is not for him.

Fifty-two per cent of India shits in the open; that makes over five hundred and twenty million people—two-thirds of Europe—defecating in fields, beaches, marshes, alleys, lanes, parks and pavements; alongside railroad tracks and on road shoulders, under bridges and behind protected monuments; it is a large country. Just twelve per cent of it is covered by what could be called a modern sewerage system. Of the several hundred million Indians therefore—an entire US—who depend on Devji's caste to remove their shit for them, not one, not one, is chastened and squirms in shame, for instance, while taking a crap.

'Where *does* our shit go, exactly?'

'*Not* at the dinner table, I mean, *really.*'

Elder Daughter dutifully changes the topic to the general dreadfulness of *The Merchant of Venice* but she remains curious and determined to dig. In two days, she ferrets out the essentials of that modern sewerage system.

'Our toilets are connected to these underground pipes that take the shit away to a large, mercifully underground, tank, in which bacteria—practically our *relatives*—swing into action and decompose the crap and after some weeks, by means of a soakaway, it seeps into the surrounding soil.'

'*Soil?*' squeaks Younger Daughter without however glancing up from some text on her mobile phone, 'OMG.'

But that is not all. Every two months or so, some employee of the nearest municipal setup has to clean that septic tank, to do what in the civilized world is done by a machine, an impressive vacuum apparatus mounted on a pumping truck. Elder Daughter learns from Karishmaben that it is invariably someone from the Valmiki or an equivalent caste who descends into the tank and that that kind of government job, reserved for the truly fortunate amongst them, is the highest that an Amritbhai can aspire to. Heaven is a septic tank. Between shitting in the fields and that heaven are a dozen gradations of toilet, examples of all of which are to be found in the Petwada area; all of them, with varying frequency but without exception, are cleaned by the Valmikis.

'You all began coming here to school at the age of five,' says Karishmaben to the assembled, uncomfortable, uncomprehending students, 'I picked up a basket to accompany my mother on her morning rounds.' She tries to smile. 'How can you say no at the age of five?' She pauses before adding, 'There are two million of us across the country.'

Devji, silent in the sun, watches the teacher arrive on his bicycle. The teacher, a Mahajan by caste, is four months old at that school. He parks against the lone pipal sapling, chains and locks the machine. 'Good morning, sir!' sing—in English—those of the students whom he passes on his way to the northern-most room of the shed. He emerges in a minute without his shoulder bag, holding instead a tin plate before his chest; he begins on it a frenzied rat-a-tat with a spoon. The bell.

The students form rows to sing first the National Anthem and next the National Song. None of them is fully certain which is which, so it helps that the teacher leads. Devji, still waiting for Ragi, stands alone behind everyone else; he leaves a gap of more than a metre between the last row and himself. It is good that they face east so that his shadow falls behind him. The teacher stands in the verandah opposite his charges. He has put the plate down but retains the spoon; beating time with it—one-two-three-four—he breaks into the national anthem; a subdued mumble from the boys and girls, like the murmur of a sleepy ocean, indicates that they have joined the singing. They sing first of the overlord of India's destiny and the oneness of the country; they move on, in the National Song, to its fertile fields and radiantly green harvests, and bow down to it as the mother and giver of all; mercifully, not a whisper in either song of the idea of equality.

Assembly over, the students disperse. Noisily, those of the senior classes pick up their satchels from the heap in the corner and enter their respective rooms. Devji's classmates, giggling and jostling, settle down on the floor of the verandah. He remains standing in the sun, glancing about every now and then for Ragi, till things quieten down. He feels even more blue because he is alone. Had Ragi been present, the two would have shared the chore. The four more senior Valmiki students are certainly not going to help, it is not their day on the roster. Finally, when it looks as though class is about to begin, he trudges off to clean the school toilet.

Its four walls are slats of rusty tin; it is open to the sky. There is shit all around it but that Devji will have to deal with later. He takes off his rubber slippers; it is necessary to be barefoot for the job. His implements are the rusted iron bucket and mug, a stump of a broom, a second, cleaner bucket and a piece of carton that says Cadbury that are kept—that *he* keeps—behind the tin slats. The toilet itself is rudimentary; two chipped and stained cement blocks with a large tin pot between them. It is heavy, full. Holding his breath, Devji pulls it out, lifts it, clumsily overturns it into the bucket. Not neatly done. He dumps it on the ground so as to step back a few paces to breathe. He returns in a few moments to the task. With the mug, he scrapes off what he can from the pot.

The bucket, as long as he can remember, has never had a handle. It is now full, heavy. He crouches, places on his head first the fragment of carton, and then lifts the bucket on to it, stands up, carefully, unsteadily and, holding it with both hands, moves off towards the stagnant drain.

At its edge, careful not to step on any excrement, he leans over and, without lifting the bucket off his head because he cannot, and attentive to not losing the piece of cardboard, dumps the filth onto the filth of the drain.

Behind the school lie the maize fields of the six richer Chowdhari families. Alongside the track that leads to them is the hand pump that serves that part of the village. The water it draws up is hard and brackish and tastes of a mix of oil and salt. Devji returns to the toilet, leaves the dirty bucket beside the dirty pot, picks up the clean bucket and trudges to the pump. He is in luck, there are people there. He waits some steps away from it for the two women to fill their own pots and buckets. When they are done, the elder one, Ganiga the oil merchant's daughter by his first wife, asks the boy, matter-of-factly and without rancour, to move back a few paces from his bucket. Muttering an incantation, she then steps forward and fills it from on high with water from her own. She is kind. Devji stands still until the women have left, then picks up his bucket of water and returns to the school toilet.

It is cold and oily, the water. With the fragment of broom, he cleans, as best he can, the pot, the bucket and the mug and replaces them. He returns to the hand pump for more water. There is no one else there. He waits. He could lose his right hand if someone sees him touching the pump. Ganiga's daughter comes back, hissing repeatedly and with rapidly decreasing good humour, 'Hello! Hello! I can't hear you!' into her mobile phone. She obliges Devji again. With the second bucket and the stub of soap that has lodged in his pocket ever since he can remember, he scrubs the flecks of shit, real and imagined, of his classmates and other villagers, off his hands and feet and hair.

He goes back to class. As always, he keeps a metre between

himself and the edge of the verandah but the students in the outer flank—as always—unthinkingly cringe as he passes them. For the last year, whenever they have done that, Devji has been reminded of Chikka's last day in school, of his all at once lashing out, but quietly, at Nirmal and Sujaan and the others. *Why are you shying away like that, you sons of pigs, from the thought of your own shit?* How much, Devji remembers, he and Ragi had had to suffer thereafter.

At the back, the last row, as often, sits right on the edge of the verandah. There is no place left for Devji. Half-relieved, he squats in the dust behind and beneath the others, his shoulders level with the loops of their half-pants, the sun nice and warm on his back. Maths is three-quarters over. Fractions. He waits. He is sort of, for the moment, content. No one can see him and denigrate him for just being.

For days, Elder Daughter digs deeper and deeper and the subject of her research gets more and more murky. She is distracted by the things that she can't follow.

'I don't get it. All these makers of modern India would've crapped in dry toilets and then someone would've slunk in through a hole in the back door to take their shit away. So what did *they* think of their shit-lifters? Dadabhai Naoroji, Bipin Chandra Pal, Motilal Nehru, Annie Besant and Bhulabhai Desai? Did they all say, Let me just go to the loo and then while some half-human carts the poo away, I shall slip on a jacket and tie and go to a meeting where, in devastating English, I shall demand freedom for my country?'

'Well, I doubt whether they thought of shit as often as you do.' But Father pauses. *Why is he trying to defend the indefensible?*

'And democracy and equality and all that shit. Karishmaben says that at every election, they all flock to her part of the village and with folded hands do a house-to-house for votes. But of course nothing changes. "Their doctors don't examine us, their police don't register our cases, they don't allow us music at our weddings, our area has no electricity and no taps."'

'Man, the world stinks,' murmurs Younger Daughter to her phone.

It is to lessen that stench, explains Karishmaben, that with the years, inevitably, the Valmiki youth take to hooch, the adolescents to adulterated heroin and the girls to strong tobacco, supari and paan. Intoxicants help them, she says, to remain switched off their entire lives.

They began to switch on—agonizingly slowly, flickeringly, as it were, in sparks, fits and starts all over the country—in the mid-nineties of the preceding century.

It is, let us say, 1995. The Valmikis of Petwada do not yet know that Parliament two years previously has passed an Act about them and what they do for a living. The Employment of Manual Scavengers and Construction of Dry Latrines (Prohibition) Act, 1993. It is available on the Net but since a mere two per cent of them—some twenty male and a dozen female adults—can just about, fumblingly, write their names (but not read what their neighbour has written), that is not going to do any good.

'And what does it even *mean,* manual scavenging?' breaks in Elder Daughter, glancing accusingly at her parents. 'A vulture is a scavenger, a coke addict rooting about in a rubbish dump is, it could be said, scavenging manually, but the Valmikis in contrast are plain and simple shit-lifters, that's what they are. It's an Indianism, manual scavenging, like eve-teasing, a horrid euphemism that hides the horror under the carpet.'

'Dust,' corrects Mother, feigning her famed absentmindedness. 'Ask the maid.'

'Or Harijan. You call them people of God, that doesn't turn the shit in their baskets to apples from Himachal, that's what Karishmaben said.'

It's more than twenty years ago today, and yet Mainaben remembers so clearly who came first to Petwada. They all seemed to arrive within weeks of one another and the cops of course came much later and—naturally—raised the most dust and annoyed and frightened everyone the *most* but the *first* visitors, she remembers, were those young enthusiasts from the new-leaf organizations of faraway Ahmedabad and New Delhi. The journalists joined them on their sixth or seventh visit, not before that.

'*You are human beings. It is not worthy of you, what you do. To carry the shit of others for a living is not what you were born for. And now at last, after four thousand years, it is against the law.*'

What on earth could they mean. At first—at second and at third—the Valmikis *really* didn't follow what was being discussed with them. Soon, however, the elders—Amritbhai's late father, for instance—were forbidding the community from paying heed to the views of those subversive unemployables. They want you to give up your jobs and become even poorer than before. And then when someone else is working in your place, at what your ancestors have been doing for generations, those maverick rascals'll give you a couple of slogans for food—munch munch—before going back to their cities forever.

The young bustlers did go away but only to return, again and again. And one day, they were accompanied by journalists in jeans carrying cameras and microphones. The next time, Mainaben and Nanko Devi, feeling unreal, saw photographs of themselves with baskets of shit on their heads in *Outlook* and *The Times of India*. 'Dr Bhimrao Ambedkar's struggle has been revived with renewed force,' they were told, 'and this time it will not end without victory. Jai Bheem.' Nodding her head despite feeling numb, Mainaben mumblingly repeated, 'Jai Bheem' and Nanko Devi slipped both, the magazine and the newspaper, into plastic and kept them under her one silk sari—her grandmother's—in her one iron trunk.

It is hot in the sun and Devji is thirsty. Maths and Hindi are over. Mahajan Sir is taking time off from Social Studies to decide with the class what they will do for the Independence Day Cultural Celebrations. Devji is tense even though there is no question of his being involved in anything, of his joining, for instance, the choir for patriotic songs from Hindi films, or participating in the skit on the Rani of Jhansi or reading out the best class essay on the Father of the Nation. The hands of some of the others shoot up every now and then in response to Mahajan Sir's demand for names, Devji continues to look down at his fingers trailing arcs in the dust. If he raises his hand, it would not actually be seen. In fact, the previous year, round about the same time, when Heena, sitting behind the last row in *her* class had suddenly stood up and, in great agitation and breathing in spasms, started speaking, for a few moments, no one had understood where the voice was coming from.

The essay selected the previous year to be declaimed on Independence Day, on the subject of *Gandhiji and His Timeless Wisdom,* was being read out before the class by the writer Smriti Kumari. The sagenss of the Father of the Nation included the nugget that castes like the Valmikis 'do for society what a mother does for her child. A mother cleans her child's excrement and safeguards his health. In the same way,' castes like the Valmikis clean up to preserve 'the health of the whole community.'

It was then that Heena all at once stood up and, hissing and weeping and gasping for breath, prevented the redoubtable

Smriti Kumari from warming to her theme. *'If shit-lifting is so noble, why don't you all do it! Why is it only us, and always us! Why do you sprinkle water on everything we touch! He lies, the Father of your Nation! Ask him to carry a basket of shit on his head first and then talk!'*

Quick as lightning, Marar Sir personally organized her thrashing. Almost all the boys and girls of the other castes in her class participated. It is okay to touch Valmiki skin with one's slipper or footruler. In any case, one washes up thereafter. No broken bones for Heena fortunately. Just bruises and throbbing legs and a nose that wouldn't stop bleeding.

From that day onwards, says Karishmaben, she stopped going to class. No more education for her. She began instead to accompany her mother on her morning rounds. In place of the toilets at school, she chose those of the village. There is no escape for us from the latrines of others. But at least she helped her family with the monthly income.

For two days after Heena's revolt, Devji remembers too well, he did not go to school. No one noticed. On the third day, his sister asked him, not very kindly, 'For how long will you continue to miss your only decent meal of the day?'

Eleven forty-five. The students on the verandah watch—and those in the rooms hear—the school lunch, in aluminium vats on a cart behind a tricycle, come in. It is usually weevil rice, watery dal and potatoes but it is warm. The four students on lunch duty—one of the Darbar caste, one Bharwad and two Vaghris—skip away to help with the arrangements while the rest while away the quarter-hour that remains in a haze of inattentiveness. At twelve, Mahajan Sir again beats a rat-a-tat with his spoon on his plate. Noisily, joyously, the classes break up.

Silently, Devji waits under the pipal sapling with the Valmiki children of the other classes. Space for them in the shade is further curtailed by Mahajan Sir's parked bicycle that—God forbid—they, even accidentally, touch. They watch the students on lunch duty bring out the teacher's table from the first room and arrange on it the vats. The others, in complete disorder, enter the last room to fetch the plates stored in the cupboard. They then line up before the vats to be served. Mahajan Sir chides each one who has not gone to the handpump to wash his hands. All those caught out rush off, laughing, to comply but nevertheless lose their places in the queue. With their laden plates, the students go and sit cross-legged on the floor, in untidy rows, down the entire length of the verandah. Slowly descends on them the silence of contentment.

The students on lunch duty then serve the teachers and next themselves. The teachers enter the second room to eat at the table, the servers join their classmates on the floor. That is usually the sign for the Valmiki children to go behind the school shed and pick up their plates from where they are stacked in the open against the wall. For identification, the back of each plate has been scratched with an X. Devji and his caste members queue up but outside in the sun, away from the verandah. Ganjambhai Valand, the Panchayat employee who has brought the food, now heaves the near-empty vats away to the cart. Devji and the others place their plates in the dust alongside its wheels. Careful not to let the ladle touch any plate, Ganjambhai serves the Valmikis. He then turns the tricycle about and prepares to leave. Those plates too near the wheels of the cart he pushes away with his foot. Devji and his caste-mates pick up their plates and go and sit and eat under the sapling.

After lunch, they will trudge to the handpump with their plates and the clean bucket, wait aside for everyone else to finish and for somebody to fill the bucket with water, wash their plates and stack them again against the shed wall. They will be thirsty but they couldn't possibly carry bottles to school and no one drinks the water of that handpump. While class begins again, they will stroll back home—half-an-hour's walk for most of them—drink and drink and take their time about returning. Devji though would have to because he has to clean the school toilet again at four.

Jai Bheem.

But how long it took—months, years actually—of tortuous, tormenting cogitation and discussion, of unwillingly giving ear to the persuasions of the worker activists—'You cannot avoid the struggle. Government is upper caste and your poverty, your life bereft of dignity, are its doing. Come, file your affidavits in court. Nothing can be worse than this, so rise, rise and say, Jai Bheem!'—how long it took for Mainaben, Lakshmania, Munira, Kusumi, Nanko Devi and the other women to allow their spirits to buckle, to cave in, and then slowly to begin to blossom, for them to conclude: *But is it possible? Could anything be worse than this? This stinking nightmare that has been my life since the age of five. In the monsoon I cannot undo my hair in public because the shit of my neighbours has seeped into it and under my fingernails. Even after twenty years, I cannot look at turmeric without wishing to throw up. This cesspit that is my world, in which, at my marriage, my dowry was how many toilets per day I did, and in which I've watched the flies rise from a pile of excrement to settle on the face of my infant because, having no choice, I had to carry her to work, that world, could things get worse and is it possible to sink even lower into it?*

'And worse I may be yet,' blurts out Father, unable to stop himself, ashamed to have a head full of useless quotations from another world that pop out unbidden and unwanted, uncontrollable like the onslaught of some acute digestive disorder, 'The worst is not as long as we can say, This is the worst.'

His exclamation is directed at his daughters who, in preparation for their skit for School Day, have been roaming around the house, ever since they got off the afternoon bus, in yellow gum boots, grey transparent raincoats, orange rubber gloves that reach the elbows, dentists' face masks and towels around their necks. Wandering about from room to room, banging into furniture, continually in danger of toppling over in their outsize boots, they practise and improvise their lines.

'Look at me, ladies and gentlemen,' declaims Elder Daughter in Hindi, pushing her mask up into her hair and glaring at her parents, 'and tell me, What's in a name? For I have several. Let us say that I was born Heena. But I am a child of the Valmiki caste. So back home in the village though, no matter what our names are, we are called, depending on which part of the country we have the misfortune to live in, Thotamma or any of its variants. Garbage-Woman. Shit-Woman.'

Younger Daughter steps up to stand beside her sister. 'What's in a name. Because the Acts of 1993 and 2013 call me a manual scavenger. *Manual*.' She lifts up her orange gloves like a boxer taking guard. 'Like a sculptor or artisan or something. Whose material, however, is excrement. And the municipal corporation calls me a conservancy worker. Like a protector of wildlife. Or of monuments.'

'*Monumental* gobbledegook, brothers and sisters,' butts in Elder Daughter. 'Because the Act of 2013 states that if I wear *protective* gear,'—she rapidly begins, as she speaks, to tap her boots, gloves, raincoat, mask and towel—'I shall *not* be deemed to be a manual scavenger. A change of name again! So what will I then have become? I pause for a reply.' None is heard. She then begins to prowl about the room in a round-shouldered crouch, chastising, in near-hysterical whispers, a piece of blackboard chalk that she holds up in front of her nose; it is the gait and manner of the Class Teacher Mrs Mendiratta. 'To be a manual scavenger and carry shit about for a living is a crime. So far so good. But if I wear this plastic shit, I am no longer, by definition, a manual scavenger and so *can* descend into a septic tank and wallow in excrement upto my neck.'

'Allow us,' Younger Daughter steps forward again, wobblingly, to centrestage, 'brothers and sisters of the upper world, to tell you about life in a septic tank.'

The tank, then reveal the sisters in a rapidfire exchange, is typically a concrete box measuring twelve feet by ten by ten. It is full of shit, water, bacteria, cockroaches, rats and other vermin. The bacteria are busy 24x7 decomposing the shit; they know of no other life. The chemical reaction involved in their activity uses up almost all the oxygen and releases into the air of the tank methane, hydrogen sulphide, carbon dioxide and carbon monoxide. Excrement therefore is not the only reason why the tank stinks to high heaven. To fight the stench and the nausea, the Amritbhais first get plastered. Then they find that they can't breathe and that there they are, in their plastic gear, surrounded by decomposing shit, in ambient temperatures that exceed 55 degrees Celsius. Often their last thought before passing out is that their wives above ground might just have a better deal. The statistics? The rate of death amongst conservancy workers in the city of Bombay alone is 349 per year.

'At that point,' Elder Daughter breaks off to explain to the pop-eyed parents, 'we want to get Karishmaben to come up and talk about her mother's revolt.'

'Except that she's terrified and refuses. Not before all the parents, she says.'

'Your brooms have no reeds left and your baskets are holes held together by string. When were they last changed? Why don't you ask the Panchayat to buy you new equipment?'

That was how Mainaben's revolt began.

The new Panchayat office building stands, white and low-ceilinged and stifling, in the open space between the PHC dispensary and the Civil Supplies ration shop. The alley to—and the few square metres around—it are where the Darbar cattle and the Korama pigs, chewing the cud, offal and the fat, love most to while their lives away. On a sweltering June day, having finished their morning rounds, a dozen Valmiki women stroll through the mud and dust towards the Panchayat; diffident, doubting, their faces veiled behind the ends of their saris, they have occasionally to push out of their way a ruminating cow or engrossed sow. Animals—each one of the women noticed long ago in her life—never, whether muttering mantras or curses or silently, feel the need to move aside for them.

They stop at the bottom of the four steps, they look at one another. They wait. A crowd of idlers gathers. Not a marriage or festival or funeral, what's going on? A *delegation?* Of *Valmiki women?* Ganjambhai Valand emerges on the verandah from one of the rooms. 'So many of you to clean one toilet, is it?' he jokes.

'We want to meet Harshadbhai Thakore,' announces Mainaben.

Whyever should shit-cleaners want to meet the sarpanch, you think he has nothing better to do, he's busy, he isn't here, tell me what the problem is and I'll tell him, you're crazy if you think he can face the village again after being called out to meet *you,* to listen to *you,* just go away, et cetera.

At that moment, without knowing exactly what she is doing, Mainaben becomes a sort of leader. The others are uncertain, the excursion has been stressful and some would be only too glad to melt back into their lives. 'Very well. It's important, so we'll wait here for the sarpanch,' declares Mainaben and sits down in the dust at the foot of the steps. The other women, almost as taken aback as the bystanders, find their knees buckling. Surprised at themselves, they join her in her sit-in.

It doesn't last very long, about twenty minutes or so. The women have lunches to cook and families to tend, a hundred responsibilities. But the earth *has* teetered, just a little. Eventually, Mainaben has to reveal to the unspeakable Ganjambhai the purpose of the drama. He is surprised, amused. Anything to do with shit he finds funny. He demands a petition on paper.

'We can't write,' confesses Mainaben sadly. 'Neither can you.' He does stop smirking.

The petition, drafted the week before, is in the hands of the activist unemployables who observe the first phase of the revolt, the fruit of their labours, from the sidelines. It covers everything, all the points that the Valmiki women have not even dreamt of.

Under Section 19 1) of the Act by which you have been created, it is the duty of the Panchayat, states the document, to function as a unit of self-government in order to achieve economic development and social justice for all. Section 19 2) of the same Act details your responsibilities that include, among others, the obligation to provide for sanitation in the area under your jurisdiction. Not to supply new and adequate equipment to the Valmiki women (after all, your contractual employees) for their daily chores therefore violates several laws of the land and is liable to attract judicial action. It is further brought to your attention that the cost of twenty brooms and baskets amounts to less than a thousandth of the annual budget of your Panchayat. It may moreover be noted that you are also duty-bound to provide to the Valmiki women detergent for their equipment, soap for themselves and three dedicated water sources in the village for their use.

You would otherwise be accused of violating Article 14 of the Constitution and the provisions of The Prevention of Atrocities Act of 1955.

Fuckall happens (apart from the earth teetering just a bit). The petition is read out to the members of the Panchayat. They are bemused and outraged and finally decide not to do anything on the grounds that they can't because the budget for that year has been committed elsewhere.

On the surface, things return to routine from the very next day. The village, having—naturally—heard of the visit of the delegation, for a week or two, mocks the Valmiki women when they turn up in the morning. 'But you haven't brought your new equipment today! Saving them up for your daughter's dowry, is it!'—that sort of thing. But inwardly amongst the cleaners, in their blood and their spirit, they do sense that their visit with their demands to the lowest level of officialdom was unprecedented; the darkness has been cracked apart a fraction, now to shatter it. No matter how slowly they move, the only way to go is forward, they do sense that. They wait. The next step, it will come.

'How much they increase our work, these activist hoodlums,' declares the assistant sub-inspector in charge of the demolitions, 'and how much they deserve to be grabbed by the scruff of the neck and have their noses rubbed—' he gestures expansively at his surroundings—'in excrement.' He is balding and genial and pleased with himself at a job being done well by others. 'They are everywhere, ingratiating themselves in Valmiki hovels, drafting petitions against the government, grovelling in the Supreme Court, everywhere. And everywhere encouraging disorder.'

It is a dull winter morning. The police roll up early in two jeeps followed by an open truck in which loll a dozen listless labourers. The convoy stops in the shit zone, the strip of no man's land where the village of Petwada prepares to become the municipality of Botadpuri. Eight dry latrines, narrow cubicles of tin with no roofs and half-doors all askew—the pride of the Panchayat—face the village; myriads of tiny piles of shit surround them for several metres in every direction, like a depiction, in excrement, of the Milky Way.

Mainaben and Kusumi are at work at those latrines that morning. Without being asked to, they step back and, puzzled, watch the constables direct the labourers to shatter, with crowbars and rods of iron, the flimsy walls of tin and the cement blocks that they hide. In half an hour, the blocks have become rubble and the truck, ferrying the labourers and the slats of tin, and snorting and wheezing and disgorging black, noxious fumes that give to the winter air the shade of ashes, has chugged away.

Before getting into his jeep, the assistant sub-inspector beckons Mainaben and Kusumi with his baton. He, chummily, taps the first with it on the backside and then, wagging it in the second's face, declares, 'Dry latrines do not officially exist from today, here or anywhere else in the land. They have all been more or less demolished, they've all—save for a few hundred thousand scattered here and there—disappeared overnight. And so the Act has been implemented, your Honour, that is what the country is going to tell the Supreme Court. Do you follow?' He beams at them both with benign, fatherly lust. 'To shit in a dry toilet, and to carry shit away from it, have both now been declared offences. So when you go to work tomorrow, you could very easily, if and when we want, carry on from there to jail.' He chuckles at the wondrous ways of the government. 'If you own a dry toilet, don't shit for three months. In that period, apply to the authorities for a loan to convert it to a flush toilet.' Continuing to smile at the women, he extends his open, upturned left palm in the direction of his driver. Reverentially, the latter places in it a sachet of perfumed, carcinogenic tobacco. 'But Petwada is not going to get sewerage in a thousand years, so who's going to remove the filth of the pit attached to the *flush* toilet?' He tears the sachet open with his teeth and showers its contents into a maw wide as a hippo's. 'Sisters, you are in luck.'

Four pm. School is almost over for the day. The last class is Sports. The girls play kho-kho, the boys kick a ball around in the dust, Devji goes off to do the toilet. By the time he finishes and cleans up, he is alone, the other students have disappeared.

He walks home quickly, following Newton's fourth law of motion that states that a child returns home from school at twice the velocity that he expends going to it in the morning. Dump the bag, a drink of water, then off again to mooch about, chew the fat, play some tennis-ball hand-cricket with his Valmiki chums before setting off, round about six o'clock, with his two plastic bags and his grandfather's stick, on his evening round.

His first stop, as always, is the back door of the house of Raghubha Darbar. The lane that leads to it is in fact a five-foot-wide gutter, perennially muddy, filthy, stinking of rotting food and stagnant water and humming with flies and mosquitoes like an amplifier of a music system left on with the volume at maximum. Devji, for fear of slipping, treads most cautiously. With the stick, he taps politely on the door, twice, and waits. There was a time not so long ago when they had to tap and then kneel in the muck to wait. That stopped because of his grandfather who just couldn't bend his knees on account of his arthritis. Raghubha's wife had at first been so shocked at his pride.

She opens the door, head half-hidden behind the veil of the end of her sari, nods at Devji, he is expected. She disappears, returns in a moment, flings at him something heavy wrapped in newspaper, shuts the door. He, leaning the stick against his leg, catches the packet with the dexterity of a cricket professional; he places it carefully in one of his plastic bags.

The Raghubha Darbars give the best food; invariably the largest number of stale rotis and always something to go with them, dal in a tiny polythene bag—typically a little too sour because it's gone off—or day before yesterday's potatoes. In any case, Mainaben never fails to recook whatever is given, usually adding chilli in three forms—dried red, fresh green and as powder—to mask that faint, unmistakable stench of rottenness of the food.

Sometimes the back door just doesn't open, or the leftovers thrown out are so putrid that they stink in flight even before they reach Devji's capable hands. To leave them in the muck at his feet would be so insulting as to cause an Incident; he usually takes it all home and lets the boss of the household decide.

Onward to the back door of the house of Devipujak Barot. Pigs in the back alley and rats the size of piglets. They eat better food than us, Mainaben had screamed, on that morning of her famed revolt, on her return from Devipujak's house, hobbling in pain, bleeding, round of houses left incomplete. She'd then been in her seventh month and Amritbhai, apprehensive, had suggested that day that she rest and send her daughter instead to do her circuit.

'My children go to school. They'll go to college. They are not going to touch other people's shit.'

Devji knocks. He waits. A rat pauses near his foot to contemplate his slipper.

That evening in March of the previous year, a good six weeks after the police, in knocking down the dry toilets of the Panchayat, have shown the Valmikis, but in a glimmer, that nothing in life on earth is impossible, Mainaben, carrying her basket and broom, pushes open the back door of the house of

Devipujak Barot, enters, and thrusts ajar the toilet immediately on her right. It is full, filthy, shit all over the place. On any other day, she would've been inured to the sight and stink but she's been feeling queasy all morning. She reels just a little, her foot slips, she collapses half on the pot, overturning some of its contents on herself. The thud of the fall and the wailing bring Padmaben Barot scurrying to investigate. One look, two exclamations and the lady of the house scoots off again only to return a few moments later with a bottle from her puja room and the long-handled broom from the kitchen. Muttering the appropriate incantation, she first purifies herself by sprinkling Gangajal on her torso and the top of her head; she then offers the reed-end of the broom to a prostrate Mainaben to hoist herself up with.

Mainaben can't; the pain in her abdomen is too acute. She remains flat on that floor for an hour and twelve minutes; the shit on her, around her, mean nothing to her. She has lost the baby, she is sure of it. It takes that long for Padmaben to send the servant to the Valmiki quarter to fetch help; no one in her household can touch that woman curled up on the toilet floor, naturally. Amritbhai is out cleaning a tank in Botadpuri; to drag him away would entail the loss of a day's wage. Ultimately, Gudiyadevi and a couple of other women half-carry Mainaben home.

It is Padmaben who opens the back door to Devji; she knows who it will be, she shuts the door in his face; it is the sole pleasure that life has left to her.

The boy's mother has made her the laughing stock of the village.

For, three days after her fall in the toilet, Mainaben, haggard, distraught, limping, leads yet another delegation of Valmiki women to the Panchayat. At the foot of its steps, they make a bonfire of their broken brooms and tattered baskets and swear over its flames to abandon, from that day forth, the occupation of their caste. They are filmed by a scruffy television crew. Interviewed. During which (horror of horrors) wretched Mainaben actually mentions Devipujak Barot by name. 'I have had to take this decision because of what happened to me a few days ago in the house of...she was occupied in sprinkling Gangajal on herself while I was losing my child...she will have to drown many times in several buckets of holy water before she finds salvation (the last delivered quietly, in tears, shattering in a subdued way).'

'You and your sister have more sense than your mother,' declares Padmaben as she flings her newspaper packet at Devji. She says it every day. Three quarters of the village agrees with her, virtually everybody, that is, other than the Valmiki women.

After the bonfire and the TV interview, the mood in the Mainaben household is blue; several tempers are frayed. Aghast at his daughter-in-law's conduct, Amritbhai's father hobbles off the next morning, with his stick and everything, to clean the dry latrine of Devipujak Barot. That his son simply cannot have; he proposes a compromise.

'Heena can take over your work in the mornings; in any case, she's stopped going to school, she has nothing to do. And Devji can do the food round in the evening. Why should we lose out on both your salary and the food?'

Have you no shame, how dense *are* you, what am I trying to fight for, et cetera, from Mainaben, screaming, for a day and a half.

Though preserved in alcohol, Amritbhai's brain turns out to

have enough current to emit a spark or two. 'You should revolt in stages. First you. Then when you are nicely settled in your state of rebellion, then the children.'

Mainaben never says yes to the arrangement. Like a street dog curled up in repose, on a pavement in the winter sun who, whenever a stray from another part of town passes within ten metres of him, growls to himself but otherwise does not react, she murmurs abuse every morning when Heena leaves to do the round that was her mother's and she frowns in the evening and mutters other phrases of invective when Devji returns home with two plastic bags of stale food. She says that she feels exactly like a mother bird who has escaped her cage without caring for the fledglings that she has left behind.

Amritbhai is impressed with the simile and says as much. She is up to something or very soon will be, he knows that; but as long as the few rupees and the stale food continue to dribble in, he lets her be. She is trying to do what he himself should be doing but he's been manacled since birth by his birth. So has she, he acknowledges that. Well. They can neither read nor write and everything—a sewing machine, a driving licence, the tools of a plumber's profession, the apprenticeship to a bicycle repairer—everything costs money. They don't have either the cash or the papers to open a bank account with. Nothing, they have nothing except the children, her two silk saris, her six silver bangles and the hereditary right to the excrement collected every day in a dozen dry latrines of Petwada. He watches her get ready to pawn the bangles.

'I'm going to start a tea shop. Umed Solanki will give me a loan.'

'Except the Valmikis who don't have the money, no one in the village is going to drink tea made by those beautiful hands. You know that.'

'There is a world beyond Petwada. Heena will accompany me.'

The offers of change, when they do arrive, come from that world.

'What did your mother say about the dark glasses?'

'I wore them this morning. Tops they are. Didn't tell her that you gave them. But she knew somehow. Heena didi probably.'

Devji can't take his eyes off Chikka. He hadn't even recognized him the day before till he'd opened his mouth. After a year in Bombay, Chikka is taller, he wears jeans, he smokes and he's done something to his hair; it rises straight up like the bristles of a black toilet brush from a skull otherwise shaved clean; even more wondrous, he has a mobile phone.

Chikka shakes his head in sorrow and scorn at the plastic bags of food in Devji's hands. 'In Bombay, after a day's work, we eat kebabs and swig rum before going off to have ice-cream at Chowpatty with the sweeper girls.'

He's been nagging Devji, Come with me. You could work with me in the hospital morgue. It's nothing, you drag a body out, dump it on the table, you clean it, it's nothing. The doctor dawdles in a corner, smoking and saying, here, shave his pubis, cut his stomach, crack his skull, it's all science, man. And I already make sixty rupees a day, that's almost twice what my father gets here. And then in the canteen you do the dishes and you're fed free.'

'I'll have to ask my mother. She'll never allow me to leave my studies.'

And the next day: Did you ask?

'No. Heena didi might be leaving. How could I in the middle of all that drama? One posh lady with a bobcut came to visit us and tried to sit on the floor with us crosslegged. First she couldn't and then later, when it was time to go, she couldn't get up. My mother yelled at my father in front of her for not removing his junk from the top of the trunk and giving her that to sit on.'

It is not surprising therefore that Devji does not pay due attention to what the posh lady offers. She has been a regular visitor, she oversaw the drafting of the petition for the Panchayat; her organization, she says, runs a school in New Delhi in which she would like to place Heena and a couple of the other Valmiki girls; there, they would earn some money and some self-respect. In return, the posh one expects the girls to join and take seriously the evening literacy classes at the school.

'How do I know that it isn't a sex racket?' asks Mainaben pensively.

Slapped in the face, the posh one makes to get up and discovers that she can't. Heena, helping her up, whispers to her, 'I'm willing. I'll go with you.'

Devji is certain that he will never escape his daily routine and leave the village with Chikka but what he wants to know is, why him? They *were* the best of friends but that was a year ago.

'Have you asked any of the others? Ragi? Bhiku? And would they give me a job just because I know how to carry shit on my head?'

'You think it's *fun* to work with corpses? Those on the payroll play cards while we do their job for them. And then they give us a fraction of their winnings.'

It emerges in a roundabout way that it is lonely at night in the verandah of the shed—alongside the hospital morgue—that stores defunct medical equipment. Would be nice to have someone to chew the fat with about home when you can't sleep and are wondering what that thump-thump next door was.

Being too certain of her response, he can't possibly ask his mother, particularly when she is so apprehensive and upset over Heena's imminent departure for the wider world, so he asks his sister instead.

'Don't be stupid, what are you saying,' snaps she in response, barely following what he mumbles, so apprehensive and upset is she herself.

The thought of his days, of his daily routine, *without* her at home, is what has finally decided him. 'What is the posh lady's mobile number? I'll sms you from Chikka's phone once I reach Bombay.'

'You're so stupid,' she hisses. 'And mad.' Then adds, even more sibilantly, 'Don't say Heena in your stupid message. When she asked me my name, I am Karishma, I said. Sounds better for Delhi. Okay?'

Devji carries with him his school bag but first he dumps its contents into the drain that he has had to visit, twice a day, for years and places in it instead just his new dark glasses.

Mainaben is inconsolable at the simultaneous departure of her two children; she wails all night, she tears her hair, she beats her breast, she stops functioning.

'They aren't dead, you know,' points out Amritbhai, wise and sozzled and ready to pass out, 'they've left in search of a better life for themselves. And they are happy.'

Mainaben would have recovered in time because it takes care of these things, time does. But watching her husband quietly, humming to himself, spend the remainder of the loan from Umed Solanki on hooch puts her back on her feet in four days.

But where is she to go, what is she to do? She finds herself less burdened; in freeing themselves, the children have also set her free. She has discovered that she likes bustle and being in the public eye, she has always been hot-tempered, a lover of fights in which she can rave and rant, *and* she is unlettered. Where else can she go but into politics?

'I'm going to contest the Panchayat elections against Harshadbhai Thakore,' announces she, trembling at her temerity, yet determined to have the time of her life.

One last loose end.

Elder Daughter's skit does not get past the Class Teacher Mrs Mendiratta. 'I shall have to tell your parents to get your head examined...Now don't be so upset!! Social uplift is a never-ending story but if it is really such an Issue with you, why don't you sponsor one of the girls—Karishma, for instance—for the beauty parlour training course that she seems to have found at Jamrudpur?'

So it happens. But Karishma's adventures in a South Delhi beauty parlour is really quite another story.

Foreigner

The India Buggers. That's what Bhuvan still calls those Europeans bitten by the India bug. Marie Claire liked the phrase and was amused by it when, way back in July 1990, round about the time that Pink Floyd played on the Berlin Wall, he had first said to her:

'You know, you are a quintessential India buggerina.'

He was younger then. On his way to work those days, he would stop at the Samrat Hotel to swim and she came all the way from Europe to New Delhi, she said, for seven weeks every year, for which she pinched and scraped and saved up for the other forty-five, to tan. Straight from Immigration to a mattress beside the Samrat swimming pool that she did not leave, save for the hourly dip in the water, for fifty days. No Fatehpur Sikri, no Shekhavati, no Benolim beach.

Even today, were she to be asked if she considered anything in life to be more fundamental than a decent tan, she'd be lost in thought for days. There on her mattress on the grass, for lap after lap Bhuvan had noticed her, stretched out on her back behind her huge sunglasses, thighs wide apart, trying to brown as much of her private parts as possible without actually peeling off her farce of a bikini. The waiters at the Samrat loved her. All day, they took turns to come and chat to her pubic area and respectfully ask it whether it was in need of anything, a nimbu soda or perhaps a fresh fruit juice.

She came to India every year to tan and to get to know people, she said.

He'd finished his laps and was dawdling in the shallows, hating the thought of the traffic jams that he would have to negotiate before arriving at work when she slipped into the water and swam the most graceful butterfly that he'd seen outside a TV screen. Like a tireless dolphin, he said to himself, though I can't tell her that because it'd sound as though I meant that she isn't very slim.

Oh. She's older than I'd at first thought, said he to himself when she stopped beside him for a breather. Forty, forty-two even. But beneath the crows'feet and loosening skin, she had a nice face. Rather, her nature, her ways, seemed to have refashioned her features and given her a laugh that could be heard in Europe. When she wasn't laughing though, her eyes, grey green, were curiously opaque, almost dead.

'That was the most graceful butterfly I've seen outside a TV screen. Like a tireless dolphin.' He was relieved that she smiled in response and didn't hit him on the head or anything. And before leaving for the university that morning, a good quarter of an hour later than usual, he asked the supine form on the blue mattress, 'Are you sure you've been coming to the Samrat regularly for the last several years? Because I've been swimming here since 1983, you know, and we haven't met before, have we?'

After a moment, 'Claridge's,' she murmured in response to the sky without however taking off her dark glasses.

Her English accent told him that she was French but he wasn't going to risk his Alliance Francaise French with her. Her ethnicity, if not her nationality, was confirmed the following Wednesday, the day that the French School on Aurungzeb Road ferried its kids in the morning to the Samrat for a swim; suddenly the sleepy and smelly changing rooms were swarming with noisy, white-skinned children who looked through Bhuvan and made him feel invisible in his own country; outside near the showers, he could hear Marie Claire trilling with the female teachers of the school in French.

'Where do you stay?'

'Not very far from here. Nizamuddin East.'

'Oh, that's a *nice* part of town. Practically a French quartier.'

She was leading up to something. He waited for her to spell it out in black and white.

It was raining, bucketing down, on Monday morning. Bhuvan liked swimming in the rain because it usually kept more people away from the pool. Marie Claire, paddling about in the water and, in the absence of the sun, looking so depressed and grey as to have become quite another personality, said, even before saying 'Good morning', 'This is an odd hotel. Everyone I meet looks like a policeman.'

'He probably is, you know.' He needed to wrap up the conversation before starting on his laps. 'You are right next to the Prime Minister's house, did you know that? And I think the top floors of the Samrat have been handed over to Intelligence, Security, Special Protection, that lot.' Then, 'See you later,' he added before pushing off the wall to the patter of the rain.

It mildly annoyed him to see that, having sailed past, she was waiting for him at the deep end of the pool to continue her side of the conversation. 'And those policemen whom I see in the hotel lobby are so acutely moustached. It's a very Indian-Asian-Middle Eastern thing, isn't it, the moustache. You hardly see it in west Europe. You arrive in Delhi in the middle of the night and suddenly all the men are moustached.'

Bhuvan had shaved his, on the advice of his elder sister, in February of the previous year. He had been about to leave for Khan Market to have his passport photos done when Tripti had said, 'An Immigration official is a highly prejudiced entity. He is suspicious, exacting and a damned nuisance. He is *paid* to distrust. He prefers to see, for a start, on the other side of the glass, an uncovered head and a face clean-shaven. At London Heathrow, he is even likely to be a British Indian. Genetically, he resembles you. Then he opens his mouth and speaks BBC. He won't follow your English. You would've heard that English gets you nowhere in continental Europe; *yours* won't even get you out of the airport. Timorous, dazed, you'll ramble in vast, sophisticated, disorienting, cheerless Heathrow, stopping frequently to comprehend their currency and to buy soft porn. Europe—that universe—is a marvelous place for picking up glossy adult literature and shopping for it is a pleasantly social experience. In your trolley, the erotica basks snugly amongst your carton of cigarettes, your Givenchy and your single malts; you choose a cashier of the opposite sex to whom you, a man of the world, hand the magazines over without blushing.'

And that was not all that she, a formidable diplomat's redoubtable widow, had had to share with her younger brother on his maiden trip, that winter of 1989, to London, Heidelberg and thereafter to Paris.

'You'd do well to remember, Bhuvan, that you are travelling to another planet. On the plane, on that animated flight map on the video screen that charts your progress, you will notice, with surprise and relief, what you've never remembered from your Junior School Geography, that Europe and India belong to the same land mass, and that if, journeying north-westward from, say, New Delhi, you cover a distance a mere few hundred kilometres more than, roughly, Porbandar-Kohima-Calcutta, you will fetch up at the gates of Europe. Such thoughts will germinate in you the glow of well-being—"How large India is, a teeming continent, I'm positive that I'll take to Europe."'

Tripti chooses her words well; she loves the polished manner in which she speaks. 'When you survey your fellow travellers on the flight, you might catch a glimpse of the planet that you're hurtling to. The only restless, fidgety people in the plane will be Indians—continually being chided by the air hostesses for swapping seats, for ambling in the aisles, for carrying three pieces of hand baggage per head, each filled to bursting with deep-fried vegetarian food. Everybody else—shall we say, the Europeans?—will be glowering at his reading matter; smeared on his white skin will be that cherished, invisible cold cream that guards him—or her—from all unexpected, adventitious mortal contact. Where he—or she—comes from, where you're off to—you'll discover that they've so arranged their gadgets and appliances—Left Luggage Lockers, fizzy-drinks vending machines, push-button visiting-card printers—that you experience near-zero human contact, that you can traverse your day there by interacting entirely with apparatuses and electrical devices. It is that belief of theirs, I suppose, in the sacredness of the individual's space. They keep to themselves, to each his own, and then they commit suicide. Not quite like *our* overloaded planet—here, everyone, all the time, longing for contact, brushes against, or bumps into, everyone else—now and then, just for the heck of it.

'And their beggars wear Levi's.'

Tripti takes a gulp of her single malt and reluctantly gets up from her armchair to check where in his luggage her brother has secreted away the two kilograms of Mysore Pak that she has asked him to carry. The search does not deflect her from the pleasure of hearing herself. 'Bemused, on the occasion of my first visit to see Jean-Francois after his departure from India, having just bought, as a souvenir, an ordinary brownish canvas shoulder bag—at an astronomical price!—at the Paris Opera House—Fabrique en Pakistan, declared the piping of the bag—I was chewing over why I'd yielded to the wretched, touristy hard-sell, when this middle-aged man—a white, a mottled greyish-red—waylaid me to cadge a cigarette. By my standards, he was irreproachably dressed. Correctly-faded jeans, needlecord jacket. He then shambled off to a nearby litter bin, foraged deep and long, and picked out a fast-food carton—French fries and leaky ketchup. In contrast, my kind of beggar—I couldn't but recall—a human spider crawling about outside Howrah Station on his stump of a hip, with the head of Jimi Hendrix and a right arm that petered out in a pinkish knob at the elbow, swathes the base of that stump in blue polythene. Wherever does Europe lock up its hideousnesses, its deformities? Everything is ordered and takes its place so that even when Satan drops in, a la Bulgakov, he too, ever heedful of the niceties, will be dressed to kill.'

She interrupts herself with an 'ah!' of triumph to remove, from the bottom of the tightly-packed suitcase, two cardboard boxes wrapped in scarlet polythene and sealed with beige Scotch tape. She places them on top of the unwieldy Gladstone that Bhuvan hopes to pass off as cabin baggage. '*Europe Round the Bend, Europe in Bits and Pieces*'—fetching titles for the right kind of handbook, don't you think? After all, when *they* show up here, their luggage dribbles surviviors' guidebooks and V.S. Naipauls, doesn't it?'

Marie Claire's reading material, forming an untidy semi-circle round the head of the mattress beside the pool, indicated that she preferred to browse through five things at a time. *Le Nouvel Observateur,* a Sunday *Le Monde, Teach Yourself Sanskrit* (in English), Tagore's *Kumudini* (in French) and a glossy guidebook on the Golden Triangle that, Bhuvan learnt on examination, was not about some kind of chastity belt but a touristy epithet for Agra, Jaipur and Fatehpur Sikri.

'You are quite a serious swimmer,' she said to him, smiling, when he had finished but was still in the water, 'What do you do during Delhi's awful winters?'

'I mope. I run in Lodi Gardens moping. And you? How do you tan during those six rainy, freezing, sunless months in old Europe?'

'I've been meaning to ask you,' she responded, suddenly rushing into it as though they had wasted too many days in pleasantries and time was running out, 'You know of a place where I could stay for the remaining four to five weeks or so?'

Bhuvan to Tripti that evening at dinner: 'Well, if it's okay with you, I could propose that Marie Claire use our second-floor barsaati for a month or till mid-September or whatever. Apparently, she's been to some estate agent in Meherchand and obviously no one's interested in renting out for a mere one month. In any case, she couldn't follow *at all* their English and they'd glance at one another and smirk whenever they heard her Hindi.'

Tripti has washed her hair that evening, was not interrupted during that process and is therefore in a good mood. 'I don't know. She's a foreigner and I suppose that's a good thing. We should still sign the usual lease for eleven months and take three months' rent in advance as a security deposit. You never know. Much better to have everything down in black or white.'

'And. Black *and* white. Well, if a contract for *eleven* makes you feel in control for one month. You—we—had signed with Cecilia and look how that ended.'

'You'll have to tell her about that before we decide anything. Have you told her?'

'You know, I go to the Samrat not to find tenants but to swim.'

They make up their minds not to do anything. Not in a

hurry, at any rate. Give her the address, let her come and see the place. Maybe she'll find the rooms too stifling. What about rent? The flat is furnished and we pay the electricity and water, so we should start with twelve and be ready to come down to a cut-off of eight. Cecilia paid seven thousand, didn't she? And so what? No landlord discusses tenants past with tenants prospective.

The address was conveyed the following morning (before Bhuvan began his laps) and, it being Friday, he proposed that Marie Claire drop by over the weekend to see the rooms. On returning from work that evening, he was—almost disagreeably—surprised to learn that she had visited Nizamuddin East at eleven that very morning.

One glance at Tripti's face told him that the two women, unexpectedly, had hit it off.

'Unannounced. No phone call or anything. Rang the bell. There she was on her motorbike. Someone's motorbike, at any rate. No crash helmet. She was in the neighbourhood, she said. A lie, of course. In this humidity, no one is simply *in* any neighbourhood. At first, I thought I'd send Khulamati to show her the rooms because I haven't been up there, you know, since Cecilia and then what the hell, I said, I went with her myself.'

The flat hasn't been opened in three and a half months. Two rooms, not small, equipped with the serviceable, handmedown furniture of the parents that Tripti, as often happens, has no wish to use and yet cannot give away. Suddenly the landlady, she goes across to the windows and, hoping that the bamboo chicks don't fall apart in her hands, rolls them up to let in the light. Musty, dusty, quiet, and yet the flat appears to be glad to have visitors after such a long time, its air is welcoming. She turns to observe Marie Claire—who retains her knapsack on her back—cast an eye around, open the door of the bathroom to see what that is like, peek into the kitchenette, fiddle with the tap of the kitchen sink and unbolt the door of the second room that gives on to what is by far the most attractive feature of the flat, its large terrace.

'Ohhhh—nice!'

It is. The terrace corresponds in size to the drawing room and dining space of each of the floors below; it is screened from the neighbouring houses by the verdure of the pipal, neem and gulmohar trees that were planted by the gate and along the boundary wall by an earlier generation. What is more, through gaps in the greenery, all that one glimpses, a bare twenty metres away, are parts of the spectacular sixteenth-century tomb of Abdul Rahim Khan-e-khana.

Is she *crying?* asks a puzzled Tripti of herself. I mean, the flat's nice but surely not *that* nice? She feels it to be a good time to initiate a discussion of the rent. Marie Claire's contribution to the conversation, as she wanders about the rooms again, touching a vase, moving a lamp a fraction, is desultory, almost disinterested. They settle on a round ten thousand rupees, to be paid in advance in cash, for the entire six weeks of her stay. Happy at the outcome, Tripti invites her downstairs for a celebratory cup of tea.

'Chai. A l'indienne. Certainly. Thank you. But may I join you in a minute? I just want to...' Marie Claire waves her arms about to encompass her new world '...experience these rooms by myself.' Tripti notices that her new tenant's eyes are brimming over again. An allergy, perhaps. Foreigners.

'I have my car,' offers Bhuvan next morning at the swimming pool of the Samrat, 'if you need any help with your things.'

'Oh thank you but I don't think,' counters Marie Claire, 'I'll be ready before lunch.' And then continues in the same breath truly as though the new topic runs naturally on from the old, 'Your sister is one of the loveliest women I've seen—' wincing as she pulls on her swimming cap '—at least here in India.'

Bhuvan is surprised; he finds the remark almost distasteful. 'Whatever does that mean? Wouldn't she be as beautiful in Paris?'

Marie Claire laughs, that guffaw that can be heard across the seas. 'Mon dieu, one has to watch out for your post-colonial sensitivity!' She glances at Bhuvan affectionately, slips into the water like an eel, 'Beauty is all context, at least for me. There is nothing French, you know, in Tripti's loveliness.'

One last subject Bhuvan touches upon when he has finished with swimming for the day and is about to leave for the changing rooms. He never dawdles by the pool or lolls about in sunglasses in a deckchair, sipping a nimbu-soda and trying to look cool. 'I don't need to tan, as you can see. I hang about in the sun for three minutes, I get heatstroke.' But that he pauses above her mattress, dripping water on the flagstones, makes Marie Claire take off her goggles and squint up at him.

'Yeah...just thought you should know before...you know... you sort of instal yourself above our heads...the last tenant, Cecilia—a lovely girl—Italian...wonderful...she...uh, early April...that ended in a bit of a mess.' He pauses, not quite knowing how to continue, waiting to be asked for details but Marie Claire says nothing, grimaces, puts her dark glasses back on.

Rue du faubourg Saint Denis, Paris, late-February, 1989. Bhuvan at lunch with Jean-Francois Arumugam and Milou (some six months after, knocking about in Provence with a Jean-Francois on the edge of one of his breakdowns, Bhuvan thumbs through his first French Tintin and understands—with a spasm of shame—where Milou has come by his nickname). Jean-Francois's father is Tamil, from Pondicherry, his mother Vietnamese. Bhuvan had not known that such combinations existed. Both Milou and Jean-Francois introduce themselves, laughingly, as out-of-work dancers (What exactly is an out-of-work dancer? asks Bhuvan of himself. Shut the fuck up and live and learn).

Salad and cold meats for lunch, red wine, cheese, bread that makes his gums bleed; for dessert, Khulamati's Mysore Pak from one of the two boxes that have survived the sardonic scrutiny of several customs officials in their long journey across Europe. Overhead, unwinking, a tripodal landmine, the white ceiling fan that Jean-Francois has actually carted back from Pondicherry, an unwieldy memento to remind him of his father's birth and his roots. Conversation has been more heroic than sparkling because Bhuvan's French is sort of worse than the ghastly English of the other two. FM on the radio.

'My daughter will join us for coffee, she said,' announces Jean-Francois, grimacing with theatrical sorrow at the rapidity at which the Mysore Pak is being gobbled up.

He is Franco-Vietnamese-Tamilian; now when he is blue, which is often, he feels a foreigner wherever he is. His father left Lawspet, Pondicherry for Paris's rue de Metz in December, 1948; parts of his extended family followed him in 1963. Jean-Francois himself goes back once every three or four years to reconfirm that once one has left home for good, even one's descendants are homeless everywhere.

Milou is from Fez, hooknosed, muscular, in a singlet despite the weather, extravagantly virile, as though playing at living in the pages of a Jean Genet. The two are the first homosexuals who live together that Bhuvan has met.

It feels unreal—but he is fascinated—an engrossing play—to meet, in flesh and blood, two men who cohabit more or less like husband and wife (with a child too—their damned dog, a gigantic beige sausage on pigmy legs, unstable, unfriendly, sedate, self-centred, bloody expensive. When Milou had been living in Marseille, he would shuttle up to Paris to tend the beast *each time* Jean-Francois waltzed off on a tour with his dance troupe). Bhuvan is a little mortified to find himself watchful of the usual hints of physical intimacy—a squeeze of the arm, a pat on the bum, a peck on the cheek, but there is none of that. The two seem delighted to play host to a stranger with whom they have nothing in common other than one absent acquaintance. Conversation for the time being centres on cares of a ponderable sort: for example, should Jean-Francois sink over a hundred thousand francs in a good many months in the dentist's chair and a full set of permanent false teeth? What did Bhuvan think?

All at once, on the FM, a welcome diversion. Marvin Gaye whinnying, *I Heard It Through the Grapevine.* All three know the song and hum along with histrionic gusto, glad to find, at last, the spark of a connection in their pasts.

I bet you're wonderin' how I knew
'bout your plans to make me blue
With some other guy you knew before
Between the two of us guys you know I loved you more.

Splendidly evocative the song, appears to be for all—

It took me by surprise I must say
When I found out yesterday

yet Bhuvan soon detects, watching the other two lipsync, happily and free of care, that they didn't know the lyrics *at all*—

Don't you know that I heard it through the grapevine
Not much longer would you be mine

and that they didn't care in the least; it was just another soul-thumping tune and this divine voice wailing away in a foreign language.

Oh I heard it through the grapevine
Oh I'm just about to lose my mind

And so it was okay to singalong in tribute, make an O of your mouth and tunefully emit some sounds that respectfully aped the heavenly original.

Honey honey yeah.

In discomposing—almost ridiculous—contrast, he could've written a brief essay, off the cuff, on the Motown Sound.

The centre of the world is how Bhuvan has read London being described. One would hardly have thought so in Paris. That is its first lesson for him. For a week, he has walked its boulevards and avenues, has resisted being overawed by the city of Haussmann; that determination of his has been made easier by his being distracted instead, being overwhelmed in fact, by the astounding irrelevance of English in that world. No one speaks it, no one needs to, no one wants to, it is of no importance, but it isn't even his language, why should he care! And then, of what use is it, asks he of himself in his dismal, ex-colonial, Anglocentric befuddlement, and to whom should I boast, here amongst these elegant creations in ashlar, that I can recite all of J Alfred Prufrock by heart?

Afterwards, he does realize of course that being a foreigner has its uses; he accepts fast enough that it is of minimal significance that continental Europe and the Indian experience of English would never connect. At the same time, while growing accustomed to being splintered, again and again, on his subsequent visits to Paris, Heidelberg and Barcelona, he, in bits and pieces, begins to view language itself, the diverse idioms of men, in a new, deferential light.

Meanwhile, it appears imminent that the second box of Mysore Pak is to be opened and Milou, grinning from ear to ear, has constructed, unaided and for Bhuvan's approbation, his one full, grammatically correct English sentence of the day—'In England, Europe is the light at the end of the Chunnel'—and while he is being applauded, the doorbell rings.

'Bhuvan—Cecilia.'

With Simon and Garfunkel yelling away in his head, Bhuvan exchanges smiles with a large, cheerful girl in Indian pyjamas and some kind of torn teeshirt. She dumps her enormous jute backpack on a chair and joins Jean-Francois and Milou in clearing the table and putting the cafetiere on. In the few days that Bhuvan has been in Paris, he's taken hugely to the poisonously strong Arabica that he has found the world drinking out of those diminutive white cups that look as though they've been pulled out of some elaborate doll's house. He's recalled, with amusement, the coffee that he's been quaffing back home for over fifteen years—one heaped teaspoon each of sugar and instant coffee churned into a mug of frothy, piping-hot milk. Mon dieu, the world *was* a mixed bag, wasn't it? He must remember not to ask for milk with his coffee. Jean-Francois would probably smirk in embarrassment and Milou would look uncertain. Then Milou, grinning again, would say, We don't *have* milk, would a Danone yogurt do?

It is Cecilia who has the yogurt with two generous squares of Mysore Pak mashed and stirred into it. Jean Francois and the other two nibble frenziedly—like squirrels pressed for time—on the Gianduia chocolate with hazelnuts—puro cioccolato—that Cecilia has brought them from Milan. Coffee lasts till four in the afternoon—by which time it is dark and rainy outdoors—primarily because she provides the required connections, the rapport. There is all at once no need of Marvin Gaye; she has taken over. She is warm, congenitally cheerful; her gaiety is intelligent and infectious, it irradiates her face and renders her mannish features beautiful. She speaks French with Jean-

Francois and Milou, Italian on the phone with an unnamed friend and Hindi with Bhuvan.

'Oh why did I choose India as my field of study?...Well, after the punctiliousness of social relations in Europe, the spontaneity and warmth of your hospitality is exactly like a brandy by a cosy hearth in a Prague winter.'

It is necessary, to give a sense of how odd that sounds to Bhuvan—and that for several reasons: one, the sentiment itself he finds quaint and almost palpably untrue; two, just to hear Hindi—accented but flawless—from the pale lips of a young female Caucasian feels totally bizarre, like seeing the Bolshoi without warning break into Bollywood bhangra, and three, the Hindi itself. He hasn't heard those words outside his High School Sanskrit class—it is necessary, to as it were provide a visual counterpart to how peculiar he feels, to render it in the original Devanagari:

यूरोप के अत्यौपचारिक सामाजिक व्यवहार के बाद भारतीय अतिथि-सत्कार की स्वतः प्रवृत्ति व तपाक का अनुभव ठीक एक प्राग के शीतकाल में किसी सुखदायी चूल्हे के निकट बैठ कर ब्रांडी पीने की अनुभूति से तुलनीय है।

'I am your guest,' he responds to her, smiling, in English, 'and as per the laws of Hindu hospitality, you cannot pull my leg.'

'But I was not!' She stops smiling, looks crestfallen, hurt, and continues in English, 'I just like to practise my Hindi as often as I can.'

'Then Hindi it will be/ Between you and me,' he returns in that language, eager to revert her to her gaiety, feeling almost criminally guilty at having been the cause of her fall from it, 'even though it isn't my mother tongue, and even though we would be depriving our hosts of the pleasures of our sparkling conversation.'

Cecilia turns to provide Jean-Francois and Milou, in rapidfire French, a précis of the foregoing exchange; Bhuvan uses the opportunity to visit the loo and thereby, for a time, to escape the Hindi.

Marie Claire shifts into the terrace flat on Saturday, at four o'clock, in a fine drizzle. The rain doesn't appear to bother her. She arrives on the motorcycle with a stranger riding pillion and playing coolie; he is Indian and has been entrusted with managing her bags, carrying one on his back and holding another squeezed in between him and her.

'Who on earth is that?' icily demands Tripti of the world in general and Khulamati in particular. 'The flat has been leased to her alone; she can meet her lovers in the swimming pool.'

She learns, while the hellos are being said and the bags carted up two floors, that the coolie is Rajan. He is bearded, from Bhopal, and less for those two reasons than for his manner of eternal, smiling contentment, does resemble rather strongly the late-lamented, dear-departed Rajneesh Osho. Behind his shining spectacles, his eyes gleam with serenity. Heaving the two bags up two floors does not disturb his breathing because he has clearly found the Answer. It lies in having no home, no address, no suitcase. He had one, large and maroon; it was whacked that very morning at Paharganj when he had put it down to turn and hug some long-lost type. Just like London Victoria, remarks a still icy Tripti.

They, she and her brother, have been invited up to the terrace for a housewarming cup of green tea. They accept because she intends to find out at the earliest whether the beard is part of the tenant's belongings. No, it seems at first and at second glance. All indications suggest that after the tea, Marie Claire will bed the beard and then pack him off. 'He will come and go,' whispers Bhuvan appeasingly to his sister,

'I guess, during the sleepiest part of the afternoon. Khulamati can keep vigil after lunch.' What impresses him the most is how quickly, within half an hour, the flat so orderly, silent, dusty and peaceful, has, thanks to the Marie Claire effect, begun to resemble an overflowing ashtray.

How does she do it? asks he of himself in wonder. The larger bag has been dumped on the mattress and opened; she has pulled some clothes out and heaped them on the carpet. She has then abandoned the idea of unpacking in favour of lighting her first cigarette on the premises, thus leaving her luggage to resemble a cotton pillow the stuffing of which has been attacked by a pack of gambolling puppies. The second bag, almost all the contents of which have been removed and piled up all anyhow around it in the search for her lighter, is, perched on the edge of the round table, about to topple.

'Could I use one of these bowls for an ashtray? But it seems a shame, they're so pretty.'

'And cheap. Cottage Emporium. The earlier tenant'd bought them. Perhaps you could try not smoking instead.' But watching Marie Claire, not listening to him, wander from table to cupboard to kitchen, observing the out-of-focus look, the exhaustion, on her features, Bhuvan adds to himself, She can't concentrate. She wants to be alone, to flop down somewhere to unwind, why did she invite us up in the first place?

She is the sort of person, though, who settles down quickly wherever she is. If she can't, she leaves—snap!—like that. By the evening of the first day, she looks as though she has begun to feel at home, in the humidity, in the rain, in Nizamuddin East. For, at eleven at night, long after an early dinner, she accepts graciously Khulamati's offer of a long, leisurely full-body oil massage.

Marie Claire has to strip for it. It takes close to an hour. The room is silent, lit by two lamps, its peace enriched by the whisper of the drizzle on the terrace. Yes, she admits to herself when it is over and Khulamati has left, that was strange but quite marvellous, that peculiar intimacy with some old unknown woman who murmurs nonstop to herself in a language I can't follow, whose hands know my body almost perfectly, almost as well as me, who makes no demands other than a modest fee of two hundred rupees. Yes, quite quite wonderful.

Khulamati is ageless, half-blind, almost gaga, and a temperamentally wonderful cook, maid and factotum. She sleeps every morning till nine or till whenever she is woken up. She murmurs obscentites to herself in Bhojpuri all day. She has been with the family long enough to consider whatever it possesses to be hers. Her needs being simple, she appropriates all that she requires—small change, Tripti's Mont Saint Michel soap, Bhuvan's Yardley talcum powder, a peg of rum. In her lazy, good-natured way, she bitches for hours about Tripti and Bhuvan to the servants of the neighbourhood and about their employers to her mistress. She awakens only when, during her massages, she finds herself giving pleasure to a supine form by skilfully kneading its inert flesh.

Marie Claire is the first white skin that she has massaged. That novelty is an added delight that does not diminish with the days. She kneads her up and rubs her down two nights a week, usually Tuesdays and Fridays. She babbles without pause during those sessions, liberally sharing both fact and fantasy, about her childhood in Motihari, her marriage at the age of nine to an alcoholic from Ara, how adroitly she had helped Tripti murder her brute of a husband, and so on. Marie Claire cannot follow a word of the Bhojpuri, naturally, but is lulled by its cadences and so helps the narration along by purring on occasion a word or two of encouragement.

She is told that she ought to up her sessions to three a week, that correct massaging—and she is in the best hands in north India—can painlessly and permanently depilate the pubic region—and that is so important from the point of view of health in the torrid zone. Also that her skin is too brown, too dry, because she burns herself too long in the sun every day. That is not good. That the earlier tenant'd absolutely refused, laughing each time, to get herself massaged, saying, I don't need it, I do hatha yoga regularly, then she—Khulamati here looking up a little, and indicating the ceiling with her raised eyebrows—left us so shockingly, poor girl, all because of that goat of a boy from Mussoorie.

During the day, as a rule, Khulamati babbles to Tripti all that she has gabbled to herself and to other people the night before. 'I told Marie-madam last evening about Cecilia-madam and that pink rascal from Mussoorie.'

'Yes, but did she understand?' responded Tripti, following, from tub to pot and from floor to floor, their shirker of a gardener like a Victorian sleuth his quarry. 'There is no dearth in Nizamuddin East of people like you. Who gossip in a tongue that no one can make any sense of. But if she understood, then at last she knows. Now she'll say that the rent's too steep and demand that I return her security deposit.'

Nothing of that sort happens, half-disappointing Tripti who finds short, sharp altercations with neighbours, tenants, vendors of fruit and brother to be good for her circulation. The massages continue; towards the end of the second week of her stay, however, the tenant surprises the masseuse by asking her to teach her the techiniques of her skill and secondly, whether she, Marie Claire the student, can practise them on her the preceptor, Khulamati.

The single loo in Jean Francois and Milou's apartment is long, low, narrower than a corridor and crammed with books in shelves painted navy blue. It has a tiny wash-basin tucked in amongst the racks, a WC at the far end beneath a plastic exhaust fan and alongside it, a—what Bhuvan realizes almost immediately must be—bidet. There are books on ballet amidst the lotions on the white table, and on the history of modern dance in boxes that sit one on another, all anyhow, on the floor. The wallpaper, even the little that one can see of it around the shelves, is overpowering, pinkish, with a motif of a thousand blond cherubs astride what look like courgettes. The door has no latch, bolt or lock. He doesn't like that. It is either accidental or perhaps they enjoy surprising each other in the toilet. He pisses hurriedly. He would've liked to rinse his penis—a ritual dating from the fearsome discussions of his adolescence, of the unendurable torment of foreskins that do not retract—but isn't certain whether and how to, in that loo. A tap on the door and Jean Francois enters without pausing. Bhuvan tenses just a bit. Jean Francois beams to relax him and starts to wash his hands.

'Thought you came in to see,' says Bhuvan drily, still a little offended at the unannounced entry, 'whether I knew—' nodding here towards the bidet '—what *that* was or whether, like Henry Miller's Hindu in a pension in Paris, I was going to move my bowels in the wrong receptacle.'

Jean Francois, drying his hands, laughs; he hasn't followed a word but is certain that it is a witty remark. He is in good spirits; it is the wine and the presence of Cecilia. 'She's off again, on a field visit to north India, to some small towns I haven't even heard of. You'll see more of her in the next few months than me.'

'That's wonderful. She's lovely.' But Bhuvan hasn't finished yet with the theme of an Indian in an Occidental toilet. 'You know, for me, the representative image is that of Peter Sellers in the film *The Party*—d'you know it? He plays a preposterous Indian and creates an enormous mess in the loo with the flush and the toilet paper and everything.' He, waiting for Jean Francois to show some sign of exiting the toilet, waves his hands about at the books surrounding them. 'One is—I am—certain to fumble here in this...dryness. I—we—tilt so towards water—ritual baths and open drains, peacocks in a drizzle, one river as mother and another as goddess, a billion mortals imploring heaven for rain.' Without ceasing his drivel, he makes the first moves towards squeezing through between Jean Francois and the shelves to get to the door. 'We could never juxtapose books and a water closet, because in books—even in a French translation of Mickey Spillane—reposes wisdom.'

Almost as though to shut off his vapouring, Jean Francois grips hard his forearm. 'I didn't want to ask you in front of Cecilia because that would embarrass her no end. You are to send me news of her. Please. I worry.' He smiles as though to show that he doesn't. 'She goes away to study Hindi in Mussoorie and for three full months, I've no news of her. No phone call, no letter, no address to which I can write. When she left, she had no idea of where she was going to stay. After one month of waiting, I phoned Tripti. Do you remember?'

She writes letters, explains Cecilia, like a diary. One, two paragraphs a day, to Jean-Francois, to her friends and others, describing what she is doing and thinking at that very moment, and the view from her window, the sounds from the street, and then, fragile that she is, she rereads what she has written and is dejected, crestfallen, at its quality. So she doesn't post her letters and yet doesn't have the heart to throw them away. See a thing through, Cecilia, Jean-Francois has often admonished her (and he himself so well-known in his circle for backing off midway even from an idea—leave alone an act—undertaken).

As with her letters, so with her life. She tends to abandon, go away from, events unfinished and encounters incomplete because she feels that she has in them come off badly, let herself down; and so she hears herself being told: Yes, move on, it's time.

They depart from the lunch together, she and Bhuvan. They both have the Metro to catch from Gare de l'Est. In that cold, dark and windy evening, their silence is companionable.

'Aren't you going to, like all your countrymen, ask me why, in Bologna, I chose, of all places, India as a field of study?'

'No.'

She laughs. 'It was sparked off in 1982 by the film *Garam Hawa*. You've seen it, surely?'

He doesn't see Hindi films at all but that is not the kind of detail that he wants to share with her. 'Who hasn't? An absolutely *wonderful* film. A landmark in the history of world cinema.' She giggles at the fulsomeness of the praise. He directs the conversation to safer ground. 'You learnt your phenomenal Hindi in Mussoorie? I didn't even know that it could boast of a language school that churned out pundits at short notice.'

'I stayed three months in fact with a family there. We spoke Hindi of course.' A sort of catch in her voice makes him turn towards her. Oh dear, are those tears, he wonders, or the cold? 'I have never met nicer people in my life.'

She met them, as people do in stories, serendipitously.

In the June of 1988, Cecilia Padovani left Bologna for Mussoorie—travelling via Milan, Moscow, Kabul, New Delhi and Dehradun for a little less than two days—less because of her passion for Hindi than out of an overwhelming need to flee her life. For four unremitting months, she had watched, week by week, her aunt die of leukaemia; that distress, itself cancerous, spread out and infected everything else in her routine and her relationships. Thus her new boyfriend galled her by his grasping and exploitative tactics and her two other flatmates, bickering constantly, compelled her all the time to take sides. It was demeaning and exhausting, life was; she had terrible headaches, she consumed nothing but coffee, why did nobody ever leave her alone? And at the university, the disinterest of her supervisor in her thesis was surpassed only by his deep ignorance of its subject. Yes, she needed to slip away, if from nothing else, then from the urge, getting more compelling by the day, to end the whole damn thing, slash her wrists, walk out of the fifth-floor window of one of the university buildings. But which one?

Her life followed her, of course, as the crow flies, right across those seven thousand kilometres. Her depression was both numbed by the increasing fatigue and imperceptibly lightened by the distractions, the novelties, of the wider world—the perils of Aeroflot in the passage to Moscow, the mountains, all chocolate and icing, bearhugging Kabul, the eternally crotch-scratching male population on the streets of New Delhi, its individuals small, misshapen, deeply uncivil, permanently on heat. They accosted her, without letup, with offers of bed and board and bed, from the moment she cleared Immigration till the night, in the April of the following year, when she tied tight her Fabindia dupatta around her neck and wondered whether it was time to move on. She could take care of herself but it was tiring. 'Doelaar doelaar change pound doelaar?' 'Sightsee sightsee me Qutb Minar you Kamasutra.' Leers, hisses, pinches, sounds of sucking. 'Light your fire baby night fever night fever.' I should be doing my thesis instead, she told herself in the impossibly stifling train to Dehradun, on why the males of north India scratch their crotches so often in public. Is it the heat? Ill-fitting underwear? Fungus? I am well-hung? Shouldn't they just wash themselves more often?

Three people in the train had given her the addresses of six different places to stay in in Mussoorie. Dayal Lodge, Hill Crest Guesthouse, Valley View Hotel, B & B My Guest, Batra

Boarding and Dining Hall, Summer Queen Residency. With her backpack and lugging her suitcase, she trudged to each one of them. She had not reckoned with the summer rush of tourists in the hill station. Three of the boarding houses were full; was she willing to share rooms? she was asked. Two she didn't care to enter because they looked too sleazy; at the sixth, the one closest to the Language Institute in Landour, the man at the counter, being too intent on eyeing her bustline, couldn't reply coherently to her questions. So at eleven in the morning, she sat on the steps of the Kulri Post Office, clasped tight her shins, rested her chin on her knees and wondered.

'May I be of help, Madam?'

Kaushalya Rawat is young, short, roseate, happy to be plump; she resembles a little the young Woody Allen, down to the thinning hair, and is keen to practise her English on a foreigner stranded in an unfamiliar town.

Some conversation, and then:

'No, Madam, I suggest that you accompany me home, have some tea and lunch, and then some rest. Then we'll see where in Mussoorie we can find rooms for you worthy of your status.'

Cecilia didn't say no because she wanted most of all a break from her wretched suitcase; she stayed with the Rawats, however, gratis, till the first week of September. At the end of ten days, she fumblingly offered Mrs Rawat—Auntie-jee—three hundred-rupee notes but the matriarch would not have been more offended had Cecilia stroked her derriere before the other members of the family. She would have stayed longer with them—for the goodness of her hosts had a benumbing effect on her thought process—but she woke up in time to see that her visa was going to expire in ten days.

The Rawats stayed in Barlowganj. Two rooms on the first

floor and an open verandah at the far end of which, in two separate wooden boxes, were located a toilet and in the other, a tap and an iron bucket that designated the family bathing space. They bathed far too often and always frightfully early. They found, like much else about Cecilia, her habit of washing herself only occasionally during the week both intriguing and amusing.

The single bed in the second room was taken up by the paralysed Mr Rawat. His wife slept beside him on the floor. On three steel trunks, one atop another, at the foot of the bed, sat the TV so that the poor man was at least not denied his entertainment. In the first room, between the work table that was also the dining table and the bench and the sewing machine placed on top of more trunks slept, on the floor, Kaushalya and her younger brother, Vikramsinh. To make room for Cecilia, he immediately moved to sleep alongside his mother in the second room.

The family survived on Mr Rawat's modest pension and the little that Kaushalya earned from the private tuitions that she provided to a handful of students scattered over town. Cecilia gathered from Mrs Rawat that it was high time that they married off their daughter—and the mother'd been scouring the countryside for the appropriate match, and receiving in their open verandah prospective parents-in-law from Dehradun, Haldwani and Kathgodam—but arranging for Kaushalya's dowry would eat up the family savings; besides, they would then also lose her income.

Cecilia gave the matter some thought. 'Why don't you marry Vikramsinh off first? The dowry that he will bring in will offset the outgo on his sister's.'

The Rawats laughed so much that Cecilia, after a minute or two, stopped grinning and began instead to examine her nails. They needed paring.

As she told Bhuvan a few months later in Paris, these were the nicest people that she'd ever met in her life.

'So what do your parents do? Are they both working?'

The Rawats are tremendously excited with the arrangement. It makes them giggle all day long. For, to improve her facility in the language, Cecilia is to speak to them exclusively in Hindi while Kaushalya and Vikramsinh, in order to better their English, are to respond only in that tongue. Such fun. The biggest gainer in this daily exercise is the man in the bed. Old Mr Rawat hasn't chuckled so much in months.

'My parents?' Cecilia's first impulse is to cook something up. That would certainly be easier than finding the equivalent words in Hindi. And then—glancing at Mrs Rawat's handsome features behind that bottled-up expression—would it even make *sense,* her parentage, here in this part of the planet? But what the hell, she is not going to belittle one world for the amusement of another; grinning, give it a shot, she says to herself, and begins. 'I have one mother and three fathers. My mother was very young when I was born. My birth, you could say, was not planned. My first, biological, father, passing through Europe in the summer of 1964, came from and went back to Boston in America. My second father, whom my mother married, is—was—is a curator of museums, from Milano, in Italy.' She smiles at Kaushalya trying to look expressionless. 'So that is where I grew up. Then they *both* remarried. My third father is a dancer who lives in Paris in France.' With a soft squawk of excitement, Vikramsinh rushes off to a trunk, rummages, returns with a tattered Oxford School Atlas in which, on a map of the world, he attempts to plot, like steps on a dance floor, the peregrinations of Cecilia's real and putative progenitors. 'I later divided my time between

Bologna where my aunt—who brought me up, really—lives—used to live—and Paris.' A momentary waywardness tempts her to add the rest of it, that her second father has changed partners again, that her third father is bisexual, that her mother has moved on too, but she desists. Mrs Rawat, she is sure of it, hasn't understood a word of her stream-of-consciousness Hindi but Kaushalya looks a bit goggle-eyed though.

It is Mr Rawat in his armchair, however, who is smiling and eager to learn more. 'And your religion, Cecilia beti? You are Christian and go to church?'

'Well, not really,' She grins, happy to discomfit again. 'No one I know goes to church anymore. Not regularly. Maybe at Christmas and Easter. My mother is Roman Catholic and my father Jewish.' She is not sure what Jewish is in Hindi, she tries Yehudi; it sounds crazy, as though she'd said, my father is Yehudi Menuhin, I'm on first name terms with him. 'So I don't know, religion, it's not a big thing with me.'

'And you are non-vegetarian. Even beef.'

It was what Cecilia missed most of all in Mussoorie, a perfect rare steak, all blood and juice on the inside. That was the stuff of her daydreams and when she lay awake at night, thinking of life in general and the death of her aunt, of all that had happened, what she'd left behind, what had hurt beyond bearing and what had given her pleasure, her thoughts would unfailingly stray to her aunt in the kitchen on many a sunny Sunday forenoon; salame di pollo, manza in insalata con radicchio, carpaccio con ravanelli, filetto in conza, fagiano all'uva. That had been one of her aunt's pleasures, to see faces light up at her table; give, keep giving, that had been her.

To catch her flight, Cecilia took the direct bus from Mussoorie to New Delhi. Everyone cried. She swore to look them up when she returned the following year for her field work; she wondered if she really would. She promised to write, in Hindi. Vikramsinh accompanied her all the way to the capital, a nine-hour ride through the heat and rain and humidity of the plains.

His presence was not unwelcome—he was a sweet good-looking kid—but it was totally unnecessary. But that was his way; he'd dogged her for three months; every morning, he'd walk her to her Hindi school in Landour and when she'd finished for the day, he'd be there, ready to walk her back.

'Don't you have your computer classes to attend?'

He would smile and lie in response. 'The servers are down,' or 'I finished early,' or 'The programmer has gone to Dehradun.' Everyone doted on him at home, so it seemed uncharitable to let slip, during her bilingual chats with the Rawat family, that the young man was happily wasting his days away, waiting. On the afternoons when Cecilia emerged from the Institute with Emile and Sasha, the two students from Reunion, and it seemed that she was going to stroll part of the way with them, Vikramsinh would suddenly do an about-turn and dart away and then, keeping safe distance, trail them; if at any time it appeared as though she were about to stop, look back and ask him not to be laggardly and walk with them instead, he would, in anticipation, pivoting on his heel, swing around and begin scampering away even before she could open her mouth. It's the French that we're speaking, she would say to herself in exasperation that was only half-comic, it's too foreign for him, and maybe also because my friends aren't white but I mean, what the hell, he must be at least twenty years old.

He was overwhelmingly solicitous during the nine hours to New Delhi. In the grime and chaos of the bus depots of Dehradun and Roorkie, he bought Cecilia ThumsUp and lemon soda, in the traffic jams after Muzaffarnagar, thick tea and Parle Gluco biscuits; sometime after Meerut, heart in mouth, he reached out and held her hand. She didn't even notice, that is to say, it didn't matter.

Of course they were running late. From Kashmiri Gate, they took an auto-rickshaw to the airport and asked him en route to stop at The Oberoi. The poshness of the hotel lobby awed Vikramsinh and made his steps falter. She couldn't care less, she had little time to waste, she needed a fix. Leaving him to struggle with her suitcase, she marched straight to the delicatessen and, ordering three hundred grams of smoked ham and four mince pies, began tearing at the packets and, with feral vigour, wolfing down the meats even before she had paid up.

'I'm sorry but it's been three long months. Try some?' she asked and without waiting for him to recoil in horror, added, 'No one will ever know.'

'Okay, thank you,' and gingerly accepted a mince pie, then a slice of ham, and finally another mince pie.

She was sated soon enough, she calmed down, the feline light in her eyes dimmed, she started to look sheepish and indeed, vegetarian. Back in the auto-rickshaw, she began to worry about tapeworms from the pig meat entering her bloodstream and swimming their way up to set up house in her brain.

'Do you think that ham was safe?'

He was so happy to be with her and away from home that not a word of what she said registered with him.

He had never been inside an airport before. She bought him an entry ticket. Mentally, she was already in Europe. They said goodbye at Security. He was trembling and in tears. She fought down an unexpected welling-up within her, held him by the shoulders and because she was certain that they would never meet again, kissed him on the lips.

Khulamati has become altogether a different personality. At night, bubbling and bashful, she is a coy mistress being rubbed down by a white masseuse; and daydreaming of the peace and pleasure of her massage sessions in which she both provides and receives such contentment and well-being, during her waking hours, she is mentally further away than she has ever been before.

'You don't notice anything but she's now a hundred per cent senile,' comments Tripti to her largely inattentive brother, indicating with a spoon the casserole of gelid mutton stew that Khulamati has brought out of the fridge and placed, not in the oven, but directly on the dining table. 'Hello, I'm talking to you, young man. It's those motorcycle rides that you've been enjoying of late sitting behind Marie Claire and no doubt encircling her by the waist. You can now think of nothing else. I've told you a dozen times already, it's a most unmanly thing to do, ride pillion behind a lady.'

Bhuvan doesn't do that so often, take a ride with Marie Claire; on a Saturday perhaps, when he doesn't have to go to work and they are both headed for the Samrat for a swim. Mindful of local custom, she offers to let him drive but he declines.

'I have a licence for a car but not a motorbike.'

'But what does that have to do with it?' She seems genuinely puzzled.

'Oh. Maybe we should take the car then.'

She rides the motorcycle in an exhilaratingly terrifying Indian way, beeping its horn without pause, racing through traffic signals when they turn amber, and without encumbering herself with a crash helmet. Over the days, after the swim, they fall into the habit of roving the green, sun-dappled avenues of Lutyens's New Delhi, of lunching at Café Bankura alongside the Cottage Industries Emporium. In the city of his upbringing, Bhuvan has never ridden before with a woman; it is a chastening experience.

Vicious, savagely venomous, obscenities are hurled at them, thick and fast, from passing cars and two-wheelers, even from pedestrians on the footpaths. Marutis and Padminis veer in frighteningly close to them, and along with the deafening music, disgorge abuse all the more spiteful because she is white. He is shaken by the discovery that their mere reversal of seating positions—and roles—on the motorbike can incite such lustful ill-will in complete strangers, a malevolence made more stark by its contrast with the lushness of the verdure of Lutyens's city, with its wide avenues and gardened roundabouts, its colossal trees of peepal, neem and jamun, those splendidly extinct colonial bungalows hiding behind armed guards and barbed wire, a city peopled by savages so uncouth that he squirms to admit that they are his countrymen, that he is to be counted with them.

She is amused at his reaction, and not a bit contrite or embarrassed; a woman's response, a now-you-know-what-it's-like-for-us-every-minute-of-our-lives-here smirk that remains on her features all through their Saturday lunch at Café Bankura.

Imperceptibly, Bhuvan is drawn into Marie Claire's strange, expatriate on-vacation life with the India Buggers. Her friends and acquaintances, almost all white, are journalists, unqualified teachers at the embassy schools and the cultural institutes, students of Indian music, dance and esoterica, freelance photographers, documentary film-makers, exporters of Indian bric-a-brac. A few of them hold undemanding, fairly lucrative jobs that help, for the time being, to resolve their visa problems. Several others pick up again as much from the largesse of Welfare in their mother countries as from their incomes in New Delhi. The Buggers travel frenziedly within India—Mandu, Orchha, Kumbalgarh, Diu, Kannur—places that Bhuvan is not at all certain that he can spot on a map;

when the country maddens them, they fly home to recover, in order and cold silence. But while here, with time, many of them nicely commingle their habits, their fixed ways, with local custom. Thus, at Nizamuddin, at pot luck, at an informal dance party that stretches into the wee hours of the third Sunday of August, Bhuvan enjoys idlis and alu chaat with ratatouille; the hostess is Spanish, at ease in her Kolhapuri chappals, salwaar kameez and Lacoste polo, smoking bidis with her plonk.

And Marie Claire is on the dance floor with Andre.

Bhuvan is privately quite relieved that Rajan, who seems to have been relegated to rainy Tuesday afternoons, has been replaced in public by this Andre who is an official in the Cultural Section of the French Embassy. His wife is Punjabi and his marriage is the way he likes his whisky, on the rocks. Bhuvan's heart sinks and becomes a hernia at all this endless effusion of wit. Andre is large and beefy, bespectacled, long-nosed, black-haired, he resembles a huge, rather good-looking penguin. 'Do you mind if Marie and I speak French?' is what he asks Bhuvan. 'All day long, I have to speak English when I have to deal with the Indian government.' He then sashays off with her to frisk about on the dance floor.

They dance splendidly, with both frenzy and grace. Bhuvan, who has never formally learnt how to dance and doesn't know anybody, any Indian, who has, is astonished that someone of Andre's bulk can shimmy and twirl so fluidly. They have to stop, abruptly, when Andre's glasses fly off his nose. They are instantly scrunched by some dancing shoes. The rock'n roll and shuffle and moonwalk temporarily stop while Andre retrieves his spectacle frame and the hostess, for the moment less at ease, arranges for that part of the floor to be cleaned up. When the dancing resumes, Andre decides to opt out, to relax on the rocks instead and Marie Claire coerces Bhuvan to partner her.

She is crying on the dance floor. She is rocking and rolling with tears in her eyes. Bhuvan leans forward and, feeling silly, shouts into her ear. 'Is anything wrong?'

She shuts her eyes, smiles, shakes her head.

'It isn't my dancing, is it?'

They walk home from C Block at three-thirty in the morning. He is about to unlock the door to his rooms on the first floor when he feels, partly because of all that burgundy, that it would be unchivalrous not to see her to her flat first. He mumbles something and climbs the stairs after her. She unlocks her door and turns to him. They kiss. It is their first. Her mouth tastes of olives and red wine.

The rooms are stifling and in their usual mess. Without glancing at each other, they lift clothes, papers, letters, books, apples and massage oil off the bed and dump them on a jumble in some other part of the room. In the process, something that he sees—but he doesn't recollect what till twelve days later when, on the eve of Marie Claire's departure, while helping her to pack, he comes upon it again—dimly nudges in him, and just for an instant, a sort of unpleasant memory, of the kind of event that one wants to efface from it. But just then they disturb a gecko on the prowl between the mattress and the wall. *Ahhhhhhh!* she shrieks in a sort of gasp. Giggling, he shoos it away outdoors.

Later, he smokes, after a gap of a decade and feeling that the occasion demands it, a post-coital cigarette.

For twenty-five years, once every six months or so, Marie Claire sends Bhuvan picture postcards from different parts of the world. The first unexpectedly is from Berlin, a shot of Roger Waters on the Wall. Bhuvan responds always but not more frequently, with cards that they bought together, in that strange last week of their brief affair, at NGMA and on Janpath. They exchange emails too but those are even more impersonal. They never meet again, in part because well, she moves on but also because she believes that he, deep down, is uncomfortable with what he once called her hardness of heart.

He regrets it instantly of course. He is driving her to the airport for her Austrian Airlines flight to London. He hopes that she hasn't heard, looks straight ahead through the windshield like a good driver should, waits for a few seconds to change the subject to one that will not depress them further—'You sure you have your passport? Ticket? Some rupees for overweight baggage, a cup of chai, that sort of thing?'—but she saves him the bother.

'In the mid-sixties,' she speaks slowly, softly, she pauses, it is a delicate subject to discuss with a foreigner, 'abortion was illegal in France. Unlucky women had to go to Amsterdam or London for the operation. And if they had no money? Knew nobody?' She looks down at her beringed fingers in her lap. 'Men never understand what women go through.'

Between late-February and April 1990, there in the terrace flat in Nizamuddin East, Cecilia sank into gloom every evening. Nothing went right. She had letters of introduction to Professors of History and Political Science in Delhi University and JNU; she could never meet them. Grinning with embarrassment, she trooped down to the ground floor every morning and used Tripti's telephone to try and contact them. The numbers, alternately, were first busy and then rang forever. After one exasperating week, she undertook expeditions to the two universities located at antipodal ends of the city. Vikramsinh accompanied her.

He was another cause of her low spirits. It had been quite a shock to see him, glowing, at the gates of the airport when she exited after having spent fourteen hours with Aeroflot. He had grown a moustache in the intervening five months but that did not make him beam any the less.

'But what're you doing here? How could you've known which flight I was on?'

He was very proud of his achievement and certain that she would be too. It depressed her terribly to learn that since all he had known were the city of origin of her flight and the month of her return, he, throughout the weeks of February, for hours and hours on end every day, had waited outside the airport for all the flights originating from Europe.

'But you're mad. Does your mother know what you're up to?' Tears had welled up in her eyes. It was her fatigue and his beaming stupidity, and the conviction that her visit would be a disaster because it had started so badly. 'I'm going to stay in Nizamuddin East with someone I met in Paris and whom I don't really know well. And when do you return to Mussoorie?'

From the sound of it, never. 'I stay in Palam Gaon.' Simpering, he gestured above and to the left of his head at the rosy future ahead of them. 'Just two-three kilometres away. Advanced computer course I'm doing. What is the address in Nizamuddin East? I'll follow on my bicycle.'

A city spread over more than a thousand square kilometres, with some of the planet's most dangerous traffic in it and this simpleton from the hills traversed it a dozen times a day on his cycle, zig-zagging through auto-rickshaws and public buses, zipping down the wrong side of the road to avoid a traffic signal, frequently letting go of the handlebars in order to comb his hair.

He was ready to be there outside Bhuvan and Tripti's house from morning till night. Whatever advanced computer course he was supposed to have enrolled in, it clearly did not insist upon any attendance. Recalling his family's kindness in Mussoorie, she had to bring him in, she couldn't very well leave him smiling on the pavement. She also had to mumble an explanation to her landlords.

Bhuvan was amused. 'Ah, I see. A beau.'

Beau he wasn't but he had his uses. All day long, while waiting to be kissed on the lips again, he, manifesting the family genes, made the world immediately around him a better place to live in. He arranged things, he, grinning, asked her for money and went shopping for essentials, he cooked some simple vegetarian stuff for two, he washed up after, he watered the plants. And outdoors too. He accompanied her to daunting places like the Foreigners' Regional Registration Office. He helped her fill up the form for an Out-Of-Turn Temporary Telephone Connection On Priority Basis. He in fact was the only company she had when nothing seemed to go right. He knew, for instance, which buses to take for which university.

The older Indian universities are vast, open, disorienting spaces. Each has well over a dozen busstops. Only an old, old hand skilled at avoiding reality, at enrolling for MPhil after MPhil after MA after MA, would know where to alight to go where. For Cecilia and Vikramsinh therefore, locating the right departments took hours.

'Oh Professor Jyotirgamaya has left to become HOD in BHU.' 'Oh Professor Vanamali is in Tokyo on sabbatical.' 'Professor Mukhiya? Oh but he retired last year.' 'Professor Rajhans? There is no one in this department by that name. You could try Sociology.' 'Professor Dev? He's European Studies, though. He'll be around somewhere. Or at home.'

'May I leave him a note?'

'Of course. In his pigeon hole in the Staff Room.'

'Where could I get his telephone number from?'

Cecilia left Professor Dev a page, explaining who she and her thesis guide back in Bologna were, what she was doing in India, and what sort of help—*'with your letters of introduction, I could meet the specialists in my field and the doors of university libraries would open for me'*—she was looking for. While she wrote, sitting on a bench in the March sun, Vikramsinh protectively stood by her, proud of the ease with which her Reynolds ballpen glided over the page.

The month of March slid by with even more facility. The linesmen came, six of them, to instal one telephone. The first person she called was Jean-Francois in Paris. The instrument rang and rang but no one picked up. She didn't like that, it didn't make her feel any better. Perhaps it's me, she half-joked to herself. Both here and in Paris, they know it's me calling and don't want to talk to me.

She wrote a letter to the Rawats in Mussoorie. She began in Hindi and then gave up and switched after the first paragraph. She gave it to Vikramsinh to post. He was a perfect errand boy, whistling and rushing off on his bicycle. Nothing happened though with Professor Dev introducing her to academia and those fabled university libraries. Every morning she dutifully dialled the number given her and the phone dutifully rang and rang and rang. Did she have the spirit to visit that wretched Staff Room again? Instead, she did what work she could with the suitcase of books, photocopies and drafts that she had.

Sundays were nice. For on Saturdays, Vikramsinh took long to say goodbye (giving Cecilia several opportunities for that farewell kiss) and went off to Mussoorie to return to beam only on Monday. Cecilia did nothing on Sundays but recover, just bask in bed in the silence. The entire house in fact was quiet because after an early lunch, Tripti and Bhuvan too always went off to play some serious bridge somewhere, returning only after dinner, exhausted and yet with the energy to dissect till midnight, in muted civilized banter, on the patch of lawn on the ground floor, over a couple of drinks and in the smoke of the anti-mosquito incense, the blunders in the other's play.

They were essential, those hours of calm on Sunday, for her introspection and her self-respect. This wretched thesis is not going anywhere, but maybe it's me, I'm just not the research type. Then she would hear her aunt say grimly: Face what you are, and what you started, and finish it; and then Cecilia would grin at the ceiling fan and respond, aloud, *Don't worry, I will because I promised you I would.* And then there would be lunch at some leisurely moment during those blessed hours of silence. She would get up, make herself some strong black coffee, and open the fridge and gaze with amusement and affection at all that Vikramsinh, before leaving, had prepared for her for the weekend. He was naïve and cute and his thoughtfulness in fact a blessing, she would think, undecided between the dal and the capsicum-tomatoes, but nothing was going to happen between them. For one, she had had enough of relationships for a while; for another—deciding on the dal and shutting the fridge—that all white women sleep around like crazy, she was just not in the mood to pander to that stereotype. She had sometimes seen that hope in his eyes. No, she was having none of that. And yet what she did like about him was that he did not importune or press, he was happy just to be with her.

The first of April that year was a Sunday too. She should have listened to her instincts and stayed in bed. She felt queasy all day. At two in the afternoon, not having been able to speak to Jean-Francois even once, she phoned Paris. A woman picked up. That was unnerving.

'*Maman?*'

Roger Waters answering the phone from the Berlin Wall would not have surprised her more. Her mother had travelled for half a day to arrive in time to take care of that damned dog for just a few hours. Jean-Francois was at a dance workshop in Dijon, he and Milou had had a tiff and Milou had left for Marseilles, perhaps never to return. Her mother understandably was in a foul mood; mother and daughter were bickering within seconds. They had last met at the funeral of Cecilia's aunt. They had bickered then too.

Cecilia, feigning someone at the door, disconnected quickly. She lay down again and waited for her heartbeat to return to normal. Her mother always had that effect on her, to hurt and be hurt, to ruin your life as you have ruined mine. Were she to be asked for the truth, Cecilia that afternoon would have said: This research is garbage, a pretext. I have travelled half way around the world only to get away from my past and the people who inhabit it. But as long as one is alive there is no escape.

At three thirty that afternoon, just when she had begun to calm down and not feel hunted, without warning and so suddenly as almost to make her scream with fright, a loud, rude rat-a-tat knocking at her door.

Her hand holding the cup shook, she spilt a little of the hot tea on herself; before she had time to react further, however, the rapping on the door, impatient, peremptory, was repeated.

She put the cup down on the floor and stared, mesmerized, at the door two metres away from her head. Whoever could it be? No one knew where she stayed, she was expecting nobody, she had no friends, certainly none who would invade her seclusion in the manner of the police on the hunt for a criminal, and Vikramsinh always turned up in the morning and never knocked, instead whistled one of his five thousand Hindi film tunes. She was not going to open, she decided, until her annoyance overwhelmed her disquiet.

'Who is it?' And then asked the same question in Hindi.

In reply, the rat-a-tat was repeated even more imperiously.

She was livid when she opened the door, ready to hit out.

A small, darkish bald man stood on the top step, grinning at her in a mirthless and peeved manner. His moustache was small and rectangular, his spectacles golden. He wore a grey safari suit with a design of stitched fish scales on the breast pocket. While Cecilia glared at him, he tried to sidle past her into her room.

'Yes please? You are?'

She had to let him in. It was Professor Arjan Dev, doyen of European studies at the Public Policy Institute at the university.

Not looking at her, murmuring to himself and continually and noisily clearing his throat, Professor Dev began to prowl around the room. He peered at the papers on the desk, examined the pile of books on the suitcase, seemed to sniff the air in an effort to unravel what she had been up to. She removed the cup from the floor before he could trip over it. Feeling slightly unreal, she opened wide the door to the terrace and put two chairs out so that they could sit in the open to discuss whatever that nasty bit of work had come for. When she re-entered the room, he was sitting on her suitcase and riffling, with great interest, through a diary that he had found in the jumble on the desk.

'How may I be of help, Professor Dev? Please put that down, that is my personal address book.'

He nodded as though to confirm her guess but made no move to comply, so she stepped up to him and snatched the diary out of his hands. He let go reluctantly, his fingers seeming to linger on its cover as though on the hand of a beloved.

'I noticed a couple of addresses in it that could be useful to me.' Professor Dev stood up and puffed his chest out because he needed more air for what he had to announce. 'I have been invited to Leiden for a conference on The European Idea of Caste in India. I am looking for people with whom I could stay in The Netherlands, who could receive me at the airport and all that.' Giving Cecilia a chance to jump up to make a dozen suggestions, he paused to swing his arms about and rock on the balls of his feet.

'I'm sorry, I know absolutely nobody who could be of help.'

He grimaced delicately at what to him was clearly a lie. 'How is that possible? As a European scholar, you would know others in the field in every major centre of the continent.' He continued to peer and squint into every corner of the room, occasionally glancing at her face to gauge whether her expression gave away the location of her most secret belongings. 'Networking, I assure you, is an integral part of scholarship.'

'Thank you, Professor Dev. But I'm from Italy and you've been invited to The Netherlands.'

'Then you give me some money. Dutch guilders or French francs. I will give you rupees at a good rate of exchange.'

It was extremely important for her to get him out of the room. She couldn't breathe with him hovering between her bed and her desk; it felt like a cockroach crawling on her skin. 'Why don't we sit outside and discuss it?' She moved towards the door to the terrace. He moved towards the address book on the table. She lost her temper. 'I have no money to spare. Just because I'm white doesn't mean I'm rich.'

'But that is just not possible. Are you not a Jew?' retorted Professor Dev, totally undisturbed by her anger, even disappointed at her lack of cooperation, her mendacity, and at the same time quietly triumphant like the player with the winning hand. 'I've studied your continent for three decades, my dear, and Europe has all along known its Jews.'

She did not speak, she couldn't. More than hurt and rage, an overwhelming sense of fatuity prevented her from thinking. This is my fault, for being who I am, this could only have happened to me. Her eyes filmed over; she stood still in the middle of the room and waited for more ghastly things to occur. Professor Dev asked her for a glass of water. She didn't seem to hear his request and did not move towards the kitchen. At last, after an age, still darting glances at the four corners of the room, continuing to half-smirk and half-sneer as though to say that he was outplayed but not trounced, down but not out, that he could well return better-armed and with more ammunition, he moved with abysmal lethargy to the door to the stairs. Cecilia followed inches behind him, seemingly ready to grab his elbows to physically prevent him from changing his mind. She stood on the top step and watched and heard him descend to the ground floor. She then bolted the door and rushed to the terrace to see him leave the premises. Naturally, he didn't bother to shut the gate behind him.

That sense of futility, of worthlessness, touched off in her by his remarks, his mind and his presence, did not diminish with his departure; instead, having once been given life, it grew by the hour, nourished by the bile of her own inadequacy. She spent the rest of the day lifeless on her yoga mat on the terrace floor, unaware of the play of the April light on the verdure surrounding her, of the pigeons warbling around the water tank, of the branches of the champa bobbing to the hopping of the crows. At some point—perhaps as dusk fell and the sky turned rapidly the colour of grime—POP! the bubble—or the balloon—burst and in a light so sharp that her head seemed to throb in its clarity, she could ask herself, *My god, what am I doing here, I don't belong here, this is not my country.*

Then, in a series of steps that calmed her by their appearance of logical progression, she concluded: Just pack up. Cash in on that open return ticket. Go back home. Once in Bologna—well, one thing at a time.

She ate nothing that night and fell asleep suddenly, out of exhaustion, with all the lights on. She woke up next morning with a terrible headache. That did not surprise her. Vikramsinh did not turn up at eight. That did. Well, one thing at a time. She took an auto to Connaught Place and spent the entire forenoon getting her plane ticket done. That made her feel lighter and yet at the same time more depressed. Once back in the flat, she shivered with nausea at the mere memory of Professor Dev; then she felt choked with foreboding at Vikramsinh's continued absence. He was dead, she was sure of it, crushed on his silly bicycle by some monstrous truck or bus or BMW. Otherwise, he would've phoned her. She willed herself to clean up her rooms, pack her things, put in order what remained of her time in Nizamuddin. She went downstairs to tell Tripti that she had to return suddenly to Bologna because of some academic foul-up on the part of the university administration.

'Administrations all over the world are the same, my dear. They exist to confuse and annoy and obfuscate. Never mind. When are you leaving? Friday, you said? I must ask Khulamati to make some Mysore Pak that you can take home with you.'

In the evening, in a room so orderly as to make her feel that she had already gone away, Cecilia sat down and wrote two letters. The first was to the Rawats in Mussoorie, brief, lukewarm, in Hindi. *Hope you received my earlier letter, I'm sorry I won't be able to meet you this time because I suddenly have to return home*, et cetera. She would make an effort, she decided, to post it before she left.

The second she wouldn't, she knew. It was practically a confessional diary written, on handicrafted paper from one of the Janpath boutiques, mainly to clear her head. She covered page after page in the days remaining to her, and she put everything in it: her aunt's death, the breakup with the boyfriend, Professor Dev's visit, Vikramsinh, his continued absence, how she was certain that he was dead, but surely it wasn't her fault?, the futility of her research work, how unintelligent it made her feel; and she put in her life in Nizamuddin, how nice in fact the flat was, and Tripti and Bhuvan were, everything, down to waving goodbye on some mornings to Bhuvan when he went off to the Samrat for a swim.

Imperceptibly—but inexorably—over the days, the diary changed focus to become a letter addressed to the last person from home that she'd spoken to, her mother. The adjustment in tone surprised her but not for long: well, why not, she argued with herself, smiling, especially since it was unlikely that she was ever going to post it. On Thursday morning, when she felt that she'd for the moment said all that she wanted to say, she even put the pages in an envelope and, just to feel that she had at last accomplished something, addressed it to Toulouse, the last mailing address she had for her mother.

On Thursday afternoon, she had visitors. Vikramsinh, Kaushalya and their mother, all fairer than ever, and all beaming.

They didn't stay long. Mrs Rawat in particular had wanted to meet Cecilia in person and, as she said, seek her blessings for the future because it was entirely due to her talismanic presence in their house that things had turned out so splendidly. For on Monday in Dehradun, Vikramsinh had seen and liked Aradhana, the only daughter of the widower Havaldar (retired) Brajmohan Singh Rathore. 'She's fairer than any foreigner,' butted in Vikramsinh, beaming and blushing.

And what was more, the personable Havaldar (retired) himself had been quite, quite taken with the Woody Allen charms of Kaushalya. So it would be a double marriage! and all the family worries over!

'And all because of you, beti. You do good to someone, God does good to you.'

They—all smiles—left after exhorting Cecilia a dozen times to attend, no matter where in the world she was going to be, the two weddings in November.

After their departure, she wandered from room to room and out on the terrace, without pause, till well after six. Then when the light began to fail, she switched off the ceiling fan in the bedroom, placed her suitcase, heavy with books, directly beneath it, stood on it, knotted her new Fab India dupatta firmly around her neck, threw its other end over the motor of the fan and trussed it tight. She wasn't depressed any more, she was fed up, just fed up. She kicked, with effort, the suitcase away.

At the airport, Marie Claire wants to say goodbye in the car itself but Bhuvan says that that is just not done in India. He deposits her at the gates and takes a good forty minutes to drive off to the car park, walk back, buy an entry ticket and locate her at the Austrian Airlines counter. He stands beside her in a queue that moves more slowly than mud. Her face is lined and haggard, the white roots of her hair show up markedly, she hasn't slept at all.

'Well, thank you once again,' she smiles, 'for all that you did for Cecilia. And for posting her letter to me. Otherwise we'd never have met.'

He grins twistedly, shrugs and just to make conversation, is about to say, You could've told us, you know, who you were, but looks at her face and murmurs instead, 'I shall concentrate in your absence on the butterfly.'

At Security, they kiss but not too passionately because the cops are watching. She walks away, he watches her go. She turns once to wave, he raises his hand in response. His attention is distracted for a second by the loudness of the saffron of a Sri Lankan monk; when he turns back, he suddenly can't spot any more her reddish-brown head amongst the other foreigners.

Sailing to Constantinople

(For Vijay Nambisan)

'You have been asleep, my dear sir, for a good nineteen hours.' Captain Taylor smiled indulgently—but without much humour—at his guest. 'Would you care for a cup of coffee? Or would you join me directly for dinner?'

On his makeshift bed atop the chest in the captain's dining cabin, the guest didn't seem to have heard. He sat slouched, staring at his fingers curled up on his knees like withered tongues. The captain waited a moment, then speared a generous portion of roast duck and had carried the fork towards the napkin under his chin when the guest slowly—like a bell tolling ponderously—began to shake his head—either in denial of the number of hours that he had been unconscious, or of the offer of coffee or the duck.

'Here be demons,' he muttered, his crimson eyes staring without blinking at the candles flickering on the table.

'Certainly, my dear sir, certainly,' agreed Captain Taylor comfortably and returned to his duck, roast potatoes and red wine. He chewed and sipped for a long minute and wondered whether he should launch, like a second boat from a sinking ship, another theme of possible interest to his guest. He reminded himself that he was in no hurry to make his acquaintance; they had a voyage of two hundred days ahead of them. 'We would have passed St Andrews' Church—or at any rate, that part of the country—within, I should imagine, some four hours of leaving port. Of course, one would have seen nothing from the ship. But I understood yesterday from Mr Fonseca Soares when he escorted you on board—' fixing his abstracted and inattentive guest here with an eye the expression of which was increasingly ready to turn less benign '—that you most particularly wished to espy a church on your day of departure from these shores. I may add, though, that the—as it were—igreja of Santo Andre was built by the Portuguese some two hundred years ago—late sixteenth century, I should think—whereas you, my dear sir, would be Church of England?' While waiting for confirmation, the captain masticated and sipped and smacked his lips. 'Quite likely therefore that there *be* demons within that edifice.'

On the previous day—one of the finest that the sailors had experienced during that month of January of 1807 anno domini—an hour before the *Christabel* was due to embark from Goa, its merchant owner, Mr Henrique de Castro Fonseca Soares, had come on board accompanied by a tall, slim, youngish Englishman whom he had presented to the captain as the guest of whom he had spoken the previous week. Captain Taylor had been busy, naturally, overseeing the loading and storage of the last of the raw silk and the pepper, the placement of the dunnage and the barrel chocks between the casks, going through the manifests with the mate and the purser; he could be forgiven for not catching the guest's name. He nodded pleasantly enough and while shaking hands and muttering a preoccupied 'welcome on board', merely noted how haggard the stranger's face was, lined, saddened and as though made wise by some frightful spiritual experience, the head of an old, old man on a young man's body.

'Come sir, Khan will take you down to the captain's cabins and see to your immediate needs. He is my personal man and worth his weight in—shall we say—cardamom.'

The guest's eyes had flickered with momentary warmth in acknowledgement of the deferential and personable Khan; he had then absentmindedly turned to the merchant owner to mutter his gratitude and his goodbyes. Captain Taylor noted that Mr Fonseca Soares, looking distinctly relieved, had urged the guest to descend to the captain's accommodation and rest himself after his exertions. Both merchant and master had then observed the two, servant and guest, negotiate the bales and chests, the rigging and the cordage, and the milling, shouting deckhands, to reach the hatch at the stern that gave on to the quarterdeck and, servant leading, disappear down it.

'It is considerate of you, Captain, to take on the responsibility of providing my guest passage to Europe.'

'It's your ship, sir, and I am in your pay. I'm sure that he will offer the surgeon and me some company during our long nights of calm. Of which I am entitled to expect some on this voyage—before Mogadishu at any rate and certainly before we cross the Line.' He paused because it had seemed that Mr Soares had wished to speak but the merchant owner thought better of it, nodded a couple of times, bid the captain good fortune and farewell and, accompanied by the attendant from his trading firm, disembarked. With light step, remarked the captain.

At that very moment in the quarterdeck, Khan put down the trunk and a valise on the bed atop the chest in the dining cabin, stood upright and had begun to explain matters when the guest stopped him by holding him by his strong shoulders and kissing him on the lips.

'Not a word. *Not a word.*'

'Sir.'

The guest took a turn or two about the confines of the cabin, stroked the bulkhead as one would the flank of a horse, examined the china in the cupboard riveted beneath the tongue-and-groove panelling to the left of the hatch, upturned the hourglass even though the sands had not yet run out. The cabin reverberated gently in the bang and thump of the ship's impending departure.

'I love all things, Khan, both great and small.' He smiled at the servant in a manner that caused the latter cautiously to step back a foot. 'I love man and bird and beast. That is what the dear Almighty enjoins us to do because He made us and loves us. So I, created in His image, love you, your cat and the lice in your hair. Do you find any fault in the argument?'

'God is most astonishing, sir.'

'So is your English, I do not hesitate to add.'

On surer ground here, Khan's tone became a little less irresolute. 'God is most kind, sir. I have spent over twenty years at sea. I began as a cabin boy and rose to be serang. I have travelled to the most distant lands through the most tempestuous waters. I—' An unexpected, enormous yawn from the guest, sustained for several impossible seconds, brought Khan back to the responsibilities at hand. 'But you would want some repose, sir. Would you require anything else from me?'

The other did not reply. He picked up his trunk and his valise, heaved them to the ground, then seated himself on the bed and began slowly to slide his posterior back and forth, glancing alternately to left and right to see whether the mattress slid with it. Khan paused uncertainly for a moment and moved to climb to the top deck only when it became clear that the guest had forgotten his existence.

The monsoon winds, blowing down from the north-east, were propitious for the ship. Its lateen sails, responding faithfully to the steady gusts, pushed the vessel evenly through the changing waters of the Arabian Sea. Fishermen's dhows and the junks of coastal traders became, with the days, sights increasingly rare. The older sailors, the seadogs, gazed at the stars, observed the changing species of bird and fish, watched the ocean ripening its colours—cobalt, gunmetal grey, olive green, midnight blue, aquamarine—and without the help of charts or compass or sextant, knew very well where they were.

'We be passing Socotra round about today or early tomorrow. There, some hundred nautical miles starboard.'

A fortnight into the voyage and the captain's dining table, intrigued and amused by the eccentricities of the ship's guest, took great pleasure in his company in part because it was so rare. He avoided the mate and the surgeon and the purser, particularly the surgeon, as one would the vectors of some fatal, contagious disease. The instant he sensed the approach of a habitué of the dining table, heard a salutation even as he saw a pair of lower limbs dangling from the hatch, he arose from his bed, readied his reciprocal greeting and in a moment, disappeared up the rungs the other had just descended.

'Stay, sir! A glass of wine with the curried goat!'

The invitation would inevitably hasten the ascent of the departing legs.

The surgeon, James Gillman, the guest interested particularly. 'I wish to examine his proclivities, you know, Captain, for the advancement of medical science.'

'Certainly, my dear James, certainly, if you can hold him to any lengthy conversation. Another glass of port, Khan, if you please, for the good Doctor.'

'He doesn't seem to sleep or eat, he paces the deck all night looking down at the water or far out to sea.' Gillman's eyes glinted with nervous, scientific excitement. 'His distemper—which may with equal propriety be named either Somnambulism, or frightful Reverie, or Epilepsy from accumulated feelings, is alarming. He falls all at once into a kind of Nightmare, and all the Realities round him mingle with, and form a part of, the strange Dream. All his voluntary powers are suspended; but he perceives everything and hears everything, and whatever he perceives and hears he perverts into the substance of his delirious Vision.'

'Khan has the most fabulous tales to recount of his conversations with him.' Recalling a couple, the mate chuckled drunkenly and glanced up at the attendant standing just behind and to the right of the seated Captain. 'Tell us once more, my good man, so what does he gaze for hours at the water for?'

Night after night, indefatigable like a man possessed, blind to the beauty of the moonlight silvery on the water, the guest paced the width of the stern deck—exactly thirty-nine feet in the beam—paused at the bulwarks, at both starboard and aft, to peer for several long moments down at the waters, so incandescent on the one side and blacker than night on the other, and not seeing what he sought, turned to retrace his steps, with frantic strides, as though believing that it—whatever it was—had slipped under the keel to frolic in the sea at his back.

Night after night, Khan, dispatched after the captain's dinner to see that the oddity did not fall—or jump—overboard or break a leg on a companionway, observed him in silence, enjoying in tranquillity all that the guest was oblivious to—the sea breeze on his skin, the tepid smell of salt in the air, the masts against the moonlight, the lookout high above, the distant laugh from the lower deck, the lulling creak and sway of the ship and overarching all, the vastness of the waters mirrored in the midnight blue of the skies. Slowly, with the hours, the figure moving on the stern deck, tireless, relentless in his pacing, seemed to blur into the ebb and flow of the moon and the waters, become as inevitable as the rhythms of the night. Khan, sitting on his haunches against the bulwark, dozed off, and several times awoke with a start to find the guest still pacing or a heap in a corner, unconscious to the world.

It was on the eleventh night after the ship's departure from Goa that the guest shook Khan awake to ask, 'And have *you* seen the water snakes? Or is it your deafening snoring that keeps them away? What is it, are they invisible only to *me*?'

Docilely, the attendant arose, yawned, stretched his limbs, looked over the gunwale at the black and opaque water and, still foggy, mumbled, 'Water snakes are not found in mid-ocean, sir. They are harmless and typically inhabit river banks, shallow streams and estuaries.'

'Don't lie to me. Do not try to fill my head with your heathen drivel.' The guest, greatly agitated, once more held Khan by the shoulders and turned him about to face him. To avoid the kiss, Khan swiveled his neck and expectorated into the sea with Gujarati gusto. 'They are splendid, many-coloured creations—blue, glossy-green, velvet black—one of the jewels of the Maker's handiwork and upon seeing them, springs of love gush from the blessed viewer's heart. But what would *you* know about that, infidel?'

'Very little, sir.' Khan tried to wriggle out of the other's grasp. 'But since I am awake and up on deck, sir, why do you not consider going down to bed?'

'Yes. Sleep. That knits up the ravelled sleeve of care.' Abruptly crestfallen, he dropped his arms from the attendant's shoulders, drooped in sudden dejection, turned, shuffled a step forward to the bulwark, looked out at the vastness and muttered in a voice of quiet desperation. 'There is no sleep for an unquiet mind. And amidst these immense waters, not a drop to drink for a sinner.'

'There is some good wine in the Captain's cupboard, sir.' Khan moved forward a step when it appeared that the guest was inclined a little too precariously over the gunwale. 'Perhaps if you care to descend, I could pour you a glass.'

'I could bite an arm and suck the blood but would that quench the thirst in my soul?'

Khan stepped back a pace and hid his own arms behind his back. 'No better time to sleep, sir, than when I am above you. That would be in line with your beliefs.'

On the second night of the ship's voyage, Captain Taylor had discovered, upon the guest surfacing from a slumber of over nineteen hours, that the latter desired that Khan the attendant share his bed.

'I adhere to Pantisocratic articles of faith, Captain,' he had announced, his crimson eyes staring at the master of the ship as though he were one of its privy seats. 'All humankind is equally precious to the Creator and I am bound by my faith to share with my fellow creatures whatever has fallen to my portion.' Not caring for his interlocutor's amused expression, he, punctuating his utterance with vigorous thumps on the makeshift bunk that he hoped not to be alone in, had elaborated, 'It goes against all that I hold dear to have another human being—equal in all attributes, in form and feature and design—sleep on the deck of the cabin that houses my bed.'

'You had best practice your Pantisocracy on land, sir, where you will find sufficient space for it.'

'Very well sir. I too then shall sleep on the floor.'

'You shall do nothing of that kind, sir, not on my ship.' The captain's playful mien indicated not that he was being jocose but that he would enjoy carrying out whatever action he intimidated the other with. 'If the rules on board the vessel are in conflict with your fantastic opinions, I shall only be too glad to put you in a rowboat that will enable you to return to Mr Soares. I shall not be able though to spare the good Khan to accompany you, sir.' He returned to chewing his roast duck with calm, equable relish.

'Very well, sir. You leave me with no choice. I shall then sleep only during the hours that the good Khan is at his duties.

And while he benefits from his well-earned slumber, I shall pace the deck in hail and snow and shine and reflect on the ways of this and other worlds.'

Thus to Khan's manifold responsibilities was added the duty, immediately on awaking sometime an hour into the second watch, of mounting to the stern deck to invite the other to descend to his rest.

'I cannot sleep, my good man, unless you procure for me some opium.'

Along with the cotton, raw silk, indigo, pepper and Chinese tea, the opium was stored in casks in the hold. The proper loading and storage of cargo in the belly of the ship was of fundamental importance to the correct distribution of its weight and consequent stability. Apart from the barrel chocks, vast quantities of dunnage in the form of wood shavings, chips, pieces of horn, coir and rattan were stuffed between casks to impede their shifting and under them to prevent any possible damage to their contents from the infiltration of water. The cargo, being the reason for the very existence of the merchant vessel, was frequently checked to make certain that all was well. Furthermore, deckhands repeatedly descended into the hold in search of cordage or straw or sea biscuits or canvas or carpenter's wood. 'It would not be advisable—indeed, it would be impossible, sir—to pilfer some opium from the cargo without anyone noticing and reporting the matter to the captain.'

'I credited you with more sense, my good man. I was thinking of your giving me some of your personal stock.'

'I have none, sir. Besides, if the Captain were to learn—'

'*Selling* it to me. For a gold sovereign.'

Thus it was that when the ship, well into the fifth week of its voyage, and blessed during that entire duration with propitious weather and a good wind, was less than five hundred nautical miles away from Mogadishu, its first port of call, its guest increasingly began to be found reclining against the bulwark in some obscure corner of the lower deck, providing amusement to the deckhands by the very theatricality of his presence, sharing their ribaldry without paying attention to a single word, oblivious to the filth and fetor of his surroundings, smiling beatifically at whoever addressed him, and responding in speech so slurred that the surgeon was moved to remark that he, the oddity, had not had the need to be indistinct to be incomprehensible.

'You do not see, my dear Gillman,' murmured the guest, addressing him with unexpected familiarity, 'what I see. I readily believe that there are more invisible than visible Natures in the Universe. But who will explain for us the family of all these beings? What do they do? What places do they inhabit?' A guffaw ending in a snort from the cook's storekeeper made the guest smile, glance in the rascal's direction, and raise his right arm to bless him in his ignorance. 'The Heathen Divines—the Hindoos in particular—have very much philosophized about the invisible world of Souls, Genii, Manes, Demons, Heroes, Minds, Deities and Gods. But of doubtful Value are all these Things.' In the swaying light of the horn lantern, he paused once more to stare at the surgeon, to learn from his expression whether his sharing his assessment of the very same things would prove to be of equally uncertain worth. The surgeon seemed to pass the examination, for the oddity continued, 'I know a little of the subject, sir, for I, with the assistance of Mr John Shore of the Asiatic Society at Calcutta, have studied the Hindoos for six long years.'

'And what conclusions, my good sir, have you arrived at?'

'That the goddess Kali, in one of her incarnations, roams these waters in a spectre ship. I need to see her, to experience the Unnameable so as to set my mind at rest. I have travelled the high seas for a decade towards that end but to no avail.' Suddenly listless, defeated, he reclined his head against the bulwark. 'Perhaps my soul will find repose only after I complete my researches upon our arrival at Constantinople.'

'Of acute interest to me, sir, are the subject matters of your speculation.' The surgeon arose to return to the light and fresh air of the upper deck. 'But duty calls. I need to report to the Captain that Billing here, though undoubtedly indisposed, has not yet, thank the Lord, displayed any of the symptoms of scurvy.' He looked down at the immobile guest. 'So you are to part ways with this vessel at Lisbon? I was given to understand that we would have the benefit of your instructive conversation all the way to Southampton.'

The guest's eyelids flickered momentarily. After a pause, he disinterestedly posed the question to the surgeon's departing derriere. 'Are we not bound then for Constantinople?'

It surprised no one, and amused every single soul on the vessel, to learn that the guest had boarded the wrong ship.

His error in fact rendered him even more popular, in particular since he himself seemed to see it so philosophically. To the jesting deckhands who accosted him all day with—'I smell kebobs in the air, sir! We be approaching Constant Pople!'—the guest, perhaps jabbing at a chest with a forefinger, would gravely elucidate, 'There be daemons, my good man, and there be Fate. The daemon of my individual spirit has played at dice with Fate and lost. It is evident to me, as the one chosen to be the battlefield, that I am not destined to reach Constantinople without struggle. So be it.'

And Captain Taylor, recalling the haste and happiness of Mr Fonseca Soares's departure from his own boat, correctly concluded that the mission of the merchant owner had been at all costs to unload his oddity on some unsuspecting master mariner.

'I should in all fairness add, Captain,' Mr Soares had disclosed over tankards of ale in the verandah of his mansion in Fontainhas on the Saturday preceding the ship's departure from Goa, 'that I am acquainted with your prospective passenger but as the son of an old and esteemed friend. The father, you are no doubt aware, as one of the Directors on the Board of the East India Company, is a weighty personality in our line of business.' Outside in the garden, a servant gathered coconuts and argued excitedly with another in Konkani. Mr Soares pursed his lips, and his forehead creased at an unpleasant memory, but he nevertheless continued, 'The son is harmless and utterly charming but, you will learn, not quite right in the head. Hasn't been for the last ten years or so. Not since his betrothed upped and married his father. And they wanted him to be best man. Can you imagine?'

In the days that followed, suggestions streamed in from all quarters on the best course of action for the guest.

'You could consider disembarking at Mogadishu,' cheerily proposed the Mate as he oversaw repairs to the planks of the orlop deck; a native of Riga, in fleeing from both poverty and prison, he had abandoned the land of his birth to find a measure of calm mainly in ceaseless wandering. 'You join there one of the traders carting his wheat up to Djibouti or even Alexandria. Then from its port, you hop on a boat crossing the Mediterranean. If you keep your wits and your weapon about you, you won't get robbed and you won't get killed and your soul should reach the city of your aspirations, mate.'

'It has also been known sir, for the last three hundred years, by another name,' offered the surgeon, tending to a nasty gash on the guest's forehead, the outcome of an opiated stumble on the stern deck. 'Istanbul is the heart of the Ottoman empire. That would affect whatever you are hoping to find.'

'I am in search, my dear Gillman, of the spiritual and mental descendants of Michael Psellus. Are you familiar at all with the doctrines of that luminous eleventh-century neoplatonist? And his masterwork, *De Daemonibus?* I thought not.' In disappointment, he jerked his head out of the other's hands. They followed it as it twitched from side to side to evade them. 'His beliefs—and the heirs who sustain his tradition—reside not in any quarter of any Mohammedan city but—' he tapped the side of his forehead that had not been receiving the surgeon's ministrations. The hands of the man of medicine grabbed him by the throat. '—here, in the psyche. And to *understand,* to see the relation between the Visible and the Invisible, between different forms, to grasp that a fish may be a daemon, and a bird a polar spirit, one would need the primary Imagination that I hold to be the living power and prime agent of all human perception and a repetition in the finite mind of the eternal act of creation in the infinite I AM.' His eyes filled with tears at the obtuseness of the man of science. '*I am.* So close—spiritually, phonically, metaphysically—to the Hindoo Om. Do you not see? Save me, does *no one* see the connections?'

Khan was not impressed by the disclosure of the guest's final destination. 'I have visited twice, sir, the land of the Ottomans. That is no country for old men,' declared he to the guest over a pipe shared clandestinely during the first half of the second watch. 'Four years ago, I was robbed of my bejewelled dagger—at knifepoint—one night in Kapalicarsi. Just behind the Beyazit mosque. And my magnificent turban too. And to think that they are likely to have been fellow Sunni Muslims!'

'Perhaps they merely wanted to see, you handsome man, whether the hair on your fine head was more grey than your beard. How old *are* you, Khan, if I may be so bold as to ask?'

The attendant did not know and didn't much care.

'I have known someone who was three hundred years old. Dreadfully skinny with glittering eyes. A tattered coat upon a stick.'

'A yogi in the Himalayas, sir, no doubt. But wearing a *coat?*' He returned the pipe to the guest.

'No. A sailor. He said that he had been the first to sail the Pacific. That would antedate Ferdinand Magellan, I remember thinking later while reflecting upon our meeting. In fact, I've done little else for the last ten years.'

In the gloom, Khan nodded sagely in acceptance of the wonders of the world and waited for the pipe to come back to him.

In part because of the attendant's seemingly inexhaustible supply of opium, the succeeding weeks were quiet for the guest. Rather, things did happen, events occurred, but mentally he remained far away from them, perhaps in some distant city of his own making. Outside the harbor of Mogadishu, for instance, when the rowboats were lowered for taking in fresh water and provisions, in particular umpteen baskets of lemons and limes and clementines to counter any outbreak of scurvy in the weeks to follow, and the natives in their dinghies surrounded the ship like the mob besetting Jesus, clamouring to sell their livestock, fowl, coconuts, bananas, tubers, grains, salves, baubles and novelties, the guest for hours observed the noise and bustle, the stir and hurly-burly, with remote, glassy eye. Then again, he slept through the passage across the Line and did not appear to hear when, upon his waking the following afternoon, Captain Taylor jovially welcomed him to the southern hemisphere of the globe.

Even the long-expected storm that overwhelmed the ship some two hundred miles outside Mozambique no longer seemed to mirror the turmoil within him. The squall drenched him, buffeted him against the bulwark of the quarterdeck—eventually knocking him senseless by making him slip on the planks behind the boom of the main mast—but it did not excite him. The hands, frantic with furling the sails and heaving overboard the anchor and lashing down the tarpaulins, let him lie in the rain for a couple of hours, carting him down only when he was soaked enough to go down with a grippe that confined him for a fortnight to his mattress in the dining cabin.

Thereafter the calm. Two months into the voyage, four thousand miles done, and one fine day in March, Captain Taylor awoke to discover that his ship had ceased to move. By the middle of the third watch, the sails had slackened, by noon the breeze had dropped to a hint of a whisper and the sea imperceptibly had turned to glass. The sun that had been warm and life-giving turned coppery, then bloody; the vessel seemed to have sailed into a painting or a poem, a world eternal but lifeless.

On the third day of that paralyzing immobility, the Moslem deckhands tied to the three masts little green paper flags on which had been scribbled praises of the Prophet. The Mohammedan seadogs amongst the crew suggested to some of their companions that they bathe in the ocean to cleanse themselves—and the ship—of the impurities that they had committed with their younger shipmates; only then—with the kindness of Allah—would the blessed breeze from the north return. The guest observed the tempers rise and the squabbles turn bloody, then the bodies become listless and the spirits sink into despair—all without expression.

'What's that you're up to, Khan?'

The attendant had laid out, on pieces of discarded map on the gunwale of the stern deck, portions of meat in little heaps that resembled offerings to a god. 'Oh, just arranging some leftovers from the Captain's table, fish and duck, for my old friend who sometimes drops by in this part of the world at this time of year.' Khan smiled while adding, 'It's good to see you, sir—after months—at last take an interest in the material world around you.'

The guest stepped forward to the gunwale and stooping, peered at the leavings with peculiar intensity. 'Your friend is a spirit, I take it. But in what form? Does it have *that* shape that I've waited to see for ten long years?' Without pausing for a reply, he abruptly straightened and in great agitation looked all about him at the cold blue heavens; he screamed his subsequent questions at them. 'Where *are* we exactly? How far from the Polar seas? Is it possible that at long last it will fly this far to the Cape? For *me?*' and again, without giving Khan a chance to respond and dropping his voice to a reflective, half-mad, murmur, added, 'It's grown wondrous cold.'

With a height of a little over five feet and a wing span of just under sixteen, and in colour an effulgent white more dazzling than snow, the albatross appeared with the sun at dawn. Uttering sharp cries and gliding through the mist on those enormous wings with the grace of some supernatural being, it circled the ship twice, three times before alighting to peck at the food on the gunwale. It being a bird of good omen and moreover the harbour—for most sailors—for the souls of departed India sea-captains, the watch was delighted to report its arrival to the ship in general and Khan in particular.

The news drove the guest into a frenzy. Oblivious to the world, he paced the stern deck for two nights and a day. 'Where are you!' he would scream at the icy blue sky. 'Reveal yourself to me!' On the third morning, not having eaten a morsel or sipped a drop for forty hours, he lost consciousness and collapsing, hit his head quite brutally against the edge of the roof of the master's cabin.

'It's important, my good sir,' said Captain Taylor, 'to distinguish cause from effect and see things with that imagination that endows the understanding with clarity. Now that you are calmer of mind, all passion spent, we would urge you to go back ten years to that wedding at which you were a guest, that event in your life that rendered you sadder and wiser and—not to put too fine a point on it—deranged you beyond any medical assistance.' He glanced briefly at the surgeon seated at his customary place at the dining table. Gillman, looking down at his notebook, nodded his approval of the captain's choice of words. 'So deranged as to be prevented from *seeing* with your imagination. *What exactly happened on that occasion?* I put it to you, sir: You were to attend a wedding at which you were next of kin and *you were prevented from doing so.* Is that not so? Reflect upon it! Whose wedding was it? In your words, sir!'

'My father's,' whispered, after a silence of close to a minute, the shadow supine on the mattress.

'I see. The bride being your mother?'

'No, my betrothed. Red as a rose was she.'

'With more than one gardener. I see even more. Your father did not remark upon your absence from the wedding?'

'He was furious. When I explained to him that I'd been detained by an old coot, an ancient mariner who had spun me a yarn about ice green as emerald, a ship with naked ribs and his fellow sailors having hung a dead albatross about his neck, my dear father began foaming at the mouth. *Have you even seen, you imbecile, how large an albatross is?* I cannot forget his question. He was so savagely livid that well, he disinherited me and forbade me to enter his house. Any of his houses. I could not laugh or wail.'

'With reason, my good sir. And your father's substantial wealth, upon his death, will now be made over to whom?'

'To my love.'

'Who, as you say, is like a red red rose. I see all. Is it not possible, I put it to you, my good sir, that she was also being tended by a *third* gardener? Possessed of a long grey beard, a glittering eye and a storehouse of voyagers' tales that would rival the Hindoos? An old codger well-travelled, well-versed in the black arts and the no-less ebon sciences, an acolyte perhaps of our contemporary Viennese physician, Thomas Mesmer and adept at employing his sensationalist methods? Who had been instructed by the rose to remove the thorn that lay in the way of her acquiring a fortune that would challenge the wealth of Constantinople? I put it to you.'

At that moment, no doubt to allow his primary imagination to better reflect on the new suppositions that had been put to him, the guest, with a groan, relapsed into unconsciousness.

Pleased with the acuity of his own analysis and at last, as a consequence, warming to his guest, Captain Taylor placed the capable Khan in charge of his recuperation. 'Get up on deck, go, take him with you, do your mumbo-jumbo and arrange for him to see that damned bird at close quarters. Else I fear that he might give up the ghost long before we reach Lisbon.'

The miracle occurred on the second day after the ship had left Cape Town and set her course for Sao Tome. Khan did his calculations and muttered his incantations facing Tristan da Cunha fifteen hundred miles to the south-west. An hour later, a dot appeared in the distant blue. The guest shuffled forward to the gunwale and, as mesmerized as he had been by his betrothed's third gardener, watched the speck grow larger and larger.

Nothing in his imagination had prepared him for the albatross.

On that first day, the bird stayed with the ship for a mere quarter of an hour, gliding, circling, beating its wings, uttering its wild cries, and at last, alighting on the gunwale a foot away from Khan, pecked at the offal in the palm of his hand. Speechless, breathless, with open mouth and transfixed eyes, the guest observed its every move and feature, the effulgent whiteness, the elegance of its wings, their prodigious span. Only when it was airborne and sailing away like a ship in the heavens, its wings pumping like enormous bellows, did he seem to descend to the world around him. He said nothing however, half-smiled at the watchful Khan and then, looking away at the now-distant visitor, abruptly became more pensive than ever.

The albatross returned at the same time, at noon, every day for a week. The guest was always there to welcome it. He said very little, he merely watched the bird, observed its closeness to Khan, the way the attendant cooed to it in Gujarati. The guest's physical and mental health, though, improved markedly with each visit of the bird. Then on the following Sunday, they waited all day for it. In vain. Khan, seemingly more dejected than his companion, muttered, 'It'll see us no more this year. We are come too far north.' The guest merely smiled in a resigned and heroic manner.

At dinner two evenings later, he sat down at the head of the table in the captain's chair—befuddling his host not a little—and announced to the assembled company, 'I thank you for your hospitality, gentlemen. I shall avail of it only till Lisbon. The sea holds no more wonders for me. Neither do the artifices of Constantinople.' He paused and the mate, feeling that the lull had a deeper meaning, raised his glass to him in a silent, unsteady toast. 'In my reveries of the last few days, I have remarked that my love is like a dark, dark rose. She is Abyssinian. Ebon as a rose is she. A celestial musician she is, heavenly with the dulcimer. From Lisbon therefore, I shall set forth to find her and unravel the secrets of the mountains and valleys. Across France and over the Alps and eastward, forever eastward. North Italy and the Balkans, the Black Sea and the Caspian, then the land of the Kazakhs. I see it quite clearly, that is the route to take. What is a journey without the imagination? And thus I shall at last arrive not at Constantinople but the ruined city of Shangtu. In Mongolia.' He looked around at the largely inattentive company. 'You are familiar with Purchas's account of his Pilgrimages? Then you know it as Xanadu.' He turned to the loyal figure who'd been gesturing to him for the last several minutes to vacate his chair. 'What say you, Khan? Do you not wish to accompany me?'

Robertus Heimric, Welcome Back

Upon turning twenty-four, Peter returned to the town that he had so abruptly left while practically a baby in his nursemaid's arms. He had then not even been called Peter; he'd been Robertus, but they'd altered so many things at that point—identities, possessions, habitations, vocations, towns—that a new name for an infant had been small change. He remembered nothing of that departure; his memories did not stretch beyond his turning three in their meagre lodgings at Hanover, and his playing in the mud with irregularly-shaped beads of glass.

Robertus became Peter in part in remembrance of his elder brother. One oppressively overcast day in June twenty-three years ago, the original Peter, then aged seven, had gone out to play with his friends and had forgotten to come back. 'The rat-catcher is going to show us how he sets his traps,' had said Peter to his younger brother's nursemaid before scampering off down the alley to join Hans, the two Johanns and several others whose names the nursemaid did not know.

The journey from Hanover took an entire day and utterly exhausted Berta. Peter Robertus had suggested to his wife that she not accompany him, that she stay back in Hanover with her mother-in-law for the one week or so for which he would be away. That Berta had steadfastly refused to do. She did not want to hurt her husband's feelings, he being a good soul, but frankly, his mother, with that perennially cloudy look in her eyes and her manner of chatting often with her vanished elder son, gave her, as she told her sister, the jitters.

'Be very, very careful,' Berta had been advised by her family and her neighbourhood. 'Never forget how powerful a witch your mother-in-law-to-be is. That is why her cadet son did not disappear along with her first.'

Robertus or Peter the Second, the good soul, having unexpectedly come into an inheritance, was returning to the town of his birth to claim it. 'Must I go?' he'd asked because he did hate the disruption and discomfort of travelling. Besides, he was apprehensive at being stared at by strangers with whom he yet shared an event in the past that not even God had been able to explain.

'Nonsense, of course you must,' had retorted his mother. 'Six acres of prime land and a two-storeyed house just off Bungelosenstrasse, why should we give that up?'

'But you've changed my name as a way of escape, I'm not who I was, maybe not who they think I am. Perhaps Aunt Clara has willed all that she had to Peter my elder brother and not me. And if he comes back to avenge my usurpation?'

Privately, he and Berta both believed that his mother fondly hoped that that was just what Peter the Original would do; indeed, that was why she insisted that her remaining son depart to claim his inheritance and thereby—perhaps—lure back from the past a ghost or two.

A distance of some fifty kilometres between the two towns, there were no cities in those days. They changed horses once on the outskirts of Springe. Mindful of Berta's condition, Peter Robertus twice told the coachman to take it easy because they were in no hurry; the coachman grunted on both occasions but seemingly not in response. To avoid conversation, for a large part of the journey, Berta kept her eyes shut and pretended to doze and Peter looked out at the fields of rye shaven of their harvest and thought about things.

He was the one survivor who remembered nothing. About his past, he thus felt clumsy and incomplete; at the same time, he sensed that the absence of memory in one so young had protected him from harm. Of the others who had not been taken, he'd been told that one boy had been blind, another deaf and a third had felt too cold. Of course he had never met any of them in the preceding twenty-three years. And no girl had survived.

'Had it not been for me,' Else his nursemaid would drone into his ears practically five times a day for two decades, 'why, you'd've vanished too, who knows. You were always crawling off on all fours after your elder brother and howling and screaming and biting and kicking when I stopped you from tumbling down the stairs or wallowing outdoors in horse manure.' Else would pause in whatever she was doing—clearing the table, hanging up the washing—to check whether her charge—older now and independent but still, she felt, her charge—looked properly abashed. 'In fact, had you not begun to choke on your porridge out of your usual wilfulness and spite, we would not even have been out of doors that morning. The weather was freakish that day, the clouds so oppressive.'

'Nothing would've occurred had the adults all—each and every one of them—not been in church that morning. That in fact was the first freakish thing to have happened.'

She didn't like it when he or anyone else commented on or analysed the incident of the Disappearance without acknowledging her—with a final phrase such as 'Isn't that so, Else?' or 'What do *you* think, Else?'—as a superior authority on the subject. She was the vedette, one of the few eyewitnesses, and felt annoyed that people should begin to forget that essential fact so quickly.

'It was St John's and St Paul's day that day, of course everyone would've been in church,' she sniffed at his obtuseness. 'I would've been in church myself had you not been so cranky that morning.'

'And where were they, St John and St Paul, that they saw nothing? In church too, is it? Or bathing in the river?'

It was dark when they crossed the Weser but the coachman seemed to know his way. The clip-clop of the horses' hooves on the cobblestones, loud in the dusk, prevented thought and instead aroused in them a nameless anxiety. A mist had followed them from the river. It being cold, there were fewer people about in those filthy, congested alleys. The horses took forever to draw up at the inn that had been recommended by the senior assistant of the apothecary at Hanover. Hanover itself seemed so far away. That, on hearing his name, the innkeeper would instantly know who he was and why he was there made Peter Robertus uneasy.

It started badly; the coachman was not happy with what they paid him. They reasoned with him for a few minutes and then, leaving him to his grumbling, entered the inn to ask whether rooms were available and whether someone could be sent to help with the luggage. The innkeeper looked them over, nodded and—there didn't seem to be any boys available, at least, they didn't see any—sent out with them a tall, taciturn young man strong as a stallion and more silent than the dead. In the forecourt dimly lit by a single lantern, the young man heaved the two trunks off the ground without uttering a word and stumped off to the room on the first floor that had been allotted to Berta and Peter Robertus.

Its fire made it feel warm and welcoming, it was otherwise simply furnished. Berta lay down and said that she felt too tired to descend for dinner. 'If they can send up some soup, cheese, bread and milk, would be nice,' murmured she sleepily to her pillow. 'If not, we won't die.' She was sturdier than a sturdy ox, a little plump and on the side of life.

'I'm hungry, I'll go down, I think.'

But she was fast asleep by then and even gently snoring.

Carrying a taper, careful not to stumble, hoping to eat a quiet dinner and go early to bed, Peter Robertus went slowly down the steep and narrow wooden staircase. He liked food, he liked eating, he didn't think much of conversation at the dinner table and was fervently hoping that there wouldn't be any. Chatter, he felt, distracting the humours from concentrating on the stomach, dissipated them instead through the mouth into the air. His heart sank when he saw the long dining table, for it looked surprisingly crowded for such a modest inn. He then noticed that none of the dozen-odd men in that tiny hall was eating; all conversation stopped, all heads turned towards him when his foot touched the bottom step.

'Robertus Heimric, welcome back.'

'I'm Peter now. Have been for over twenty years.'

'For this town, you'll always be Robertus Heimric. There's no getting away from it.'

Peter smiled appeasingly at the blur of faces and moved towards the soup tureen. A middle-aged man with red hair and close-set blue eyes abruptly asked, almost politely, and in a soft voice, 'And your mother? All well with her? Still feeding you rats' kidneys to ward off the evil spirits? You won't get any here, I can tell you.' Someone snorted. A second voice asked the red-haired man to shut up. The innkeeper's wife took off the lid of the tureen. How they all stared.

There was no sound save for the clicks of the ladle slushing about in the soup and beneath it, the chirpy crackling of the fire in the grate. Peter Robertus contemplated going up again with his bread and bowl and returning for a second helping when the townsfolk had dispersed and then wondered why he was eating when he wasn't hungry in the least, indeed, when he even felt a little queasy. The dog sleeping on the hearth suddenly sighed loudly in his dreams.

'You don't know me but your mother will remember me,' continued the red-haired man, stepping up within striking distance of Peter Robertus. 'When you meet her, you tell her, "Oh Mother, I met Kurt Weisser, and he sends you his regards." And she will exclaim, "How kind of him! Of course I remember him: he's the one who never gave up searching for our children." For months on end, through rain and sleet and snow, with lanterns and flaming torches, we, your father and I, all of us, searched the entire region, town, hill, vale, village, field, borough, province, digging in ditches and hacking through underwood for leagues in every direction, rooting about for any sign, any remnant, of his Peter and my Maria, my Hedwig and my Georg and all the other young'uns. All day long and far into the night, we shouted out for them and for almost a year, the hills and woods and lanes about the town resounded, echoed with the names of the lost children. It seemed then to some of us that Nature was looking for them too. We gave up everything else, farming and milling and our shops, to search, to *understand.*'

'And then my father died.'

'Yes, and then your father died,' repeated a short, bald man with a high-pitched voice, moving forward to the table and sitting down on the bench, 'but he was neither the first nor the last in the town to succumb to a broken heart.'

With Peter Robertus's single utterance, the ice seemed to have been broken; everything suddenly appeared less menacing and a couple of townsmen, muttering something about having to tend to their horses, even tramped out of the room. Slowly, the remaining locals, keeping Peter Robertus as the nucleus of the group, arranged themselves in various positions about the hall—on the bench at the table, against the stair rail, on the steps, by the wall alongside the fire. Peter gingerly began on his soup while they, individually and contrapuntally, in ruptured sentences, muttered oaths and lamentations left dangling in the air, started to reconstruct a narrative that they had evoked ten thousand times before. Yet each retelling seemed to ease the load accumulated since the last narration, and even stirred a faint, fresh ache akin to hope. Maybe they would get it right this time, perhaps they would resolve the riddle of imprecision; so they should go over the whole thing most, most carefully, with the finest of toothcombs, because once they got it right, the mystery doubtless would dissolve into the clear light of day, a key would turn somewhere, something would click open and at last the children, excited, laughing, at last they would return to Hamelin.

'On that day of St John and St Paul in June twenty-three years ago, the church service took longer than expected. Robertus's mother came out from it all wrought up because her husband made such a pother if dinner wasn't on the table at twelve noon sharp and she was sure to be late. They said their goodbyes to everyone at the church door and she scurried off home. At a quarter to twelve, just when she thought that she would be ready in time, she noticed the absence of her elder son and snapped with annoyance at Else the nursemaid, "I thought you were to keep an eye on him and see that he doesn't wander off with that Johann. Rush and fetch him from that rascal's house so that I can give him a piece of my mind before we sit down."

'Else returned at twenty past twelve to find the master of the house glowering at the meat that he was about to carve. Robertus's mother sat opposite him, in nervousness nattering away about the church service and complimenting herself, since her husband clearly wasn't, on how well the potatoes had been done. Else, a little flustered too at returning mission unaccomplished, brought the news that Johann wasn't at home either and *she* was late because she had gone on to Hans's house only to find *his* mother peeved and waiting for her son at her doorstep.

'Lunch was a silent and ruined affair and at two o'clock, the father was more cross than ever because he couldn't settle down to his afternoon nap till his son returned. At three o'clock, the mother told Else, "Put Robertus to sleep. Stay with him. I'm going to take a round of the town to get to the bottom of this not-very-entertaining game."

'She didn't have to go very far. She turned the corner into Rathausstrasse only to bump into Paula's parents. She didn't know them very well, Paula being a couple of years older than her elder son, but the expression on their faces, mirroring so acutely her own anxiety, obviated the social niceties. Paula hadn't come back home for dinner either. And neither had Willie.

'Feeling more sure of themselves when together in a group, they returned to the Heimric home to collect the father; he was at the front door, they didn't have to go in. As uncertain of where to head for as of what to do, silent, bewildered, angry and at last openly apprehensive, they slowly moved off towards Market Square and the rathaus. Their progress was not free of incident; it seemed that the entire adult population of the area—parents, elder siblings, aunts, guardians, grandparents, nursemaids, manservants—had foregone their afternoon naps to take to the streets. Their differing physiognomies were rendered similar by variations of one single expression of befuddled fear; across it, when they posed their questions, flickered a sort of hope in darkness. "Have you by any chance seen my Maria today?" "Joachim isn't at your place, is he?" "Wasn't Eva going with the others to see how the rat-catcher sets his special traps?"

'The group of citizens that gathered at the steps of the rathaus that afternoon numbered over a hundred.'

A ripple, a murmur, amongst the townsmen sitting on the steps in the hall of the inn caused the narration to cease. Berta, surprised at seeing the number of people in the room, had halted halfway down the stairs. Heads turned. The innkeeper's wife took a couple of steps forward to welcome her. Without getting up from the bench, Peter Robertus said, 'Come come Berta, we're all friends here having a chat. The soup is delicious, sit down and have some.'

Berta's face was puffy and her eyelids drooped with the need to sleep. Her hand slithered up and down the handrail of the stairs even though her feet didn't budge on the steps. 'Some cheese and bread, if that's possible,' she asked hesitantly, first of the innkeeper's wife and then, turning a little, of the taciturn odd-job man who had taken the trunks up. 'And some milk please.' The odd-job man didn't seem to have heard, for his expression didn't change and he didn't move from the door that led to the kitchen.

'Your husband is right. The broth is just the thing for you,' beamed the innkeeper's wife, 'in your condition.'

Berta slept badly; all night long, she seemed to hear behind the headboard the rustling and squealing of rats and was annoyed that Peter Robertus's deafening snores did not intimidate them. She got up twice, candle in hand, to check the dark corners of the room but saw nothing save dust. At nine in the morning, when Peter was ready to present himself at the Town Hall to initiate the process of conveyance of the inheritance—he was a little nervous—Berta felt swollen and exhausted and ached all over. To her husband, she suggested, 'You go on ahead. By God's grace, everything'll be fine. Perhaps later in the morning if I feel better, I'll visit the church to see the new stained glass window that they talk so much about.'

Even though the day was cold and gusty, Berta felt better outdoors. She exchanged greetings and smiles akin to grimaces with the few citizens whom she met while crossing Weiss's Common. For twenty-three years, the town had seen no births, how could any of its inhabitants look happy? There had been miscarriages, stillbirths and departures; bereaved parents had committed suicide and expectant mothers had left to have their babies elsewhere, in Luneburg, Springe and Braunschweig. After the deliveries, they had found it impossible to return to the town from which had vanished, that day in June, without a word of explanation from God or anyone else, a hundred and thirty of their children. How could they be happy? However could they breathe and talk and eat, sleep and buy and sell and go about their business without breaking, without buckling and disintegrating into lifeless flesh on the floor? However had they withstood the despair, borne the inconceivability of what had happened?

That June afternoon before the rathaus twenty-three years ago, Peter Robertus's mother at first had been befuddled by the sheer number of her fellow citizens milling about in search of meaning, then she'd been extremely vexed: Did they think that the Mayor, the councilors and the bailiff had nothing better to do that afternoon than to demarcate some boundary between the plots of two adjacent houses or adjudicate upon the course of a water channel? Then she'd slowly become bewildered again, and even calm in her bewilderment, when she'd realized that all her neighbours and fellow-townsmen, *all* those good churchgoers had children who had forgotten that day to return home.

Save for the fact that the children seemed to have vanished, nothing was clear. And that discovery was so enormously incomprehensible that it seemed to paralyse all of them; while waiting for the Mayor, the bailiff and other authorities, they gazed at one another's faces, looked away before their eyes locked and offered tidbits of information to the general mass of unknowing. One coachman said that he'd seen a group of kids going off laughing and chattering in the direction of Poppenberg Mountain. An ostler contributed that he'd overheard a dozen of them planning a bathe in the Weser and Hans's uncle, still wearing his leather apron, repeated the story of Else the nursemaid, namely, that his nephew and some of the others had been nattering away that morning about seeing the rat-catcher set his traps.

For Peter Robertus's mother, the rest of that day became a blur; and to that indistinctness, that dusk, was added, fuzzy film upon film, each succeeding day of the next twenty-three years. Search parties were organized and sent out to the surrounding hills, to the villages across the countryside, to the river. With lanterns and torches, horns, kettledrums, axes and spades, spears, swords, butchering knives and the Bible, on horseback, in wagons and on foot, they left as on a crusade, fanning out, once clear of the town, like the clumsily spreading fingers of an impotent hand. The teams of searchers looked determined and filled those left behind to wait with a sort of hope.

'They're in hiding, it's a practical joke,' said Erich's elder brother to the group around him, 'they want to frighten us. Wait till he gets back, he'll get such a good hiding that he'll wish he'd remained on Poppenberg till next winter. He's gone off, I told you—' turning here to his beer-quaffing companions '—to impress his friends by wearing my new boots for wherever they were tramping off to. Nothing doing, get out of my sight before I wallop you, you fool, I'd told him straight off. And yet he took them. Can you imagine, *my* new boots.'

On that first day, the search parties trickled in well after midnight, bone-weary and ready to drop, almost emptied of their distress by their exhaustion. They slept for three hours, ate and left again at dawn. For half the town, that became the diurnal rhythm of their lives for the next several months. They dredged the river, scoured the woods, explored the fissures and caves in the hills; they dug in ditches, sniffed around in graveyards, poked the roots of trees, excavated the boundaries of fields, they beat the vegetation to death. They enquired of the citizenry of the surrounding villages, they enlisted their help. They interrogated innkeepers, farmers, shepherds, fowlers, stablehands, ostlers, coachmen, vagabonds, journeymen, soldiers on the road, homeless wastrels and God. Before Him, as the weeks turned into years, they lit candles, kept vigils, whipped themselves, fasted, prayed and wept.

In a couple of months, the several search parties, wandering further and further away, had cumulatively covered the diocese of Minden, all of lower Saxony and finally stretched out beyond Westphalia; as far east as Moravia, East Prussia and Pomerania they'd gone, and a hundred and fifty kilometres north towards Hamburg, and north-west beyond Bremen to where the continent was stopped by the North Sea. The Duke of Braunschweig came to know of the baffling disappearance; at least his retinue was informed through the appropriate administrative channels. The Church too had to be told, particularly since the children had vanished on the day of Saint John and Saint Paul.

'And that rat catcher?' asked the Bishop of Fulda. 'Where is he?' and when no one answered, continued even more irritably, 'And the survivors? Don't they have anything to say?'

Berta was perspiring a little by the time she arrived at the church; the walk, even through those filthy alleys, had done her good. She was surprised to see, standing alongside the path that led to its doors, shifting sacks of meal from a barrow to a cart, the silent odd-job-man of the inn. 'Good morning!' she greeted him brightly; he smiled uncertainly but somehow not in response. 'Would Father Josef be here?' continued she, 'I received word this morning at the inn that I should find the time to drop by during the day.'

That was not entirely true. The innkeeper's wife had told Peter Robertus just as he was about to leave for the rathaus that the priest would be delighted to see him if he could find the time. 'I'm not going to the church, I won't, you know that,' he in turn had told Berta in the privacy of their room, '*you* go. If he asks, tell him I've gone to the devil.'

The odd-job man, appearing not to have understood Berta, continued to bend and lift and dump, raising in the process dust that in the light enclosed him like an effulgence. But she turned her head away because just then the church doors groaned open wide.

She watched the priest, hugging his arms as though he felt cold, pick his way through the pigs in his path towards them. He was a small man, Father Josef, and she was surprised by his comparative youth; she'd expected someone venerable but he looked as though he couldn't have been more than thirty. He displayed no surprise at seeing her alone; amidst the carts of hay, the snorting horses and the hubbub of the crowd headed back from the market, he was all politeness. He began to speak even before he reached her and did not stop till she had understood the burden of what was expected of her. All the while, his cloudy, unfocussed eyes, staring at her, seemed to see something else in her place.

'You know that your visit, Frau Berta—yours and your husband's—assumes enormous significance for our town. Late last night, Otto—' The priest raised a limp hand in the direction of the odd-job man '—brought me the news of your arrival. And I said to him, Do you think she'll visit our church? Or is she like her husband and her mother-in-law? They have not stepped inside the house of God in the last twenty years, is that not so?'

She glanced at him to see whether he expected a reply. But with his gaze moving from the cross on her necklace to a waggoner grumbling to himself about the quality of hay, through the whinnying of horses, grunting of pigs, the hubbub and confusion of that overcrowded lane, he continued, 'Your husband and I have met before. He won't remember. Neither do I. He must then have been less than a year old and I, in the April of that year, had just turned seven.' He suddenly hugged his arms again at that memory and, in a gesture uncharacteristic of a priest, kicked a pebble in his path. He seemed to address his next remark to the departing stone. 'He and Otto and I are to be counted amongst the survivors.'

There had been just three of them.

By the evening of that June day twenty-three years ago, when the town lost a hundred and thirty of its children, it had become clear to its citizens—and yet at the same time the discovery somehow had befuddled some of them even more—that not *all* the children had been taken; the infants and toddlers—those, like Robertus Heimric, too young to be left unattended, and those who'd remained indoors or had attended church service with their parents, they had survived (for several days thereafter, their mothers did not let them out of their sight even for an instant; they followed them to the privy and in bed at night tied one of their mutinous limbs to the corresponding arm or leg of some willing elder). And of those young ones not taken, some were totally unaware of what had occurred, and others—like the infant Robertus in his nursemaid's arms—remembered nothing. In fact, there had been only three boys who had seen the different groups of children, their playmates and schoolfellows amongst them, gambol off out of the gates of the town never to return. Blind Franz, deaf and mute Otto and little Josef who always felt too cold. *They* were the true survivors.

How they were interrogated, as by an Inquisition, for weeks on end.

What exactly did you see? What did you feel? Naturally, Little Josef bore the brunt of the examination, having to respond even when he did not know the answers; each time, the questions stopped only when he broke down sobbing or started to shake violently as a prelude to his epileptic spasms. The councillors' men waited patiently before continuing. *Was it just Peter who said that the rat-catcher was going to show them his traps? Or did others say so too? Think carefully. Which group of children did you follow? Why? Blind Franz says that he heard beautiful music from a wind instrument and that that's what tugged him forward. Did you not hear it too?*

You say that on the road to Poppenberg, you realized that you were in your shirtsleeves and so you turned back to fetch your coat. That is not quite clear to us. Were you cold? Or were you scared? Of what? And then you say that you were following Johann and Hans and the others. Why following? Why were you not with *them? We put it to you that you might have been aware that they would not return. What did you know that they did not?*

Inexorably, without believing his answers because they did not know what to think, day after day the councillors' men went on with their questions. *So you went home, put on your coat and scurried back to the road to Poppenberg. And then what?*

'Nothing! There was no one there!' replied Little Josef, in tears again at seeing the sustained befuddlement on the faces of his interrogators. 'My friends and the other groups had all disappeared, maybe into that cave on Poppenberg, I don't know. But they weren't there, I swear! It's true!'

What cave? There's no cave in Poppenberg.

Without wanting to, without even quite realizing what they were doing, the councillors' men were remorseless in their interrogation of all the three witnesses. Hour after hour, for weeks without end, they hovered and buzzed like flies around that one agonizing question. Those three boys had experienced the event and yet they lived on; how had they done it, what did they know that the others hadn't known? Whenever Little Josef was beyond their reach, either in seizure or delirious with sorrow in his mother's arms, the investigators, with desperate lack of focus and crueller than they wanted to be, recoiled on mute Otto and blind Franz. That music that only Franz seemed to have heard, yanking him onward, tugging him, tugging him out of the walls of the town, infuriated them beyond bearing because even Otto, who had lived since birth in black silence, confirmed, with loud, inarticulate groans, furious nods of the head and frenzied mime, that he too had felt it, that celestial music, on his skin, and like a vibration in the core of his skull.

'Celestial?' in a murmur demanded Father Landl of his flock. 'Or music infernal?'

It was only natural that, in their darkness and dolour, the good citizens turned to their church for succour. 'Save our son, Father,' begged Josef's parents when at their wits' end. 'If he has sinned, it must be venial, why is he being punished so?'

'He—all three of them—*have* been saved,' repeated Father Landl, 'I see in their eyes the look of Lazarus.' His next suggestion had the approval of the Bishop of Fulda. 'Give them to me. It is time that this godless town surrender its sons to the Lord and His church.'

'And that rat-catcher?' demanded for the hundredth time the good Bishop of Fulda. 'Has he returned to the nether world without leaving behind him even a hint of a trace? Or are we too scared to confront him face to face?'

He was an itinerant, a journeyman, the rat-catcher; wearing a coat of many colours, he'd arrived from the East. Yes, a funny foreigner from Moravia or Pomerania, no one knew for sure. For a couple of days, he'd been spotted amongst the down and out, the seasonal labourers, the vagrants and vagabonds who inhabited, around Sedemunder Gate, the filthiest, most insalubrious part of a poor and overcrowded town. Then suddenly one day in the middle of June, there he was in the market square fawning and proposing that, for some absurd sum of money, a guilder per head or something, he would rid the town of all its rats.

How they all laughed at him. 'A guilder per head!' chortled the Mayor, renowned in the entire district for his wit, 'That would make our rats more expensive than our children!'

The rat-catcher's blue eyes twinkled at the remark, his long nose twitched, he scratched with his pipe the lice in his blond hair, he continued to smile and persist with his offer. At last Mr Heimric, the father of Peter and Robertus, said in his no-nonsense manner:

'Look, Mr Rat-catcher, we are fine with the rats, and the rats are fine with us. If they are gone, how will our cats and dogs amuse themselves?' Mr Heimric was not a particularly religious man but something in the personality of the other pricked him into adding, 'Symbolic of procreation and the fertile earth, rats too are part of God's creation. We may let them be.'

'They are *too* fertile,' responded the rat-catcher, never ceasing to smile. 'I could restrict them, say, to half a dozen per household. As many rats as children. What do you say?' He continued to look amused even when his offer was firmly turned down and he melted once more into the mire around Sedemunder Gate.

Only to reappear a week later on an oppressively overcast morning towards the end of June; he'd at last changed his clothes, and was dressed as a hunter with a strange red hat. He chose the hour carefully; being the day of St John and St Paul, the elders were all in church listening to Father Landl. The rat-catcher wasn't alone; a group of adolescent boys from Sedemunder Gate moved out early in the morning and fanned out into the town. They were to rendezvous at eleven on the road to Poppenberg. They were paid for their pains.

For weeks thereafter, while day and night the search parties scoured the countryside of lower Saxony and beyond, some of the clearer-headed investigators, led by Mr Heimric, went ferreting around in the filthy alleys of Sedemunder Gate.

He didn't behave like a rat-catcher, we have our own, he didn't know the rates, what was he doing here? Surmise, rumour, suspicion. *Where did he stay? For how long? Whom did he meet? What was he up to for almost a week before popping up in the market square with his offer? What are you hiding from us in your head? Come on come on out with it. His outlandish proposal must have been directed at distracting us from his real purpose. How many of you've known that from well before? You want a hot rod on your genitals to jog your memory?*

Threats, inducements, recriminations, rewards. Amongst the labourers, journeymen, coachmen, stablehands, scullions and tramps, the investigators concentrated first on the families that had not lost any children. Why hadn't they?

But they made little headway. *No, so many riff-raff come and go, we don't remember any long-nosed rat-catcher. Yes, didn't I see him chuckling and filling Karolina the Free up with tankards of ale one evening? Or was that someone else? Maybe. Maybe I saw the rat-catcher and maybe I didn't. Maybe he gave me a guilder to keep my mouth shut and it will need two to get it to open. Maybe.*

Perhaps, mused Mr Heimric a couple of weeks before his death, we should look more carefully at those families that *have* lost their children.

In this long and sad history, the rest is conjecture.

But first the facts.

By early August of that year, what remained of the families of Karolina the Free, Widow Elisabeth and at least nine other inhabitants of the alleys of Sedemunder Gate, were hounded out of town. It was never established—and forever remained conjecture—that for want of money, they had sold, for the price of two guilders per head, their elder offspring to a recruiter—a child-catcher, if you will—from Transylvania; and that the recruiter in turn hired the bolder of those adolescents to inveigle, induce, incite as many other children as they could to join them on a long, long journey to a better life elsewhere. No, that was never established; had it been, those vendors of the young would have been lynched, impaled, burnt, instead of being hounded out.

And the children, it has been conjectured, would have led that better life—into which they *could* have been sold—almost anywhere in the known world; toiled in the warehouses of the port of Hamburg, laboured in the docks at Bremen, settled newly acquired lands in Pomerania, sweated blood in some distillery in Braunschweig, scavenged as scullions in some mansion beyond Cologne, drudged in the mercantile houses of Lubeck, set sail as deck hands for distant Constantinople. The vastness of that known world was forbidding; in it, nothing was certain save the emptiness, the numbness that the children had left behind.

What does it mean for the children of a town to vanish, for nature to lose its continuity? Empty rooms, silent spaces around one's heart, no chatter from the commons, no laughter in the streets. Because it didn't end there, with their vanishing; the childhood of the remaining children went with them. And with time, those left behind grew up into a sort of hollow adulthood; others left the town, some, like blind Franz, died.

Two years after the disappearance, almost to the day, he slipped into the Weser for a bathe and forgot to emerge. Mute Otto, who was with him that afternoon, explained, by means of his frenzied moans and incomprehensible gestures, that Franz had been unable to bear any more that music in his skull. Because they all believed him to be not quite right in the head, no one accepted Otto's story; they concluded that Franz's death was an accident, a footnote in the tragic history of their town.

In that walled silence bereft of music and festivity, it was deathly, at the age of ten, to ache day and night for one's lost companions, to see them in nightmares being fed upon by ghouls, to feel ancient with fear, incomprehension and sorrow. Little Josef was not alone in believing himself to be going mad. With the passage of the months, the wildest theories, the most outlandish suppositions, kept gushing—like blood that would not be staunched—out of several minds unhinged by grief. In May of the following year, for instance, Mrs Heimric asked Clara, Josef's elder sister, whether she had noticed that the population of rats in the town had declined significantly.

Yes I have. For Nature too is in mourning. So many rats drowned in the Weser, remember, just a few days before Easter. Why should they wish to drown when they can swim?

Nature in mourning manifests its formidable and complex force in ways as unexpected as God; it is as frightening and difficult to read. Impossible to tell when it is sorrowful or malicious or angry. And over what? These notions surfaced to torment the town anew in September of the following year when a shepherd's dog, rooting about, found, beneath that magnificent oak at the fork of the path at the base of Poppenberg, a child's skull.

Identity unknown and impossible to establish but the moss on its bone was fresh and living; it detonated once more into vibrancy all the nightmarish befuddlement, the affliction and agony that, exhausted, had for some months begun to droop into some sort of death.

There is not much more left to tell.

Mrs Heimric, after her husband's death, packed up and departed with her household and remaining child for Hanover where, in memory of her loss—and in hope of starting anew—she rechristened her son after his lost brother.

Twenty-three years later, Clara, Little Josef's elder sister, left, upon her death, and at the suggestion of her brother, her considerable property to the only son of her first cousin.

The lost children passed into legend. They have remained alive, in song, fable, fairy tale, myth and poem, for over seven hundred years. Rats were directly connected with them for the first time only a full two hundred and fifty years after the event. The children deserve better.

And yes, Berta Heimric liked both the house just off Bungelosenstrasse and the personality and persuasions of little Father Josef. Overcoming her own trepidation and sustained by her mother-in-law's nervous, enchanted support, two months later she gave birth to twins in that very house. The babies, a boy and a girl, hale and hearty and screaming from Moment One, shattered forever the silence of the town, and thus it was that, slowly and laboriously, in ones and rare twos, the children returned to Hamelin.

Girl

'Morning Sir!...Do you remember me?'

'Uh...Oh *hello!*...Kalpana of course! I wouldn't've recognized you! How time flies! It's been—'

'Eight years...yes...Found anything interesting?'

'Of course not. These end-of-season sales are really meant to display the junk that no sucker's bought for years...And you? You must be working? Job-hunting? Or doctoral studies somewhere?'

'In Paris. Yes.'

'*Oh.* Did you know French in school?'

'Look, sir, if you've the time, of course—could we just slip around the corner and have a coffee or something at this new place that's come up where Empire Stores used to be? If you're free, of course.'

'Tea for me. My stomach can't take coffee anymore.'

Across the table, they look at each other, glance away, do not speak.

'In fact, I changed schools.'

'I'd heard of that. You weren't the only one.'

'Yeah...We were all in the Ninth when it happened and after the Tenth Board Exams, my parents asked, Do you want to continue or what? And I thought, what the hell, maybe a new beginning would help—Would you be very offended, sir, if I smoke?'

'Probably. Do they even allow it here?'

'This is an ashtray, isn't it?'

'It looks more like a mosquito-repellent-incense stand to me. You began smoking in Paris?'

She shakes her head vigorously. 'Though it's the most beautiful city in the world for smokers...I've been smoking since school. In fact, Raveena and I were puffing away at our morning cigarettes that Friday when we got the news. It was about seven something I think and we sidled out from behind the auditorium and I heard—'

'You'd better have your chewing gum fast. Shrek's looking for you downstairs.'

The History teacher is large and physically overpowering, with a pomegranate of a nose atop a heart of gold. She is in the quadrangle, watching—but clearly with her mind elsewhere—students enter the school and, in groups of twos and threes, go up the stairs to class. 'Has she some in? Have you heard from her yet?'

'No, ma'm...Oh it's seven thirty already! She's late! She'll be on her way.'

'Would she be coming in at all? She wasn't well.' Shrek's eyes avert Kalpana's gaze and dart askance towards the gate and then left in the direction of the Book Store.

'Wasn't well?' repeats Kalpana stupidly. 'But she was fine yesterday, Ma'm. We were all together planning her birthday party.'

'Yes...but then she went off to Simla, no, and there was that road accident just before Chandigarh.'

'Road accident?' Kalpana watches in a daze Shrek's eyes behind her spectacles slowly film over and her features crumple up like a creamish kitchen sponge. Shit, it's the stink of cigarette smoke on my breath, that's why she's crying. 'Simla, Ma'm? When did she go off to Simla?'

'You are her best friend.' Shrek takes off her spectacles, holds them up against the morning light and, with a patterned handkerchief that resembles an Anokhee napkin, begins to clean their lenses. Without her glasses, her eyes seem to brim more freely. 'Never mind about Simla and Chandigarh. Go to class now, it's almost time.'

Puzzled but not yet apprehensive, Kalpana, furiously chewing her gum, takes the south stairs. Methodical that she is, she goes over in her head the tasks that she has set herself for the day. One: try and avoid Chikna so that she does not have to return his iPod before the summer hols; two: pretend that she's seen the last episode of *Friends* even though she had to miss it because of her wretched dance class; three: remember to give her Forever 21 miniskirt to Aarushi that very day to take home so that it escapes her mother's eagle eye when she checks what unsuitable things her daughter plans to wear for that grand birthday bash next week; four: remember to tell her that spaced-out Shrek thought that without telling anyone, she'd dashed off to Simla the previous evening; five: download *Dangerously In Love* before the sleepover—

On the first-floor landing, criss-crossing it without pause, not so much walking in his agitation as hopping, furiously passing his mobile phone from right hand to left and back again, his features pale and befuddled, his mouth beneath the down on his upper lip an O of incomprehension, is Chikna. He falters in his pacing on seeing Kalpana, the phone clatters to the floor. 'She's dead. Oh my shit, she's dead.'

The teacher orders a masala chai for himself. Kalpana changes her mind about the coffee and asks the waiter to make that two.

She waits to see the latter's back before lighting her cigarette and pushing the burnt matchstick into the mosquito-repellent-incense stand.

In the classroom and outside in the corridor, the girls are crying and the boys are determined not to. Chikna tries a thousand times to call her cell phone. *The number you are trying to reach has been temporarily switched off,* says the recording, slowly and clearly and speaking to the mentally retarded, over and over again, first in Hindi and then in English.

'I never could pinpoint, sir, either then or now, exactly when and how someone said that day—or who it was who *first* came in with the news, except that it was early, within the first half-hour that Friday morning—perhaps it was D-Bottom—you remember our Class Teacher?—a lovely gentle soul—leaving the room suddenly and then returning after a bit but walking very slowly, uncertainly, as though afraid of losing her balance and then just pausing—framed in the doorway, looking at us but not saying anything—perhaps it wasn't her—but anyway suddenly it was in the air and on everyone's face—that not only was she dead, yes, but also that she'd been *killed.* Murdered the night before.'

Chikna's phone is much in demand. The girls want to call home and speak to their mothers. D-Bottom silently and generously allows Aakangsha, Mehr and a couple of others the use of her mobile. The girls sob and snivel into the instrument. Those mothers who live nearby, understanding nothing beyond the fear in the whimpering of their daughters, get into their cars and rush to school. Others demand to speak to D-Bottom. There are moments when the Class Teacher has her own phone at one ear and Chikna's at the other.

When the mothers turn up, they find schoolchildren wandering about in a daze, in groups of twos and threes, in the corridors and the quadrangle and on the stairs. The Principal—Black Chomchom to her students—grants permission for the children to go home. Some of the girls do not want to be alone in their boring houses on a hot day with nothing to do but think about a classmate's murder. Aakangsha, Chanchal, Mehr and Kalpana want to go to the victim's house and see their best friend for the last time.

'No, we shouldn't do that now,' murmurs Kalpana's mother, looking as though she has just got out of bed. 'That is not a good idea.' She in fact has already been to the victim's house and met the parents—her golfing friends—and seen the body.

The walls of the child's room were a riot of blood. The girl, eight days short of fourteen, lay in her bed covered by a white flannel blanket. Her skull had been crushed and then her throat slit. Her blood had soaked through her pillow and the mattress and dripped on to the floor. Her once-beautiful head of hair was partly covered by her favourite tote bag. Sharing her bed were Bart Simpson and her other pet toys. On a side table lay some money and her iPod, its headphones still attached; only her mobile phone had disappeared. That remained missing for five years till the police, in their leisurely way, finally found it in Bulandshahr, eighty kilometres east of Delhi.

Kalpana's mother's first thought, alongside the immediate and lasting, distancing, disorienting numbness, is of the sleepover that her daughter and some of the others have been planning for the weekend. That will not be necessary, she thinks, they will never be able to clean up this mess in time.

'Maybe you could visit later,' she says to the girls. 'Because they'll first have to take the body for a post-mortem—' glancing in turn at the four uncertain faces '—to establish the cause of death.'

Aakangsha, Chanchal, Mehr and Kalpana get into Kalpana's mother's car and drive to her house. Kalpana's mother phones her boss and explains why she won't be going in to work that day. The girls dump their satchels next to the shoe rack and stand about in the drawing room. Kalpana switches on the TV even though she is only allowed to touch it between seven and nine in the evening. The girls slowly sit down. The murder is already on every news channel.

Over and over again, the screen shows the exterior and interiors of their friend's apartment. The camera catches acquaintances of the family, neighbourhood busybodies and TV folk wandering about and in and out of the flat while placid policemen, ready to be interviewed, stand by and watch. No area appears cordoned off and out of bounds. Everyone has opinions, everyone, under the benign and soporific eye of the police force, touches, tramples over and effaces clues. The anchormen breathlessly, in a dozen different ways, rehash the few facts that they know. Girl. Was to turn fourteen in eight days. Only daughter of affluent dentist parents. Murdered in her bed last night. Servant, male, missing.

'*Servant?*' ask the girls of one another, stupidly. 'Which servant? You mean that grandfatherly guy?...He's *disappeared?...* Like, how?...'

The servant is from Agrakanchi in Nepal. His passport photograph, magnified several times, is suddenly all over TV. The channels whip the scanty information on him to death. He is just seven months old in his job of cook and factotum. He is remembered in the neighbourhood as being mild-mannered and, on the whole, unexceptionable. He has at least one wife and several grandchildren back home. He is of middle height, has a moustache and, in his photo, looks inoffensive and vaguely well-intentioned. He was last seen last night by the parents of the victim. This morning, after discovering the body of her child, the victim's mother did phone the servant; someone picked up but did not speak, immediately disconnected instead. Who was that? And where *is* he?

Chikna phones. We want to light candles on her desk, all of us. You babes would want to come back for that, no?

Aakangsha, Chanchal, Mehr and Kalpana want to stick together all day. Kalpana's mother agrees to drop them back to school. 'Take more candles from the kitchen with you, she says. In case there aren't enough. 'Then I'll come back and just be with the parents for a bit, okay?'

Chikna phones again. He is more incoherent than usual. The reason for his outrage is clearer once the girls reach school. They learn in the corridor outside the classroom that Principal Black Chomchom has conveyed to D-Bottom and the other teachers that the school will not have any memorial service for the dead girl until what exactly happened the night before is clear to all.

'I mean, how weird is that?' asks an indignant Chikna of the sky surrounding his outstretched arm and his mobile phone as he takes a selfie of himself and Malini against the parapet.

'So does that mean,' asks Kalpana of LifeSkills and D-Bottom, holding in her hands the two packets of a dozen each that they've brought from home, 'no candles?'

'Well, perhaps you all could light them now,' gently suggests the Life Skills Teacher, who is new and has to be mindful of hierarchy, glancing every now and then at D-Bottom to confirm that he has chosen his words correctly, 'and that could be taken to mean that they were lit before you all got to know of the decision not to have for the present anything in remembrance.'

D-Bottom herself switches off the four fans. Kalpana doesn't want to take out her matchbox; fortunately, LifeSkills has a lighter. Without the fans, it is swelteringly hot in the classroom but the students, some fifteen of them, don't mind.

One by one, they light candles and place them on their absent classmate's desk. It's a bit of a squeeze because the incline of the desk doesn't accept any, only the flat, top portion does. They look nice, however, the candles, the smell of burning wax reminds some of the students of Deewali, they feel better. They are for the moment quite content to sit around in the heat and gaze at the burning desk and imagine, behind the flames, a figure, crouched over an exercise book, pen scratching away on a page, looking up on occasion, shyly flicking her hair off her forehead and smiling.

Of course it is Chikna's phone that breaks the spell. *Washing powder Nirma, washing powder Nirma,* sings its ring tone. 'Switch off your bloody phone,' hisses Ujjwal. Chikna answers it, listens, then announces in a voice not quite his, 'Oh my shit. They are taking the body away now for a post-mortem. They've bundled her up in some sheets to cart her off to some horrible filthy place where they'll—' his voice breaks '—cut her up to find out the cause of death.'

'I still have, you know, sir,' Kalpana pauses to pull on her cigarette with the urgency of an underwater swimmer who has come up for air, 'her pink Mango teeshirt. That's what I was thinking of in class that morning while watching those candles on her desk burn, that it looked like a birthday even though it was a deathday, that you give gifts on a birthday, so was it okay to retain gifts on a deathday. I never ever wore that pink teeshirt. Just kept it in the cupboard. In Paris and Amman and Nairobi. In any case, whom to give it back to?'

In the afternoon of May 16, 2008, Chanchal, Mehr and Kalpana, so scared that their calves flutter as they take the stairs, visit their late friend's apartment. Aakangsha has backed out. She phones Kalpana at two forty-five and blubbers between sobs. 'I just don't feel up to it...I was never part of the Awesome Foursome...none of you ever let me be...and now that she's gone, I don't want to take her place...I really just want to lie down and shut my eyes and not open them again.'

The neighbourhood, the TV-and-newspaper swarm and groups of ghoulish strangers continue, in that prodigious heat, to drift around and in and out of the apartment. Unable to be still, the parents, out of focus, bleached by shock, mobile phones at their ears, wander too from room to room, parrying questions, avoiding suggestions, circumventing thought. The policemen, still waiting to be interviewed, are fewer in number because the Prime Minister is due to visit that part of the world the next day and they and their dog squads have been detailed to go and sniff around elsewhere. Some of the women of the vicinal houses have moved in to sweep and swab and wipe out all residual traces of the crime.

The front door is wide, wide open. Chanchal, Mehr and Kalpana sidle into the drawing room and, wanting to sit down, almost rush for the vacant, three-seater sofa; they position themselves on it carefully, as for a job interview. People, familiar and unknown, wander past them without pause. Whatever it is that the girls expected, it is not this. For she has come back from her filthy post-mortem and is lying down on the divan two metres away from them. From neck to toe, she is swathed in sheets that were once white but are now the colour of dirt. Her eyes are shut, her mouth half-open, her skin is the shade of a page of their government-subsidized Hindi textbook. It is the first corpse in their lives.

They are frozen on the sofa. Her parents, in their wandering about their apartment that feels so violated, so burdensome, finally spot the girls and grimace a smile of a sort of recognition. Wordlessly, they hug their dead daughter's best friends; wordlessly, they all break into tears.

The cremation takes place at the end of that first day, in stifling heat, at the Noida crematorium. From the school, only D-Bottom and LifeSkills are present. Kalpana stands behind her mother in the shade of an amaltas tree and dully, in a disordered way, feeling uncomfortable about not owning up to possessing the pink Mango, wonders how it is possible that someone with whom she had such a catfight the previous day, whom she in tears had called a slut because all the boys liked her more, how she, now all lifeless and wrapped up like a loaf, is before Kalpana's very eyes, being slid into an oven.

The masala chai arrives, tepid water in a fancy cup, a tea bag, frothy milk in a jug. The cup is disconcertingly asymmetrical. The rim at its handle is two centimetres lower than that on its opposite side and the dip in its saucer—where it is meant to sit—is not at the centre but close to one edge. That is not what LifeSkills wants. He is a traditionalist; to him, a good masala chai is a heady brew that, stewed over the fire, tastes less of tea than of sugar, cardamom and cinnamon, and that is served in a cup that resembles, not Audrey Hepburn's hat at Ascot, but a self-effacing, ordinary bloody cup.

About such matters, Kalpana turns out to have similar views. Further, she is the new Indian woman and not inclined to take things lying down. Summoning the waiter, she explains.

'This tea bag thing I can make at home. Why should we come here and pay so much to dip dip dip in a cup that looks like the toilet bowl of my old doll's house?'

The flustered waiter takes everything away and, hidden behind the counter and following the instructions conveyed by the wriggling eyebrows of his superior, ferociously dunks the tea bags in the frothy milk. The nuisance out of the way, the face that Kalpana turns to her ex-Life Skills Teacher is angelic.

'I was to leave that week for Paris to spend the summer

vacation with my father who—about a month before, I think—had been posted at our embassy. I slept every night before my departure in my mother's bed. The first few days, none of us slept alone. None of us, in fact, slept at all. Mehr—do you remember, sir, the others of the group, Mehr, Chanchal, Chikna, Aakangsha?—of course you do. Mehr in any case shared a room with her sister but she didn't sleep a wink for weeks on end. And Chanchal—I remember—slept with her parents and it was her father's snoring that helped at night to keep her mind off the murder.'

The next day is Saturday and the first of the long summer break. Kalpana wakes up late because she could doze off only at five in the morning. It is in fact her mother's voice—high-pitched, distraught, emphatic—on the phone with someone, that, and her mother saying—'Will you hold on? I'll just shut the bedroom door'—and the door clicking shut—that series of unusual morning events that actually dredges the girl out of sleep. Dazed and trembling, with the fear of the previous day rising within her like nausea, she watches the shut bedroom door. What filters through it to the daughter are not the words that the mother is saying but the tremor in her enunciation.

Kalpana is aware that her dead friend's parents are to leave that morning for Haridwar by car to immerse in the Ganga their daughter's ashes. She learns soon enough that within a few kilometres of their departure, they are asked to return. Back home, the father goes up to find out why, the mother waits in the car with what remains of the daughter. The father learns that after an entire day in which they have ambled all over the flat, burping and standing at ease at corners to watch their superiors being interviewed by TV, the police constables have finally broken open the lock to the terraced roof of the apartment and found on it, rotting and swollen in the heat of May, a second corpse, that of the missing Nepali servant.

The father is asked to identify the body. The face of the corpse is bloated and horribly disfigured and in any case, the father is in no condition to identify anything. He phones his wife in the car to ask what kind of teeshirt the servant had been wearing the evening before. 'Did it have New York written on it?' She can't immediately remember and briefly wonders at the question.

Kalpana sits before the TV the entire day. Aakangsha and Chanchal are deposited by their parents at her house at different times during the forenoon. They join Kalpana before the box. The girls do not register much in the hysteria, just the essentials. Girl. Murdered. Servant, male, prime suspect, thought missing. Well, missing only from the apartment. Murdered on the roof, actually. A blow to the head and then the throat slit. One TV anchorman, short, fat, bespectacled, bearded, having shrieked nonstop for hours, has lost his voice but is not prevented thereby from drawing—mouthing—conclusions for his audience. Four inmates of this house of horrors, ladies and gentlemen, girl gone on the sixteenth, servant found today but most likely gone within minutes of girl. Same injuries to the head and neck, same manner of going. What conclusions are we to draw, ladies and gentlemen? Just what is going on here? Two down, two to go. Are the perpetrators still in the apartment?

'My parents are packing me off to Bangalore day after tomorrow,' murmurs Chanchal without taking her eyes off the screen, 'to spend time with my cousins. I mean, what purpose would that serve?'

'This servant guy,' asks Aakangsha, only to have something to say, to hear her own voice, to test it for tremors, 'has been bumped off because he saw or heard something, right?' For the twentieth time, TV shows the body, shrouded in a printed bedsheet, being carried down the stairs to the waiting van. Everyone is either wearing a swineflu mask or holding a handkerchief to his nose. Aakangsha tries to remember when she last exchanged a word with the corpse. She can barely recall his features. The magnified passport photograph that fills the screen with the frequency of a word from the sponsor does not aid her memory in the least. He'd just been someone who on occasion opened a front door and then stood aside smiling as you walked past him to your friend's room. 'So what's this bearded creep saying? What's he trying to insinuate?'

'I don't want to know. Last evening, some other creep said that the post-mortem showed no sexual assault or rape.' The words roll off Chanchal's lips almost without a hiccup.

The police force might appear clueless and somnolent but they have been in truth as active as hounds. For, on the twenty second of the month, just six days after the murder, they hone in on and pick up Chikna.

He is fourteen. His real name is Aashirwaad. He is called Chikna because he is Kashmiri-white (and to be fair, rather pimply). He is popular, he is rich, generous and heedless. He has exchanged 688 text messages with the victim in the last three days of her life. Many of them have been expressions of love. On her last night, he has tried to call her eighty-nine times on her mobile and thirty-one times on the landline. His last attempt was at eighteen minutes after midnight. None of the calls was answered by the girl.

'If this is the new India, Kalpana, I must say I prefer the old one.' LifeSkills watches with trepidation the waiter, still flustered, put down the recycled masala chai on the table. Sure enough, a little slops over into the saucer that he places before Kalpana. 'I mean, when I was growing up, we didn't have a phone at home till I was fifteen. No one, *no one* called after nine in the evening. It was unthinkable, simply not done. A phone ringing late at night meant urgent, bad news. And you kids call each other at midnight and whisper garbage into each other's ears till three in the morning.'

'Her phone was switched off that night. Some petty tiff with Chikna, who knows. That's why he tried calling her four thousand times . And I think the same evening her parents gave her, a week in advance, her birthday present of a camera. So she was far too busy clicking away to listen to Chikna's endearments. You know sir, this looks disgusting. I think I'll have an espresso after all.'

The Code of Criminal Procedure and the country's several Police Acts and Manuals all enjoin the police force to interrogate a minor with the permission—and in the presence—of his parents or a responsible adult. The police however believe that the law and its rules have been framed not for them to follow (that would be ridiculous) but to help *them* maintain law and order. Naturally. Towards that end, therefore, a white Maruti Gypsy jeep draws up outside Chikna's apartment block at four in the afternoon. It being a Thursday, his father is away at work and his mother at Vasant Vihar at her yoga-massage session with her male personal trainer, from which she always returns home, exhausted and rejuvenated, just half an hour before her husband. Chikna is before the giant screen in his father's den, dementedly zapping channels in a frenzied effort to solve the crime and bring his girl back from the dead.

He is very very scared suddenly to be summoned only to see three pot-bellied policemen in the immense drawing room of their apartment. So is the rogue of a servant deeply unhappy at that intrusion. He knows his place and it is as far away as can be from the law. Without a murmur from either him or Chikna, the cops take the boy away. Had they asked him to jump from the apartment on the fourteenth floor into the rear of the jeep, he would have obeyed instantly, also without a murmur.

'You send six hundred messages to your girl and then you phone her a hundred and twenty times in one evening. She doesn't respond, so you slip in through the window, you horny and unstable little rat, and you knock her on the head with a cricket bat, is that it?'

It is the first of Chikna's visits—in what is to be a long and distinguished career—to a police station. It has blue-washed walls and the stench of piss is so strong that he feels that he is being interrogated in a waterless lavatory. He is tongue-tied in part because he is being harangued in Hindi.

'Hmmm U hate me...I noe ma fault m such a frekin slut...I noe,' reads out the policeman with the smallest paunch—just a long papaya sleeping in his shirt and spilling over his belt. He looks up from the transcript and over his glasses, waiting for elucidation, stares at the boy in an avuncular manner. 'Slut? She was a slut? She's calling herself a slut?' In the questions, only 'slut' is in English.

'No. Slut doesn't mean...Slut means...'

'Frekin?...means fucking?...'

A second pot-belly, younger than the others, returns from another room carrying a fat dictionary without covers. He sits down within hitting distance of the boy and begins flipping through its pages. He finds what he is looking for and holds the word down on the page with a fat forefinger.

'Sleepovers...In these sleepovers, there were adults or not? Parents took part? Boys-girls or just girls-girls?...' The constable leans forward and gently pushes back from Chikna's forehead his matted hair. 'Six hundred messages between you and her and how many between her and her other friends? Huh?...So the slut didn't take your calls because she was with the servant and that's how the father found them, is that it?'

The boy nods his head at everything. He is trembling and can't trust himself to speak. He mustn't start crying. This nightmare will end only if he doesn't start crying.

A harried father and mother arrive at the police station at eight-fifteen in the evening to retrieve their son.

The police snoop and sniff around everywhere; it is their job after all. Their enquiries naturally lead them to root about amongst the chums and acquaintances of the dead servant in the network of Nepali domestics and hirelings in the neighbourhood. So on the nineteenth of the month, the force stagily swoops down on Aakangsha's house—the family is at breakfast—to spirit away Ramavtar their young Nepali factotum. He leaves unfinished in the pan the eggs that he has broken for Aakangsha's father's double fried. The family is left both hungry and speechless.

'What has he done? I've a right to know,' plaintively objects Aakangsha's father.

'What has he done? What have *you* done, sir? Ask him yourself—' here a hard thwack to the back of the servant's head the violence and utter gratuitousness of which sends Aakangsha, feeling nauseous, scurrying to her room '—You've been breeding killer snakes in your kitchen, sir, that's what *you* have done.'

Downstairs, at the back of the Maruti Gypsy police jeep, Ramavtar shares the narrow bench with Vishnu, his fellow compatriot from Jagriti Nagar in Kathmandu. Vishnu is the orderly and general attendant at the dental clinic run by the parents of the dead girl. Ramavtar is tongue-tied—very aware, very careful, of the suddenness of the seizure; in contrast, Vishnu—who has been assisting the police in their enquiries from the very first day, has been detained and interrogated since then without pause, without end, hopping from one police station to the next to stay a step ahead of activists and relatives hoping to provide him some food—Vishnu in the jeep is lolling in his seat and chatting up the khaki uniform facing him.

Three days is a long time for a Q and A. The police are clueless, grabbing at straws. Vishnu provides them several, a menu of leads. Mehr gets the details by fusing into the dining room furniture so as to better eavesdrop on a dinner conversation between her elder brother and their father.

'That Vishnu rascal,' announces Mehr's father, scowling at the water jug, 'less than a week ago, was scolded and humiliated in public, at the clinic, by his employer, for incompetence, for messing up a dental cast or something. How is his evidence to be trusted? The whole thing is deplorably shocking.'

So it is. Vishnu has let fall to the police—reveals Mehr's brother to the dining table, he being a young police officer in far-away Vijaywada, home on leave for a long weekend and privy to the official grapevine—Vishnu has let fall during that three day interrogation, through indirection and insinuation, little known facts about the dentist father of the dead girl. That he is an adulterer and debauch, hints Vishnu, nodding, sniffing and smirking, who can't keep his hands off women, that he's been for the last one year having an affair with the mother of his daughter's best friend, that knowledge of the liaison has—had—so disturbed the daughter—a lovely girl—that not knowing where to turn, she had sought—and found—comfort in the protective, grandfatherly arms of the servant. Why, he, Vishnu, knows all this because the servant is—was—really one of his best friends. And he has seen them—that Kalpana's mother (whose husband has left her and gone abroad somewhere) driving up to the clinic in the afternoon and the dear dentist debauch shutting up shop early and chuckling and the two touching each other all the time—unnecessarily, on the shoulder or forearm—while driving off in the Hyundai Santro ostensibly, *ostensibly,* to pick their daughters up from school. I ask you, if the question hasn't occurred to you already, sir, why didn't he send his driver? Hunh? Why not the driver? And then one night you are drunk and you find your daughter in the arms of that servant. You say something obscene, she retorts right back, something snaps in your head. Hunh?

But you aren't eating anything, bete,' says Mehr's father to her, frowning at her existence.

'It's the heat,' grins the elder brother, 'and all the Vijaywada laddus that I've brought her.'

'And the milk cake. And the halwa,' sings Mehr's mother from the kitchen.

'Daddy, could Dhan Singh just drive me over to Kalpana's? Just half an hour. I need to discuss my summer project with her.'

'Of course not, bete. Just look at the time!'

'You've been on the phone *all day,*' sings the mother from the kitchen, 'and in any case, I thought the Awesome Foursome was meeting tomorrow—' grumblings in an undertone here at the maid's notion of cleanliness '—to induct a new member.'

The meeting on the morrow—a lovely five-hour loaf in Select City Mall including watching *Singh is Kingg*—has to be rescheduled because Aakangsha phones to say, in a small voice, that she might have to back out. 'I don't know, I am so depressed. The cops are here again.'

Aakangsha's family was at lunch. The door bell rang, they said 'ah!' thinking that that was Ramavtar back from the cops. Instead, it was two cops without Ramavtar.

'That servant of yours has the dead girl's phone. He says you—' ice-black police eyes turn here to Aakangsha '—gave it to her.'

Gulping doesn't dissolve the lump in Aakangsha's chest, so her mother has to speak for her. 'Children share things all the time, you know that. Her friend gave my daughter her old phone when her parents bought her a new one. And then for her birthday last year, we bought Aakangsha a new Samsung Galaxy so she gave her old phone to Ramavtar. Who looked quite grateful.' Aakangsha's mother begins to simmer. 'What's he been saying? And what have you been thinking?'

The police do not let on, they look dissatisfied. They would like dates, description of circumstances, reasons and finally, after an hour and a half, a signed statement. Aakangsha provides one; beneath her signature—several squiggles within a circle three inches wide—her mother countersigns.

'This is intolerable,' shouts Aakangsha's father to his wife after the police leave, 'I'm going to complain!'

'How dozens of parents complained,' Kalpana sips her espresso, grimaces, it seems to scald her tongue, 'to the Principal! Of course, sir, you remember. Because you made an Issue of it too. I'm so glad that my mother, appalled though she was by what she saw on TV—and she had particular reason to be—never joined the queue that rushed to Black Chomchom to demand, shrieking, What was the school going to do to protect the morals of its charges?' She glances away, sees the waiter staring at the table, raises her cup to signal that she wants a second. She suddenly looks much older than twenty-two.

'Well, they—we—were all at sea too, the teachers,' LifeSkills smiles faintly at the memory of having negotiated a tricky time without loss of face, 'as bemused as all you students, yet unable to admit it even to ourselves. All I told Black Chomchom,' he grins in a sort of embarrassment at using the nickname, 'was that for the school not to mourn her death less clandestinely, more courageously—an open letter in protest to the police and the media ghouls, a candle in her name in a corner of the Hall—was to acquiesce in the sleaze.' The waiter has sidled up to their table. He is empty-handed. His presence somehow warms LifeSkills to his theme. 'She was just thirteen, I remember saying, and this is upper-middle-class, urban India. She was Anglophone, belonged to a happy, well-knit family, went to an expensive private school. She was outgoing, popular, well-adjusted. It is *unimaginable* that she was sleeping with the unremarkable, middle-aged servant of the house. And for her to do so, to go to bed with him *while her parents are at home* is way-*beyond*-impossible, is as likely as the earth one morning beginning to rotate from east to west. For the school not to make public where it stands on the issue, I told the Principal, is to make people wonder, is to incline them towards accepting the muck as truth.' He pauses to lower his voice. 'And you in particular, Madam, I said to her while she continued to stare at me stonily, have an extra special duty to perform; you have been to their house to commiserate, you share a special relationship with them because three decades ago, you even taught the father.' He is flustered at the warmth that the memory of that difficult time can still generate after eight years, tries to smile, looks up at the waiter, mimes with open palms that he'd like to see once more the menu. Kalpana points down at her espresso and raises her eyebrows and an index finger to signal again that she would like a second.

On the twenty-third of May, exactly a week after the crime, they arrest the dentist father for the double murder of his daughter and the family servant. The media goes berserk. Case cracked, announces the Director General of Police at the press conference that he has summoned; to elaborate, he proclaims, practically verbatim, the plot that Vishnu the clinic attendant has been feeding his subordinates for a week. The wicked father, announces the Director General, has been having an affair with the mother of his daughter's best friend, Kalpana by name. The daughter, deeply upset, and in some sort of retaliation, falls into the arms of the waiting servant. That fateful night, the father catches them at it and—bingo! 'A pure and simple honour killing; it is very prevalent in the country, you know, particularly in north India. You kill a near and dear one who has misbehaved because she has stained the honour of the family. Very pure and simple.' Throughout the press conference, the Director General, answering questions and explaining psychology, continues to refer to the murdered thirteen-year-old as characterless. He attracts more viewers on TV that day than the Indian Premier League cricket matches.

The arrest also takes place on TV. For Chanchal, holidaying in Indira Nagar, Bangalore, with her vacuous cousins—watching on the screen her friend's father in handcuffs, wan, enervated, rambling and ranting against the wrong being inflicted on him, surrounded by policemen ready to be famous for a second on the box, fitfully screaming that he was being framed—the monstrosity of the injustice, the unreality of it, of the disgrace and dishonour, suddenly makes it difficult for her to breathe. Gasping, sensing that even her tears are dammed up, she begins to wail, 'But he'd pick us up from school! And crack those jokes! He'd always stop at Mother Dairy for ice-cream for all three of us and say, What to do, the child always wants some for dessert and it's not polite buying for her alone!' She needs to speak to her mother. She dials fumblingly. 'Mummy! What are they doing! Mummy!'

In Noida two thousand one hundred and twenty kilometres away, Mummy makes some consoling noises both on and off the phone. She is with Kalpana's mother in her drawing room drinking tea and trying to calm down an extremely agitated woman. 'How can that policeman do this? Slander my name just like that on TV? First they drag that poor dead girl through the gutter, then they arrest the wrong man, and now they throw muck on the friends of the family. As though the murder itself wasn't enough.'

The Director General of Police is not the only reason why Kalpana's mother is so upset.

'My parents,' grins Kalpana, gazing at her phone ringing, not answering it, putting it on Silent and placing it beside the mosquito-repellent incense stand, 'were furious but for different reasons.' LifeSkills watches the orange silhouette of her caller blink on and off, on and off. 'Those were exciting times. My mother wanted to take that Director General to court, sue him for slander, character assassination, whatever. My father in Paris was furious at the whole mess. "No one I personally know has ever gone to jail before," he said, "and certainly not for murder. This simply does not happen to people like us. If it does, it means that they are not like us." How my mother screamed at him. "A thirteen-year-old girl has been brutally murdered. Instead of solving the crime, they proceed to butcher her character. Wake up! It could've been our daughter!"' Kalpana pauses, pushes her chin out at her phone. The orange silhouette, having given up hope, has ceased to blink. 'That was the maid. Wanting to know whether I'd be back for lunch.' She shrugs dispiritedly. 'That's all that we Indians ever think about. Food.'

For a couple of days, the TV and Press lot also scurry about Kalpana's mother's front door like rats disturbed by an earthquake. She steels herself every morning before stepping out to greet them. She is glad that Kalpana has left Delhi to be with her father. She herself is to join them on the twentieth of June and before leaving, would like to spend as much time as she can with her friend who has first lost a daughter and then a husband. She initially visits her every day and suddenly, it becomes every alternate day and then one in three. She can't help it. Her visits make her feel tense and pietistic and more wretched than ever.

Her friend has locked up and abandoned the apartment where the murder took place and moved in with her parents. She has been benumbed, etiolated, by grief, naturally. She is, furthermore, so horribly busy all day, so exhausted, rushing from prison to courtroom to lawyer that even though everything, *every thing*—people, events, the stars—is against her, nothing can crush her further. Thus, when she meets Kalpana's mother early in the morning or at times after dinner to discuss her day or commune silently over tea, she is calm and emotionless.

It is a sign of her mental health that her husband takes precedence over her daughter, the living over the dead. Her first duty is to get him out of prison on bail so that they can grieve for her, in tormented peace, together. The snippets of her life that she lets fall to Kalpana's mother seem to scare her auditor much more than her.

'Two young policemen, day before yesterday, took him from jail to Haridwar in a jeep. They wanted him, they said, to show them exactly what we did with the ashes, where else we went. He said that all the way, the younger policeman repeatedly told him, very conversationally, "We're going to kill you" and "We want to beat you to death." Then he would resume singing Hindi film songs of the sixties and early seventies. Shammi Kapoor, early Rajesh Khanna. And then in between stanzas, "I could so easily wring your chicken neck with these hands. You see these hands?"'

Spearheaded by the Director General's press conference, the police and the media then get together to cut to ribbons the murdered girl's character. As a first step, the cops leak to the Press all her personal emails, her text messages to her friends, her social media pages. The world soon learns that she is not talking to Mayank anymore because of what he said about the Awesome Foursome last Sunday. That Swati's got her ears pierced only because Chanchal has and if Chanchal asked her to wear a nosering on her youknowwhat, of course that cretin would. That of course Malini is a horny and greedy little slut who is turned on by Chikna's wallet and iPod and videocam and cellphone. That the reader of this mail would be kissed by the sexiest love of his life if he forwards it immediately to ten other people and be doomed to live forever with a stinking Malini-type toad if he doesn't. That Shah Rukh in *Om Shanti Om* is so *cute!!!!* as to score a straight 9.5 on the Johnny Depp scale and anyone who disagrees is a moron with no taste. That *yippee!* she and Dad and Mom are off to Singapore and Kuala Lumpur for three weeks in June and so hurry up with your shopping lists.

From such expressions of a young and impressionable slut's mind, the newspapers try to infer what happened in that Noida apartment on the night of the sixteenth of May. The principal guide to their reconstruction of the crime is that it must be juicy. One Bombay tabloid, not less yellow than faeces, publishes a plot in which the parents of the dead girl are members of a wife-swapping orgy club. On that night in May, the participants and playmates of the club meet in the Noida apartment; the girl is locked up in her room while they have a ball in the nooks and niches of the rest of the flat. The television channels and other newspapers like the plot, they run it. En route, someone adds that the murdered servant was blackmailing the murdered girl. Unless you sleep with me, I shall tell the world what your parents are up to.

For eight years, it intrigues the entire country, just what the parents were up to. How could they, for instance, have slept through their child being murdered in the next room? Well, their airconditioner was extremely noisy and the girl was suffering those days from severe laryngitis. She wouldn't have been able to scream. Oh. But why confine her in her room at night? Well, so precious, so priceless was she to her parents that every night, after kissing and wishing her goodnight, they would turn the key on her in her bedroom. But that is so weird. Why lock your daughter in at night? What do you fear? What kind of parents imprison their only child in her bedroom but leave the servant free to roam around the flat all night? With his guests when he has them?

'They stayed, if I remember right, in L Block and I, for the first few months, was a guest of my eldest sister in M. Identical flats, same size and layout. Do you remember them?' LifeSkills cannot take his eyes away from the three-quarter-inch of ash at the end of Kalpana's fourth cigarette that looms over her second espresso like a drone over Afghanistan. 'Each flat has a central drawing-dining space into which open the three bedrooms and the servant's room. The servant's room is nearest the front door.' With the cutlery, plates and cups on the table, he attempts to represent a model flat. The menu is for the moment abandoned.

'When the murder happened, I—we, the entire country, I guess—became obsessed with trying to unravel the plot. Exactly what occurred that night and who was where when. You see, the police keep saying, four people in the flat, two dead, so the other two are the killers, we don't have to look any further.' He swivels a knife twenty degrees left to indicate an open door. 'But the door of the servant's room that gives on to the drawing-dining space is always open, is never bolted. And the servant, a few hours before his death, had guests that night. And the police and the Press know that better than you and me. Long after the parents had gone to bed, Vishnu and Ramavtar came calling, watched a Nepali hit parade on TV, almost finished a bottle of whisky, left behind three used glasses and a filthy toilet. And two corpses. Between the servant's buddies getting drunk and the sleeping girl lie just the drawing-dining space and two doors, one open and the other—' the fingers of his left hand nudge a fork awry '—ostensibly locked. Ostensibly because the mother says that after she visited her daughter's room round about eleven to see to the computer router—the girl was asleep by then—she can't remember whether she locked the door. Or whether she left the key in.

'Neither my sister nor I slept a wink the first few nights. Are her daughters in their room safe? Will their heads be bludgeoned by an intruder the instant we shut our eyes?' With his mind elsewhere, occupied with choosing the apt phrase, he spears the limp, damp heap of teabag with the fork that represents the door to the girl's room. 'We grew up, you know, in Bombay. Its middle-class housing has no room for a resident servant.' He is distracted by what he has said, by whether it was what he wanted to say. The fork remains embedded in the bag like a garden implement. Dark tea begins to ooze into the saucer. 'And with girls in the house, my grandmother was quite clear. *No—male—servants*. For any domestic chore. We always had women who came and went.'

He smiles at Kalpana in a sort of grimace. The last thing that he wants to do is criticize but he must get the thought that has been gnawing him out of his system. 'Here it should've been the other way round. The servant should've been out of bounds and the girl free in her own house. Our world is monstrous, that we are not allowed to forget. In a thousand cases, one doesn't pay for one's crimes, one prospers instead, one gets away with murder and mayhem. And then, in contrast, for one's omissions, one does pay, but so hellishly, so disproportionately—not once but twice and still counting—one suffers first a punishment that is in itself a fiendish crime and then one suffers sustained, infernal injustice.'

Against which the victim's mother, despite her depression, struggles without pause. It helps to see her husband from time to time. She visits him in jail, she sees him in court during the bail hearings. What he goes through in prison helps her to fight the urge to kill herself.

'Last Wednesday, when they were bringing him to court'—her friend's voice is so low that Kalpana's mother has to strain to hear; she misses the occasional word '—he found himself in the prison van with Vishnu and Ramavtar. He was taken aback, dead though he was, and for a moment didn't know how to react. Those two appeared quite relaxed; they said nothing to him, made no sign of recognition. Just another criminal going to court. Then they handcuffed him with Vishnu.' She glances up from the polished surface of the dining table to gaze at Kalpana's mother's face. Her parents sit as motionless as installations on the sofa in the drawing room area. 'He began to struggle, to scream, to blubber and beg. "Why have you handcuffed me with him? He killed my daughter!" The policeman explained that they were short of handcuffs that day.' With her index finger, she begins to draw wandering circles on the wood. 'He quietened down once the van began to move. He could think of nothing beyond the feel of Vishnu's skin against his. Vishnu himself sighed and shut his eyes and pretended to nap. When my husband looked up from his single handcuff, Ramavtar opposite him was signalling to him with his shackled hands, first pointing to himself, then shaking his index finger in a "no" and then pointing at Vishnu, jabbing the air in his direction, all as if to say, "It wasn't me. I did nothing. He did it all."'

After a good fifty days in prison, the husband gets bail on July 11, 2008. His friends and acquaintances have all melted away, he has lost his job but at least he is free to fight. The couple move to Hauz Khas, try and pick up the pieces. In the new apartment, they arrange one bedroom exactly the way their daughter's had been, with her toys, books and favourite bedspread; enlarged photographs of her are on every wall. On the other side, over the succeeding months, the police, in their leisurely, wily way, continue to try and nail the dentist husband, send him back in. They have got their man; so bloody what if it's the wrong man. They ignore the facts that point to other possible culprits; a bird in the hand being worth two in the bush, they cook the evidence against whom they have. It is not easy but the police have always been tough. They quietly blackmail, terrorise and coerce experts and witnesses to change their opinions on the medical, forensic and circumstantial evidence. Then, because the case is convoluted and looks different with the seasons, they themselves change the murder weapon four times. They first believe it to be a hammer, then they agree with the medical men that it is likely to have been a khukri. In 2010, it becomes a golf club, a five iron; in 2013 however, they tell the trial court that it is a four iron.

Of course at the same time there are things that they do not want the trial court to hear and facts that they themselves have no wish to see. The used glasses found in the murdered servant's room, for example, that point to guests after midnight, or his blood on a pillow case recovered from Vishnu's room a few houses away. Oh, those are red herrings, scoff the police, arranged by the dentists and their defenders to muddy the waters. As for the views of obdurate witnesses like the housemaid who for five years refuses to change her opinion that the trio of parents and daughter formed an ideal family, happy and loving, that a liaison between the girl and the servant was simply unthinkable, well, the police must ensure that she does not appear in court. Tell her that they will, of course, send a police jeep to pick her up and all that, but inform the judge that she is not required to testify because the other side has won her over. The judge does not press for details. For eighteen months, he exhibits no curiosity to hear what could be said in defence of the dentists.

In May, 2008, the local police—naturally—were the first to be called in. They botched up. The case was handed over to a central investigating agency. Its team picked up some interesting scents, seemed to be closing in; the team was changed. The investigation, it appears, was *not* to conclude that the murderers are *not* the parents. And to establish that they killed their daughter, a picture is to be painted of her as a promiscuous and immoral slut. In this manner, the colours of the punishment become almost as grisly as the crime.

For the trio that remains of the Awesome Foursome—Chanchal, Mehr and Kalpana—the difference between the two, between crime and punishment, becomes a little fuzzy with the murder of the fourth member of the group. That image of the handcuffed father —Uncle to all his dead daughter's friends—on parade before the TV cameras, screaming that the police have framed him because they are too lazy and incompetent to investigate in depth, becomes for the Awesome Trio a picture as enduring and almost as terrifying as that of their dead friend swathed in once-white sheets and laid out in her drawing room on a cauldron of an afternoon.

In this dramatic manner, the children that summer are introduced to a world gone horribly wrong—to real life, in fact, to murder, injustice, dishonor and the permanent loss of dignity, to the butchering of the innocent and the punishment of the damned. They are scared; the power, the weight of the obtuseness of that world bewilders them, the imbecility of its judgements they find appalling. 'Whichever holes do these judges and magistrates emerge from?' they ask themselves in wonder. 'From an ass's,' they respond, too depressed to giggle.

It is no laughing matter. In December 2010, the investigating agency files a closure report in court, stating more or less that the parents did it but they don't have enough evidence to nail them so could they please close? The report is so worded that it encourages the examining magistrate, a woman tough as nails when it comes to other people's lives, to declare: Nothing doing. The father must stand trial. And—oh—his wife also because she was there too in the house, wasn't she?

The first judgement thus ropes in the mother, till then free, as a participant in the murder of her daughter. The second judgement, delivered in November 2013, sentences both husband and wife to life imprisonment. The trial judge enjoys a reputation for being tough and for making up his mind fast. He is to retire at the end of that November. He makes up his mind well in time and proudly reveals—to a dogged journalist after retirement—that he had started to write his last judgement in October itself, long before the defence counsel began his final arguments, the flow of which he repeatedly interrupts—but politely—with 'How much longer, saab, are you going to take?' and 'Finish it off, saab, finish it off.'

The honourable judge himself finishes the couple off four days before he retires and goes off to start a new life as an advocate at the Allahabad High Court. Which is where the indomitable couple head for too, to appear before a third judge for a suspension of the sentence of life imprisonment—for bail, in short, for those convicted so that they get a fair chance to prepare their appeal. *He* says, more or less, nothing doing, stay in jail, that's where you belong, even though if you are let out, the two of you cannot repeat the crime because you do not have another daughter to murder. It is he who will hear their formal appeal as and when it comes up.

Fortunately, that is not likely to be tomorrow. Justice is—well—as sluggish in that part of the country as elsewhere. In 2014, for instance, the appeal cases being heard in Allahabad date from 1982. The parents can therefore, for a crime that they did not commit, expect to wait in Dasna jail till 2046 or so. Time enough for them to catch up on their reading. It is no use telling the world that their daughter, their only child, long-awaited, was infinitely precious to them. When in Gandhinagar, in February 2010, they as prime suspects undergo narco analysis, they reveal, under the influence of sodium pentothal, that after what they have already lost, they have nothing more to fear. Yet they are sustained by their grit in the face of a horrible wrong. They fight on.

And to think that the father could have skipped the trial and the humiliation and gone straight to heaven! For, in January 2011, in the premises of the magistrate's court at Ghaziabad, surrounded by the police and the media riffraff, he, en route to filing a petition against the closure report of the investigating agency, is attacked by a nut with a meat cleaver. The cleaver almost splits his head in two. The nut slips through the cordon of khaki pot bellies and brings the weapon down twice, metal on bone, before the police wake up and join the melee. They then stand by and wait to be interviewed. The Awesome Trio, like the rest of the world, watches the assault on TV, sees their dead friend's father stumble, fall, blood spurt from his skull and cover his face like gravy.

The nut is a resident of the holy city of Benares. India abounds in them. In February of the previous year, he travelled a thousand kilometres to Chandigarh to attack with a pen knife a former police officer accused of molesting a woman called Name Withheld. For the dentist father in Ghaziabad, his crime being more heinous, he chooses a meat cleaver over a pen knife. He does the eight hundred kilometres to Delhi, buys the cleaver in Chandni Chowk and travels by public bus, weapon in lap, the forty kilometres to Ghaziabad not to kill but to teach, he says, society a lesson. Because they are going to different places—he briefly to jail and the dentist father to hospital—the police this time do not handcuff them together.

School reopened that first year—2008—on Thursday, July 3.

The rains are late as always and the weather close, muggy. The children neither notice nor care. What they cannot ignore in class however is that empty desk to Aakangsha's right. They sit in alphabetical order and that vacant place, with wax droppings like tiny clouds all over the small table, is extremely unsettling, even eerie. For a day and a half, Aakangsha sits ramrod straight through Maths and Chemistry and Life Skills, her hands in her lap, staring straight ahead and seeing nothing, trembling, till at last D-Bottom notices and asks. Admin is then requested and during Second Recess, a couple of boys from Stores come in to take the extra desk away. Their presence galvanizes the class and divides opinion. Some want the desk to stay as a symbol of the absence.

'So that we don't forget,' elaborates Malini. Her wisdom sparks off a shower of abuse.

'What was the point of lighting all those candles then?' asks Kalpana. While others mull over a response, Chikna with his mobile takes a thousand photographs of the desk even as the boys from Stores carry it out of the classroom. The remaining twenty-seven places are then hauled and dragged around so as to give each one of them three extra centimetres of elbow room.

It doesn't help; eventually, it doesn't matter. They all remember her; they all want to forget how she went. With the days, the memory of her mystifying and brutal departure sinks into the detritus of all that one lets fall, ignores and suppresses in the matter of getting on with living; and yet she bobs up a hundred times a day. She is missed when Peacock House, drawing up its hockey team for the Junior Inter House, realizes that their ace centre-half is no more. She is present in her chart work on *Addiction: What Are We to Do?* that adorns the class Bulletin Board; D-Bottom proposes that instead of passing the charts on to the other classes—that being the practice—they retain them on their wall all year as a memento. Chikna circulates to all his near and dear ones the last mythical snaps of the two of them together that he has created on Photoshop. Kalpana asks her mother whether she can drop out of dance class because, you know, it just isn't the same anymore. Kalpana's mother asks Malini's mother whether they can team up to take turns to ferry their children to and from school. And every time that Arora Madam the Hindi teacher takes roll call, she pronounces, after Aakangsha's, the dead girl's name, then biting her tongue, looks up, mumbles, 'Oho, soaree, soaree,' removes her spectacles and daubs her eyes with the same handkerchief that she often uses to wipe the blackboard with.

'Have you read the book? Or seen the film?'

'No-o.' Kalpana looks uncertain. 'I suppose I should.' They are done with the café and are walking towards his car. He has offered to drop her to Mandi House so that she can catch her Metro back to Mayur Vihar. 'But they aren't about her, are they? They are about justice.' She glances at him, quickly, as though to see if he could have taken offence. 'And she is fading every day, steadily, from our memories.'

'I—yes.'

'We maintained scrapbooks—Aakangsha, Chanchal, Mehr and I. I still have mine. I sit down and go through it once a year on May 24, on her birthday.' She stops, forcing him to stop, she turns to face him squarely. 'When I saw you this morning at the sale, I told myself suddenly, I want to go to Dasna jail and meet them, I want to tell them that I haven't forgotten.'

'Sure. I'll go with you.'

'My parents must not know.' She doesn't move, she will once more only when things are clear. 'In the scrapbook, I find stuff about our protest marches with banners, our candlelight vigils at Jantar Mantar and the discharge from her private parts being dissected in the newspapers and on TV. That's not her, that's not how you'd want to remember her. And all the time she is fading. And I think, I must keep cool and take it all out of my head and put it down on paper.'

Well, the girl has. This is it.

The Assassination of Indira Gandhi

Bunny threw his glass meditatively at the wall. It tinkled into large, ugly pieces. One fell on Randeep's head. 'We'd better look out,' he said, 'Cut Surd's getting violent.' Bunny took off his goggles. His eyes were very red. 'Give me a glass.' Shashi did. Bunny finished it and threw it slowly up at the ceiling fan. Jamun caught it. 'Stop it, Cut Surd.'

'Stop calling me Cut Surd.'

Mirza fixed Bunny another drink. 'These bloody Hindus, yaar Surd.' Everyone laughed drunkenly.

'I'm feeling sick.' Bunny put on his goggles. 'Not pukey, just sick.'

'Throw up in the bathroom. Not here,' said Shashi.

'Why didn't we get girls. I'm sick of just males. I want some sex.'

Shashi said, 'Rum before sundown, that's the problem. I kept saying, let's get beer.'

Bunny got up slowly from the floor. He tucked in his tee shirt. He kicked Jamun. 'I'm going out. I'm getting myself a ticket home.' He felt his pockets. 'Where are the keys? I'll leave the bike with you. Don't kill it.'

Outside, a very loud motorcycle went by. Bunny drew back the curtain and opened the window. The late-afternoon late-October light bounded in along with the noises of horns and accelerating cars. He spoke to the traffic. 'I'm sick to my balls of Delhi. A dog of a city. It's almost like Chandigarh.' Bunny looked around the room and looked out again. 'Sick.' His knees and right ankle ached faintly.

'No, Surd, this is just a bad trip. Get some ganja and some sleep, you'll be fine.'

'No, I'm just sick. Dog city.' He liked the phrase. He scratched his beard. 'Next June, I'll be apprenticed in Chandigarh, horny and alone.' Drink made Bunny articulate. 'The hep Surds call Chandigarh Chandy. Just red brick and empty spaces.' He moved around the room, leaned against the bathroom door and watched Shashi urinate. 'Your piss is yellow like mustard oil. Maybe you have jaundice.' At the table he slowly poured himself a large rum. 'These days I ejaculate too quickly. It's like school, those jerk-off competitions.'

'Fix me one, Surd, thanks.'

Bunny took off his goggles and sat them carefully on the knob of the cupboard door. 'Randeep, just fix my attendance with Kapila. I'll be back maybe in a month or something. 'Bye everybody.' He put on his goggles and left.

An orange October sun, but Bunny was only faintly conscious of it. He was drunk, but not uncontrollably. He was depressed too, but he did not know it. Bunny was twenty-three, and inarticulate and silent when sober. He put on his crash helmet and left the straps loose. He rode off at a frightening speed.

He stopped on the peak of a flyover to watch, in the mild light, the traffic and the teenagers around the ice-cream man. He said to himself, if there's a queue at the ticket counter, even a line of three bastards, I'm not going home. He rode away. But there was only one. So he bought a seat on the night bus to Mussoorie. From the bus station, he went for a haircut.

At traffic lights, at other places where he had to slow down or stop, Bunny felt quite ill. He attributed his weakness to his ennui, the drink, the inadequate sleep, Delhi's fickle October weather, his vague distaste for the way he lived his life. But self-examination was not his practice. He lived unthinkingly and encouraged in himself random impulses.

At the saloon, while waiting, he flipped blindly through a film magazine. At saloons, he always remembered his first haircut, in Darjeeling, about eight years ago, the barber's smiles and enthusiasm. He had written to his parents about it. He never wrote letters, for he found expression tiresome, but his parents had had to be forewarned before his return home. They had disapproved vastly. Even now his father, when really angry, called him a bastard Sikh.

Abruptly he felt queasy. He skipped the haircut and rode back to the hostel with a headache. He woke up Yudhvir, a friend. 'This is no time to sleep.'

'What time is it?' Red drugged eyes and porcupine hair, but Yudhvir never got angry.

'Sixish. I've got myself a ticket on the night bus home. You take care of the bike.'

'Okay.'

'And fix Kapila about attendance. I'm going to sleep too. I'll wake you up later to drop me to the bus.'

Bunny liked night bus journeys. The seats were quite comfortable, and he could sleep anywhere. The jolts even lulled him, but during the journey, when he woke up, his knees were stiff and aching.

He wasn't particularly fond of his parents. They bored him. Home was not an exciting place, but he could unwind there, sleep in the sun and eat really well. His mother opened the door. She was not surprised to see him. He always came home unexpectedly. She said, 'You look awful. Are you ill?'

'I just feel exhausted. Must be the journey.'

He went to his room with his bag. His father grunted as he

passed his parents' room. Bunny mumbled a reply. His mother came in with two blankets. It was six in the morning. Bunny slept uneasily till nine and got out of bed after ten.

His father was in the garden, in a white cane chair. 'What, Law Faculty again on strike?'

'Yes.' An easy lie, for at any time, Bunny would have found it difficult to tell his father that he had just felt like coming home. He sat down. The small lawn was an odd triangle in shape, the wooden fence a bright white. Beyond the fence, the hill tumbled down to the narrow road, the tea stalls, the shacks selling wooden Taj Mahals and walking-sticks, the Tibetans in bright quilted jackets. Then the hill lurched further down to the main road. Behind and beneath it lay the vast valley, surrounded by curve after curve of denuded hill. On a clear day, one could see thirty kilometres away in the valley the dots and dashes of the houses of Dehradun. Above it was an immense pale sky. At ten in the morning it still waited for the sun.

Bunny's mother emerged, in a salwar-kameez and a grey sweater. 'Come, breakfast is ready.'

Bunny didn't want to move or eat. 'Later.'

'What, shall I bring your food here?'

'No, I don't want to eat just now.'

His mother came up. Bunny looked at her defensively and noticed again his own face in hers. 'Are you feeling all right?' She put her hand on his shoulder. He cringed a little.

'You look horrible,' Mr Kairon said, staring steadily at Bunny over his reading glasses. *A History of the Sikhs* dropped onto the table. With a pencil he pushed stray hair into his turban. 'You've lost weight and colour. You don't look healthy.'

'Shall we call a doctor?'

'No.1 think I'll be okay in a day or two.'

'But do you feel ill?' His mother half-bent down and examined Bunny's face.

Bunny's resistance then collapsed. 'Yes. Maybe we should call Malviya.' He felt a little better. Just the admission of illness eased him, allowed him deeper breaths. His mother left.

His father said, 'What's wrong? Any symptoms?'

'Weakness. No appetite. That's all.' He did not mention the faint pain in his knees and now occasionally, his back.

Mr Kairon pushed his snout up and out till the upper lip touched his nose and breathed heavily into his moustache. He was a cliche of a man, once a brigadier, tall, with an inflexible back, now horribly active after retirement. He used his leisure for his garden and for long walks on the hill roads, and for educative books. He wasn't scholarly or even contemplative, but with the years he had been increasingly assailed by a conviction of his ignorance. One mild heart attack had even made him religious, and now his daily ritual included the Granth Sahib.

Bunny went in and returned with a camp cot. Dragging it tired him incredibly. He lay down. The weakness encouraged only unpleasant thoughts, it just allowed for images of depression, of Chandigarh and some lawyer's chambers, of law tomes and loneliness, of professional inadequacy and dislocation in a dead town.

'Fever?'

'No.'

'Stomach all right?'

'Yes, more or less.'

Then the sun broke through and warmed them. Somewhere in the house, Bunny could hear his mother giving the maidservant hell. His mother had a pleasant rich voice. To avoid his father's questions, Bunny pretended to doze.

Mr Kairon was proud of his son's good looks, but Bunny had often dlsappointed him. For one, he had not joined the Army. And though Mr Kairon admitted that short hair suited Bunny, he had been outraged that Bunny had not asked him before the haircut. Now he watched him sleeping in the sun and said, 'I hope your illness is not serious.'

They heard the gate and Dr Malviya appeared, clean, pink and busy. Bunny disliked doctors because they made him insecure. Standing over Bunny, Dr Malviya announced immediately, 'This is jaundice, Brigadier-ji. What, Bunny boy, you've been drinking a lot?' He checked his eyes, poked his spleen and liver, questioned him about his whisky and his urine, ordered blood tests, a special diet and lots of rest and left.

Jaundice. Bunny wondered if it could have been worse and almost immediately told himself yes. The blue of the sky was gathering richer tones. Light cottonwool clouds just above him, long flat strips of grey on the horizon, tiny white waves of cloud, ribbed like desert sand on the left, and the warm sun. When his father wasn't going on and on about his dissipation and abysmal lack of care, Bunny could hear different birds on the lawn and in the distant trees. He knew nothing about them, but they sounded nice.

Time outdoors passed easily. Bunny ate a little and drank some juice. Mr Kairon, perhaps regretting his earlier sharpness, asked him if he felt better. Bunny said yes. The telephone rang. Mrs Kairon picked it up, then shrieked through the large, white, open windows, 'from New York!'

'Rajwant,' muttered Mr Kairon. He rushed inside and pushed his hand out peremptorily for the 'phone. 'Here.'

Bunny turned on his side and observed them. He didn't think his sister worth the effort of leaving the camp cot. Older by nine years, his sister, like the rest of the family, was distant. He saw his father's back jerk with surprise and heard a loud, incredulous 'What!' Bunny turned back to the sky. His mother hurried out a few moments later and blurted out, 'Indira Gandhi has been shot dead. By two of her guards. Both Sikhs. In her house in Delhi.' Mrs Kairon looked around uncertainly.

The news was unnerving. 'What else did Rajju say?'

'She wanted details from us, imagine. We didn't know anything, she said it's all over American news, even BBC and Radio Australia. She was taken to hospital but she died quickly. It happened this morning at about nine-thirty.' Mrs Kairon gulped and sat down.

Just my luck, thought Bunny, to leave the dog city just when something exciting happens. His father returned to his chair, eyes agleam, intently twirling the knobs of a transistor.

'Will Rajju telephone again?' asked Mrs Kairon.

'Yes. As soon as she hears more news.'

All the radio stations played the same mournful song, 'She can't be dead. If she was dead, there'd be no voices and no drums and dholaks.'

'But something must have happened, all the stations are playing the same music.'

'But this is terrible,' said Mr Kairon, looking out over the valley.

No one spoke. Bunny turned over, now warming his right arm and shoulder. Mr Kairon said, 'In New York, the Sikhs are out on the roads celebrating and distributing mithai. Rajju didn't say so, but even Manjeet seems to be celebrating.' Manjeet was the son-in-law. On the faces of Mr and Mrs Kairon could be discerned a daze, that initial shock, and an inchoate ethnic guilt.

Bunny watched the green and dull-brown ground, the few weeds among the grass. The news thrilled him, momentarily distracted him from himself. Against the white fence and footrule-strips of sky, he visualized the blood dyeing the sari and the collapsing, crumpling female form. Maybe she had even said something to her assassins or to someone nearby. Mr Kairon got up, said, 'I'll telephone Duggal,' and went inside. The songs from the transistor continued.

Mr Kairon returned, more composed. 'Duggal says AIR is

still saying that she was shot, but BBC announced her death long ago. The killers are Sikhs, no doubt about that.'

Mrs Kairon said, 'For shame.'

Lunch was dreary and silent. Duggal arrived soon after. Bunny did not move to acknowledge him. 'Hallo Balwinder,' Duggal said, 'When did you arrive?' Bunny disliked Duggal because he called him Balwinder; Duggal disliked Bunny for his good looks, his haircut, his jeans and teeshirts and calling him Balwinder was his way of getting back at him.

Duggal was not interested in Bunny's illness. He sipped his tea noisily and said, 'This is going to cause many problems.'

'A shameful death. This is no way for a person of her stature to go,' said Mrs Kairon.

'But it's no surprise. She had it coming to her.'

Bunny eyed Duggal with amusement and contempt. What a stupid perspective, he thought. In the black and white of Duggal's mind, pain and annihilation, even jaundice probably, were merely retributive. As one sows, so one reaps, even when the harvest was a spray of unexpected bullets, or a debilitating illness. Bunny thought of his own past but could hunt out no redeeming image to refute Duggal's argument. Oh well.

His parents and Duggal continued to talk. Bunny dozed off to a constraint in the air and to polite, firm disagreement.

In the late afternoon, Mr Kairon and Duggal walked out to get Bunny's blood reports. They sensed, or imagined they sensed, a difference in the narrow lanes of Mussoorie. To them, the honeymooners looked sombre, there were lesser aimless throngs of tourists, an unusually large number of shops were shut, there were fewer lights.

The blood reports confirmed acute jaundice. After seeing Duggal off to his dental clinic, Mr Kairon stopped for bread and soap. The grocer said, very gravely, 'Kairon Saab, your people ought not to have done this,' and overcharged him just a little. The ex-Brigadier could think of nothing in reply.

When Bunny woke up, the pain in his knees and ankles had increased. Must be the weakness, he thought. He found it a little difficult to move back into the house. With each step, even the soles of his feet hurt. He was suddenly not sure that he could rely on his body for even the simplest acts. 'Tomorrow morning, I'll ring up Pammi,' announced his father over tea. 'Find out what's happening in Delhi.' In the lanes, Mr Kairon had sensed a tension, half-imagined an antagonism. Father and son had thus lost their different confidences together but would have found it impossible, as always, to share their uncertainty.

At six, TV finally said that Indira Gandhi was dead. Mr Kairon was outraged at the delay in the announcement. 'We first heard the news,' he snorted, 'by means of a call from New York, what rubbish!' Bunny walked carefully to the telephone, not wanting to exhibit his pain. 'Hallo, may I speak to Dr Malviya?...Hallo, this is Bunny here...Now my knees and ankles are paining quite a lot...I don't know, for about a week, I think.'

Dr Malviya asked Bunny not to worry, and not to take any painkiller. He attributed the discomfort to Bunny's exhaustion and weakness. 'You must've slept in some odd position during the day. And perhaps you're not used to the Mussoorie chill, having come up from Delhi.'

'Where things are hotting up,' said Bunny. In reaction, Dr Malviya sort of snorted in shock.

'What's this pain?' asked Mr Kairon suspiciously, turning away for a moment from the TV.

'Oh, nothing.'

Mrs Kairon watched her son walk slowly to his room. She wished that he would communicate more. She had placed a heater in his room. Through the window, the fading sun depressed him. The room was small, with a single bed. The bedspread was a present from Rajwant on her last visit. On it, on a yellow background romped one large red dragon. Bunny looked out at the sun and said to himself, No, I'm not weak. He closed the door and got down slowly onto the floor to exercise. At his third pushup, the floor rushed up and hit him.

He lost consciousness for a moment or two. When he came to, the cold cement against his right cheek was quite comfortable. An ant hurried by two inches from his left eye. He got into bed slowly, pulled the quilt right up and waited for the warmth. He felt defeated, empty, and now the twilight seemed soothing, like a dying glow. Moments passed and he breathed deeply. He tried momentarily to divert himself with a thought for Indira Gandhi but, like the rest of the world, she was remote and cold. They had in common only a numbness. Under the quilt, Bunny felt his knees and tried to rotate his ankles. That pain was his only distraction from that nothingness. Outside he could hear his parents, the TV and the foreign stations on the radio. All three were going on and on about Indira Gandhi.

After some time, his mother pushed the door open. 'Sleeping?'

'No.'

'What did Malviya say about the pain?'

Bunny answered, but wondered why his mother wanted to know. One's own pain was one's own, secret and unshareable, even incommunicable. Someone else's pain must be tedium, the cause of boredom and irritation. The ill were always alone, hugging their illness.

'You'd better have a hot-water bottle.'

'Okay.'

Bunny's father locked up early, at about seven. He then checked his Service revolver. From the lawn, the hills and the valley were a black menacing mass, shrouded by mist and topped by a clouded night sky. The quiet of Mussoorie normally gladdened him, but now it made him irascible and uneasy. No intermittent laughter from the teastalls below them, no wink of light from a neighbouring hill. Just the evening chill, the opaque mist, behind it the dark, and an underwater silence. Mr Kairon felt nervy, irrationally remembering the riots of Partition and the wars of '65 and '71. Indoors, the tension was alleviated only by the depression at Bunny's illness.

Dinner was short. Bunny nibbled something in bed. His mother asked him to leave his door open and to call whenever necessary.

That night, Bunny entered a private, nightmare world. His ankles and knees turned red and doubled in size. His skin burned with fever. Very very slowly, he struggled to sit up in bed. He touched his left knee and the pain stunned him. He just looked at his legs and could not believe the horror. Then Bunny heard the telephone ring and ring, loud and frightening.

At last his father picked up. 'Oh Pammi, hello...what, I hope...oh no...god...no...' From his father, Bunny heard only exclamations of shock. Mrs Kairon joined him, 'What, what's happened?'

Bunny carefully put his two pillows beneath his knees. He couldn't scream because he was not used to expressing pain or to pleading for help. His fear and his helplessness drew tears out of his eyes. His face crumpled. But he cried without sound. Jerking his head from side to side, his fists squeezing the pliant quilt, he decided to fight his battles silently and alone.

'A pogrom in Delhi.' Mr Kairon walked around helplessly. 'Sikhs pulled out of buses and butchered. Some burnt to death. Bonfires of turbans. Houses attacked and looted, torched. Hundreds dead already.' Then, Mr Kairon's slippers made the only sound.

'And Pammi?' asked Mrs Kairon.

'No problem in his area yet.'

Mrs Kairon's eyes followed her husband. 'And Punjab?'

'No news. There's a news ban there.'

To Bunny in his delirious state, it seemed that the world's chaos merely mirrored his own. He again tried to move. The pain rushed up to his hip and back. He sat motionless for what seemed ages. That night, he began to realize for the first time what he was later to get used to, that pain cannot be acute forever. After a time it turns monotonous, even becomes boring. So, sitting up in bed, he dozed a little, till some inadvertent movement wrenched him out of sleep. Awake, he would suffer, grow bored, and doze till the next wrench. Then at last, through the window behind him, he heard the chirrup of the birds and sensed the new dawn.

In this manner, he provided his parents with something other than Indira Gandhi to think about. Dr Malviya checked his heart and, avoiding Mr Kairon's eyes, said that apart from jaundice, Bunny probably also had rheumatoid arthritis. The doctor called for more blood tests and even an ECG. Rheumatoid arthritis stunned and later scared and disgusted Mr Kairon. It was *not* an illness for a young, strong, goodlooking Sikh. When the sun came up, he dragged his son out onto the lawn.

In the sunny cottage that he had bought for a song, Mr Kairon now felt helpless and isolated. He was cut off, lost in an idyllic location, while epochal events were taking place elsewhere. He looked at his son, lying there with arms folded and eyes closed, with bewilderment.

Out under the heavens, Bunny was less scared. He sensed the security of the house, aloof and removed; he liked the feel of the orange of the sun under his eyelids. He was living with people who meant well, who would never do him harm. Home. Though home didn't mean that for everybody, I mean, he said to himself with an inadvertent, horrible little smirk, look at Indira Gandhi.

Mrs Kairon brought out the portable black and white TV,

another present from Rajwant. They watched Mrs Gandhi lying in state. Initially, they all felt solemn. Bunny said, 'She still looks dignified.' Later, he looked down at his torso and then up at her aquiline nose in that grey face surrounded by flowers, and thought, Just an old woman dead before her time.

Mrs Kairon murmured obscure expressions of sorrow every time Mrs Gandhi was shown. But Bunny soon wearied of TV and returned to the infinite variety of the sky. Malviya's pills were good. If he lay still, he could even forget the pain for a while. The weeping women on TV irked and disgusted him. He watched them beat their breasts and wail on shoulders. But surely tears were more valuable than that, he thought, remembering only his own. The TV continued to spew out words of grief and immediately deprive them of meaning.

Duggal came again that afternoon and was quite happy to hear of Bunny's new illness. He and the Kairons talked interminably, about the assassins, the pogroms, Punjab, the Anandpur Saheb Resolution, Khalistan, Trilokpuri. 'A communal carnage,' said Mr Kairon, picking up the jargon of the newspapers from Delhi that had just come in. 'The riots are also directed against the financial dominance of the Sikhs in Delhi.' 'They'll announce the elections soon and this killing will win it.' 'Some young Sikhs are cutting their hair, turning out like Bunny.'

Bunny liked the discussion as background and the stray sentences that registered with him like the conversation of fellow-travellers on a long bus journey. He idly wondered what Khalistan would be like. He was a little surprised at the fervour of the elders. Religion to him was an alien and awkward thing. But listening to them, he realized that he liked his state, without roots or history. With his nondescript past and ugly future, nothing could claim him.

Dr Malviya came again. 'The fever will return. The

swelling will subside in three weeks or so. Later you will need a physiotherapist.' Over the next few days, he visited regularly. 'You must be careful, Bunny. You must not allow the pain to move into your wrists and fingers, or up your backbone. No exertion, complete rest.' 'You'll have to forget alcohol forever, or almost forever. The jaundice will pass, but the arthritis is going to stay.' Sometimes Dr Malviya turned quite philosophical. 'You will have to learn to live with pain, with limitations. Learning to live, that can be quite rewarding, Bunny.' 'Don't think of it too much, and don't talk about it with others. They'll all have stupid theories. Don't you have hobbies or something like that to occupy you?'

Bunny said no. He never read, he had no ear for music, he collected nothing. He wasn't even used to thought.

As Dr Malviya had prophesied, the fever returned, fitfully. Then when his mother asked every hour if he felt better, he couldn't even snap at her because he felt so dulled. Sometimes he would press his hand to his heart, hard, and say, You are strong. Sometimes he would giggle when he recalled that earlier, in Delhi, he had thought that he had problems, and now... Sometimes he would glaze his eyes and pretend not to recognize his mother when she bent over him because he found her concern irritating. Sometimes he played a game of exaggerating the pain, for the pain was boring and needed to be embellished.

On the second and third of November 1984, Indira Gandhi lay in state and Delhi, as the newspapers said, was in flames. On the fourth, she was cremated. On the eleventh, her ashes were flung all over Gangotri, a cold dead place. The nineteenth was her birthday. Thus the days passed for Bunny, and every day he saw the same images of her on TV.

Surprisingly, Randeep wrote him a letter. 'My dear Bunny, where do I begin? I can't believe that I really saw what I am about to describe to you...'

I can't read this rubbish, said Bunny to himself, and crumpled up and threw away the letter. Hours of introspection had made him love and long only for his own self. His mother sensed this as she watched him spend his hours examining the sky. 'I wish there were more people of your age here, my son.' Randeep's letter had broken Bunny's cocoon and the world had rushed in. He thought of his friends and his Delhi life with distaste. He couldn't return there. He hated his past, it had given him his illness, and he distrusted his future, it would bring no respite. And yet this is the real me, he said to the sky with a shudder, and this the real world.

He bathed after the first few days, using an aluminium chair. The skin on his feet was thin and wrinkled. His toes looked like pieces of ginger. He thought, I had once been innocent, when I had assumed I could sprint a hundred yards with ease.

Then Mr Kairon asked once, on a bright morning, again over tea on the lawn, 'Bunny, will you grow your hair? And wear a turban? For my sake?' The ex-Brigadier did not know what role to assume, that of a liberal Sikh, a nationalist Sikh, or what Duggal called a true Sikh. 'And for Chandigarh, when you're a lawyer.'

Bunny said yes immediately. He would have said yes to any request, it was not important. There were still months before Chandigarh, and the disease and the assassination had made it clear that the world was a wonderfully unstable place where anything could happen. The two events ratified his inaction. One had to wait for the mad event, that was all. Where were the certainties? In the sky and sun? To the questions, there were no solutions; there was only one life, a sort of life. Ambition was an absurdity; so-much-to-do-and-so-little-time-to-do-it-in, how pointless an outlook, here, look at Indira Gandhi, Bunny used to think, and often smile at the recollection.

Acknowledgements

My thanks to Sanjay Subrahmanyam, Namita Gokhale, Iti Khurana and Ameena Saiyid for their help in locating obscure background information for 'History Lesson'.

Many thanks to Amritananda Chakravarty and Ranjit Mankeshwar for their help with 'Three-seven-seven and the Blue Gay Gene'. Most of all, thank you, Anand Grover.

Many thanks to Bhasha Singh, Manjula Pradip and Martin Macwan for all their help with 'Can't Take This Shit Anymore'.

Many thanks, for their help with 'Girl', to Vandana Luthra, Bhalachandra and Lalita Chitnis, Anita Durrani, Vidushi Durrani, Masooma Jha and Neesha Barua. Most of all, thank you, Avirook Sen.